LOST AND
FOUND IN VENICE

Joanna lives in the south of England with her family, in a house with far too many books and a cat who often ignores her. She hates to fly but loves to travel, prefers paperbacks to ebooks and adores American sitcoms.

Alongside her writing, she has a love of movies, eating out and socialising with her friends. Her family are her world and her husband is the love of her life. She completed both a BA (Hons) in English Literature and a master's degree in creative writing, all while her children were little.

These days, she can often be found scouring the internet for her next book destination, failing miserably at the daily crossword and writing her next novel sitting absolutely anywhere but at her desk.

Lost and Found in Venice is Joanna's second published novel with Orion Fiction. Her debut, *Love is in the Air*, was published in 2023. She is currently working on her third novel, which takes place at the top of a volcano.

LOST AND FOUND IN VENICE

Joanna Knowles

ORION

An Orion Paperback
First published in Great Britain in 2024 by Orion Fiction,
an imprint of The Orion Publishing Group Ltd.
Carmelite House, 50 Victoria Embankment
London EC4Y 0DZ

An Hachette UK Company

1 3 5 7 9 10 8 6 4 2

A CIP catalogue record for this book is
available from the British Library.

ISBN (Mass Market Paperback) 9781 3987 1766 4
ISBN (Ebook) 9781 3987 1765 7

Typeset by Born Group
Printed and bound in Great Britain by Clays Ltd, Elcograf S.p.A.

MIX
Paper | Supporting
responsible forestry
FSC® C104740

To my wonderful Mum and Hugh,
because your love story began in Venice,
this book is for you.

Chapter One

'Thank you for calling Wanderlust Wishes, where we work hard to make all of your travel dreams come true.' Rosie pressed the receiver back into the base on her desk, relaxed her cheek muscles into a grimace and took a deep sigh. 'I hate my job.' She lowered her forehead and let it drop onto her desk with a thud.

'Oh, come on now, don't be such a negative ninny,' Audrey, her colleague, said, tapping the desk opposite Rosie's to get her to sit up. 'So, you're slightly off meeting your quota this month—'

'Slightly! I'm so far from it, at this rate, I'll be owing the company money.' Rosie groaned, her voice muffled by the cold, hard desk close to her face. 'The gap between what I have earnt and what I should have earnt is so large that the Grand Canyon could easily fit between the opening.'

'See! Look at you,' Audrey said, sounding upbeat. 'Even at the bottom of the leader board, you're still able to reference travel in your woes. You're a natural travel salesperson. Who else here knows the exact location of Kiribati? Or the currency of San Marino? Or what country travellers need an ESTA form for?'

Rosie shrugged, and then couldn't help herself, and muttered, 'Central Pacific Ocean, the euro and the United States.'

'See!' Audrey said, slamming a hand on her desk, causing Rosie to sit up in her chair. 'December is always a tricky month; we all know that. Just you wait, I bet the next call you receive will be someone booking a huge trip . . .'

Rosie's office phone on her desk rang sharply and Audrey looked at Rosie, her face positive, her eyebrows raised into her hairline as if to say, *See?*

Rosie picked up the phone, the tension already evident in her arm muscles. She planted a smile on her face, convinced it was able to project itself down the line and into the caller's psyche.

'Good morning, Rosie at Wanderlust Wishes here, how may I help you today?' She listened to the speaker, her face impassive, her eyes focused on Audrey.

'No, of course,' Rosie said, nodding as the speaker continued. 'Absolutely.' Audrey's face lightened with every word. 'Yes, I'm here until 6pm today, so I'll look out for you.' She said her thanks and gently placed the phone back down.

'See! I told you! How serendipitous was that?' Audrey said, raising her arms and doing a little jig in her office chair.

'Hmm,' Rosie said, pushing back her own chair and straightening down her pencil skirt as she stood up. 'That was Nigel from the magazine distributors. He'll be dropping off next season's brochures sometime today.' She raised one perfectly arched eyebrow at Audrey and grabbed her bag, hoisting it over her shoulder unceremoniously. 'It's officially time for a coffee.' She looked at Audrey, whose triumphant face had been replaced with dejection. 'Gingerbread latte from Jonah's?'

Audrey nodded. 'Go on then, it is nearly Christmas. Whipped cream on top, please.' She licked her plump lips together, her orangey-pink lipstick contrasting fabulously with her dyed silver bob.

Rosie walked around her desk and out of the store into the gloomy, dark skies of the high street. The weather matched her mood. It was only two weeks until Christmas and the shop frontages were filled with festive sights, all promoting their wares for sale.

'Christmas,' Rosie said to no one in particular as she walked towards Jonah's Café. 'I'll need a Christmas miracle at this rate.'

Chapter Two

Rosie scurried along the busy high street, just as the darkening clouds decided to release their load – purely onto her, it seemed. A torrent of slushy, icy rain splashed onto her vintage cashmere coat and last season's beige ankle boots.

'No, no, no,' she said, jogging as best she could in three-inch heels.

She could feel her hair flattening to her scalp with each step, thinking of those thirty minutes tonging it this morning in an effort to add some curl to her long, straight blonde hair. Her mind reverted to the office and the large umbrella stand full of branded umbrellas for staff use. Why hadn't she taken one when she left? Her fingers had literally grazed the stand when she grabbed her coat.

She lifted her purse over her head in an effort to stem the worst of the rain, but it made no difference. By the time she reached Jonah's, she had rain dripping from her nose and hair, and her boots were mud-spattered and most probably ruined. She pushed open the door with a little more force than intended and it almost slammed into the table for two behind.

'Shit, sorry,' she said, holding up a hand in apology before shaking herself down like a wet dog.

There was no queue, which was unusual, so she walked directly up to the counter.

'Bad day, Rosie?' Jonah asked, tossing a tea towel over his shoulder, a habitual gesture Rosie had seen him make many times. His big, dark eyes, warm under bushy brows, had a look of fatherly concern as he took in her bedraggled appearance. He removed the tea towel from his shoulder and handed it to her over the counter, which she took gratefully and began to pat her face.

'A bad month, actually,' she said, wringing out her hair and placing her dripping purse on the counter. 'Two gingerbread lattes, with whipped cream, please,' she said, giving him an appreciative smile. 'And has Martha been baking her infamous Christmas cranberry and cinnamon cookies this morning?'

'They're fresh out of the oven,' Jonah said, gesturing to the swinging kitchen door, where the sound of whisking was audible. 'Want me to grab you some?'

Rosie told herself she didn't need them – that the latte was enough – but then she reminded herself that December was the month for indulgence. That Martha's cookies were a Christmas special and were only available in December.

'Go on, then,' she said, her stomach growling in agreement, 'make it a dozen.'

Jonah's eyebrows nearly disappeared into his mop of salt-and-pepper hair.

'Good girl! Cookies remedy any bad day,' he said, winking.

'They're for the office, too,' she felt the need to explain, but he just laughed and disappeared into the kitchen.

The coffee shop door opened, a blast of icy wind blowing through. A buxom woman marched towards the counter, wrapped in a designer raincoat with a matching umbrella and hair so fixed into a tight chignon that it could have held in a hurricane. Wide-leg woollen trousers skimmed her ankles, revealing sturdy-heeled boots that Rosie realised were both a fashion statement and a necessity from the way she stomped towards her.

Jonah reappeared through the double swinging doors carrying a white box with the lid still open and the cookies visible, their sugary deliciousness reaching Rosie's nostrils and making her want to dive right in and eat them all in one go, her tastebuds activating immediately.

'Here you are, Rosie,' Jonah said, closing the lid on the cardboard box and placing the box on the counter. 'Still hot from the oven.'

Rosie went to take the box just as the woman sidled up next to her, her sodden, pointy elbow budging Rosie to one side.

'Excuse me,' Rosie said pointedly, taking a step to the right.

The woman either didn't hear or didn't care and began to speak.

'Jonah, I need a dozen of your finest Christmas cookies, please.'

Her tone was demanding and carried an air of expectation. Rosie got the impression that this was not a woman who took disappointment well.

Jonah looked down at the box, then back up at the woman. 'Good morning, Mrs Winthorpe-Smythe! I'm ever so sorry, but there will be a bit of a wait for the next batch of cookies. Martha has just put two further trays into the oven.' He shrugged, sliding the box towards Rosie a little more. 'Maybe a half-hour wait, maybe more?'

'Well, this simply will not do, Jonah. I don't have time to wait around in here while your wife fulfils her baking duties, which I'm sure could have been done before the working day actually started . . .' she said, lowering her voice snidely.

'We have many tables still available; I could offer you some coffee while you wait?'

Jonah was still smiling, but Rosie could see his eyes narrowing. He turned away from the lady towards Rosie without waiting for a response.

'That'll be ten pounds, please, Rosie. Martha put extra cinnamon in them this morning. They are pure Christmas magic.'

Rosie opened her purse to extract a ten-pound note but was interrupted by the lady once again.

'Wait a minute,' she said, her eyes widening in realisation, 'are those a batch of Christmas cookies in that box?'

Jonah nodded, his eyes not leaving Rosie's.

'Then I will pay double for them. Hand them over.' She beckoned the box over with her hands, letting out a deep sigh as if this was all just too much of an inconvenience.

'Er, no, sorry. These are mine.' Rosie placed the note onto the counter and slid the box safely into the crook of her left arm.

'But you aren't in a rush,' Mrs Winthorpe–Smythe said before turning to Jonah. 'Jonah, I'm offering double what they are worth. No shrewd businessman would turn down the opportunity to make a profit on what is effectively sugar, flour and fat!' She looked exasperated, as if trying to negotiate with toddlers.

'I mustn't be a very good businessman, then,' Jonah said, waving Rosie off and removing the note from the counter. 'Enjoy, Rosie. See you soon.'

'But, but . . .' The woman stood there; her large chin dropped, revealing a rather large mouth.

Rosie noticed a touch of lipstick on her top two teeth. She looked infuriated.

'Well, in all my days . . .' She turned to Rosie as she made her way to the door. 'Our generation are to be respected, young lady. What you have just done is tantamount to daylight robbery.'

Rosie turned back as she reached the café door, her arm still clutching the box tightly. She deliberately looked away from the woman and made eye contact with Jonah. 'Thanks, Jonah, always a pleasure. And the icing on the cake? I didn't even need this many – a half a dozen would have been enough.' She beamed at them both brightly, turned and walked out of the café back onto the street, laughing to herself as she held the still-warm box in her arms.

Chapter Three

'Rosie? Can I have a word, please? In my office?'

Rosie looked up from her half-eaten cookie, a sugar dusting already covering her cream silk peekaboo blouse, to find her manager, Benjamin, glaring at her from the doorway to his office. He angrily jerked his head in the direction of Audrey's desk, where she had clients seated with her, discussing a cruise.

'Sorry!' she said in a hushed tone, surreptitiously trying to brush the crumbs onto her navy skirt.

His foot began to tap on the linoleum floor.

'Coming, boss,' she said, standing up and knocking her left knee hard into the leg of the desk. 'Shit,' she said, wincing, which resulted in a darker glare from Benjamin.

She hobbled around her desk and sheepishly past the clients at Audrey's desk, slipping past him into his office. Before closing the door behind her, he disappeared onto the shop floor and returned with the box of cookies in his hand.

He stepped back into his office, closing the door behind him, which was never a good thing. Benjamin had always insisted on an open-door policy, which Rosie soon realised was more for his benefit than theirs. Benjamin, or Bastard Ben as he was known to the girls in the office, was notorious for his sleazy, overt gazes at female clients, passers-by, shop assistants, delivery personnel; basically, anything with a female chromosome. He was divorced – Rosie, to this day, was still surprised anyone had agreed to marry him – and the rumour was that he had slept with most of the city's north-west female population. With no siblings and no children (that he knew of), he had been spoilt from the minute he could talk and it seemed that, for now, he was demanding the attention of women in their twenties.

'Take a seat,' he said, his face serious and his hair slicked back in his usual style, greased to a statuesque peak that wouldn't look amiss on the stage of *Grease*. But there was no mistaking his attractiveness. He was chiselled and preened to perfection, with long, fluttering eyelashes and dark, almost black eyes. The gym was his second home and he knew how to work a room so that within minutes he had the whole crowd in the palm of his hand.

But Rosie couldn't see him in that way. Her mother, before she died, always used to say that *you're only as attractive as your last good deed* and Rosie had used that advice with every new relationship, every new friend.

'Everything OK, boss?' she asked, sitting opposite him in a plastic chair while he reclined in an executive leather desk chair. She was sure he did this deliberately so that he always held the upper hand.

'Well, not really, actually,' he said, pushing his thick-rimmed glasses further up his nose.

Rosie knew that the glasses were superfluous and were simply clear glass, but he liked how they made him feel efficient.

'I've been checking the figures and you are down on your quota. Why is that, Rosie? We can't have head office find out we are not meeting our targets – that'll reflect badly on the company.'

On you, Rosie thought. He didn't want to have to deal with all the paperwork and questions, which, as manager, he would inevitably end up doing.

'Benjamin, I am doing everything I can to make a sale. I have contacted everyone on my database, I have issued flyers, I have even resorted to stretching further out of our location area. People are not wanting holidays. They have Christmas to deal with, and a cost-of-living crisis, and rising bills . . .'

'Yes, yes, yes,' Benjamin said, holding up the palm of his hand in her direction as he interrupted her. 'We all know times are tough. But how come Audrey is meeting her targets, and Elinor, and Isadora?'

'Well, to be fair, Isadora is on maternity leave, Elinor is only part-time and works weekends, our busiest time, and Audrey is just awesome at her job.' Rosie shrugged, unwilling to be compared to the others. They were all brilliant at their jobs. It wasn't them at fault, it was the unrealistic sales targets.

'And you used to be awesome at your job,' Benjamin said, leaning forwards and folding his arms across his chest. 'What's going on with you, Rosie? The last eighteen months or so, your sales have been consistently falling. But I know what you're capable of. Why the change?'

Rosie shrugged, her cheeks flushing. Why the change? She really didn't know. She had noticed her interest in the job waning over the last year, finding herself looking at job adverts online as if she were shoe shopping, looking up at planes in the sky and wishing she were on them, feeling a sense of restlessness that had settled in the pit of her stomach. None of this was she willing to divulge to him, though.

'It's just a slow month, boss. It might pick up in the next few days, with people wanting to get away for some winter sun.' She smiled encouragingly, but he didn't look placated.

'Well, it had better pick up soon,' he said, waving her away from his desk, indicating their meeting was over. 'For your sake, and mine.'

As she stood up, she gestured at the cookie box and he followed her gaze.

'Oh, yeah, thanks.' Lifting the lid of the box, he grabbed five of the cookies and placed them on his mouse mat, piled one on top of the other.

'Help yourself,' Rosie muttered sarcastically under her breath as she grabbed the box before he could take more and walked out of his office back to her desk, deliberately leaving the door open wide.

Her head was beginning to pound, as if the room had suddenly lost cabin pressure. She slumped into her chair just as Audrey's guests rose to leave.

'You're going to love every second of your cruise, Mr and Mrs Arthur, I guarantee it. What a way to spend Christmas!'

They leant down to shake her hand and left in a buzz of titters and excitement, their hands clasping their tickets, brochure and currency.

As soon as the door closed, Audrey pushed back from her desk and made her way around towards Rosie, her wheelchair making its familiar little squeak as it always did when she angled left. She gave a big push with her arms and flew forwards with speed towards the cookie box now situated on Rosie's desk. Opening it, her eyes widened at the sweet sight, and she grabbed a cookie and took a large bite.

'Sod it, I need sugar!' she said, her eyes closed in delight.

Within seconds, she had polished off an entire cookie and helped herself to another two.

'If Jonah's wife wasn't married, I'd marry her just so that she could bake me cookies every day. These are amazing.'

Audrey licked her lips and Rosie couldn't help but look at her. She was so pretty; her features were delicate and she dressed with the ease of someone who had a natural sense of style. Despite them both having to wear the company uniform, Audrey had a knack for making any outfit look brilliant. She was wearing navy blue trousers instead of the tight pencil skirt that Rosie wore and her feet were adorned in blue velvet brogues with thick gold buckles that sat neatly together on the metal foot stand of her wheelchair. Her cream blouse was tied in a knot at her tiny waist and she had restitched the thread with a vibrant orange. Around her neck she wore a navy-and-gold patterned scarf that had been tied into a large, loose pussy bow. Her nails were painted electric orange and her wrists were weighed down by numerous bangles of various colours.

'As if you ever need to worry about how you look in a dress,' Rosie said, taking a sip of her now-cold coffee and wincing in disgust. 'You could wear a bin bag and still look amazing.'

Audrey shrugged. 'Shut up, you.'

They both continued eating in comfortable silence before a ringing could be heard from Benjamin's office. He picked it up, beginning a conversation.

Audrey continued, 'So, what did Bastard Ben want with you?'

'Oh, you know, the usual. Empty threats, disappointed glares – he's just nervous I'm going to make him look bad.'

'He does quite well by himself,' Audrey said. 'He's already in trouble with HR for messaging Emma from accounts.'

Rosie loved a bit of office gossip and Audrey was amazing at extracting it from various sources.

'Really? Emma, who recently married Henry from reservations?'

Audrey nodded. She was opening her mouth to continue when the shop door flew open and an icy gust of wind blew in, scattering the papers from Rosie's desk, whipping her hair into a frenzy and almost sending the cookies flying, but Audrey had protectively grabbed at the lid to hold it down. Audrey took her snacks very seriously. The door closed again and Rosie looked up to see who had come in, pushing back strands of hair from her face and straightening in her chair in an effort to look professional, not the windswept, cookie-crumb-coated woman in her late twenties that she actually was.

But when the dust had settled, she found herself looking up at a familiar face. A face that was neither smiling nor looking at her. Rosie followed the older woman's glare and they fell on the box of cookies. Her gaze slowly moved back to Rosie's face and it was at this point Rosie recognised her. It was Mrs Winthorpe-Smythe from Jonah's Café. Empty-handed. With not a cookie crumb in sight.

Chapter Four

'Can I help you this morning?'

Audrey had pushed herself forwards to greet the new client, but Mrs Winthorpe-Smythe had clearly recognised Rosie and headed straight for the chair set out in front of her desk.

'No, thank you, my dear. It's this lady who I believe can help me today.' She smiled at Audrey but bypassed her chair completely and took a seat opposite Rosie. 'I would like your assistance, please,' she said, smiling, as she removed her gloves and began rifling through her large designer bag.

She pulled out a Filofax as fat as a loaf of bread and removed two elastic bands from it, holding bundles of envelopes, Post-it notes and papers together. As the last band was removed, the Filofax burst open in her hands like a magic trick.

'So, here is my dilemma,' she continued, searching through the endless scraps of paper until she found the one she wanted: a piece of A4 paper folded into quarters. She flattened it on the desk in front of her and Rosie noticed a list of what appeared to be names scrawled in swirly cursive handwriting. 'I urgently need to book a package deal for ten people, plus a tour guide for a holiday beginning Friday, 19 December, for five days.'

Rosie looked at her, surprised. 'Madam, we book holidays here, but do not offer tour guides or accompanying staff for any of our trips. I'm not sure you have the right place, here.'

Rosie looked down at the list and felt a bit disheartened. Booking for that number of people would definitely take her over the required quota for the month. Even if it did mean conversing with the likes of this cookie addict.

'Mrs Winthorpe-Smythe, if you please,' she said, looking unfazed at Rosie's response. 'Herein is my problem. I am the manager of a prestigious award-winning care home. I assume you've heard of it, Heirs and Graces?'

She paused while Rosie shook her head to show the opposite.

She rolled her eyes and continued, 'Well, as part of their world-class service and hospitality care package, the residents are taken abroad, once a year, by a tour operator and guide, and this year, the chosen location is Venice. However, the travel company we have always used has gone bust and we are now left with ten disappointed residents only days before they are due to fly. And this is where you come in.' With a large, painted fingernail, she pointed at the piece of paper and slid it across the desk towards Rosie.

'Mrs Winthorpe-Smythe, I would obviously love to help you with this difficult situation—'

'Good,' Mrs Winthorpe-Smythe said, smiling and looking satisfied.

'—however, as already mentioned, we are not a company that offers escorts, guides or accompanying staff for our customers' trips. If your residents require assistance, then I'm afraid you would have to organise that yourself, or you would need to chaperone them.'

A silence fell. Rosie looked at Mrs Winthorpe-Smythe as the woman glared back at her, appearing to size her up. Her face was passive and Rosie suddenly imagined her leaping across the desk, grabbing the box of cookies and making a run for it as fast as her boots would allow. She surreptitiously used the edge of her elbow to shift the box away from her.

'I'm sure there's something you can do. I am willing to compensate you handsomely,' she said, her smile returning.

She was one stubborn middle-aged woman.

'I'm afraid there isn't. We aren't covered by our company insurance to travel with our customers and head office simply wouldn't allow it. I can, by all means, book the trip for you today, but I cannot organise any assistance.' Rosie smiled, standing firm. Yes, she may need this sale, but she wasn't willing to risk her job, or her sanity, by agreeing to travel with a bunch of crazy old OAPs.

Mrs Winthorpe-Smythe turned to look at Audrey, who was now back behind her desk, clearly hoping for a different answer from her. But she shook her head sadly, agreeing with Rosie.

'Right, fine,' Mrs Winthorpe-Smythe said, whipping back around to Rosie. 'As manager of Heirs and Graces, it will fall on me to accompany them then. I would like you to please book for the following dates, and this was the original hotel, who have agreed to honour the booking, providing I book today.' She found another folded piece of paper and handed it to Rosie, with flight times and address details scrawled on there. 'Shall we get started, then?'

An exhausting hour and a half later, Rosie tied up the last few ends of the holiday package and handed over both an itinerary and a receipt to Mrs Winthorpe-Smythe. They had both drunk a strong cup of coffee, made by Audrey, but the cookie box had remained sealed – Rosie unwilling to offer any to her customer.

The cost of the holiday had been astronomically high, mostly due to the last-minute flights and the time of year. Rosie was already feeling the relief of knowing that she had not only reached her quota, but also far exceeded it, which would guarantee her a nice little Christmas bonus.

'So, all that is required from you now is confirmation of who might need travel assistance at the airport, but other than that, you are all set!' she said happily.

Mrs Winthorpe-Smythe smiled back, the itinerary placed on her lap. 'Thank you,' she said, beginning to gather her things. 'Despite my initial impression of you, you have actually proved to be quite competent.' She stood up. 'This morning must just have been a bad moment for you, but I forgive your rudeness, you have been most helpful.'

She smiled at Rosie, who sat frozen in her chair, absorbing the insults.

'I don't believe it was me that was rude,' Rosie said, trying to remain calm and keep the professional smile on her face. 'I think it was simply a misunderstanding on your part.'

'My dear girl,' Mrs Winthorpe-Smythe said, a patronising smile on her face, 'you're young, you'll learn in due course.' She pulled on her gloves and headed towards the door. 'With age comes wisdom, you see. Your behaviour at the café was not only immature and embarrassing for yourself, but you made the café owner quite uncomfortable, too. Over a trifling matter of some cookies.' She indicated the white catering box on Rosie's desk and shrugged as if she felt Rosie a lost cause. 'But as I say, you have redeemed yourself this afternoon.'

Rosie, feeling lost for words and with anger boiling inside of her, chose her words carefully.

'How kind of you to point out my errors,' she said, reaching across her desk and opening the cookie box, which had one solitary cookie remaining. 'I will endeavour to improve on my manners immediately.'

At which point she took a huge bite out of the last cookie in her hand, allowing the crumbs to fall onto her blouse and desk with abandon. She let out a contented groan, closing her eyes in pleasure, and when she opened them, Mrs Winthorpe-Smythe's face was thunderous. The woman ripped open the door and walked into the rain and cold.

As the door closed behind her, Rosie collapsed back into her chair and began laughing, with Audrey staring at her in total confusion.

Chapter Five

'So then what happened?' asked Bee.

'So then I ate two more cookies and I am now riding a massive sugar high,' Rosie said, nodding for her wine glass to be topped up by Nav, which he duly did.

'She sounds like a total *witch*,' Bee said, making the symbol of lower-case 'b' with her fingers and nodding in the direction of the twins who were playing on the floor beside them.

'Oh, an absolute *witch*,' Rosie said, nodding and smiling at Arya and Aisha, who were both looking up at her with their gorgeous chocolate-brown eyes.

'But on a positive, you've hit your quota, so now we can all relax and sort out what you're wearing to your work's Christmas party tomorrow,' Bee said, placing a hand on Nav's leg as he perched on the arm of their huge sofa beside his wife.

'Auntie Rosie sleep with me.'

Sam, or Samaj as he was formally named, toddled over to Rosie and placed his sticky hands on her knees, arms raised. She picked him up, enjoying his warmth as he snuggled into her chest.

'I am, little buddy,' Rosie said, leaning down and rubbing her nose against his, the two of them giggling together. Rosie felt a rush of love for this tiny human being.

Bee was Rosie's best friend. They had met when they were both placed in a sandpit in preschool and a boy had bashed Rosie on the head with a plastic watering can. Bee being Bee had pushed the boy forwards so that he face-planted in the sand and came to Rosie's aid. And in a nutshell, she had been doing that ever since.

When Rosie's parents died suddenly in a car accident when she was fourteen, it was Bee who was by her side throughout. It was Bee's bedroom she shared when she had nowhere else to live, Bee's parents who stepped up to become her legal guardians, who soothed her and hugged her at the funeral. It was Bee who helped her to study for her exams, get dressed for her first date, ride in the car to prom together. It only seemed natural that they went to college together, then university, choosing to study different courses but on the same campus. Rosie studied tourism management while Bee studied fashion design, but they made sure that they shared accommodation. Despite finding their own pathways with different friends, they still gravitated back to each other as if they were two magnets drawn together by an invisible pull.

After university, they both came home, deciding to set up back near Bee's parents, in the family home that Rosie had inherited once she had come of age. It was a tough time adjusting to living back in her parents' house, but with Bee by her side, and by renting out two of the other bedrooms to long-term lodgers, she was able to distance herself from her childhood memories and begin making her own.

They both found jobs – Rosie with Wanderlust Wishes and Bee with a small art gallery across town – and they found themselves falling into a comforting routine in which they happily ambled along for a few years until the arrival of Naveed.

Bee had been travelling back from London having visited an art exhibition and negotiated some art pieces being loaned for her own gallery, when the train she was due to take home was suddenly cancelled. Not only did this mean she had to wait at Waterloo for the next three hours, but it also meant that she would miss her connecting train further down the line.

She had angrily stomped over to the nearest café, to find every seat taken, resulting in her standing with a hot cup of coffee, leaning against a wall. While feeling sorry for herself, she had felt a tap on her shoulder and, on turning around, a gorgeous man with a wheat-ish complexion and a head full of tight dark curls was standing there, offering to share his tiny table for two in the corner of the busy train station café. She accepted, they began talking and before they knew it, two more coffees and two hours had passed, and it was time to catch their train.

In a serendipitous realisation that they both had tickets to travel on the earlier, now-cancelled train, and on realising that they were only two stops apart from each other on the line, they decided to meet up again the following weekend. And that was it, the start of a relationship that, in what seemed like only moments, had led to a marriage, two-year-old Samaj and twin one-year-olds Arya and Aisha.

Rosie hadn't been left out, though, and Nav knew from the start that Bee came as a package. He was a laid-back guy who had become accustomed to their late-night phone calls and last-minute sleepovers, and he understood that Rosie was a massive part of her life. He welcomed Rosie like a sister and the three of them gelled well. Rosie was even godparent to all three of their children, with Nav's brother being godfather. Bee truly fell in love with Nav and their marriage was as content as they come. Rosie felt nothing but happiness for them both. But that didn't stop her from feeling lonely.

Sam started to snore in Rosie's arms and Nav walked quietly over, extracting Sam's little body from hers and carrying him upstairs.

'Give me five minutes and I'll get these munchkins to bed, too, then we can properly begin . . .' Bee said, naturally scooping up both twins in her arms and kissing their necks so that they squealed in delight. 'Give Auntie Rosie a kiss goodnight,' she said, leaning them down so that their heads were level with Rosie's.

They both duly leant in and landed big, wet, milk-scented kisses onto her face, which made her laugh, and she kissed them right back.

'Goodnight, my gorgeous Double As,' Rosie said to their tired little faces and they both smiled sleepily before snuggling back into their mother's arms, their matching bottles clasped in their hands.

Their nickname, Double As, had come about when they were both about two months old. Bee, who wanted to breast-feed them, was up at all hours, tandem feeding them both, and Rosie had remarked that when they were being fed, it was like they were both being charged up, like AA batteries. The nickname had stuck, despite Nav's obvious objections, and as Rosie looked up at their tiny matching sleep bags and identical mop of dark curls, so like their father's, she couldn't help but feel a twinge deep inside her. She always said she didn't want her own children, but when Bee started having babies, Rosie realised that she had a lot of love to give, and not just to Bee's three.

Bee disappeared, so Rosie pulled her phone out of her pocket to check for messages. There was one from Audrey asking for *immediate photos of outfit choice!* along with two emails, both work-related, so she ignored them, and then she found herself scrawling through social media. She kept a low profile on most platforms, preferring not to display her (rather boring) life for all the world to see. But that didn't stop her from nosing at everyone else's life. Yet as she scrolled, she found herself sighing. It was all parties, eating out, holidays, and she was here, sitting with a glass of wine, while her two favourite people in the world were upstairs dealing with their own children.

Rosie gulped down the rest of the wine in her glass and stood up to help herself to another. If there was one thing she loved about Nav, it was his ability to buy only the best wine, and to install a huge wine fridge in their kitchen. She helped herself, like she always did, and on the spur of the moment, she whipped out her phone and snapped a quick photo of the bottle, her glass, and Nav and Bee's, too. The background was blurred, but the twinkling lights that Bee hung around the gazebo in their garden were captured, making the photograph sparkle. From the photo alone, she could be anywhere. Rosie uploaded it with the caption: *Friday night fizz! Let the festive fun begin!*

She scrolled a bit more until Bee walked back into the kitchen, holding her own phone aloft.

'Let the fun begin? What fun?' she said, Rosie's recent post lit up on her phone. 'My fingernails have toddler shit under them and my bra hasn't been washed for weeks. I feel grotty, knackered, and I somehow managed to mix up my mascara and lipstick this morning and ended up with mascara lips that made Aisha cry.' She grabbed a handful of takeaway menus from a kitchen drawer and placed them on the table between them. 'I wouldn't say I was ready to party.'

Rosie blushed. 'I know, I'm pathetic.' She grabbed the menus and began rifling through them absent-mindedly. 'But my social media makes me look crap.'

'Social media isn't real! It's just everyone's shiny, fake perception of what they want people to see,' Bee said, grabbing the wine and topping up both her glass and Rosie's. 'I assume you're staying over?'

One perfectly raised eyebrow arched in her direction and Rosie nodded, watching as Bee slopped in a generous amount into the tangerine-coloured wine glasses that had been bought on their honeymoon. The white wine looked like liquid amber.

'So, did you find anything suitable to wear, then? No LBD stranded at the back of your wardrobe, desperate to be worn?' Bee slid onto a bar stool next to Rosie.

'Nope. I tried on everything I owned last night and everything is either too tight or too revealing.' She gestured down to her soft tummy, evident in a pair of leggings, and her chest, which was currently bursting to escape the top three buttons of her blouse.

She made a mental note to try to curtail that Christmas cookie habit from this moment onwards. And her wine habit. And her pasta habit . . . Her stomach grumbled in disgust. She grabbed at a pizza menu. Bee's eyes lit up.

'Then it's time for *Fashion by Bee*!' she said, jumping down from her stool, her wine sloshing in her glass. 'I think I have just the thing. C'mon.' She grabbed at Rosie's wrist and led her towards the door, passing Nav along the way. 'Order dinner, darling. And don't forget the ice cream for afters!'

Nav saluted them as they passed him, standing to attention in a mock-serious manner. Rosie laughed, allowing herself to be led upstairs.

Chapter Six

'No, Bee.'

'C'mon, it looks great,' Bee pleaded, grabbing the corset element of the dress and tugging it a little higher so that Rosie's nipples weren't so obviously on show.

'No way. They'll think the company has hired a stripper.'

'Now that's rude. This is my dress.'

'Yes, and with your tiny B cups, this would look fantastic. But on my Double Ds, I look indecent. I'm not wearing it.'

She unzipped the corset with difficulty and her breasts made their escape, bursting forwards and releasing her lungs in the same breath. She was not shy in front of Bee. They had seen each other naked thousands of times over the years. She stepped out of the dress and tossed it onto the bed in Bee's spare bedroom, or as Bee liked to call it, her dressing room.

The room itself was large, with a double-aspect window that overlooked the city and with one wall that was floor-to-ceiling wardrobes, while the other remaining wall was floor-to-ceiling mirrors. Rosie had paraded around in this room numerous times, dressed in various outfits: Bee's bridesmaid dress, christening outfits, Christmas party dresses – and it appeared to be fancy dress this evening.

'I need something more . . . conservative,' Rosie said, walking back over to the wardrobe and rifling through the various rails that stretched back at least two deep.

It wasn't quite a walk-in wardrobe, but Nav had done his best when building it, to make it large enough to hold sixteen rails in total: four along the bottom, two rails deep, and four along the top.

'It is work's Christmas party, after all. I need to look professional.'

'Basically, you want to look dull,' Bee said, rolling her eyes, pulling out a black dress from the end of a rail. 'How's this, then?'

'Didn't you wear that to Nav's uncle's funeral last month?' Rosie said, touching the maxi dress, which had a high neckline and long sleeves.

'It's certainly conservative.' Bee shrugged, tossing it onto the bed. 'I'm not one for blending into the background, so I'm not sure I'll have anything.'

She disappeared head first into the bottom rail and Rosie wondered if she'd disappear altogether. Her voice was muffled, but she continued talking, her body pushing ever deeper into the wave of clothes, her feet standing on shoe boxes to gain traction. She twisted back as she began holding out hangers with various outfits, their fabric creased from being constrained in such tight circumstances. Then she stopped, her bottom still protruding between blouses.

'Hold on a minute,' she said.

Rosie could hear the scrape of something heavy and solid being pulled through the rails and into the light of the bedroom. It was a large wooden chest. Bee's eyes were wide in delight.

'I completely forgot about this!' She looked towards Rosie, who shrugged in confusion, and grabbed at a dressing gown from a nearby rail.

It was canary yellow and had an obscene amount of yellow feathers stitched into its lining, but it was warm, and Rosie was no longer half-naked.

'Do you remember this?'

'No? Should I?' Rosie said, rubbing her hand along the curved wooden lid and finding her fingers now covered in a layer of dust.

'From university! My final year? The outfits I didn't end up using but were just too pretty to be thrown away!' Bee's voice rose in excitement and she dropped to her knees in front of the chest.

There was a vintage lock on the front – a large brass hook that swung into a clasp and a red ribbon tied around the hook in what must have been an elaborate bow but was now flattened and knotted.

'Grab me my fabric scissors,' Bee said, pointing at her beloved fabric table beneath the window.

Rosie did as she instructed, handing them to her. Bee effortlessly sliced through the fabric and the ribbon fell to the floor. She unclipped the clasp and seconds later, they were both staring at the inside of the chest, which was full of fabric of various bright colours.

'Wow,' Rosie said, coming forwards and kneeling beside Bee.

Rosie ran her hand gently over the powder-blue silk that was folded on the top of the pile. Bee lifted the fabric and stood up, allowing it to fall gracefully to the floor. It was a full-length dress, with the tiniest of intricate beads sown into the sweetheart neckline and around the waist.

'Wow,' Rosie repeated.

'Oh my gosh, I remember this one! I almost used it in my final piece but decided to go for a darker colour.' Her cheeks were flushed and she was hopping from one foot to another in excitement. 'There is bound to be something for you in here, I'm sure of it,' she said, marching to the door and walking out into the hallway. 'Nav!' she called down to the ground floor. 'Bring us up another bottle, will you? This might take a while . . .'

An hour later, and both Rosie and Bee were lying face-up on the spare bed, slices of now-cold pizza on plates beside them on the bed. The plates were hovering delicately on mounds of clothes like porcelain boats on stormy seas. A bottle of wine lay empty on the carpet below their feet. Bee was wearing a pair of silky ruby-coloured dungarees with gold heels and a fluffy green bolero over her shoulders. Her arms were covered to her elbows with gold fishnet arm warmers and around her head was a huge multicoloured faux peacock feather attached to a velvet hairband that lay across the white bedding. She was a cross between a 1940s wealthy aristocrat and a starving artist.

Rosie, on the other hand, was wearing a classic silver satin dress that, if she was standing, trailed almost to the floor on her. The dress itself was plain over the bust but ruched from the waistline down, in a way that meant it shimmered when she walked. While the neckline was high from the front, it fell low down the rear, into an excess of material that scooped at her lower back. It was both flattering and comfortable, and more importantly, it didn't feel tight around either the bust or the tummy, so Rosie wasn't self-conscious in it.

Her feet were currently bare and Bee had loosely tied a lightweight black satin scarf around her neck that, on closer inspection, had tiny toucan birds printed onto the fabric. Around her left wrist was a large gold bangle of a single toucan, its vibrant orange beak and white chest intricately painted on.

'I sometimes forget how talented you are,' Rosie said, lifting her arm and turning the bangle around so that the bird faced the ceiling.

'Gee, thanks for that. Am I meant to take it as a compliment?'

'Of course!' Rosie said, laughing and turning to her left so she could kiss Bee on the cheek. 'It's just that I don't see many of your creations any more. Since the kids have come along, you're barely darning a sock. You're just so talented. It's a waste, 'tis all.'

'I know, I miss it terribly. But I will rise again once the kids are in school. Like a patchwork phoenix from the woven ashes.' She sat herself upwards and extended her arm towards the door, pointing at her fabric table. 'Armed with my trusty sewing basket in one hand' – she planted her other hand on her waist – 'and my Singer machine by my side, I will reveal myself as the ultimate sewing superwoman.' She held her pose for a second and then fell back onto the bed as they both began laughing. 'So, is that the outfit, then? Have you decided?' Bee asked, touching her hip.

Rosie nodded. 'It is. I love it. Thanks, Bee. You always know how to make me look good.'

Bee shrugged. 'I know. But are you sure I can't quickly whip up a toucan fascinator for you? I could have it done in a few hours, max . . .'

But Rosie was shaking her head, feeling the light-headedness that came from drinking wine. 'A toucan on my head is a step too far, I'm afraid.'

Bee shook her head, letting out a giant hiccup before saying, 'Ah, go on. Who can? You can! Go on, wear my toucan!'

This caused another fit of giggles and Nav, who was walking past the door, rolled his eyes, chuckled and pulled the door to, knowing from previous experience that neither woman would be in any fit state to move from the spare bed tonight and that he would be sleeping alone.

Chapter Seven

Rosie awoke with a start as one eyelid was yanked open by a pair of sticky little fingers. She groaned, wincing at the bright light from a spaceman torch that was being shone into said eye.

'Not now,' she groaned, removing the tiny hand gently and burying her face in the pillow.

But the hands persisted and before she knew it, the covers were being lifted and a tiny warm body climbed in beside her. Rosie then heard a giggle, so she gingerly turned her head to check the source. As she did so, a pounding began in her temples. She groaned again, but the giggling continued. She found herself staring into the wonderfully bright eyes of Sam, his warm body cosying up to hers.

'What are you laughing at, little pickle?' she whispered, more for her sake than his.

'Auntie Rosie, you're so silly. You've gone to bed in a party dress!' Sam said, covering his mouth with his hand, still giggling. 'Mummy says I'm never to go to bed in my clothes and that only pyjamas can be worn to bed. Mummy is going to tell you off.'

He lifted the covers again and pointed at the silver dress that she was still wearing, along with the arm cuff and, for some reason that she couldn't remember, Nav's hiking socks. She rubbed her face with the palm of her hand, waiting for the hangover to properly begin, his giggles acting as a soothing tonic for the time being.

'Oh, I have, haven't I!' she said, whispering to him and stroking his cheek, noticing he was wearing his favourite fluffy onesie. 'What a silly billy I am.' She rolled over to see if Bee was still beside her, but her side of the bed was empty. 'Where is Mummy?'

'She's downstairs, making a *hugover* breakfast for you. What's a hugover?'

Rosie didn't think he could be any sweeter and she pulled him into a hug, whispering into his hair, 'It is when I sleep over but wake up needing lots of hugs.'

'Oh, I'm brilliant at hugs!' Sam said, wrapping his little arms around her waist, sounding very proud.

'Yes, you are, sweetie, yes, you are,' Rosie said, wondering if children were the remedy to all hangovers.

An hour later and Rosie realised that children were definitely not the remedy. If anything, they exacerbated the hangover. Their demands, their cries, their determination to play with toys that appeared to break the sound barrier, all of it just made her feel worse.

After her cuddles with Sam, things had looked positive, with Bee having made chocolate-chip pancakes and strong coffee and offering her pain relief. Bee was neither hungover nor tired. In fact, sleeping in the spare room had meant that she had achieved a nine-hour sleep fest and had drunk the pint of water before sleep that Nav had sensibly left out for both of them, cancelling out any dehydration and reducing any hangover.

But then the twins had woken and Sam then dropped his plate of pancakes on the floor, causing his favourite blue plate to smash, and then all three children appeared to activate their maximum volume of screams to the point where no amount of bargaining or cajoling seemed to make a difference. It was at this point that Rosie made an excuse to leave. She did feel a bit bad – taking the dress, the bangle and Bee's favourite pair of strappy wedges with her – as Bee juggled a twin in each arm and a wailing Sam around her left leg.

'I'll drop them off tomorrow, I promise.'

'Keep them,' Bee said, shrugging. 'I'll never get to wear them again and they look better on you anyways.' She smiled at her. 'You're going to look fabulous tonight, honestly. Just try to enjoy it, please.'

'I will, I will,' Rosie said, grabbing her overnight bag and giving the children a quick kiss.

But Bee grabbed her hand to stop her from walking away, looking serious.

'Rosie, please. You see everything as a chore. Birthday, Christmases, parties, weddings . . . Ever since your mum and dad died . . .' She tailed off, not needing to finish the sentence, her face full of concern. 'I just want you to try a little harder to live a bit more. You deserve it.'

'I do live,' Rosie said, blushing and looking away. 'I live just fine, thank you very much.'

'OK,' Bee said, hoisting one of the twins a little higher on her hip. 'When was the last time you went out, apart from either here or work, in the last month?' Her eyebrow rose questioningly.

Rosie went to respond, opening her mouth, but no words were forthcoming. She thought over the last few weeks. Sure, she'd been busy with work trying to meet her quota, and she'd felt too tired for the gym, or eating out, or socialising. She thought of the three Christmas party invites she'd turned down only last weekend, preferring instead to re-wallpaper the second bedroom. And when was the last time she left the city? She couldn't even remember.

'Exactly,' Bee said, looking both satisfied and sad. 'You don't live, you just exist. You work, you sleep, you stay holed up in your parents' house as if there isn't a whole world out there waiting for you. And it is, waiting for you. You're an oxymoron! You work for a travel agency, but you don't travel! You have a kitchen enviably larger than mine and you don't host! You admire the love you saw between your parents, yet you seem in no rush to find your own. You're almost thirty, Rosie.' Her voice rose. 'Travel! Find love! Find passion! I can't remember the last time I really saw you passionate about anything, Rosie. And that makes me so sad. It would make your parents sad, too. I know it would.'

That last comment smarted. Rosie had adored her parents and she hated the thought that she might be disappointing them, and she knew Bee knew that.

'And what about you?' she said, anger flaring suddenly, like a match to a flame. 'You gave up all of your dreams when you married Nav. You were going to travel, become the next big thing in the fashion world. And you gave it all up to change nappies and talk about preschools.'

She knew it was childish, and hurtful, but she felt attacked. So what if she didn't go out that much? She was happy at home. She looked at Bee, who didn't rise to the bait.

'My plans are on hold while I change direction for a bit and focus on some pretty awesome lane-changers,' she said, kissing both twins, who had stopped crying from the tension in the room. 'I still fully intend on going back to fashion. I'm passionate about it. But what are you passionate about, hey? Like, truly passionate about?'

'I'm passionate about a lot of things,' Rosie said, her grip on her bag handles tightening.

'Such as?' Bee asked, lowering both twins onto the kitchen counter and placing her hands on their knees.

'Such as my work—'

'Your work that saw you almost miss your target and causes you undue stress,' Bee said, interrupting her. 'Anything else?'

Rosie shook her head. 'Where has all this sprung from? What's your problem?'

'I don't have a problem—'

'It sure feels like it to me,' Rosie said, turning away from her and heading towards the front door.

'Rosie, please. It's only because I care,' Bee said, unable to follow as the twins were wriggling to get down.

'Or maybe you just want to rub your stupid happy life in my face. You clearly think you're better than me.'

Rosie had opened the door and looked back at Bee for only a moment before pulling the door to and heading down the three steps from the townhouse onto the pavement.

She felt so angry that she stomped forwards, ignoring glares from passers-by as she bulldozed through them on her way towards the main street. She continued walking, despite the heavy rain that began to pound her head and shoulders, until she came across a bus stop and stopped, her fingers raw from carrying the heavy bags.

A bus pulled up and she got on. With dripping hair and a splitting headache, the twenty-minute journey across town didn't help to lower her anger. The bus was packed with Christmas shoppers and mothers with prams and the noise felt intolerable. She appeared to be the only person alone.

It was only when she walked the five-minute distance from the bus stop on the corner of her road to her door that her anger subsided. As her functional mind kicked in, she remembered that not only did she not have her house keys, but also that, in her anger and haste, she had left her car outside Bee's house.

Tired, hung-over and soaked through from the freezing rain, Rosie slumped onto her front step and dropped her head into her hands, her dripping hair causing tiny puddles on the mosaic paving slabs her father had installed years ago. Rosie remembered watching him level the soil and lift the large slabs, while she had sat crossed-legged on the grass, her eight-year-old voice singing songs to keep him company. An ache ripped through her chest and bubbled up her throat. She missed him. She missed her mother. She was so lonely. A loud sob escaped, and it was at this point that, finally, the tears began to flow.

Chapter Eight

After being cajoled into Mrs Benson's house next door and dried down like a wet dog, Rosie was now nursing a hot cup of honey tea in her neighbour's front room beside the electric fire. Mrs Benson had been her elderly neighbour since the day she was born. A widow in her late eighties, she had been both a chore and a pleasure to have in close proximity. She was incredibly useful to store a spare key with, to direct post and parcels to, and when Rosie's parents died, she was an ever-present figure with a steaming casserole dish to make sure Rosie was well fed.

But she also had the unfortunate habit of being a gossip, a curtain-twitcher and a woman who had so little going on in her own life that she relied on the excitement of others. Which is why she had been on Rosie's drive within minutes of her bursting into tears, with an umbrella and her walking stick, saying all the right things to encourage Rosie into her house to 'tell her everything'.

'What you need is a good man in your life,' Mrs Benson said, carrying in a large, crimped plate of sliced cake and fanned biscuits.

She placed it on the small table beside Rosie before sitting down in her own armchair opposite her.

'That was Sid's chair,' she said, nodding in Rosie's direction. 'He always liked to sit facing the window so that he could see the world go by. He used to say, "Times are changing, Beatrice. The world moves on, yet here we sit, unchanged." He would often read the paper and shake his head in disbelief. He never could quite keep up with the speed of how things change.'

Mrs Benson looked wistfully at the small artificial Christmas tree that stood on a small table in the corner of the room, her glazed eyes caught in the past. The lights were switched off and the decorations looked vintage, as if plucked from the 1940s.

Rosie took a bite of her biscuit and it seemed to draw Mrs Benson back into the present. Her head turned and she focused in on her.

'So, what are we to do with you, then?'

'Well, I'd love my spare key, if that's OK? I have a party to get ready for tonight—'

'A party! Oh, how fabulous!' Mrs Benson said, clapping her hands together, her lined face crinkling like crepe paper into a smile. 'At yours? That house is such a perfect place for hosting.'

'No, no. Not at mine,' Rosie said, placing the half-eaten biscuit on her saucer and removing the towel from around her shoulders. She was no longer sodden, but her clothes were beginning to stick to her uncomfortably. She shifted herself. 'It's my work Christmas party this evening and I need to get ready for it.'

As if on cue, the carriage clock on the large mantelpiece began to chime, indicating it was already three o'clock.

'I really should make a move.' She saw the look of disappointment on Mrs Benton's face and immediately felt guilty. It was obvious this old woman was lonely, but she'd processed enough emotions already – she felt burnt out. 'Thank you so much for being so helpful. You're such a kind neighbour.'

She hoped the compliments would soften the blow of her leaving. It worked.

'Oh, my pleasure!' Mrs Benton said, her cheeks flushing the palest pink against her sallow skin.

She got herself upright with the help of her stick and walked into the hallway before returning with Rosie's spare key.

'Here you are.'

Rosie took the key from her outstretched hand and smiled gratefully. 'Thank you.'

She walked to the front door and collected her belongings before turning back to Mrs Benton.

'What are your plans for Christmas, Mrs Benton? Will you spend it with family?'

Mrs Benton flushed again, but this time her eyes turned away from Rosie before answering.

'Oh, you know, I'm still deciding. Edward is busy with his hotel and Edith says she already has her hands full with the in-laws visiting from New Zealand. It's a very busy time for everyone . . .'

She tailed off, fiddling with the netting hung over the small window next to the front door. There was a small tear in the netting and Rosie noticed her eyes narrow in frustration at the damage.

'Yes, I bet. But I'm sure they'd both love for you to visit,' Rosie said, hoping that Mrs Benton wasn't about to spend her Christmas alone.

'Yes, well, as I say, nothing decided as yet. But enough about me, you go! Have a bath, curl and set your hair, draw on your stockings! You never know, perhaps you'll find the man of your dreams tonight!' She tittered like a schoolgirl and opened the door, allowing a cold gust to blast them both.

Rosie stepped out into the wintery conditions.

'I very much doubt that.'

'Ah, doubt is merely the dismissal of believing,' Mrs Benton said, wrapping her knitted cardigan tighter around her middle. 'Remove the doubt and true love will find its way in.' She waved Rosie off down the garden path before shutting her front door and disappearing into the warmth of her house.

As Rosie walked the few steps into her own front garden and up her path to the front door, she couldn't help but think of Mrs Benton's words. Did she dismiss every opportunity? Was she closed off to new experiences? Did her self-preservation mean she was blocking out the chance to live properly?

Unlocking her front door and walking into the warmth of her own house, she realised how silent and how huge the hallway felt. It was by no means a grand house, but it was built with the intention of being occupied by a family. There should be wellies piled up against the large radiator to her left and a pile of discarded toys on the wide stairs. She removed her coat and placed it on the almost-empty coat stand, which she realised should be full of anoraks, blazers and jackets of all shapes and sizes.

As Rosie made her way up the stairs and into the family bathroom to run herself a hot bubble bath, she looked around at the neatness of everything. The row of cosmetics, the single bath towel, the empty washing basket. With the bathwater gushing out of the tap, she walked into her bedroom and examined the contents, its tidy furniture and lack of personality easily visible. It wasn't even new furniture. It was her parents'. She hadn't yet put her stamp on this house, instead choosing to hold onto her parents' choices.

Bee's voice reverberated through her mind, like an announcement at a theme park: *I can't remember the last time I really saw you passionate about anything, Rosie. You don't live, you just exist.*

'I'll show her,' Rosie said, peeling off her wet clothes and leaving them on the landing carpet. 'I can be passionate. I know how to live.'

Four hours later, Rosie was feeling a lot more confident. She had soaked her worries away for a good hour in the bath before climbing out and wrapping her warm, wrinkly skin in her dressing gown and making herself an early dinner. Fried eggs and reheated cauliflower cheese with crispy bacon worked wonders on the hangover. She then spent another hour pampering herself by painting her nails and blow-drying her hair.

She kept her make-up to a minimum, like always, but doubled up on the eyeliner, thickening her brush stroke so that she had a definite emphasis around each eye that only seemed to make her eyes seem larger than they already were. She dressed them with three layers of mascara and only a hint of gloss to the lips. Her eyes had always been her best asset and tonight she wanted to show them off. It felt good to focus on her good parts for once, rather than constantly berating herself for her flaws.

Finally, it was time to slip into Bee's dress. She had deliberately hung it in the bathroom for the duration of her bath so that the creases fell from the dress and as she climbed into it, the silky-smooth fabric glided over her curves sexily. She didn't allow herself to think of Bee and how this was her dress; she only focused on how it made her look. She added the toucan cuff and a few other simple pieces of jewellery before spritzing herself with her mother's favourite scent and calling for a taxi. While the party was only a ten-minute drive from hers, she had no intention of either walking the distance or taking public transport.

With her heels securely fastened and her small clutch containing just her phone, credit card and house keys, she headed out through her front door when she heard the double beep of the taxi. As she gingerly walked the front pathway towards her gate, she caught sight of Mrs Benson running over from her side of the garden towards their shared low-level fence.

'Yoo-hoo!' Mrs Benson called, her yellow towelling dressing gown and wellington boots moving at a good speed for someone in their eighties. 'Rosie! I have something for you.'

She was waving her left hand in the air in front of her, but in the darkness, Rosie couldn't see what it was. With the taxi waiting, its engine humming, she walked over to Mrs Benson.

'Mrs Benson, it's too cold for you to be out here at night,' she said, looking at her outstretched hand, which appeared to be holding something small and shiny.

'Oh, I'm as hardy as holly and ivy,' she said, blowing off her concern with the wave of her other hand. 'Here, this is for you. My arthritic old fingers can no longer squeeze it on, so I would rather you wear it on my behalf. Please?'

Rosie stared down at Mrs Benson's outstretched hand to see a large ring in her palm. She leant in closer over their shared fence and saw it was a silver ring with a circular plate depicting the Earth, the outlines of the continents etched into the silver. It was a statement ring, but also not gaudy with its simple outline and lack of gem or colour. Rosie loved it instantly.

'Oh, no. I couldn't take it from you. It looks very expensive,' Rosie declared, taking a step back, but Mrs Benson insisted, thrusting it forwards with shaking hands. She was clearly cold.

'Please, Rosie. It brought me such joy and reminded me that there is a big old world out there waiting to be explored. I want you to wear it for me so that I can live vicariously through you.'

Her face was pleading yet stern. Rosie could see she would keep insisting. She reached out and took it from Mrs Benson's hand. The ring shone under the cold winter moonlight. She tried her ring finger first, but it was too loose, so she slipped it onto her middle finger to find it was a perfect fit. And it looked fantastic against the silver of her dress.

The taxi driver beeped his horn impatiently, but Mrs Benson waved him away as if brushing off a fly.

'There,' she said, satisfied, 'it looks stunning. I knew it would. I once had hands as smooth and as beautiful as yours. Now, they are past their prime, a bit like me!' she said, letting out a chuckle. 'Now go. Enjoy your evening and I look forward to hearing about it soon.'

Without waiting for a response, she turned and walked back a little unsteadily to her open front door, turning to wave as she stepped over the threshold. Her yellowy golden silhouette was outlined by the hallway light behind her.

'Thank you so much,' Rosie said to her retreating form, rubbing her hands over the surface of the ring, her fingertip tracing the indents of the world.

The taxi driver beeped again. She walked towards him and opened the car door, giving Mrs Benson a little wave before climbing inside. Rosie felt exhausted already, and the evening was only just beginning.

Chapter Nine

The Wanderlust Wishes Christmas party was being held at a swanky hotel in the centre of the city. The company had hired one of the function rooms and all staff had been invited, from every region. Bastard Ben had reckoned there would be well over one hundred people there tonight and on first sight, Rosie quite believed him. The large room had been set up with tables and chairs situated around a large dance floor, and the room was dimly lit, with numerous disco balls turning and projecting a kaleidoscope of colour on the moving bodies.

The dance floor was packed already with swaying people and there was a DJ in the corner, surrounded by his sound equipment, his head down, music pumping from various speakers in the room.

Rosie looked around for a familiar face but couldn't see anyone, so she decided to walk to the bar to obtain some liquid courage. Wanderlust Wishes as a company always rewarded their employees and this year was no exception. Not only was there a free bar, but there was also a rather impressive long table of food. As she walked around the periphery of the dance floor, her view opened to the back of the room, where she was stunned to see a nine-foot chocolate fountain in action, with chocolate waves flowing downwards into people's glasses, bowls and in some cases, open mouths.

She reached the bar and ordered a large glass of white wine. Her chest felt tight and she was uneasy about her appearance. All her confidence from last night seemed to have evaporated after her fight with Bee and now her silver dress seemed to be clinging to all of her curves in the wrong places. She also hadn't realised how low-cut the back was, so she surreptitiously took sips from her glass with her back to the bar. She pulled on the toucan scarf subconsciously, trying to swivel it around so that it draped down her back, but she ended up almost simultaneously garrotting herself and spilling her drink down her dress.

'Rosie!'

She turned to see the familiar sight of Audrey moving towards her through the crowd. Instead of the usual work uniform, she was wearing the most fabulous, collared sequin palazzo jumpsuit that seemed to sparkle with every movement of her wheelchair. Her shoes were midnight-blue velvet ankle boots with heels that sparkled with faux diamonds. Her silver bob was pinned up and curled, so that tendrils fell around her pretty face, and Rosie didn't think she had ever looked more beautiful.

'Audrey! That outfit! You look insane!' Rosie said, leaning down and kissing Audrey on the cheek. She smelt of bubblegum and rose petals, like always.

'I know,' Audrey said, twirling her wheelchair around so that Rosie could get a 360-degree look, her confidence enviable.

'And those boots,' Rosie continued, examining the heels. 'Can I borrow them?'

'Sure,' Audrey said, shrugging. 'It's not like they'll get much use from me.'

She said it jokingly, but there was a tinge of sadness to her eyes as she said it. Rosie knew that she hadn't always been in a wheelchair. She was seventeen when she was hit one night by a thirty-eight-year-old drunk driver as she walked home. He had been arrested and served his four-year prison sentence, but in one split second, Audrey had been given a life sentence in a wheelchair.

But that hadn't deterred her from her path. Within six months, she was back in college and began campaigning for alcohol awareness in lots of rallies. She even visited schools to try to steer young minds away from drifting into a life of alcoholism. It was at one of those schools that she had met her future husband, a gentle soul called James who had been the headmaster of the secondary school. Within half an hour of meeting her, he swore to himself that he would ask her to marry him. Which he did – three times.

Each time she refused, stating their incompatibility. He took that to mean her disability, so he sold his house and bought a small plot of land in the nearby town, where he brought in a contractor to build an accessible bungalow that was as unique and as pretty as his future wife. It was on his fourth time of asking her to marry him, after surprising her with a visit to the newly completed house, that she accepted him through her tears. They had lived in that house and been married for over a decade now.

Those boots will always look better on you, though, and you know it,' Rosie said. 'Drink?'

'Sure.'

They both moved towards the bar, Rosie ordering a bottle of house red. She knew that was Audrey's favourite. The barman placed it on the counter, along with two glasses, and gave Rosie a wink. She flushed.

'Well, hello there, my lusty ladies.'

A familiar leering and clearly drunken voice caused Rosie to turn around, to find Bastard Ben walking towards them, his eyes focused about six inches down from Rosie's face. He was wearing a smart-cut designer suit with a loosened narrow tie, the top two buttons of his shirt undone. His hair was stiffly styled, as always, but his eyes were glassy and it was clear that he was making use of the free bar.

'Don't call us that,' Audrey said, rolling her eyes.

'Why not?' Benjamin said, attempting to lean against the bar but misjudging the distance, causing some of the liquid in his drink to splash onto the floor. 'Whoops, steady as she goes,' he said, a snort coming out of his nose. 'You work for Wanderlust Wishes. Therefore, it is fitting that I call you the lusty ladies.'

'It's insulting, that's why,' said Audrey.

'Insulting?' Benjamin said, giving Audrey a wink. 'It's a compliment.'

'It just sounds pervy. And I don't like it, so don't say it,' Audrey said, taking the bottle of wine from Rosie and placing it between her legs before spinning around and moving towards a table.

While Audrey's back was turned, Benjamin leant forwards and placed a hand on Rosie's hip, his fingers slowly stroking the fabric of her dress.

'You look so hot in this dress,' he said, moving a little closer.

She could feel both his heat and his warm, alcoholic breath against her cheek. His fingers kept stroking. Her instincts told her to step back, but the stroking was so nice and she couldn't remember the last time she had been touched. She closed her eyes for the briefest of seconds, enjoying the sensation.

'How did I never notice how smoking your body was before?'

'Probably the nylon uniform I wear every day to the office,' Rosie said, moving away from him, his voice snapping her out of her stupor. 'Best get over to Audrey. She has the wine and I,' she said, holding up the two glasses crossed between her fingers, 'have the wine glasses.'

But he moved towards her again, his roaming hand snaking its way around her waist towards the base of her spine where her dress fell away to bare skin.

'How about a quick dance?' he persisted, his fingers working their way up her spine.

She shivered, which he took as a sign to continue.

'Or a bit of fresh air?' He nodded towards the exit.

For a millisecond, she considered it. Embarrassingly, the idea of a quick fumble and some male attention was something she hadn't had for a long time now. But common sense prevailed and she remembered him for who he was, Bastard Ben.

'Thanks, but Audrey is waiting for me.'

She gave him a quick smile before turning on her stiletto heel and walking away from him. She could feel his eyes watching her as she went and her emotions felt conflicted again. What was going on with her? How desperate was she?

It turned out Rosie was extremely desperate.

A couple of hours later, and what appeared to be three bottles of wine down, Rosie was decidedly drunk. They had sunk the first bottle quickly, with Rosie grabbing the second bottle, and with every glass, more people seemed to appear at their table. Employees from other branches who they had met at previous events joined in with the drinking and their table soon became the most raucous in the room.

Rosie had eaten almost nothing all day, yet she had kept drinking. Her stomach grumbled loudly in frustration, but she ignored it in favour of doing shots with Isadora, who was on her first night out since having her baby and was also determined to make use of the free bar. Rosie's head was beginning to spin and she noticed uncertainly that when she turned her head, her vision didn't always follow immediately. The room swayed in time to the music and the dance floor was lit by a kaleidoscope of colour that Rosie found both hypnotic and unsettling. After the third shot, she felt an arm around her waist and turned to find Isadora pulling her onto the dance floor.

'C'mon, let's dance!'

Isadora was clearly drunk and she stumbled onto the dance floor with her eyes half closed and began to gyrate to the music. To Rosie, she looked like the sexiest human being on Earth, so she began to copy her, their bodies moving in time to the music, and other people joined them, until the dance floor was a heaving mass of sweaty, drunken bodies.

Rosie could feel the bass of the music pulse through her legs and up into her torso, encouraging her to sway and swirl in time to the music. She didn't care who watched or who saw her – she was lost in the music, her drunken mind allowing her the freedom to live purely in that moment.

That was until a hand slipped around her waist and pulled her close. A hand that found its way to her lower back, as before, and was joined by a second hand on her hip that gently moved in motion with her. Rosie tried to focus, but her vision was blurring, and the face seemed too close, too intimate.

But the masculine aftershave smelt amazing and she leant in, resting her head on the person's shoulder and wrapping her arms around his neck. The music changed to a slower beat and she pulled the person closer, enjoying the sensation of being held.

'Well, this is a surprise,' she heard him say, and the voice registered with the conscious part in her mind.

Benjamin. Her boss.

She lifted her head from his shoulder and found herself at eye level with him – and took in his large, sexy eyes with strong eyebrows and a jawline that was so sharp, the stubble looked artificial. With his straight roman nose and his lips that were slightly parted to reveal two beautiful lines of straight white teeth, she suddenly felt a stirring deep inside of her. He was so good-looking. How had she not noticed it before?

And why did they call him Bastard Ben? That was unfair. He appeared to be a total gentleman tonight, being nothing more than friendly. And in his arms, it just felt right.

So what that he had been with his fair share of women . . . At least that meant he knew what he was doing. The thought of his practised hands bringing her pleasure ripped through her body and without another thought, she leant in and kissed him hard, harder than she intended.

But he didn't seem to mind. He responded, pulling her even closer so that their chests were pressed together, and she opened her mouth wider, wanting more of him.

She was faintly aware of whoops and hollers from those around them, but she didn't care. His kisses were something else. She could feel his energy and passion, and she ran her fingers through his hair, their kisses intensifying.

Wait, was someone calling her name?

She tried to ignore it, letting Benjamin's kisses take her to a place she hadn't been for a while, but the voice persisted. And appeared to get louder. She allowed Benjamin's hands to lower to her bottom and he gave her a gentle squeeze, applying just the right amount of pleasure for her to let out a little groan.

Benjamin groaned, too, but his was different. It was more of an anguished, in-pain type of groan. And suddenly he pulled away from her, bending down to grab his left foot.

'Shit, shit! C'mon, Audrey, watch where you are going!' he yelled, breaking Rosie out of her passionate daydream.

Rosie stumbled slightly, trying to find her balance without him to lean on. Then she felt a tug on her left hand. Looking beside her, she saw Audrey's concerned face staring up at her from her wheelchair on the dance floor.

'Rosie, we're leaving. Let's go.'

'What? I don't want to . . .' she began.

But Audrey didn't seem to hear, or care, as she spun her chair around with only one hand while keeping an iron grip on Rosie's hand and began to move from the dance floor towards the exit.

'Audrey, what's going on? Why are we leaving?'

The speed with which Audrey was moving seemed too fast for Rosie's blurred vision and she became aware of other bodies surrounding her as they moved towards the double-doored exit. An arm looped through hers before a hand pushed open the doors and led her into the atrium of the hotel.

But they didn't stop – they kept moving, towards the deep mahogany revolving doors, which swirled her around for what seemed like an eternity. Until she felt a blast of icy air hit her face, when she realised that she was now outside on the pavement.

With her eyes to the ground and the world continuing to spin, Rosie leant over, placed her hands on her knees and promptly threw up all over her shoes. She could hear groans and a harsh voice asking them to move along, but the last thing she remembered before passing out was having her hair held back, her back stroked and the soothing sounds of shushing. And then everything went black.

Chapter Ten

Rosie awoke to a sense of unfamiliarity. Opening her eyes to the darkness of the room, she tried to assess her surroundings and work out where she was. It was oddly disillusioning. She sat up, but immediately regretted it as the hammering in her head began, and a surge of nausea rose like a wave from her stomach into her gullet.

Knowing she was going to throw up in some unrecognisable room, she tried to push back the covers to climb out, but her bare foot did not hit the floor; it fell straight into a bucket. A yellow bucket with a handwritten sign sellotaped onto its side, with the words 'sick bowl'. Mentally thanking the unknown person who'd placed it there, she violently threw up into the bucket while her stomach growled angrily.

Wiping her mouth with some well-placed tissues on the bedside table, she spotted a large glass of water, along with a small trinket plate containing two (assumed) paracetamol, and a note saying, 'Come down when ready. No rush.' Who had done that?

She swallowed the tablets, along with the whole pint of water, and leant back against the soft headboard, waiting for the nausea to subside. Closing her eyes, she tried to think back to the night before and what had happened, but it was all a thick fog in her memory and trying to visualise it was like trying to grab hold of a cloud. Opening her eyes again, she instead took in first the room, and then her attire. Someone had clearly dressed her, as she was no longer wearing her silver gown but instead a full-length white cotton nightie that had a frilly high neck and long sleeves.

In a panic, her hands scuffled under the nightdress to check for underwear and was relieved to feel both her bra and her large support knickers still in place. So, wherever she was, she was safe.

She then took in the dim room once again, shadows forming from heavy black-out curtains. It was large for a bedroom, with a wide area of space in its centre, built-in wardrobes with low handles and a dressing table without a chair. The dressing table was full of cosmetics, bottles, perfumes and a large jewellery box shaped like wooden doors, which were open. Inside hung numerous necklaces from little hooks. Like a wardrobe for necklaces, Rosie thought. How cute.

She tried sitting up again and this time she managed it without vomiting, which she took as a sign of encouragement. Her stomach grumbled again. She needed food.

Attempting one foot back on the floor and resolutely ignoring the putrid smell of her own sick from the bucket, she found that a pair of fluffy yellow slippers had been neatly placed beside the bed for her to slip her feet into. She did so, enjoying the sense of pleasure from their softness, which was in sharp contrast to the aching in her temples. Sitting with her arms either side of her, she took in the rest of the darkened room. Aside from the built-in wardrobes, she now noticed the wall of shelves stacked with row upon row of shoes. Ankle boots, ballet pumps, stilettos, heels, wedges, all differing colours and all of them beautiful. She searched for any trainers or practical shoes but saw none. This was a shoe-aholic's room, that much was evident.

She tried to stand and found that it didn't lead to any catastrophic effects, so she delicately moved towards the shelves. The shoes were so well cared for. Each one was like new, the soles barely scuffed and the heels still clean. And as Rosie approached, she recognised one in particular. A pair of midnight-blue velvet ankle boots with heels that sparkled with faux diamonds were positioned on the middle shelf and, on closer inspection, were not as clean as the others. In fact, Rosie noticed that parts of the velvet were splattered with a dried yellowy substance. As she leant in, she caught the unmistakable smell of vomit mixed with alcohol, and a flashback raced into her mind from last night – of her throwing up all over the pavement and again over Audrey's shoes.

She knew where she was. She was at Audrey's house. And she had no idea of how she got there, or how she was going to repay Audrey for the damage to her beloved shoes. More importantly, how she was going to look her in the eye when she left the room and had to face both her and her husband. Her cheeks flushed with embarrassment and she made her way back to the bed before collapsing onto it, her unfamiliar nightie floating down around her as she let out a long groan.

There was a knock at the bedroom door only minutes later and Rosie stiffened, not wanting anyone to see her in her current state. But then Audrey's muted voice came through the solid door.

'Rosie? Rosie? I have some toast and a cup of tea for you here. Would you like it?'

Rosie's stomach rumbled its answer. She wanted that toast.

'Yes, please. Just leave it on the floor. I'll come get it.'

'That's OK, I'll bring it in.'

'No, no . . .' Rosie began, but Audrey had already opened the door and wheeled herself in, a tray resting on her lap with a plate of toast and a mug.

'Come on now, I don't care what state you're in. You threw up all over me last night and I'm still here, making sure you're alive, aren't I?' She gestured to the tray.

Rosie groaned again. 'I'm so embarrassed. I'm so sorry,' she said, taking the tea from the tray and wincing as Audrey checked the contents of the bucket. 'Sorry again,' she said, sipping the wonderful sugary tea, which felt like the most beautiful liquid in the world. It warmed her sore, dry throat.

'Blimey, girl. How long have we been friends for? I can handle a bit of sick, and so can James. He's done his fair share of having to clean up after me,' she said.

At the mention of his name, he appeared at the doorway, with long rubber gloves on both hands and a cheery smile.

'Clean-up on aisle nine,' Audrey said, pointing at the bucket, and before Rosie could protest, he whisked the bucket away and out of the room like a cleaning ninja. Audrey handed Rosie the plate. 'Here, eat. You'll feel so much better.'

Rosie did as she was told, taking a tentative bite from the first piece. On realising how hungry she was, she wolfed down the second slice and picked up the crumbs with her fingers.

'Told you,' Audrey said, winking at her and taking back the plate. 'James!' she hollered. 'Fire up the frying pan, she's in need of a bacon sarnie.'

'Righto,' James called back from the kitchen. 'Give me ten minutes and I'll have two bacon sarnies ready and waiting.'

'What a guy . . .' Rosie said, leaning back, her shoulders slumped.

'I know. I struck gold with him,' Audrey said, looking over her shoulder towards the hallway. She then turned back to face Rosie. 'So, about last night . . .'

'I know, I'm sorry, I'll pay for the shoes to be professionally cleaned,' Rosie said, pointing towards the shelves of shoes.

But Audrey turned her head towards the shoes and wafted away the notion with a wave of her hand.

'Shoes? Oh, I don't care tuppence for those shoes. I'm talking about Bastard Ben!'

'What about Bastard Ben?' Rosie asked, not understanding.

Audrey's eyes were wide. 'Er, about you practically going to third base with him right there on the dance floor?'

'What?' Rosie said, shaking her head. 'There's no way I would do that!'

'Er, are you sure?' Audrey said, pulling her phone from her jeans pocket and swiping the screen until she found what she was looking for.

Audrey triumphantly turned the phone screen around so that Rosie could view it. It was unequivocally, unmistakably, a clear and close-up video of her and Benjamin in a passionate, and clearly drunken, embrace while the dancers around them cheered and hollered. She felt the familiar rise of bile in her throat but managed to swallow it down.

'No, no, no . . .' she said, shaking her head in disbelief. 'I didn't, I couldn't . . .'

'You did and you shouldn't have, Rosie. What were you thinking?' Audrey said it kindly, but she was shaking her head in disbelief.

'I-I-I don't know,' Rosie said, lowering onto her pillow face down and groaning. 'I don't remember.'

'Oh, Rosie,' Audrey said, brushing Rosie's hair off her face onto the pillow kindly. 'Don't worry about it now, just rest. I'll get you your bacon sarnie.'

'Let me see it again,' Rosie said, gesturing towards Audrey's phone.

Audrey hesitated, clearly debating whether or not it would be a good idea. But then she handed it over before heading back into the hallway. Rosie pressed Play, watching with horror her body react to Benjamin's touch and how desperate she looked. She couldn't remember any of it, but watching how her fellow employees cheered and laughed at her made her blood turn cold.

'Oh, Rosie,' she said to the room, 'what have you done?'

At which point her phone trilled from within her bag on the bedside table, indicating a message. She bent over the mattress to fumble through the small bag and retrieved her phone, noticing with embarrassment that she had twelve messages from various employees, all wanting the goss. But the latest one made her sit up straight, the toast crumbs on her chest falling onto the duvet. It was from Benjamin:

Hey, gorgeous, you left too soon last night! I had to party on without you! How about we pick up where we left off tonight, my place, 7.30pm?

'Oh, no, no, no, no . . .' Rosie wailed into the darkness, causing Audrey to return.

'What's wrong? Need the sick bucket again?'

Rosie said nothing but handed her phone over to her. Audrey read the message, her eyes wide.

'Oh, Rosie,' she said, shaking her head. 'You have got yourself in a bit of a pickle, haven't you?' She then spun her wheelchair around and called out, 'James! Sod the bacon sarnie, we're in need of something a little more hardcore. Can you get the car ready, please?' She then turned back to Rosie and with one strong sweep of her hands, she pulled the cover back, a waft of cold air causing Rosie to shiver.

'C'mon,' Audrey said, gesturing to the wardrobe. 'Get dressed. We're off to Jonah's.'

Chapter Eleven

'Ladies! Always a pleasure, never a chore. Take a seat and I'll be with you momentarily.'

Audrey wheeled over to the nearest table as James moved a chair out of the way for her while Rosie followed slowly behind. Her feet dragged across the tiled floor and she knew that even with a face-full of make-up, she was looking less like her namesake and more like a crushed mouldy green apple. She slumped into a chair opposite Audrey and lowered her head onto the table.

'Ooo, rough night, was it, Rosie?'

Jonah's voice seemed close and Rosie painfully lifted her pounding head from the table, finding his kind eyes looking at her. She nodded, wincing.

'Self-inflicted?' he continued, and Audrey answered on her behalf.

'You could say that.' She looked up at Jonah, her face serious. 'We're going to need three of Martha's specials, please. As quickly as possible. And three large coffees. Thanks, Jonah.'

'Oh, my. We haven't had to do one of those for a while,' he said, his face mock-serious.

He walked away from their table and towards the counter. Lifting a large golden church bell that was situated on the mantelpiece, he rang it with a solemn air and Martha appeared at the kitchen door, her hair tied back via a silver scarf and one perfectly sculpted eyebrow raised.

'Three of your specials, my dear.'

She nodded and disappeared back through the swinging door as a waft of sweetness emanated from the kitchen.

The coffee shop was busy, as usual, and the regulars looked towards Rosie's table.

Rosie didn't speak. Nor did Audrey or James, until Jonah appeared back at their table carrying a tray of three large coffees and a generous jug of cream. He placed them on the table and disappeared back to waiting customers at the counter. James poured cream into all three mugs, followed by two sugars for Rosie, and slid the coffee across the table towards her.

'Drink this,' he said kindly, and she lifted her head to the warmth and sweetness of the coffee.

She sipped at it slowly, the hot liquid warming her cold lips.

'So,' Audrey said, 'we need to respond to Benjamin soon or he's going to think you're up for tonight. Pass me your phone, Rosie.'

She did as instructed and Audrey used Rosie's finger to open the phone with a swipe.

She read the message aloud again, making Rosie wince, and said, 'We need to let him down gently. James?'

James nodded and said, 'Don't say you're not interested. A man hates to hear they are not desired. Just say you don't think it'll be professional to continue with anything romantic and that you are dedicated to your work.'

'Ooo, that's good,' Audrey said, her fingers moving quickly across the screen.

'And say that while it was fun last night' – Rosie's pallor turned a little green at the memory, but he continued – 'you're not looking to date anyone at the moment.'

'I don't think it's a long-term girlfriend he's after,' Audrey said. 'More like a quick shag.'

'I know, but as her boss, he can't exactly say that, now, can he?' James said, encouraging her to type that.

Audrey did and then pressed Send.

'Done.' She placed the phone on the table just as Jonah appeared with a larger tray piled with plates and bowls.

'Martha's lentil and bacon soup,' he said, placing the steaming bowls on the table in front of them, followed by three large plates. 'Along with her infamous egg-coated, deep-fried cheesy toast' – three more plates were placed on the table – 'and to finish, her dark chocolate and peanut flapjacks, covered with pumpkin and sesame seeds. Full of zinc and vitamin B, guaranteed to cure any hangover this side of the British Isles.' He placed the last plate, piled high with flapjacks, in the centre of the table and handed over some cutlery.

'Yum,' both James and Audrey said, grabbing spoons while Jonah slid a soup bowl closer to Rosie.

'Eat,' he said kindly. 'It'll help.'

Rosie smiled weakly and took the spoon from him, trying a bit. It tasted so wonderful – warming and smooth – that she kept eating, her stomach grateful for the sustenance.

Moments passed as the three of them ate in silence, each savouring the deliciousness that was Martha's cooking. Then Rosie's phone trilled into life with a message. All three of them paused, their spoons midway to their mouths. Audrey picked it up and handed it to Rosie, who unlocked the screen. Audrey then read the message aloud:

'You? Act professional? Give me a break. You were up for it last night. But fine, have it your way. I'll see you Monday at work. I expect to see your dedication to the job produce a lot of sales next week, based on your professionalism, OK?'

'Wow. He truly is the epitome of an arsehole, isn't he?' James said, and both girls nodded. 'This message alone would probably see him being served a disciplinary,' he continued, tapping the side of his temple.

'But I voluntarily participated. And it was outside of work hours,' Rosie piped up, finally feeling better enough to talk. Martha's cooking was seriously pure magic. 'Plus, I'm on dodgy ground with regard to sales anyways – he's already spoken to me about that.'

'But you sold that booking last week. That geriatric booking to Italy! He can't complain about that.'

'No, he can't,' Rosie said, taking a large gulp of coffee, 'but I'm sure he will find something to complain about.' She sighed loudly. 'Why do I get the feeling that next week is going to be one huge shitshow?'

Neither James nor Audrey had an answer to this and they sat there in silence, finishing their food. If only they'd known how right Rosie was.

James dropped Rosie off at her house an hour later, Rosie's car sitting stationary in the driveway. After thanking them and waving them off, she approached her beloved Mini Cooper to find Bee sitting in the driver's seat, asleep. Rosie stifled a giggle. Bee was a beauty to look at: cropped blonde hair that framed her face and huge oval blue eyes that made her look like an anime character. Her bee-stung lips, from which her nickname originated, required neither gloss nor lipstick and she was sexily soft in all the right places. Unless she was asleep. Then, she looked terrible.

It was a long-standing joke that when Bee slept, she became a fairy-tale version of her ugly sister. Her face would crumple, causing lines and a whopping double chin. And her tiny button nose was cute, but caused her to snore, her little nostrils flaring with every breath. The snoring inevitably produced saliva, which would often drip out of one side of her mouth like a thread of liquid glue. As Rosie peered through the driver's window, she could see a long, gloopy trail of dribble falling from Bee's mouth onto the seat belt on which her head was resting.

Rosie knocked on the glass gently, not wanting to frighten Bee, but she was out cold, her snoring audible even through the closed door. She knocked a little louder this time and Bee stirred, her hand rising to wipe away the dribble subconsciously. She shifted in the seat, clearly uncomfortable.

Rosie knocked a third time, causing Bee to startle and make eye contact, her eyes sleepy. She rubbed her eyes with her fists balled and then lowered the window.

'Hey, sleepyhead,' Rosie said, smiling sheepishly. 'Thanks for bringing my car back for me.'

'No worries,' Bee said, stifling a yawn.

'Have you been waiting long?'

Bee checked the time on the dashboard.

'Whoa, yeah, I have. I got here over two hours ago,' Bee said, looking shocked.

'Oh, Bee. I'm sorry. You should have called me.'

'Don't be sorry. I've just had the best nap I've had since the twins were born,' she said, stretching her arms out in front of her before opening the car door and climbing out.

'And anyways, I had to come over to apologise for being such a bitch to you. I shouldn't have said all those things – I'm sorry.' She looked at Rosie, her brow crinkled in anxiety and her eyes searching Rosie's for forgiveness.

'No, I'm sorry,' Rosie said, pulling her close into a tight hug. She felt warm. 'Everything you said you meant with good intentions.'

'And I don't think I'm better than you, I really don't.'

Bee was flushed and unusually tentative as she pulled back from Rosie, rubbing her hands together nervously.

'I know, I was just being mean,' Rosie said, taking hold of her hands and squeezing. 'You're my best friend. You're only looking out for me,' she said, feeling the beginning of tears. 'And you're right. I do just exist. I am so stuck in the comfort of the mundane that I'm too scared to take any risks. Risks mean danger.'

'I know. Look, what you had to go through with your parents is enough to make anyone anxious. I think you're amazingly strong, Ro-Ro. And I am so proud of you.'

Her words sounded so sincere that Rosie properly began to cry.

'Let's never argue again, yeah? I can't bear not having you in my life,' Rosie said, giving Bee another hug.

'Agreed,' Bee said, breathing a deep sigh of relief. 'Now, can I please come inside and pee? My bladder is ridiculous since having kids. I almost ruined your car-seat upholstery and you've only just had the fabric shampooed.'

Rosie laughed. 'Of course, c'mon.'

She turned and walked to her front door, unlocking it and laughing as Bee barged past her and headed straight into the downstairs bathroom, slamming the door behind her. Rosie heard her groan with relief and she stifled a laugh as she walked into the kitchen and switched on the kettle. Pulling out Bee's favourite mug and hearing a yell from the bathroom demanding biscuits, she chuckled. All was well with the world again.

Chapter Twelve

Rosie took a very deep breath before pushing open the door and walking from the icy-cold exterior into the warmth of the office on Monday morning. She scanned the room quickly for any signs, smells or sounds of Benjamin. Audrey was already there and she shook her head silently, indicating that he had yet to arrive.

Not knowing if that was a good or a bad thing, Rosie shuffled over to her desk in her hiking boots, the ice outside making the walk from the car park to the office almost treacherous. She sat quickly, pulling off the boots and slipping on her work court heels.

'Do you think he's coming in?' Rosie said, looking over at his closed office door.

Audrey shrugged. 'I would have thought so. Doesn't he have that online management meeting this afternoon?'

'Oh yes, he does,' Rosie said, her stomach dropping at the thought of having to face him today.

She switched on her computer and watched it wake up, its screen glaring at her. She looked over at Audrey, who was looking at her, concerned.

'Are you feeling better today?' Audrey asked.

'Do you mean, have I got over my hangover? Yes, I have, thanks. I'm fully rehydrated, my stomach is lined with carbs and after three washes, I have finally removed all traces of dried sick from my hair.' She lifted a thick strand of freshly conditioned hair in Audrey's direction as if to prove her point.

Audrey laughed. 'As far as hangovers go, yours was pretty spectacular,' she said, nodding, 'but I also meant how are you feeling?'

Rosie thought about it, taking a moment before responding. 'I'm feeling a little lost, actually. Like I'm adrift from everyone and everything. Like I haven't yet found my feet. Do you know what I mean?'

'I do. I felt like that for a few months after my accident,' she said, shifting in her chair. 'I remember not really knowing who this new version of me was, or whether I could adapt to a new life that I hadn't chosen. It's tough—'

'I don't mean to compare my life to yours . . .' Rosie interrupted, blushing, but Audrey held up her hands to stop her.

'You're not, and my troubles are no more important than yours. We all have our difficulties, Rosie,' she said, smiling. 'It's not a comparison, it's a friendship. I want to help.'

'Thank you,' Rosie said, grateful for her friendship.

Audrey went to respond, but the door flew open and they both turned to see Benjamin waltz through the door, his cashmere coat collar pulled up towards his sharp jawline. A gust of wind flew in with him and he continued his pace straight past their desks.

'Morning, Audrey,' he said, nodding in her direction, but his stride didn't let up.

He approached his office door, opened it and closed it without so much as a look back. He didn't even acknowledge Rosie's existence.

'Wow, that's childish,' Rosie said, rolling her eyes.

'We know him well enough to know he's not one for confrontation. Or negotiation,' Audrey said. 'Plus, you've bruised his ego.' She shrugged, picking up her mug, the steam rising from the fresh coffee. 'Leave him be. He'll have to talk to you eventually.'

'I'm in no rush,' Rosie said. 'It'll be quite nice to know that I don't have to hear his slimy stories or about his latest conquest. Oh . . .' she said, realising her error. 'Well, maybe not his latest almost-conquest,' she said, stifling a chuckle.

Audrey snorted into her coffee. As the first customer came through the door, Rosie kicked into action.

'Good morning and welcome to Wanderlust Wishes. How can we help you today?'

Chapter Thirteen

The rest of the week continued as expected. Benjamin ignored Rosie as much as was physically possible, darting in and out of his office like he had rocket launchers on his heels, and emailing her only on a need-to-know basis. She actually quite enjoyed the peace and quiet, and it gave her the opportunity to focus on increasing her sales and planning for the next quarter.

The days went past in a blur of last-minute bookings and admin duties and before she knew it, Thursday had come around. She found herself tying up the loose ends to a Mediterranean cruise booking she had taken from an elderly couple earlier that morning and was munching on the remainder of her chocolate reindeer from Audrey. Christmas music was audible via the small speakers in the ceiling and Audrey was humming along.

'The last working week before Christmas,' Rosie began. 'In my opinion, the best working week of the whole year.'

She readjusted the tinsel that was wrapped around her noticeboard behind her desk and double-checked for any unopened doors on her Advent calendar in the hope that she had inadvertently missed one. She hadn't. She turned to Audrey, who rolled her eyes and threw across another shiny chocolate from her desk, which Rosie caught with precision. When it came to chocolate, Rosie was a modern-day Joe DiMaggio and could catch a Quality Street Strawberry Delight with barely a flick of her wrist. She unwrapped it and popped it into her mouth with a happy moan.

'Don't you just love Christmas?' she said.

'Abso-blooming-lutely,' Audrey said, adjusting her antler headband and winding up her Father Christmas music box for the umpteenth time.

She smiled as it began turning, the melodic chords of 'Silent Night' echoing around the shop floor. At that moment, the door to Benjamin's office opened, emitting a frosty chill into the warming festive atmosphere. With a face like the Grinch, he strode out and headed straight towards Audrey's desk.

'Audrey, I want you to sit in on the meeting this afternoon. They want my star employee this month, and you are it!' He perched on the side of her desk and tapped a finger on her keyboard.

She looked confused.

'But Rosie made that huge sale last week. She has far exceeded me on sales based on that,' she protested loyally. 'It should be her really.' She looked around him at Rosie, but he lent over, blocking her view.

'Oh no. I've crunched the figures and it's definitely not Rosie. You have come out top and I want you to represent our branch.'

'But—'

'No buts,' Benjamin said, interrupting her, a sharp undertone to his voice. 'It's you I have chosen and it's you who will be joining me this afternoon, OK?'

Before Audrey had a chance to answer, the branch door blew open. Rosie turned to see Mrs Winthorpe-Smythe waltz into the branch and head directly towards her.

'Morning, young lady.' She threw off her woollen cloak and tossed it on the back of the customer chair in front of Rosie's desk. 'We have a predicament, and you are just the person to sort it for me.' She sat down and gave Rosie a questioning glare. 'Well? Are you on mute?' She folded her legs under her chair and chuckled at her own joke.

'Mrs Winthorpe-Smythe,' Rosie said, holding out her hand to shake. It was surprisingly dry and warm. 'How may I help you today? Last-minute insurance for your holiday tomorrow?'

She turned her focus away from Benjamin, aware of his presence still dampening her Christmas buzz. Even the musical box had wound down to silence. She began typing away, bringing up the details of Mrs Winthorpe-Smythe's large booking.

'There are eleven of you in total, aren't there, travelling Friday morning from City airport to Venice? I can give you a quote for insurance now, or if you want to sort airport transportation—'

'It's neither of those things, I'm afraid,' Mrs Winthorpe-Smythe said, leaning forwards and waving away her suggestions. 'I am afraid I need to cancel the whole trip, effective immediately.'

'What? Why?' Rosie said, aware that Benjamin had turned around to listen in, along with Audrey.

Rosie panicked as she visualised a huge hourglass being turned upside down, but instead of sand pouring through, it was her commission falling through its centre in a wave of gold coins. A cold shiver ran down her spine.

'Oh, my dear, I am so torn,' she said, her face changing to one of theatrical dismay. 'My dear, darling younger sister has had a fall, quite a bad fall, and has shattered her hip. Not only does she require surgery, but she is most distressed as her four beloved Pomeranian puppies are home alone while she is laid up in her hospital bed. She is in such a state. She lives alone, you see, and she is desperate for me to go to her and help out. And as her dutiful sister, I couldn't possibly say no.'

'But Mrs Winthorpe-Smythe, cancelling with only twenty-four hours' notice invalidates any chance of a refund. I may be able to transfer the flight tickets to another date, but it won't be cheap.' She began bringing up different screens and picked up her phone to call the airline.

'Oh, but I am so torn,' Mrs Winthorpe-Smythe continued, wiping away an invisible tear from her dry eye. 'I cannot possibly let down my residents. They wait all year for their annual holiday and the thought of disappointing them when they are almost packed, medicated and wheelchair-ready makes my heart sore.'

Rosie looked at her, sensing she was getting to a point.

'If only I wasn't so needed,' Mrs Winthorpe-Smythe cried. 'I'm so vital for so many, you see. If there was someone who could go in my place, then I could nurse my sister without disappointing ten darling, sensitive and selfless pensioners, who just want to taste different air and experience the world.' She looked at Rosie pleadingly. 'They don't deserve to have their one chance of happiness taken away. Who knows how long they might have left?'

'Mrs Winthorpe-Smythe, is there no one who can go in your place? Didn't you say that you're in charge of the residential home? Surely there must be someone you can delegate this task to in your place?'

'My dear, would I be here if I had already come up with a solution?' Mrs Winthorpe-Smythe said, leaning forwards and placing her elbows on the desk. 'Is there anything you can do to help me? I'm at a loss!'

'Like I said, I can try to move the holiday to a future date, or get a partial refund, but at this moment in time, it seems unlikely.'

'But it has to be this week. I promised them Christmas cheer, not January dreariness. Is there really nothing you or the company can do? Are there really no exceptions to Wanderlust Wishes' rule that the company do not offer travel guides or companions? I would be happy to compensate the company handsomely for the inconvenience . . .' She tailed off, side-glancing over at Audrey and Benjamin, ensuring she had total control of the room.

'I'm afraid we don't offer tour guides for any of our package holidays, that's just company policy . . .' Rosie began but stopped speaking when Benjamin walked over and placed a hand on Mrs Winthorpe-Smythe's chair.

'Madam, apologies for butting in, but I could not help overhearing your sad predicament.' He offered a hand and she shook it, giving him a weepy damsel-in-distress gaze. 'First, may I say how sorry I am to hear about your sister. But she is clearly lucky to have such a kind and compassionate sister, and I'm sure that with your warmth and care, she'll be back on her feet in no time.' He walked around Rosie's desk and gestured for her to move over, taking centre stage. 'And secondly, at Wanderlust Wishes, our primary goal is to make all of our customers' wishes come true.' He smiled one of his most professional grins and straightened his tie. 'My name is Benjamin and I am manager of this branch. I can assure you, Mrs . . .' He paused, clearly having no clue what her name was.

'Mrs Winthorpe-Smythe,' Rosie added.

'Yes, Mrs Winthorpe-Smythe, that I will personally work with you to come to a happy resolution for us all.'

Mrs Winthorpe-Smythe let out a sigh of relief, fanning herself with her hanky, which only a few moments ago she had been dabbing her eyes with. 'Oh, Benjamin, aren't you just a total delight,' she said. 'I would be ever so grateful for your expertise.'

'And I would be so happy to help,' Benjamin said, turning his attention to Rosie for the first time that day, a stiff smile fixed across his face. 'Rosie, could you bring me and Mrs Winthorpe-Smythe a coffee, please?'

'Oh, yes, that would be delightful,' Mrs Winthorpe-Smythe said, looking at Rosie. 'Milk, please, no sugar.'

'I-I . . .' Rosie stumbled over her words, feeling side-stepped.

'Let's not keep our customers waiting,' Benjamin said, giving her a glare that spoke volumes. 'Chop-chop, Rosie. I'll take over here.' He placed a hand on her chair, indicating that he wanted to sit down.

She stood up silently and stepped away from her desk as he slid into her chair like a snake.

'So, Mrs Winthorpe-Smythe, here at Wanderlust Wishes, we like to offer a personal service to each and every one of our VIP customers, and you are no different. We can make this work for you.'

'Oh, thank you, thank you,' Mrs Winthorpe-Smythe gushed, leaning forwards and patting his arm in a motherly fashion.

'You're so kind.'

'My pleasure,' Benjamin said, gesturing for Rosie to hurry up.

She looked at Audrey, who simply shrugged silently, so Rosie disappeared through the staff door into the shared kitchenette. Popping on the kettle, she leant against the worktop and crossed her hands over her chest. Benjamin was such a selfish magpie, sweeping in and stealing her shiny, costly sale from beneath her, his beady eyes scavenging for the trinkets of others.

Her frustration rose with the temperature in the kettle and by the time it reached boiling point, so had she. She angrily prepared four mugs of coffee and placed them on a tray before grabbing from the top shelf Benjamin's contraband biscuits that were only reserved for him. She ripped into the packet, stuffing two into her mouth before arranging the rest on a chipped plate. Leaving a mess in the kitchen, she made her way back into the shop.

'—so, as I was saying, we can arrange transportation to the airport as part of our modified package and we will ensure that Rosie will be there at the airport to assist them with the checking-in process.'

Rosie picked up the end of his sentence. She looked over at Audrey, whose face was flushed, and she looked pained. She passed her a mug of coffee and slipped her two biscuits before walking back to her desk and handing out the other three mugs – one for herself – and the plate of cookies. Benjamin's eyebrow rose at the sight of the biscuits, but he grabbed two before continuing.

'I'm sorry, did I hear my name being mentioned?' Rosie said mock-innocently, watching as Mrs Winthorpe-Smythe took another two biscuits, leaving only one on the plate.

Greedy cow. 'I hope I'm not in any trouble,' Rosie said, smiling.

Benjamin shot back a triumphant look, his smile widening.

'Of course not, Rosie. You're a total star. But yes, you did hear me say your name!' He chuckled, biscuit crumbs falling from his hand into the little gaps of her keyboard, making her wince. He continued unaware. 'As part of our excellent service here at Wanderlust Wishes, I have assured Mrs Winthorpe-Smythe that you are our star performer this month and you like to live by the motto that one should always *provide excellence, at all costs—*'

'When have I ever said that?' Rosie interrupted, but he held out a hand towards her, indicating for her to quieten down.

'And as our star performer, Rosie, and with your Christmas bonus only days away, we know that you'll be the prefect representative on this trip, don't you agree?'

The tone was light, but she could see from his eyes that he was unwilling to negotiate here.

'We'd hate to lose this booking when there is so much on the line . . .' He tailed off, letting the unspoken threat hang in the air, before continuing, 'By which I mean we couldn't possibly let down all those lovely residents who have their hearts set on their once-in-a-lifetime holiday, now, could we?' He smiled at Mrs Winthorpe-Smythe.

'But it's Christmas in a few days . . .' Rosie could feel panic rising, causing her to break out in a sweat.

'All the more reason to give those residents a true Christmas miracle,' he retorted, taking a huge gulp of coffee while surreptitiously winking at her.

Her cheeks flamed. She knew exactly what he was doing. She had embarrassed him and this was his idea of punishing her in a way she couldn't refuse. She couldn't afford to lose this sale, or her job, and she knew that if she didn't go, the atmosphere in the office would only worsen. She looked over at Audrey, to find her friend looking almost tearful.

'Rosie,' Benjamin continued, typing away at her computer, 'I've added you as a travel representative to the group booking and booked an extra seat on the flight. We were lucky – there was one seat remaining and it happens to be with the group, too.'

He turned to Mrs Winthorpe-Smythe, who was looking at Benjamin with a look of awe and, Rosie noted, smugness, too.

'Thank you so much, Benjamin. What a blessing you are! You have cleverly sorted the whole mess out, without so much as breaking a sweat. Clever boy.'

The woman's eyes darted to Rosie, but her mouth stayed closed. Ensuring Rosie had her full attention, Mrs Winthorpe-Smythe grabbed the last lonely biscuit from the plate and took a giant bite, crumbs falling, before licking her lips. Revenge is a biscuit best served crumbled, it seemed.

Chapter Fourteen

Half an hour later, Rosie's voice was hoarse from all the shouting with Benjamin. She had gone from attempting to negotiate her way out of the trip, to pleading, but to no avail. Benjamin wouldn't budge.

'The flights have been booked and the final details have been arranged, Rosie. I don't want to give you an ultimatum, but if you refuse to go, it might be a deal-breaker with your position here. I've been told that the numbers nationwide need to reduce by 10 per cent and while I didn't want to have to nominate anyone . . .' He tailed off, one eyebrow raised, speaking volumes. 'Now, let's get back to being professional, shall we? Customers are waiting.' He pointed outside, where people were walking past slowly, their heads down.

Not one of them seemed interested in coming into the branch. By the time Rosie had turned to face Benjamin again, he had disappeared back into his office, closing the door behind him. Rosie let out an exasperated gasp.

'Argh, that total shit!' she said to Audrey. 'He's tricked me. If I pull out of the trip, I'm most likely fired, and if I go on the trip, I'm stuck in a foreign country with a bunch of nearly dead OAPs who will no doubt need constant attention. I'll be left hijacking my own gondola and using my own arms to row away from them.' She felt breathless and her fists were clenched.

'I know. He's a total shithead,' Audrey said, sighing deeply. 'I don't know how to get you out of this, if I'm honest, Rosie.' She shrugged, wheeling her chair around her desk and turning the Open sign around to Closed. 'But I do know one thing you can do. Take the rest of the day off. Go home. Pack. Eat. Find your passport. He's not going to leave his office before closing time now. If you must go on this trip, go on your own terms.' She opened the door and nodded her head towards the pavement. 'Go.'

Rosie didn't need telling twice. Her mind felt full and it was nice for someone to think for her. Someone with her best interests at heart. She shut down her computer, grabbed her things and threw on her coat, not bothering to change her shoes. Her festive tinsel had fallen down again and lay forlornly on the floor.

'So much for an enjoyable last few days in the office,' she grumbled, tossing her empty Advent calendar in the bin.

'Well, technically, it is your last day in the office . . .' Audrey began, but stopped short when she noticed Rosie's expression.

Sighing, Audrey wound up her musical box again, gazing at the image of Father Christmas as he twirled his way around his porcelain Christmas tree, and waited until Rosie was ready to leave.

As Rosie gave Audrey a tight hug, she took one last look at Benjamin's closed door, wondering how one drunken mistake could have lead to her Christmas being ruined. Her second thought was that she hoped Italian wine was both cheap and plentiful.

'So let me get this straight,' Bee said, pouring them both an eggnog as she sat cross-legged on Rosie's bed. 'You get a free all-expenses-paid last-minute holiday to one of the most desired destinations in the world and you don't want to go?' She pointed at one of the two jumpers Rosie was holding up for her to choose. 'Are you crazy?'

'Well, when you twist it and make it sound like a holiday—'

'Which, effectively, it is. You're not having to go into the office every day, you receive a daily allowance and you get to eat out every day, and all while staying in a decadent hotel in the middle of Venice. In the run-up to Christmas. That sounds like a holiday to me.' Bee shrugged and downed her drink.

'But I'm effectively chaperoning. What if one of them runs into one of the canals?' Rosie exclaimed, throwing two blouses into her open suitcase.

'Honey, if they are as decrepit as you say they are, no one will be running anywhere!' She laughed as Rosie threw two pairs of jeans into the already messy suitcase. 'Where's your passport?'

'On my bedside table,' Rosie said, pointing to the left of Bee.

Bee leant over and grabbed it. She brushed off a thin layer of dust before opening it.

'When was the last time this was used?'

'Um . . .' Rosie said, pausing for a second and sweeping some strands of hair from her face. 'Definitely pre-Covid? I'm not sure.'

'By the look of your passport photo, it was pre the Stone Age!' Bee said, tossing it onto the bed and moving on to Rosie's backpack. 'What is all this crap?' She tipped the bag upside down, letting the contents spill onto Rosie's bedding.

'No, don't! I'd packed that already!' Rosie yelled, coming over to the bed to gather her things.

'You don't need all this shit,' Bee said, holding up each item and tossing it on the floor. 'Wet wipes? You're not a baby. Pencil case? Are you going on a school outing? Sun cream? Honey, it's minus two out in Venice at the moment. You don't need half of this crap.'

She continued tossing items over her shoulder without a care, while Rosie winced as she saw her belongings tossed aside.

'A calculator? Seriously?' Bee continued. 'A giant bar of chocolate?'

'In case I get hungry,' Rosie protested, watching as Bee ripped into the packaging and began eating.

'You're not trekking in the Himalayas, Rosie. And surprisingly, they do have food in Italy. Bloody amazing food, too. This,' she said, taking another large bite from the bar, 'is not needed.' Her eyes widened as she spotted a brand-new lip gloss on the bed and opened it before painting her lips with it.

'Help yourself, why don't you?' Rosie said.

'Thanks!' Bee said, ignoring any notes of sarcasm and continuing with her decluttering task. 'We'll have you fit to fly within the hour.'

'And then what?' Rosie said, dropping clothes on the floor in defeat and downing her glass of eggnog.

'Then, we gotta get you to bed, young lady. At this rate, it'll be a Christmas miracle if we get you packed in time before the taxi comes. Chop-chop,' Bee said, pulling herself onto her knees and wafting Rosie away.

Rosie sighed and returned to her wardrobe.

Rosie still couldn't believe that Benjamin had tricked her into this. Only this morning she had planned a semi-relaxing festive week.

'I'm so upset I'm going to miss Sammy's nativity play. I was really looking forward to it,' she moaned as she searched through her pile of jumpers.

'Oh, seriously, Rosie. He's playing the part of the stable door. Stable. Door. No lines, no speech – just standing still and smiling. I'm his mother and even I don't want to go. It's going to be a haven of germs, pushy parents and tiny low seats. You won't be missing anything.'

'I guess I can ask him to act it out on Christmas Day—' Rosie began.

'If you do that, I'll pelt you with pigs in blankets. Just make sure you buy me something really pretty from Venice. I hear that the Venetian glass is phenomenal. I expect amazing presents this year, you have no excuse,' Bee demanded. 'And a giant Toblerone from duty-free for Nav, obviously.'

'Oh, obviously. We mustn't forget Nav,' Rosie said, rolling her eyes. 'Speaking of which, what have you got him for Christmas this year?' Bee always gave him amazing presents each year.

'I've outdone myself this year,' Bee said proudly. 'This year I've managed to secure an F1 driving experience at his favourite racing track, Brands Hatch. He's going to be over the moon,' she said, smiling. He is going at his favourite racing track, Brands Hatch.' she said, smiling.

'Nice!' Rosie said, impressed. 'And what do you think he's got you for Christmas?'

Bee sighed dramatically. 'I've told him the only thing I want for Christmas is for his parents to disappear early Christmas Eve to his brother's house.'

Rosie laughed.

'The only person I want walking around my landing or helping themselves to milk and cookies in my kitchen late on Christmas Eve is Father Christmas himself,' Bee declared.

Chapter Fifteen

Even after 5am on a Friday morning, the City airport was crazy busy. Thousands of families milling around dragging their luggage and children behind them, their Christmas holidays having begun. It felt odd. Bee was right when she said Rosie hadn't travelled in a while. In fact, she couldn't remember the last time she flew somewhere or travelled out of the country.

She searched the airport departure boards that hung above her and was both relieved and disappointed to see that the flight was both on time and active. Reading her check-in desk number, she turned left and began navigating her way through the throng of people, crying kids and skiing equipment, a loud mix of languages filling the airport.

'Desk nineteen, desk nineteen,' she muttered to herself as she walked along the concourse of check-in desks, counting the numbers.

Queues had already formed, despite the early hour, and as Rosie spotted her check-in desk, she sighed – her queue was clearly the longest. People looked tired and bored, and as she joined the end of the line, she checked her watch for the umpteenth time. Looking down the line, it was clear that her group of ten hadn't yet arrived. The queue was full of families, young adults and what looked like a hen party consisting of a group of eight middle-aged women dressed head to toe in white, with an excess of feathers, Lycra and sequins. They seemed far too excitable for 5am and Rosie made a silent prayer that they wouldn't be seated anywhere near her aisle during the flight. She checked her phone again but turned as she heard her name being called over the PA system:

'Miss Redbrush, Miss Redbrush, please make your way to the information desk in the departures hall. We have the rest of your party gathered here for collection.'

Odd, Rosie thought. She'd assumed she would meet them at the check-in desk, but no matter. She pulled herself out of the ever-growing queue and dragged her suitcase behind her as she headed for the correct desk.

The airport was huge and, without realising, she headed in the opposite direction for a good ten minutes before she heard her name over the tannoy again:

'Miss Redbrush, Miss Redbrush, please make your way as quickly as possible to the information desk in the departures hall. We urgently require your assistance. Thank you.'

Rosie imagined that she detected a distressed tone in the speaker's voice, but she was distracted by her arrival at the incorrect information desk. After receiving correct directions, she headed forwards. The departures hall seemed louder than before, with voices rising above the general hubbub of the crowds milling around. As she continued walking, the loud voices seemed to separate themselves from the crowd, their yelling and arguing getting louder with every step.

'Someone's having a bad day,' she muttered quietly, turning left as instructed.

The voices grew louder as she continued, both male and female, and it was clear an argument of sorts was ensuing.

She looked up, seeing a large sign for the information desk ahead of her, but she couldn't see the desk itself owing to the hustle and bustle of the airport. People swarmed around her like excited flies on an overripe peach and she had to meander around people like she was negotiating potholes in a deserted road.

The dissatisfied voices rose to a crescendo just as the crowds parted and she was greeted by the view of ten irate pensioners grouped beside the information desk.

Approaching, she took in the white-haired, flushed, disgruntled bunch, of whom three were standing beside the counter, with the other seven leaning on their suitcases, on the counter or on each other. A couple had walking sticks and one elderly woman had hopped up onto an airport bin. They all had the same expression: frustration.

The man behind the information desk was equally flushed, his hands held up defensively as he tried to negotiate with the man in front of him – a tall, sturdy man easily in his eighties, wearing a shiny pale-blue three-piece suit, polished shoes and white-grey hair that was styled like a lion's mane. It was feathered around his face and sat comfortably on his shoulders. He was speaking calmly, but his voice still rose above the rest, as if he had spent his life addressing crowds from a stage. He was smiling, but in a way that showed dominance. It seemed he wasn't used to losing a fight.

Rosie approached with caution, as if she were a photographer in the wilderness having spotted a herd of woolly mammoths. She slowed her pace as she took in the others. A couple of elderly men stood beside the tall man in the suit, also trying to show dominance, but one was leaning heavily on the desk, his blotchy face red from anger or exertion, she wasn't sure. The other was trying to join in the debate happening in front of him, but his words were blatantly being ignored. He was scrawny and short, his trousers held up by large red braces over a white shirt. There were sweat patches evident under his arms and he kept wiping his brow like he was under direct sunlight.

Her eyes moving away from the desk, she took in the other seven. Another man stood bent over, examining his suitcase padlock with what appeared to be a magnifying glass. The elderly lady sitting on the bin was swinging her legs forwards like a toddler, her smart court shoes banging the metal bin like a drum, much to the annoyance of the others. She was wearing a pair of orange velvet trousers and a gold high-neck jumper that looked like it came straight from the 1970s. Which it probably did.

The other five of the group were standing between the bin and the information desk, one man and four women; all elderly, most of them white-haired, apart from one buxom lady who had hair the colour of pink candyfloss. The others were all dressed for travel in raincoats, mackintoshes and all sorts of travel attire that included both straw and pillbox hats.

Rosie couldn't delay it any longer – the poor guy behind the information desk was looking like he might cry – so she took a deep breath and moved forwards, calling out, 'I'm Rosie Redbrush.' She raised her hand in a small wave in their direction and felt the gaze of eleven pairs of eyes on her, one belonging to the guy behind the desk.

'Oh, wonderful!' the guy said, gesturing her to come forwards quickly. 'Miss Redbrush, here is your party ready for departure. I have assisted them as best as I can, but they are insisting that you were meant to meet at this point half an hour ago and that you were also meant to have organised special assistance in advance so that these people' – he gestured to the group – 'would have help accessing the flight. As I keep informing them, special assistance needs to be booked in advance for a group of this size and as it stands, we don't have enough resources at this time to help. If they could just wait another twenty minutes, then—'

'Miss Redbrush.' The tall man stepped forwards, interrupting him, and took her hand before shaking it. 'A delight. My name is Horace and I am the leader of the group. This is Albert' – he gestured to his left – 'and this is Walter' – he gestured to his right. 'The others are Enid, Dottie, Shirley, Winnie, Olive, Norman and Mildred.' He pointed them out individually, but Rosie found it hard to work out who was who.

'Lovely to meet you all,' she said, giving them a small wave back and stepping forwards to the desk. 'Now, tell me what the problem is and I'll see what I can do.'

Chapter Sixteen

By 7am, Rosie was ready to abandon ship or, more appropriately, ditch the departure lounge. It had taken her a good hour to persuade the group that the check-in desk was only a few minutes' walk away. After queuing for ten tortuous minutes, they were finally all checked in and their luggage had been dispatched from them. With much huffing and puffing, she successfully got them through security, averted their eyes from the duty-free shops and finally got them to the gate. Or she thought she had got them all to the gate.

She lost Enid in the perfume area and Horace in the toilets, resulting in her having to get a male security guard to go in there and call for him.

They had called for final boarding twice already and while she had managed to get eight of them onto the aircraft, she was now trying to persuade both Olive and Norman that flying was perfectly safe, and that there was no reason to panic, speak to the captain or see the fuel levels before boarding. The boarding crew were beginning to lose their temper and she could see not only the holiday not happening, but also her bonus slipping away faster than her patience. She needed them to get on the flight, and she needed them to get on now.

'Olive, Norman, please. Planes take off every minute and are one of the safest ways to travel. Plus, if you two don't get on board now, they'll close the gate and the others will experience Venice without you.'

'I don't care,' Olive said, her bottom lip sticking out like a toddler's would.

'It makes no sense. We're not birds, we're not meant to fly,' Norman argued.

'And I'm not sitting in row thirteen. That's unlucky.'

'There is no row thirteen on aircraft, don't worry,' Rosie said, hoping that was true and not just some urban myth. 'I get it. You both haven't flown before. It's scary. But also exciting! Imagine telling your grandkids about your travels when you get back for Christmas. Imagine walking the streets of Venice! Travelling is a privilege,' she pleaded, nodding at the approaching staff. 'Don't take it for granted.'

'Miss? We need to close the gate now. Will you be boarding?' the lady asked, her uniform starched to perfection.

Rosie looked at them both questioningly. 'Are we?' Her heart was pounding, her palms sweaty.

Olive and Norman looked at one another, their eyes showing silent communication.

Olive then turned to Rosie and the airport staff.

'If we do board, we would like free drinks to settle our nerves.' She looked at Norman, who nodded. 'And we want seats with extra legroom. I simply cannot travel without being able to stretch out my poor arthritic ankles, and we all know Norman has a bad back . . .' She tailed off as Norman hunched his shoulders down into a stoop. 'Deal?' Olive gave the airport staff worker a glare that showed she wasn't to be messed with.

The lady rolled her eyes, checked her watch and said, 'Fine! Can you just please get on the flight now?'

She pulled out her walkie-talkie from her belt and advised the captain that the two passengers were boarding now and of their demands. She gestured for them to follow.

Rosie looked to Olive just in time to catch a sneaky wink and a conspiratorial smile at Norman before they both followed the lady to the aircraft entrance, with Norman's back suddenly strong and straight, and Olive's ankles seeming to be able to skip in two-inch heels.

'They just totally played the system!' Rosie said to the now-empty gate. 'They are octogenarian outlaws! What am I getting myself into?' she said to herself before grabbing the handle of her cabin suitcase and walking onto the aircraft.

'Madam? I really do need you to take a seat. The captain is keen to push off from the gate now.'

'Of course, I'm so sorry. I'm just making sure all of my party are where they should be,' Rosie said, standing in the aisle and counting the heads of those she could see.

As promised, Olive and Norman had been moved to row one and she could see the rest of the group in row seven, with Horace's head rising clear above the others. He gave her a reassuring nod. The rest of the passengers looked less impressed. They clearly suspected that she was the reason the plane was still on the tarmac.

The crew member gently placed a hand on her elbow and Rosie turned to look at her. She was very pretty, with a headful of curls that were swept back into a tight bun. She had large, welcoming eyes and a smile that, to Rosie, looked genuine and kind. She spoke softly.

'I'm sure everyone is on board, don't worry. Plus, we've had clearance from the gate that the numbers add up, too. Can I show you to your seat?'

'Of course, thank you,' Rosie said, showing the flight attendant her ticket. 'Seat 8C.'

'Follow me,' the flight attendant said, giving her a broad smile.

Rosie noticed her name badge pinned to her blouse. Her name was Maya.

They arrived at row eight and Maya indicated for her to sit in the aisle seat.

'As soon as we are up' – she pointed skywards – 'I'll come over and double-check we have everyone where they should be. Until then, try to relax.' She pointed to the seat next to her, which was unoccupied. 'You're lucky, you've got no one next to you! Make the most of all the space; that seat is a no-show.' Maya smiled and walked away, closing the overhead lockers as she made her way to the front of the plane.

Rosie looked at the middle seat with contempt. That was the seat purchased for Mrs Winthorpe-Smythe. Something told her that she had been set up royally from the word go. Did she ever intend on going on this trip? Did she even have a sister?

After reaching the intended cruising altitude of 35,000 feet and Maya had assured her that all ten of her group were on board, Rosie pulled out a large file from her backpack and began reading it on the drop-down table. It was a list of the group themselves – their names, their ages, medical conditions and any allergies:

Horace Anthony – 81 – high blood pressure – self-medicates.

Norman Nuttell – 79 – recent hip replacement/eczema – risk assessment required for each activity/eczema cream administered himself.

Walter Tulip – 80 – high blood pressure/high cholesterol – self-medicates.

Albert Eastbourgh – 76 – slightly anaemic – where possible, red meat and iron-rich foods. Suffers with IBS.

Enid Smithson – 77 – glaucoma – awaiting operation. Extremely shy and soft-spoken. Very easy to lose.

Dottie (Dorothy) Winters – 70 – anxiety/panic tendencies – recent widow. Buddy her up in a room with someone.

Shirley Fryers – 73 – acid reflux/gastritis – self-medicates, but avoidance of alcohol is advised.

Olive Tanners – 74 – coeliac disease/autoimmune disease – follow the BROW acronym: avoid barley, rye, oats and wheat. Gluten-free food only. Olive is very aware of condition and will travel with a translation medical card.

Winnie (Winifred) Dubois – 68 – menopause – Winnie likes to act like she's forever fifty. She isn't in the menopause. She is slightly deluded. But for convenience, go along with her belief.

Mildred Schmidt – 84 – arthritis in wrist/chronic inflammation – inflammation currently under control and wrist strap worn for relief.

It read like a badly written OAP dating website and she couldn't believe she was going to have to spend the next week with these strangers, in an unknown country, and with the responsibility of caring for their health, their wellbeing and their happiness. No pressure.

She sighed loudly, rubbing her forehead as if she had a headache. The trolley rattled past her in the aisle but stopped beside her. With her head still in her hands, she felt soft fingers on her shoulder.

'Here.' She heard the gentle tone of Maya beside her and when she looked up, she found a plastic glass filled with orange juice and a plastic flute of champagne being offered to her, with Maya nodding at the table. Rosie slipped the paperwork from the table onto the empty seat beside her and Maya set the two drinks down.

'I feel like you might need this.' She handed Rosie a napkin and gave her a friendly wink.

'Oh, thank you,' Rosie said, fumbling to find her purse inside her handbag on the seat beside her.

'No, no. It's on me,' Maya said, pulling out a couple of chocolate bars from the trolley drawer and placing them on the table, too. 'I get the feeling you might need all the energy you can muster today. Enjoy.'

Before Rosie had a chance to thank her, she turned to the left side of the aircraft and began taking their orders. Rosie looked at the table in front of her, her stomach growling in anticipation. She picked up the orange juice and greedily gulped down half the glass before lifting the champagne flute and pouring the contents into the plastic tumbler, essentially making herself a Buck's Fizz.

Taking a bite of the first chocolate bar, she turned to the next few pages inside the folder and found herself looking at a pretty intensive itinerary: wine tasting, Rialto Market, Doge's Palace, Basilica di San Marco Murano . . . the list appeared to go on and on. She craned her neck and saw the group in a state of relaxation. All of them were asleep, their heads lolling onto shoulders, their gentle snores blurring with the hum of the aircraft. From the state of her party, she couldn't envisage them walking off the aircraft without a tea break, yet alone traipsing all around the city of Venice.

'This won't be too bad,' she mumbled to herself as a cabin crew member placed a plastic tray of what resembled breakfast in front of her.

If only she'd known how wrong she was.

Chapter Seventeen

'Ladies and gentlemen, this is your captain speaking. As you can see, we have landed safely at Venice Marco Polo Airport with a bit of a bump but ahead of schedule. The local time here is almost eleven o'clock. The weather is a tad wet this morning, but we hear some wintery sun is on its way. May I take this opportunity to thank you for travelling with Oasis Airlines. On behalf of all the staff travelling with you today, may I wish you all a wonderful day and if you are not returning with us in the coming week, a very merry Christmas.'

Rosie stretched her arms upwards, banging her right hand on the compartment above her. She yawned and stared out of the small aircraft window, its glass covered in diagonal streams of raindrops as the aircraft slowed to a comfortable speed and headed towards its gate. The skies looked grey and uninviting, with no hint of blue skies.

All around her people began moving, eager to disembark. She looked across the aircraft to see her group attempting to gather their belongings and she followed suit. She thought it best that she try to act like a leader, although her instincts were telling her to slouch into her seat and catch the return journey back to England.

Sighing, she stood up and stepped into the aisle, acknowledging Horace as he handed down bags from the overhead compartment with ease, his height giving him leverage above others. Grabbing her own backpack, Rosie made her way down the aisle and to the exit. She spotted Norman and Olive still seated, draining the last drops of their free alcohol, their eyes slightly glazed and their childish giggles audible. Rosie felt icy-cold blasts of air sneaking their way around the legs of the passengers and as the plane emptied, she found herself staring at the cabin crew as they offered each person a monochrome 'Happy Christmas, enjoy your stay.' But as she reached Maya, Rosie gave her a grateful smile and could see Maya's return smile was genuine.

'Enjoy Venice,' Maya said, giving her a wink. 'And try not to lose anyone.'

Rosie chuckled. 'Thank you.'

As she stepped out into the chilly air, she pulled her scarf a little closer around her neck and looked ahead, taking in the airport just as a crackle of thunder rolled around the skies.

'Venice is welcoming us!' Horace said, standing behind her.

'Or warning us to stay away,' Rosie quipped, taking tentative steps down the airstair and onto solid ground and wondering again what she had got herself into.

'I've got to hand it to her, she's not tight with her money,' Rosie muttered to the lapping water in front of her as she waved at the private water taxi driver who was standing beside a beautiful shiny wooden taxi boat at the airport cruise terminal.

He was holding a small blackboard with 'Mrs Winthorpe-Smythe' written in white chalk, and was dressed in smart cream chinos, a crisp white shirt and a striped navy-and-white boating blazer that fitted him in a way that screamed expensive.

'Mrs Winthorpe-Smythe?' he said, his Italian accent strong.

Rosie nodded, taking in his sculpted salt-and-pepper beard, which framed his strong jawline and accentuated the vividness of his blue eyes. His build was stocky and she could see a tuft of chest hair just visible below the open collar of his shirt. She hated that normally, but here, in Italy, it felt sexy. He smiled – showing straight teeth and full lips. He was one of the most attractive older men she had ever seen and she found it hard not to stare.

'Yes,' she said finally, stepping forwards along the wooden planks over the water and nodding again shyly.

He took her hand and brought it to his lips, kissing it, before addressing the whole group.

'*Benvenuto a Venezia*! Welcome to Venice! My name is Lorenzo and I am honoured to be your driver for today. You are lucky customers indeed! For today only, I will throw in a guided tour on our way to the *bellissimo* city of *amore*!'

He made grand gestures towards the city with his arms, which made Rosie think he was more suited to the stage than driving a boat. As if on cue, the grey clouds broke apart and a winter sun lit up the dock around them like a spotlight. With each rehearsed movement and flare of his arms, she couldn't help but feel the beginnings of excitement prickle her skin as Venice seemed to come alive around her. The moving waters sparkled under the warming sun and the long-standing buildings seemed almost mystical under a golden hue.

'*Salire a bordo*, climb aboard, everyone, and let your magical journey begin!'

His smile was wide and with a slight twirl, he waltzed towards the water taxi and placed a rubber-soled shoe on the shiny mahogany gunwale before holding out a hand. The boat barely moved and Rosie gestured for the group to climb aboard.

'Rose?'

Rosie turned around to see Dottie standing behind her, her wizened face creased like tissue paper and her pale hand trembling slightly as she adjusted her handbag on her shoulder.

'It's Rosie, actually. But how can I help, Dottie?'

'Um, it's the water. It looks a little choppy,' she said, indicating to the calm Venetian waters, which looked almost stationary, aside from the gentle lapping of water against the wooden mooring. 'It might cause travel sickness or we might get caught up in a tidal wave from all those large boats out there.' Dottie gestured towards the few small boats that were sailing gently and at low speed. 'Should we take another form of transportation?'

Rosie looked at her to see if she was joking, but then her mind flitted back to the list of characteristics. Dottie was panicking. Rosie placed a hand on her bony shoulder and gently tried to steer her towards the boat. For a short, frail older woman, she sure was able to hold her own and Rosie found her unmovable.

'Dottie, it'll be fine. It looks really clear,' Rosie said, smiling kindly as she tried again.

The rest of the group had all climbed onboard and found a seat; both Norman and Olive were looking a little green about the gills.

'But is there no other way to get to the hotel?' Dottie continued, resolute.

'Well, there is, but this is the quickest route and it is already paid for,' Rosie said, thinking how much she did not want to deviate from the tight schedule that Mrs Winthorpe-Smythe had created.

'*Signora*?' Lorenzo called to them both. '*Tutto OK*?'

'Yes, yes,' Rosie said, looking at Dottie and pulling at her hand gently. 'Just coming.' She lowered her voice and whispered, 'I promise you it will be OK and I'll hold your hand the entire time we are on the water.'

The others started complaining, yearning for their hotel beds, and Dottie looked around Rosie towards them nervously, indecision etched onto her face. Exhaling, she reached to her neck to rub her fingers across a delicate gold chain. Rosie could smell liquorice on the woman's breath. Dottie took a step on the dock, muttering to Rosie as she passed her.

'Young Rose. Don't make promises that you can't keep.'

Chapter Eighteen

'My friends, there it is. *Piazza* San Marco.'

Rosie looked up from staring at a small photograph of St Mark's Square in her guidebook to find herself staring at the real thing ahead of them as Lorenzo gesticulated widely towards the square, his smile wide and proud.

'Isn't she a beauty?'

The boat was quiet as they took in the sight before them. The infamous buildings, seen in films, written about in literature and immortalised in paint, grew more real as they approached the wooden mooring dock. Rosie looked down again at her guidebook and back up to the real thing – there really was no comparison. Seeing St Mark's Square alive with both birds and people and hearing the faint sounds of music waft towards them gave Rosie the first real frisson of excitement about being in Italy.

'Wow,' was all she managed, but Lorenzo still smiled at her, acknowledging her awe.

They stayed silent as he slowed the taxi and expertly manoeuvred his way into the busy dock, finding a free slot among the tall wooden posts that jutted towards the sky. Their trunks were decorated with red-and-white ribbon wrapped around each pole like welcoming maypoles, guiding the mix of gondolas and small boats towards the land.

'Now the tide is low, so it might mean a bit of a step up onto the dock, but looking at you all, I'm sure that a group as young and as athletic as yourselves will spring up like little joey kangaroos,' he joked as he secured his taxi to the dock with rope. Reaching out to one of the thick wooden poles, he nimbly hopped from the taxi onto the dock, defying his age, and clicked his fingers to a nearby young man, who jumped forwards. After a quick exchange of dialogue, the man hopped into the taxi and began unloading the luggage as if he were moving bags of air. Within moments, the luggage was off and one by one, the group were assisted onto dry land.

'Thank you,' Rosie said, shaking Lorenzo's hand before quickly adding, 'sorry, *grazie mille*.'

His face lit up at her attempt at Italian and his bushy eyebrows rose respectfully.

'Your accent is *molto bene*, very good!' he said, nodding. 'Have you been to Italy before?'

Rosie blushed. 'Never.'

'Well, you were clearly born to visit, then.'

He let go of her hand and shouted at the young boy, gesticulating wildly to show his disapproval that he had wandered off, thinking his job was done. The boy walked back towards them, his hands shoved into his trouser pockets in an adolescent fashion, and mumbled something under his breath. Lorenzo rolled his eyes, took a pile of notes from inside his blazer and handed it to the boy, who stuffed it into the back pocket of his jeans as if it were wastepaper. He then lifted both hands to his lips and blew an almighty wolf whistle that caused most of the party to jump. But it was clearly a call to arms, as within seconds, four other young boys were at his side and he began talking to them.

'These young men will escort you to your hotel. I have told them where to go and they will assist you with your luggage to make the journey more accessible,' Lorenzo said, gesturing towards the luggage beside him.

Rosie remembered her manners and pulled out her purse, ready to tip him, but he shook his head, placing a large, well-manicured hand over the top of her purse.

'No tip necessary. Go, have fun. I'll see you in five days.'

Letting go, he jumped back into his water taxi and Rosie watched as the boat stuttered back to life and began its return journey, with Lorenzo waving back at her. She turned to see the five young men all waiting for her to follow. Wanting to appear authoritative, she smiled broadly and addressed the crowd.

'Righty-ho, let's go!'

On her command, the boys led the way, heading directly through St Mark's Square, causing a crescendo of pigeons to rise into the air like a feathery wave, Rosie's gaze rising with them as she took a deep in-breath. There, rising proudly into the sky, was the bell tower of St Mark's Basilica, with the golden statue of Archangel Gabriel at its pinnacle, glowing majestically in the afternoon sun. Lowering her gaze, she took in the grand buildings surrounding her, St Mark's Campanile and the Doge's Palace.

She had seen it all before, the buildings, the square, and when she closed her eyes, she was instantly transported back to her grandmother's front room where, positioned above her large fireplace, there was a huge replica of Canaletto's version of her exact view now. She had been a child then, sitting on her grandmother's threadbare rug and staring up at the painting, imagining a life behind the brushstrokes. Of bustling market stalls and the chatter of Italian conversations, all stuck in that captured moment of time, forever encapsulated in paint. The painting was so much more than just an image of a faraway city. To a young Rosie, it was the opportunity for adventure, the intrigue of her grandmother's many travels, and the notion that the world was so much bigger than the comfort of the familiar.

The only difference here was the startling twenty-foot Christmas tree that stood proudly in the centre of the square, its branches festooned with baubles and lights that seemed to twinkle even in the daylight. Atop the tree sat a beautiful golden star.

Rosie breathed in and smelt the Italian air, recognising an eclectic mix of ground coffee, engine fuel, pine needles and terracotta tiles as they warmed in the sun. She listened to the voices of people milling around her – the disjointed conversations and various languages. A cacophony of human interactions that made Rosie feel like the Canaletto portrait had finally come back to life, its characters free to move, interact, breathe again. She opened her eyes and took a full turn, soaking in the atmosphere like it was air. She smiled. Her grandmother would have been proud of her.

'C'mon, Rosie. Are you with us?'

Rosie turned to see that Horace had stopped to look back for her. The rest of the group were still making their way forwards, slowly following their luggage to the other end of the square.

'Sorry, I'm coming,' she said, tightening her grip on her own luggage and stepping forwards, passing the three red flagpoles that stood proud in a line in the centre of the square.

She was thirsty, hungry and tired; but all that seemed to disappear as she greedily lapped up the sights around her. Four handsome men, clearly Italian and clearly wearing expensive suits, walked past her, one of them giving her a sexy wink as he brushed past her shoulder. She couldn't help but smile back.

As she approached the Christmas tree, a woman passed in front of her, taking a huge bite from a slice of pizza that smelt so phenomenal that her taste buds activated and she licked her lips excitedly. Guitar music floated around the square, its strings amplified by the reverberations from the surrounding buildings, and she found herself smiling widely. The city felt alive. It hummed with an energy and a history that felt magnetic, drawing Rosie in. Another group of pigeons took flight and her own soul soared with them.

Maybe this trip wouldn't be so bad.

Chapter Nineteen

'*Signora* Winthorpe-Smythe? A delight to welcome you and your party to the Grandioso Canale Vista! My name is Eduardo and I am the manager of the hotel. Please, come with me and I will assist you in checking in.'

Rosie was impressed. The hotel was far above her pay grade and entering through its heavy oak revolving doors had been like stepping into a lobby that belonged to a nineteenth-century Italian duke's residence. The walls screamed opulence, with golden panels painted on more dark wood and large beams that criss-crossed above their heads, each beam holding a grand chandelier that lit the lobby via tiny shards of ornately carved glass. There were Renaissance paintings encased in gold frames and behind the reception desk was a mirror so large that it spanned the length of the huge desk and gave the effect that the lobby was even larger than it was.

The furniture was plush velvet and ahead of Rosie was a very grand shallow staircase, the carpet so luxurious that Rosie had an urge to take off her shoes and socks right that minute and dig her toes into its softness. It led up to the first floor, where it split in two, wrapping itself around the edges of the building.

At the top of the stairs was a huge glass window, stained with the image of St Mark's Square, its colours vivid in the afternoon sun. Adjacent to the staircase were two sets of lifts, their gold doors polished to almost a mirror. As she stared, she heard the ping of the lift doors and the shoosh as they opened, releasing a bellboy pulling an empty gold luggage trolley behind him. He was dressed in a similar uniform to the rest of the staff, a smart trouser suit of merlot red, with large gold buttons visible on the waistcoat and jacket.

The rest of the group collapsed into the plush sofas and leather high-backed armchairs with audible groans and Rosie left them to follow Eduardo to the check-in desk.

Barely moments later, having explained Mrs Winthorpe-Smythe's absence and displayed passports and relevant documents for a smooth check-in, she was being handed a set of key cards for the group. They had conveniently and discreetly been placed in ground-floor rooms, apart from Rosie's room, which was on the top floor. Rosie wondered if Mrs Winthorpe-Smythe had done that deliberately.

It soon became clear that it was deliberate, as the door opened to her own room and she found herself entering a suite larger than the entire square footage of her own house. It was huge. And opulent. And as she walked from room to room she couldn't quite believe that Mrs Winthorpe-Smythe had been happy to give this up to care for a sick sister.

She tipped the bellboy and threw herself on one of the two large sofas, wondering for the umpteenth time how she had ended up here, in Italy, as the caretaker of a bunch of total strangers. She decided it was only fair that she let Mrs Winthorpe-Smythe know of their arrival, so she pulled out her phone and searched through the intensive information pack for her number.

She found it odd that the information was so thorough and detailed, yet the contact details for Mrs Winthorpe-Smythe were on the back page and in a font smaller than the rest, with the caution that she 'use it with discretion and only in an emergency situation'.

Rosie decided to ignore the second part and dialled the number. It rang for a long while before it was finally picked up.

'Hello?'

Rosie noticed the line was crackling and there was a whistling around her voice, making her sound like she was in a wind tunnel.

'Mrs Winthorpe-Smythe? This is Rosie Redbrush here.'

'Sorry? I can barely hear you?'

Rosie heard the movement of the phone and the rustling of what sounded like thick gloves being removed.

'Eddie? Hold my skis, will you?'

Skis? Rosie thought. Had she heard that correctly?

'Sorry, who is this? I'm at the piste start line and the network is terrible here.' The phone muffled and she heard Mrs Winthorpe-Smythe yell, 'Go! Go order me a hot toddy when you reach the chalet.' Her voice quietened and she returned her attention to the phone again. 'Sorry, who is this?'

'It's Rosie, Rosie Redbrush. From Wanderlust Wishes? I wanted to inform you that we have arrived safely in Venice.'

There was a silence on the end of the line, which made Rosie wonder if they had been somehow disconnected.

'Hello?'

'Yes, of course.' Mrs Winthorpe-Smythe sounded distant, her voice hesitant. 'Thank you for letting me know. What a relief.'

Rosie heard excited whoops and yelps in the background and alarm bells began to ring.

'How is your sister doing? I do hope she's recovering well.'

'My sister? Oh, yes, my sister. She is doing just great, thanks.'

'And her injury? What was it you said she did again? It sounded nasty.'

A slight pause, then, 'Oh, yes. Terrible, really. She, um, her ankle recovery is slow and she is still mostly bedbound.'

'Her ankle? I thought you said she shattered her hip?' Rosie said, anger beginning to bubble inside. She knew when she had been duped, and this woman was ignorant enough to think Rosie wouldn't find out. 'Mrs Winthorpe-Smythe, would it be possible for you to pop into the office tomorrow, please? There is a disclaimer form that the hotel is asking for and I need you to sign it ASAP, so that my manager can send it over. I'm sure your sister could spare you for just a moment.'

There was a silence. Rosie heard a conversation taking place in French and her anger grew. But she waited for Mrs Winthorpe-Smythe to reply, enjoying her discomfort.

'Actually, I don't think tomorrow will work for me. You see, my sister has a hospital appointment and it might take up most of the day . . .'

She tailed off, leaving Rosie to persevere.

'Oh, of course! We at Wanderlust Wishes pride ourselves on providing personal and excellent customer service, so why don't I arrange for my colleague to pop over to your sister's, thus relieving you of any concerns?'

'No!' Mrs Winthorpe-Smythe shouted before taking a deep breath. 'No, no. That's so kind; however, I am currently unavailable for the foreseeable—'

'Because you're on holiday,' Rosie interrupted.

'What? Of course I'm not. I'm caring for my sister,' she insisted, but Rosie knew she'd cornered her.

'Mrs Winthorpe-Smythe, please don't insult me. I can hear the ski lift operating in the background. You're not caring for any sister, are you? You're skiing. And instead of doing the honourable thing of supporting and chaperoning your own residents, you offloaded them onto a complete stranger, with no care or thought for any of them. Or me. Or my plans for Christmas.' She took a breath, realising that she was panting and her hands felt shaky. 'I feel obligated to tell them the truth about you, Mrs Winthorpe-Smythe, about how their supposed care-home manager lied and treated them like dirt.'

'No! Don't. I'm sorry,' Mrs Winthorpe-Smythe shouted, her tone panicked. 'I'm sorry,' she repeated. 'I acted selfishly, I know, but I knew they would be in capable hands with you.'

'Or are you just worried that they'll have lost trust in you and leave your residential home, hurting both your reputation and your pocket?' Rosie interjected.

'I, no, I . . . of course not!' Mrs Winthorpe-Smythe stuttered.

'Mrs Winthorpe-Smythe, I am here now and I will honour your residents by providing them with a satisfactory holiday as that is what they deserve. And that is the kind of service we like to offer at Wanderlust Wishes, but I can tell you now,

I expect your next decade of holidays to be booked through our company, and in particular, me. How does that sound?'

She couldn't believe she was acting with such force. She was sweating, but her anger was keeping her voice level and controlled.

'That sounds fair,' Mrs Winthorpe-Smythe answered, her tone defeated. 'I'll come in and see you in the new year.'

'To book a winter getaway?' Rosie persisted.

'Yes, to book a winter getaway. Direct through yourself.'

'Fine. And, Mrs Winthorpe-Smythe?'

'Yes, Miss Redbrush?'

She sounded irritated, clearly wanting to end the call.

'Don't forget the cookies. A dozen of Martha's finest. Thanks.' And with that, she ended the call.

Chapter Twenty

After Rosie had unpacked and enjoyed a sublime coffee down in the hotel restaurant, she braced herself to scan Mrs Winthorpe-Smythe's itinerary. She knew she had a few hours to herself, as the entire party had unanimously agreed that room service and an afternoon siesta were necessary owing to the early-morning flight.

Rosie had left them all to their privacy in their individual hotel rooms, no doubt snoring away, and she had luxuriated in her own company – and the company of an entire plate of Italian pastries. Her anger from her phone call earlier was dissipating quicker than the high tide of the canal outside her window. She was still infuriated with Mrs Winthorpe-Smythe, but even she couldn't help but be in awe of the view outside her window.

It was a glorious day, with a wintery blue sky that made everything feel fresh. The moving traffic of water taxis and gondolas was incredibly soothing to watch. The waters were calm and the pace was slow – a far cry from the busy cacophony of trucks, cars and beeping horns that sat in endless traffic outside the office each day, their commute neither calm nor effective. Venice seemed like a city that wouldn't understand the concept of a traffic jam.

A waiter appeared from nowhere and replaced her empty coffee cup. Rosie nodded her thanks. She was not a huge coffee aficionado, preferring tea normally, so when he had first appeared at her table, asking in good English what she would like, she had asked him to bring her whatever he might recommend. Unfazed by this, he had pointed at the menu and indicated that she should order an *espresso con panna*, which she had happily agreed to.

Just five minutes later, she was sipping on the best coffee she had ever experienced. It was sublime. Rich, smooth, and with a whipped-cream head that balanced the bitterness of the bean against its sugary sweetness. The blend was gorgeous and, when mixed with a bite of flaky, buttery puff pastry, she decided there and then that she was now a coffee convert. And also that she wouldn't think about her waistline once while on this trip.

Taking another sip, savouring the hot coffee and licking her top lip clean of the frothy whipped cream, she looked down again at day two of the itinerary. It was totally unachievable. How on earth did Mrs Winthorpe-Smythe expect her to drag a group of mostly octogenarians around a cobbled city, with uneven bridges and deep canals? She had as much chance of achieving the planned agenda as she did in getting them all to re-enact Shakespeare's *The Merchant of Venice* in the middle of St Mark's Square.

She scoffed loudly at tomorrow's schedule, causing the couple next to her to glance across in concern. According to the page in front of her, after an early breakfast, they were scheduled to visit both St Mark's Basilica and the Doge's Palace, with a quick stop for lunch before they were booked to partake in an authentic Italian pizza-making workshop, lasting three hours. The evening was then booked out for an orchestral concert at the Teatro La Fenice. Even Rosie felt exhausted at the busyness of the scheduled day ahead and she was a third of the age of some of the group.

Feeling no allegiance to Mrs Winthorpe-Smythe, she decided to take matters into her own hands and screwed up the piece of paper into a ball.

'My trip, my rules,' she said aloud to the room, at which point the gentleman at the table next to her raised his hand, signalling for the bill.

A couple of hours later, Rosie was sitting at a large table in the hotel restaurant with everyone seated around from her group – all fresh from their naps and excited by their renewed energy levels.

'So, what's first, Rosie?' asked Albert, his usually anaemic pallor flushed with excitement. 'What's on the schedule for tomorrow?'

They were all feasting on a dinner of pasta carbonara, which Rosie thought she had eaten before, but it turns out she hadn't. Her plate of carbonara had no cream in it for a start, yet it was still smooth from the egg yolks, and the garlic bread that accompanied it was doughy, soaked in garlic and oil and with the most satisfying crispy edges. It was hand-pulled, like pizza dough, and was irregular in shape, so that Rosie got to tear satisfying chunks from it, which she then dipped into her pasta. She swallowed her mouthful, her eyes rolling in pleasure, and dabbed at the corners of her mouth before answering.

'That is actually something I wanted to discuss with you all,' she said, resisting the food and instead sipping her wine.

Olive shushed Albert and Walter loudly, and they all turned their attention towards Rosie.

'While I'm here to accompany you on your trip, I don't feel it fair that I dictate your activities, schedule or plans. Mrs Winthorpe-Smythe had planned an itinerary for you all that I, quite frankly, think is both unachievable and a tad selfish.' The ten pairs of eyes widened at her little dig at their care home's manager, but she kept going. 'So, I'm going to treat you all a little differently. You're all capable adults. What do you want to do while we are here? Feel free to look through what she had organised, perhaps choose a few things you'd like to do, and then we can plan something that means we will all enjoy our time here.'

The table went quiet, so Rosie handed the creased but now flattened-out itinerary to Winnie, who was sitting next to her, and indicated for her to hand it around the table. It felt good to take control and as she looked at each of the faces in turn, she could see that they, too, revelled in having a portion of power handed back to them.

These people weren't just pensioners. They were once young, possibly beautiful, hopelessly romantic, striving for success. They were engaging human beings with individual hopes and aspirations like the rest of the world. Growing older gave them valuable insight and knowledge, but this was countered by their weakening bodies and wrinkling skin – grouping them as a frail age bracket who had reached their sell-by date.

'What would you all like to do? This is your holiday, your time. Some activities are already booked, but don't worry about that, I can negotiate any changes.'

Rosie wondered how much of that was true. Her Italian was sketchy and from working at the travel agency, she knew most of the bookings would have been non-refundable. But she kept that part quiet.

Deciding to skip dessert, she left the group chatting away animatedly and took her coffee to the hotel foyer, choosing to take a seat at one of the plush armchairs that were positioned sporadically around the large room. The reception desk was busy with what looked like a large group booking, and she could make out strong American accents being bandied around by the visitors as they shuffled together, suitcases bashing against one another as their owners checked in.

Rosie loved people-watching. It was something she had done since she was little and she would try to piece together stories from snatches of conversation, accents or body language, guessing imaginary relationship statuses or fanciful backgrounds. When her parents had died, the people-watching had stepped up a gear, with her retreating into imaginary worlds for strangers that involved magic and love, rather than real-life accidents or death.

The revolving doors to the entrance of the hotel kept making a satisfying whooshing noise as hotel guests came and left, with Rosie spotting the twinkling waters beyond. Venice was lit by what looked to her like lanterns and she could just make out the moving boats passing by and the soothing sounds of the hum of their engines. The city at night had a magical aura about it that made Rosie want to step outside and let it engulf her.

'Rosie?'

A voice interrupted her thoughts and she turned to find Horace standing beside her, holding a piece of paper in his large hand. She noticed his bluey-grey veins protruding through his aged skin. He gestured for her to take the paper.

'Here you go. We've gone through the existing itinerary and this is what we have decided on unanimously.'

His smile was genuine and she took the sheet from him, noticing a thick cigar poking out of his blazer pocket. She loved that he dressed for dinner. She felt severely underdressed in her denim skirt and pink jumper and made a mental note to make more of an effort for the rest of the holiday.

'Thanks, Horace,' she said, smiling, scanning the page to see lots of scribblings and crossings out.

Tomorrow's schedule was now reduced to two outings: one to the Doge's Palace late morning and then to the concert at the Teatro La Fenice in the evening.

'Now this seems much more achievable, don't you agree?'

'I do, my dear,' he said, resting an arm on the back of her chair. 'I am also here to inform you that the rest of our party have already gone to bed for the evening, but I am going to take a little meander outside. Would you care to join me? I'm afraid I am a bit of a night owl.'

'That would be so lovely,' Rosie said, realising she did want to but just didn't feel confident enough to walk the streets alone in a strange city.

She stood up and he gallantly waited as she pulled a thick purple woollen scarf and matching hat from her bag and wrapped it around her neck in an effort to stay warm. She even managed to locate a pair of fingerless yellow gloves at the bottom of her bag and pulled them on, too. Smiling up at him, she led the way towards the revolving doors and out into the night.

Outside, there was a narrow, cobbled walkway that led away from the hotel and ran parallel to the canal. The sky was clear and the buildings on either side of the water were reflected like a mirror image. The night was cold and Rosie could see her breath ahead of her as she waited for Horace to join her. She wrapped the scarf a little tighter around her neck and shoved her hands into her skirt pockets.

Moonlight cast a soothing glow over everything and as they walked, Rosie glanced at the tall buildings, most with their shutters closed, as if the city had fallen into a deep slumber. Small lanterns swung from building to building, some emitting a warm yellow, others multicoloured, and other than the soothing jazz from a nearby bar, the city felt like it had been hushed by the night.

They fell into a slow, comfortable pace side by side, and Rosie noticed that Horace had pulled the cigar from his blazer pocket and popped it into his mouth but made no effort to light it. They walked a few more paces before Rosie had to ask.

'Are you not going to light it?' She pointed to the cigar and he shook his head.

'Horrid habit, smoking. Gave it up when I got married fifty years ago under Evie's orders. Terrible for your health, you know. But I am a creature of habit and after Evie passed away, I found comfort in carrying one around.' He shrugged as if that made sense and removed the cigar with his left hand.

In the moonlight, Rosie caught the glint of a simple gold wedding ring.

'I'm sorry to hear about your wife passing,' Rosie said. 'Was it recent?'

Horace didn't turn his head to look at her but replied, 'It'll be nine years ago on Sunday. Nine years of missing her.'

Rosie didn't know what to say. She knew grief. She missed her parents every single day.

'Tell me about her,' she said as they approached a left turning onto a brick bridge that reached over the water, its arch so low that Rosie wondered if boats could even squeeze underneath.

They paused at the tip of the bridge and Horace stopped to take a breath, leaning on the stone walls that ran at elbow length either side.

'She was . . . my everything.'

He pulled out a folded photograph from his inside blazer pocket and placed on the bridge wall, flattening it out with the palm of his hand. The photograph was old, in sepia, and was slightly frayed around the corners. The image was of a young couple, smiling widely, their eyes excited. The man was clearly a younger version of Horace, his hair dark and slicked over, his shoulders broad and his stance proud. He was wearing a smart suit and even in the poor-quality image, Rosie could see the shine on his shoes.

'This was our wedding day,' he said, pointing at Evie. 'She insisted on wearing this yellow polka-dot dress that she'd purchased for a shilling from some market stall. I tried to convince her to buy something new, something expensive, but she wouldn't hear another word on the matter.' He chuckled at the memory. 'She had a fierce mind and a strong heart, and she challenged me to become the best version of myself every day.' He pointed at her long hair in the photograph, which cascaded in waves down to her shoulders and continued, 'She refused a veil, a corsage or any type of bridal headwear, preferring simplicity. Instead, the morning of the wedding, she made a daisy-chain crown from daisies in her parents' garden and wore that. She looked beautiful. I called her my blue-eyed beautiful daisy queen.'

He refolded the photograph and placed it carefully back in his pocket, close to his heart.

'She had little sayings for things and was particular in her habits, especially her morning tea. She refused to get out of bed without a cup of breakfast tea every morning, despite my insistence that the day should start with coffee. She would state, "A morning without tea is like a sunrise without birdsong." Every day. Until the day she died.

'And she insisted on propriety, too,' he said, continuing with a softness to his tone. 'Sundays were for church, roast dinners and a game of Scrabble. Always at St Michael's and always in that order. She used to say, "One should wear their Sunday best for church and for medical people." I used to tease her, though, as she pinned a hat to her head and searched for her gloves. I used to argue that both God and medics would be equally uninterested in our outwardly appearance and more concerned with what's going on inside.

'She had a fondness for gardening, was terrible with a needle and thread, but she hosted the most amazing dinner parties. We were always the talk of the town with our dinner parties. Evie could whip up a fondue single-handedly while simultaneously laying the table and seasoning the potatoes. She did everything with poise and found enjoyment in the strangest of places.' He stopped for breath, enamoured with the memories.

'We were blessed with children, five in total, and she was the finest mother I had ever seen. She could simultaneously love them and discipline them in equal measure, and she insisted on them eating daily seasonal produce from the garden and home-baked bread, still warm from the oven. I used to tell her she had yeast in her veins, but even now I can't walk past a bakery and smell fresh bread without thinking of her.'

He began walking again, across and back down the other side of the bridge.

'I am a lucky man indeed. I found my love and was fortunate enough that she loved me back. I had almost four decades of her and I consider it the most special of gifts. Even grieving her feels comforting in some ways, as it is a reminder of how blessed I have been.'

They stepped off the bridge and onto the cobbled street and began walking back towards the direction of the hotel, but on the other side. Horace turned to look at Rosie.

'And what about you, my dear? Are you currently consumed with the heady emotions of young love? Are your diaries full of romantic scribblings and tender love letters?' He paused before continuing, 'Is there a young person out there lucky enough to court you?'

Rosie chuckled at his outdated terminology and replied, 'Nope. No love scribblings for me. Not yet, anyway.' She tried to sound nonchalant, but there was a tiny ache in her chest reminding her that she was alone.

'Ah, you are simply at a blank page of your next chapter,' he said, smiling. 'Your time will come.'

Rosie smiled back, hoping he was right. She felt a long way away from finding true love. Benjamin was proof of that. Her romance history so far was such a disaster, she fully expected someone to cordon off her love life with police tape. She realised it had been a long time since she had truly let someone get close enough for it to be considered a real relationship.

She looked away from him before continuing, 'My parents both died when I was fourteen and since then, I've got pretty good at being on my own.'

Horace stayed silent as they continued walking and Rosie wondered why she had shared such personal information. She was about to change the subject to tomorrow's agenda, when they passed a small square to their right, with people seated at tables outside a café, a small chapel and a fountain with a cherub in the centre, its mouth spouting a stream of water into the basin below. An old woman, dressed in black from head to toe, was carrying a wicker basket and was passing between the small café tables, trying to sell her wares.

'How delightful,' Horace said, gesturing for Rosie to follow him into the square.

Tucked just out of sight of the main street and adjacent to the café was a row of stalls, each selling differing products. The smell of garlic and olive oil wafted over as they entered the square and made their way to the stalls. The first one was a young woman selling the most delicate lace in the form of gloves, fans and larger swaths that could be used for multiple purposes. The second stall was offering Italian mottled paper, reminiscent of marble with its swirling patterns in various colours. A4 writing paper, A5 notebooks and diaries covered the stall and Rosie was drawn to the notepads like a bibliophile in a first-edition bookshop. She had always had a weakness for a notebook and had a stack of them in her living room – too pretty to be defaced with actual words or thoughts, though. More of an ornament to be observed.

She picked up a gold-covered notebook and flicked through the pages, each unique in its mottled design and pale enough that she instantly felt drawn to the idea of sketching in it. She hadn't sketched for years.

'*Quanto costa*? How much?' she asked the man who was chatting away in quick Italian to the stallholder next to him.

He looked across at her and said, in English, 'Ten euros.'

Placing a hand over it on the table, she reached into her large bag, searching for her purse with her cold fingers. Her bag was the reverse of Mary Poppins's bag. While it was big enough to host an entire family of squirrels and their winter storage of nuts comfortably, it was virtually impossible to ever find anything.

As she scavenged through discarded tissues and old tube tickets, her purse appeared to have hidden itself magically in one of the many apparent portals concealed within the lining of the bag. She began to get flustered as the seller began tapping his fingers on the wooden post holding up the awning above his wares and she started to pull items out randomly, the heat rising from her neck upwards. Antibacterial gel, random lidless pens, make-up brushes, a pair of ballet pumps held together with an elastic band and, randomly, a red plastic toy tractor, the origin of which she did not know. The purse, however, was nowhere to be found.

'Just one minute. I know it's in here . . .' she said, forgetting her efforts to speak Italian. She pulled out what she thought was her purse, but it turned out to be a mouldy, flattened sandwich wrapped in layers of cellophane. 'Yuk,' she said, stuffing the sandwich back into the bag and continuing her search.

'*Dieci euros*,' a deep voice said from beside her and she looked up to see Horace hand over a crisp note to the waiting seller.

He took it, tucking it into his money belt, and then proceeded to wrap the notebook in brown paper before securing it with white ribbon.

'*Gracie voi*, thank you,' the seller said, passing over the neatly wrapped purchase to Horace and then turning back to his conversation with his neighbour.

Horace waited for Rosie to ensure everything was back inside her cavernous bag before turning around and suggesting, 'Shall we grab a nightcap?'

He nodded in the direction of the café and without waiting for Rosie to answer, he began walking over to an unoccupied table, squished between other al fresco tables that were full of people enjoying the sharp night air.

'Let me pay you,' Rosie insisted as she fumbled over to the table, holding her bag and now the new paper package.

Throwing herself down into a metal chair, she yelped as she located her purse. Siphoning out a ten-euro note, she handed it across the table, only to find Horace pushing it back towards her.

'No payment necessary,' he said, gesturing to a nearby waiter.

'But I insist,' Rosie said, pushing it back in his direction.

But he simply shook his head. 'Then you kindly purchase our nightcaps and we'll call it even.'

His smile was kind and before she could argue, a waiter had appeared beside their table, his shirt crisp and his smile friendly.

'*Due caffè corretto, per favore*,' Horace said in perfect Italian, and the waiter nodded before disappearing into the building.

'Coffee?' Rosie asked.

'With a little extra,' Horace said, smiling.

Music started up from inside the café and Rosie saw a man walking out, playing a hand accordion slowly and romantically, the notes so melodic that Rosie instantly felt her shoulders drop and relax. They listened in companiable silence as the music continued, its soothing sounds lulling them into a comforting state. There were patio heaters dotted around the courtyard, adding to the ambiance.

Their coffees arrived and they clinked cups before Rosie took a sip, her eyes broadening as the warmth and strength of brandy set her tongue alight. It was the strongest brandy coffee she had ever had.

'Yikes,' she said, placing it back down into its saucer, instead taking the small amaretto biscuit on the saucer and nibbling on that. 'It's strong.'

'But delicious,' Horace said with a cheeky smile. 'So, why are you here, Rosie? What on earth would possess a young woman like yourself to come on an old folks' trip in the middle of winter?'

'Blackmail,' Rosie said honestly, making Horace chuckle. 'Your lovely Mrs Winthorpe-Smythe and her manipulative ways.' She went on to explain the whole sorry tale of how she was duped into coming, despite her protestations.

'Her deceit is worthy of a James Bond villain,' he said, having listened patiently while she talked. 'Yet, her plan is not without fault.' One bushy eyebrow rose in comical fashion.

'Oh, yes? And what's that?' Rosie asked, her coffee seeming to have disappeared without her realising. She felt warm and a bit fuzzy-headed.

'She isn't here,' he said, flinging an arm wide to the buzzing courtyard. 'She is missing out on visiting the most beautiful city in the world. So, I would say it's her loss and your gain. And hasn't she provided spending money in that huge, hideous plastic pouch of hers that sits in your ridiculous-sized bag?' he said, now pointing at her bag sitting on the table.

Rosie nodded, pulling out the pink plastic folder and unzipping it. Inside, hidden between all the paperwork, was another smaller but bulky plastic pouch, this one the size of a fifty-pound note. She passed it to him and he unzipped it, pulling apart the opening and pointing it in her direction.

'If we're not partaking in her silly itinerary, then I calculate that we are going to be in excess of a fair bit of spending money while we are here.'

'But this isn't my money—' Rosie interjected, but he continued.

'No, you're quite right, Rosie. It isn't. It's mine.'

With that statement, he gestured to the waiter who was hovering nearby, having spotted the pouch of cash like a hungry blackbird spotting a glint of silver.

'Two more of the same, my good man. And make them doubles.'

Chapter Twenty-one

The next morning, Rosie woke to a fug of unfamiliarity and chocolate wrappers. Rising into a seated position in the luxurious white linen of a four-poster bed, she took in the surroundings of her hotel room. The walls were papered in a royal gold with swirling red embellishments and her room was still shrouded by the tall red velvet curtains that hung from ceiling to floor, creating shadows. The bed was the comfiest she had ever slept in. Despite the crawling tentacles of a hangover creeping over her temples and towards her forehead, she couldn't help but smile at where she was.

She tentatively pulled the covers off and climbed out of bed, her feet sinking into plush carpet before stepping into the free hotel slippers, which were just as soft. She walked over to the curtains, pulling them back to find herself staring at another beautiful wintery day. She noticed the blue skies and puffball clouds and could hear the sounds of movement and nautical traffic below. It sounded busy.

She turned to check her phone for the time and was amazed to find that she had slept in far later than she normally did, and even through her alarm. The others must have already had their breakfast and were probably waiting impatiently to begin their day.

After scurrying around the room and dressing quickly, she made her way down in the lift and towards the general hubbub of the hotel restaurant, to find her whole group gathered at their allotted table, their heads together and their chatter animated.

'Morning, everyone. Sorry I'm a bit late this morning.' She took her seat and found ten pairs of eyes staring at her. She smiled questioningly back. 'Is everyone OK this morning?'

'We're fine and dandy,' Olive said, leaning over and patting the back of Rosie's hand as she tried to pour herself a coffee. Splatters landed on the white tablecloth, spreading out like acid on litmus paper. 'But how are you?'

Her tone was one of concern and Rosie blushed, assuming they knew she had come home last night more than a little tipsy. They probably thought she was extremely unprofessional.

'I am perfectly fine, thank you,' she said, ignoring the pounding in her dehydrated temples. 'All set and excited for the day ahead.'

She grabbed a piece of dry toast from the rack in front of her and took a big bite to prove her point. It tasted like sawdust in her mouth, but her smile stayed put.

'Sweet girl,' Winnie said, who sat to her left and looked equally concerned. 'We heard the kerfuffle last night when you came back with Horace, then we saw you stumble back into your room with your hoard of chocolate. Horace told us all about your situation this morning.'

Rosie's flush deepened and she looked across at Horace for clarification.

'I told them about your treatment from Mrs Winthorpe-Smythe, about her trickery in getting you here. How you never signed up for this but rather were forced into it by your dastardly boss and the cunning wit of our dear proprietor.'

Horace dabbed at his mouth with his napkin, despite looking impeccable, with not a hair out of place.

'We think she is utterly horrid,' Mildred said, piping up for the first time this holiday. 'I haven't heard of such dual duplicity since the war days.'

As Mildred was the oldest member of the group, Rosie was inclined to believe her. She could imagine Mrs Winthorpe-Smythe would have made a terrific wartime spy.

'We are sorry you had to be here under false pretences,' Winnie continued, 'so to make up for it, we have come up with a plan.'

The others around the table began nodding emphatically, interrupting each other in their haste.

'So that you won't be out of pocket during this trip—'

'And you can make the most of being stuck with a bunch of decrepit old farts for the next few days—'

'Speak for yourself!'

'Focus everyone, let her speak . . .'

The chatter was incessant and Rosie tried to interject.

'Everyone, please. I'm fine. You don't need to worry about me. I'm happy to be here.' She smiled at the ten pairs of eyes that were directed at her. 'Now, who's ready to go and see some Italian architecture?'

'Rosie, listen. We're offering you a deal,' Mildred said, lifting her hand up to get her to stop talking.

Rosie took in the support wrapped around her slender wrist but also noticed the sewn-on badge that stated: Women Rule the Earth. An OAP feminist, Rosie realised, impressed.

Mildred continued, 'You look after us and act as our guide, and we'll each contribute to a cash payment at the end of each day to pay for your time.'

Rosie went to speak, but Mildred held up the same hand, continuing, 'Look, it's a win-win situation. We have a reliable chaperone in case of any issues and you get a nice bonus while getting to enjoy the sights of Italy. It suits us, it suits you.'

Mildred turned to the others for encouragement and Rosie spotted a tiny blemish behind her left ear. Leaning in, she noticed that it wasn't a blemish but actually a tiny tattoo. Of a blue bird.

'I don't require any payment from you. I am justly paid by my employer,' Rosie continued, squirming in her seat.

'Then see it as a Christmas bonus,' Mildred said resolutely. 'If you manage to keep us all alive for the next five days, it'll be a Christmas miracle. Therefore, I feel it only fair to pay you hazard pay—'

'At the end of every day,' Olive butted in, causing Mildred to nod emphatically.

'Yes, at the end of every day. Just in case one of us bumps off during the night. You don't want to be out of pocket just because one of us selfishly decides to snuff it one night, do you?'

Rosie stared open-mouthed at them all as they all nodded and nudged each other in agreement.

'If I make it until the next morning, I thank my lucky stars—'

'I just assume each day is my last—'

'If my ticker keeps on ticking, then I'm still alive and kicking.'

'With your constant demands, we should be paying her double.'

'Poor girl . . .'

Rosie tried to keep up with all the comments, but it was incessant. They appeared adamant.

'Our minds are set, Rosie,' Horace said, his booming voice rising above the others, appearing to read her mind. 'We want to do this for you. Please.' He smiled warmly.

'Yes, and tell her if she doesn't accept the money, then we'll tell her boss she was terrible and left us all to drown in the canals,' Mildred added, and Rosie wondered if perhaps she would have been a good spy, too.

'I-I don't know what to say . . .' Rosie said, perplexed and a little overwhelmed.

'You say thank you, and then we all get up to leave. My IBS is playing up like nobody's business,' Albert said, standing up abruptly, holding his stomach and wincing.

'Agreed. Discussion complete. Rosie, you'll receive your first payment this evening. Now come on, everyone. Pop your teeth back in, get your walking sticks out – we are off to explore Venice,' Mildred yelled to the group and with a scrape of chairs, they were all wincing and attempting to stand to make their grand exit.

In their state, it was a good five minutes before any of them actually left the restaurant, which gave Rosie more than enough time to digest both what they all suggested, and also two large cream-filled croissants.

Chapter Twenty-two

Twenty minutes and a large bowel movement later from Albert, they were finally grouped together in the hotel lobby. Rosie double-checked the access requirements with the hotel concierge to make sure that the Doge's Palace was in fact OAP-friendly. She knew it was only a few minutes' walk away, yet she still felt a level of responsibility for these strangers plonked directly in her care.

'If I stay at the front, could you remain at the back of the group, Horace?'

Rosie tried not to yell, but it was hard when she had an excitable group of people, all with varying levels of hearing loss. But he nodded and began to usher them out of the revolving doors, with Rosie hitting the street first. The air was cool and fresh, and as she took a deep breath in, she found the remnants of yesterday's excitement beginning to appear again. It sure was hard not to be excited in a city as beautiful as this one.

They walked slowly but surely. Their natural pace meant that they fell into pairs, side by side. Rosie noticed it was Enid who joined her side. She hadn't really spoken much since the trip began; it was mostly the louder, more confident ones who monopolised the conversation.

'Enid, what are you most looking forward to on our trip?' Rosie asked, taking note of her pussy-bow blouse and modest skirt that fell at her ankles.

Enid had perfectly coiffed hair and her demeanour was that of someone who preferred the shadows. Her large woollen coat almost dwarfed her. She blushed, her eyes wide as if she wasn't used to being spoken to.

'Oh, I don't mind, really. I'm just grateful to be here,' Enid answered, pushing her wire glasses further up her delicate nose.

'Well, yes. But surely there is something that you would particularly like to see and we can make sure we do?' Rosie persisted, wanting to provide pleasure for this lady who seemed so quiet.

'Well, if I had to put forward one suggestion . . .' Enid began, her cheeks flushing.

'Of course! Anything,' Rosie said, wanting to please.

'I would really like to see the artworks here,' Enid began.

'An art enthusiast, fantastic!' Rosie said, while Enid continued.

'. . . so that I can see as many naked bodies as possible.'

Rosie fell silent. She was not expecting that. She gazed at Enid more closely, this time taking in the cheeky smile and the youthful look hidden behind those pale grey eyes.

'Well, yes, there should definitely be some of that available,' Rosie said, stifling a snigger. 'Do you prefer paintings or sculptures?'

'Oh, definitely the 3D models,' Enid said, raising her arms and weighting her hands as if she were cupping something. 'I like to see things to scale. It's better for my cataracts.'

At this point, they both burst into laughter and Rosie wondered what other surprises might be in store for her this week. If only she knew.

The queue for the Doge's Palace had been surprisingly small for a Saturday morning. Rosie guessed it might be due to the season and the heavy, ominous clouds that looked about to crack open at any moment. She looked across again at the ginormous Christmas tree positioned in the centre of St Mark's Square, noticing the tourists gathering to stare at it, a collective buzz of wonder emanating as bright as the sparkling baubles that hung from each branch. It really was a spectacle, Rosie thought. A few people braved the outside cafés, keen to capture the atmosphere of Venice's centre point, their gloved hands wrapped around steaming cups of coffee.

Before she knew it, she had been ushered forwards by a stern-looking security guard, all dressed in black, and her handbag was pointed at, with a clear indication for her to open it. She acquiesced with a smile, pulling her bag off her shoulder and placing it down on the table, but she could hear the mutterings and complaints of her group behind her, worrying that their delicates and personal belongings were for their eyes only.

Rosie absent-mindedly watched as the security officer scanned her backpack and she noticed the large plastic folder still inside, bulging with what she knew to be everyone's passports. Tutting at herself, she made a mental note to put them in her room safe when she got back to the hotel. Carrying them around seemed both cumbersome and a little daunting – what if she lost her bag?

Getting a stern nod from the security officer, she waited while the other members of the group sniffed, grunted and groaned their way through the line and into the entrance of the Doge's Palace. Their complaints soon echoed away, though, as she entered the palace itself and took a moment to take in the vastness of the building.

It was hugely grand and overbearing, yet the palace was almost in total silence, lending a sense of stillness and privacy. It was a contradiction in parts, much like Rosie felt about herself – was she happy? Yes. But she wasn't content. Did she enjoy her job? Yes, but ironically, it meant she didn't think to chase her dreams. Without realising, she exhaled loudly, causing Horace to throw her a concerned glance.

They began their tour and Rosie was awed by the gothic architecture and opulence of the building. This awe continued as she moved from room to room, taking in the grand staircases, the high ceilings and an abundance of artwork that seemed to stare down at her. Her movements were slow – not through choice, but through having to usher her group forwards repeatedly as they complained loudly of bunions, sore knees and feeling cold. Other visitors were shooting them dirty glances, their own experience tainted by the complaints from a group of OAPs who kept wondering how much further it was to the gift shop or whether it was time for a cup of tea.

After copious rest breaks and pauses, Rosie noticed with relief that they were at the end of the tour and she could see the exit sign up ahead. Their energy levels appeared to reappear with the sight of the gift shop and Rosie decided to leave them to it, taking comfort from exiting the building and taking a seat on the long stone bench that ran along the side of the building. She already felt exhausted and this was only day one. And activity one at that.

She wondered how professional it would be if she suggested that their next activity be a three-hour sit-down at one of the many Italian cafés that offered Aperol spritzes. She looked sideways at the other visitors sitting beside her and noticed they were all mostly couples, lost in their own romantic bubble, and one family of three, with a small girl dressed in an orange coat with matching mittens and woollen hat. The parents were watching her as she danced from one foot to the other, enjoying the abject attention from both parents. It was sweet, Rosie thought, and she smiled watching them, enjoying a moment of solitude.

'Rosie!'

She turned at her name and saw her group coming towards her, each carrying gift bags. Olive and Winnie came first, comparing recently purchased key rings and Venetian fans. Mildred was arguing with Albert that he should carry her bag as her wrist was aching, while he argued that his anaemia meant he couldn't. They were loud, unaware of anyone around them, but bizarrely, Rosie was already becoming fond of them all.

She stood up and took both gift bags from Albert and Mildred, suggesting that they all head back to the hotel for a nice cup of tea and some lunch. They agreed in unison and began the short walk back to the hotel, conversations limited to who was having what for lunch.

But on their way, they couldn't help but be drawn to the various stalls selling traditional Venetian wares. Rosie noticed the sheer number of Venetian masks that hung from stalls – some beautiful, some eerie and almost frightening – and before she knew what was happening, Enid had stopped to admire them.

'C'mon, Enid!' shouted Olive, who was tapping her feet impatiently, wanting to keep moving.

Enid ignored her, staring at the masks, her fingers gently stroking the more colourful ones. They were adorned with feathers, sequins and intricate stitching that made even Rosie want to admire them. Before she knew it, the eager seller was in front of them, smiling broadly, chattering away in broken English.

'You try? Only the best . . . Authentic Venetian . . . I do you an offer.'

He was pulling masks down from their hooks and encouraging them to try them on. A mirror appeared as if from nowhere and Enid was giggling like a teenager as he slipped on a mask over her white hair.

'*Bellissimo*,' he said, indicating for her to look in the mirror.

He'd chosen well. The mask was predominantly silver, with white feathers adorning the top like a peacock. Around the holes for the eyes were the most exquisite aquamarine sequins and diamantés that sparkled in the morning sun. Delicate blue swirling designs had been hand-drawn over the silver fabric of the mask and the overall effect against Enid's complexion was as if it had been made for her.

The others had also stepped forward by this point, admiring the trinkets, magnets and masks, and before Rosie had had a chance to say no, she was being offered the chance to try on her own mask. This one was completely different to Enid's choice. It was black velvet, with gold lacing and smaller black feathers adorning the top. However, as she took it from the seller's hands, she noticed on each side of the mask a delicately drawn gold outline of the globe, its continents sketched accurately and no bigger than a fifty-pence piece.

Running a finger over the detailing, the sunlight caught the ring given to her by her neighbour, Mrs Benson, its own gold globe not too dissimilar in style or colour to the outline visible on the mask. The seller's keen eye also noticed, and he pointed to her ring and to the mask, indicating she should buy it.

'*Bellissima*,' he repeated and quoted a price for the mask.

It was far more expensive than she had thought it might be. But it was also beautiful. She could imagine placing it on her desk at work and admiring it. It would be a good reminder of this trip and how she needed to take more chances.

Feeling reckless, she nodded and delved into her backpack to find her purse. Moving her passport to one side, she grabbed her travel purse and paid the seller, who had wrapped the mask in white tissue paper. She moved away from the stall to place the mask gently into her bag, ensuring it wouldn't get damaged, and then waited while the other members of the group made their purchases.

Enid had also bought her mask but had rejected the offer of it being wrapped and was instead still wearing it, her grey eyes visible. She was smiling.

'Are we done spending money?' Olive said, looking exasperated, and beckoned for the group to keep going.

The others were looking a little puffed out, their red-veined cheeks flushed, and seemed keen to follow Olive back to the hotel for a rest.

On arrival back at the hotel, Rosie ensured that they were all settled in the restaurant before heading back to her room to freshen up. Housekeeping had been in, she noted, with her bed made and her clothes folded and hung in the wardrobe. Switching the light on in the bathroom, she found her cosmetics lined up neatly and the towels replenished.

It felt odd, she realised, being taken care of, being looked after. She headed back to the wardrobe to hang up her coat and noticed the small black safe nailed to the wall on its own. It reminded her of the passports still sitting in her bag and she decided to put them in the safe before she forgot.

She took them from her bag and placed them in the safe, moving the dial to set a four-digit combination, stopping short before closing the door. Her passport was in with all the rest.

That might not be wise. She quickly removed hers from the pack and slipped it into the inside pocket of her backpack before locking the safe. Sitting back on her haunches, she heard a strong knock at the door and rose to answer.

'Mildred!' Rosie said, surprised any of the group even knew which room she was in. 'Is everything OK?'

Mildred waved away her concern and walked into Rosie's room, indicating for her to close the door. Rosie did as instructed and followed Mildred into the lounge, taking a seat on one of the two sofas. Mildred chose not to sit and instead walked around the large suite, taking in the excess of space.

'Everything is fine, Rosie, relax. We just want to add another item to the agenda today and we wondered if you would accompany us, please?'

Rosie's plans of taking a long soak in the bath and then sitting on her balcony, all wrapped up, to watch the world go by vapourised in her mind like a magician's poof and she forced a smile onto her face.

'Of course, what did you have in mind?'

'A gondola ride.'

'Oh, OK,' Rosie answered, mentally scrolling down the list of ailments that each OAP had like a Rolodex. 'Do you think that's such a good idea, though?' She tried to be tactful. 'It's just I hear they can be quite tricky to navigate into—'

'If you are trying to imply that we are too old to ride a gondola,' Mildred began, 'then you're probably right. But we are consenting adults and it's something we would like to do. But with assistance' – she pointed towards Rosie – 'and that's where you come in.'

'Right,' Rosie answered, nervously calculating how many gondolas would be needed for eleven people.

As if reading her mind, Mildred continued, 'It would only be us women. The men aren't bothered about taking a ride, we've asked. Horace and Walter have decided to join a chess group down in the lobby, Albert's gone for a nap and we all know how dodgy Norman's hip is . . .'

She tailed off as they both nodded in agreement. Norman was forever complaining about his hip.

'So, just the seven of us. I have asked at the desk and there is a gondola station literally a minute's walk away that will take us out onto the Grand Canal and then up towards the Rialto Bridge. An hour tops.' She stood up, her confidence in Rosie's agreement clear. 'Shall we meet you down in the lobby in five minutes?'

It was a question, but it didn't require an answer, as Mildred had already walked to the door, opened it and walked into the hallway.

'Then we'll let you come back and have a few hours to yourself in this ridiculously opulent suite. Honestly, the size of it . . .'

Her voice tailed away as she walked down the corridor towards the lift, leaving Rosie still seated on the sofa, wondering what on earth she had just agreed to.

Chapter Twenty-three

'They look a little rocky.' Rosie tried to reason with the older ladies as they stood on the dock beside a row of gondolas rising and falling against the dock, like a line of galloping stallions, 'Are you sure this is such a good idea? We could try again tomorrow.'

'Nonsense,' Mildred said, stepping forwards towards the waiting gondoliers with a confidence that Rosie wasn't feeling.

The gondoliers looked nonplussed, their eyes drawn to the euros held in Mildred's hand

'It does look a little choppy . . .' Dottie said, her face devoid of all colour.

Enid also looked a little nervous and Rosie's mind referred back to her medical list, reminding her of Enid's glaucoma condition. Her heart rate rose a whole octave.

'Ladies, let's think on it and we can always come again tomorrow.' She tried to reason with them, but Mildred had marched forwards, handing over a wad of notes to the smiling gondolier.

'*Gracie mille*,' he said, smiling once more and turning to speak to the gondolier next to him.

His Italian was fast, but it was clear he was initiating help. All of a sudden, three extra gondoliers, all dressed in matching black trousers and stripey black-and-white tops, came forward, holding their hands out to assist. Rosie could see there was no alternative but to go along with them.

'I want four in this one and three in the one behind,' Mildred directed, indicating with her fingers how to split the group.

Rosie could see she had allocated the second gondola to Dottie, Enid and Shirley, which Rosie did not think wise.

'Actually, Mildred,' she began, walking over to the second gondola, 'I'm going to ride in this one. You go in the first one.'

Mildred shrugged, not seeming to care.

Rosie took the lead and went to climb in first, taking the rough, cold hand of the gondolier to step into what was an already rocking and unsteady watercraft. He directed her where to sit and turned his attention back to the others.

Enid was squinting as she took the gondolier's hand, her feet tentatively stretching out to climb onboard. There was a bit of a drop down from the dock to the first step of the vessel and after much deliberating, the gondolier took hold of her ankle and guided her foot into a flat position. She blushed deeply, her ankle exposed and touched by a man, but she let him guide her into a vacant seat beside Rosie. Rosie was sure she heard a small titter and she looked across to see the older woman smiling.

Next was Dottie, who was backing away from the edge rather than moving towards it. The gondolier was encouraging her forwards, but her eyes had glazed over and the fear had clearly set in. Shirley was standing beside her, waiting to board the gondola in front, but noticing Dottie's reversing steps, she rolled her eyes and dug deep into her beige handbag, pulling out a miniature bottle of what looked like whisky. She unscrewed the cap and forced it in front of Dottie's face, who went cross-eyed trying to focus on what it was.

'Drink it,' Shirley said. 'Now!'

Dottie went to refuse, then turned at the sound of a gondola bashing loudly against the slimy, lichen-covered building wall and thought twice. She took the bottle and downed the entire contents of golden liquid in one go. Her face screwed up with shock and disgust, but she smiled weakly as Shirley, Enid and both gondoliers all applauded. Shaking her coiffed curls like a dog shaking off muddy water, she took a tentative step forward and allowed the gondolier to guide her safely into the passenger cabin and onto a seat.

Rosie's heart was in her throat the whole time, but within moments, the professional guide had Dottie seated and comfortable, with a thick blanket over her lower half. He hopped onto the stern behind her head, grabbing his oars, ready to begin.

The first gondolier pushed off from the dock, the bow facing forwards, and dug his oar into the canal, propelling him and his passengers forwards. Shirley let out a little whoop of excitement. Rosie wondered if that miniature bottle wasn't the first to be emptied today from her purse.

Her thoughts were interrupted by the movement of their own gondola and as they set off down the canal, the only sounds audible were the lapping of the water against the boats and that of the oars dipping in and out of the water. The canal was narrow, barely wide enough for two gondolas to pass by one another. Rosie looked skywards at the crumbling brick buildings covered in moss, with lines of washing hanging between window ledges and potted winter flowers adding a splash of colour as they balanced on windowsills. A low-level brick bridge drew close and Rosie watched the gondolier in front of them deftly angle down and under it before standing up again. *He'd make a good limbo-dancer*, Rosie thought.

The sky had changed into a sharp powder blue and she could see the amber glow of the afternoon sun light up the tops of the buildings. But down where they were, in the narrow and shadowy canals, the sunlight and its weak warmth didn't touch them.

She jumped as the gondolier behind her suddenly broke into song, bending down to pass under the same bridge, his low tones belting out 'That's Amore' in time with his oar strokes. She turned to look at him and he gave her a cheeky wink. She laughed. It was all so cheesy and clichéd, but the ladies of the group were lapping it up, their eyes glazed, their hands clasped in excitement.

The gondola made its way around a bend, the gondolier navigating a sharp corner with a swiftness that defied logic. All of a sudden, they were bathed in sunlight, causing them to blink and look away. When her eyes adjusted to the light, Rosie looked up to see that they had pulled out onto the Grand Canal, their gondola falling into line with the many other boats that navigated both ways of the canal.

The waters were a little choppier, which was to be expected, so Rosie looked to check that Dottie was OK. Her knuckles were white as she gripped onto the side, but she seemed to be enjoying herself still. The gondolier stopped singing and instead began to give them an audible tour of the buildings as they passed by. He pointed out the Peggy Guggenheim Museum, the Ponte dell'Accademia, Grassi Palace and finally, the Rialto Bridge, which was larger than Rosie had ever imagined. It was more of a street than a bridge, with a whiteish–grey wall of six arches either side leading up to a larger arch that stood proud on the portico. There was a staircase in front of the arches, with people looking down at the passing boats. Rosie saw a little girl wave and she waved back, smiling.

'This is the oldest bridge in Venice,' the gondolier said, his accent strong. 'It is one of four on the Grand Canal. There are three staircases in total, with the middle one being large enough to have a line of shops either side. As we go underneath, look at the width of the underbelly of the bridge.'

As he navigated his way under the bridge, passing water buses and smaller water taxis, the shade enabled them all to look skywards, the stonework dirty and streaked with green but wide enough to feel like they were crossing underneath a wide carriageway. And the noise was everywhere: of tourists chatting, motorboat engines roaring.

Moving back into the sunlight, Rosie turned around to see that the other side of the Rialto Bridge was identical, the only difference being the faces of the tourists looking down. Restaurants lined the walkways of both sides of the canal, with waiters touting for business, holding menus up for passing tourists in an effort to grab their attention, and their euros.

'If you have time, come back at sunset. She is a beauty at sunset,' the gondolier said, referring to the bridge. 'She lights up as if she were a gift from God Himself.' He smiled, his love of his city clear.

With a quick manoeuvre, he turned the gondola around 180 degrees so that they faced the way they had come, allowing the currents and waves of the water to guide them back under the bridge, his control unwavering. They were still following Shirley's gondola, like a shadow.

'How do you do it? How do you not tip over?' Enid asked him as a wave from a passing large water bus caused them to tilt side to side.

The gondolier smiled, using his oar to steer them as easily as if he were sliding a knife into a crème caramel.

'Our gondolas are a work of art,' he said, gesturing to a small block of wood beneath his feet in which the oar had been positioned. 'This is called the *fórcola* and, depending on how I position the oar, we can go forwards or backwards.' He moved the oar to show them how it worked. 'And if you look to the front of the gondola, you will see the *ferro*, or the bow iron.' He pointed to the strange-shaped iron fixture that sat proud at the front of the vessel with a large piece of iron and six identical horizontal lines all protruding forwards. 'The top part is shaped like the Doge's hat and the six horizontal lines each represent one of the six regions of Venice.'

Rosie looked at the bow iron and how it proudly edged forwards with each sweeping stroke. The sun glinted off the black paintwork and looking at other gondolas in the canal, she noticed that they were all black, like water-based sports cars, she thought.

The rest of the journey passed uneventfully and before they knew it, they had turned and were slowly edging towards the original dock from where they had started. Shirley's gondola had already emptied and they were standing on the dock watching their arrival. As the gondolier deftly moored, he hopped out of the gondola and held out his hand to help them off.

First was Dottie, who was seated closest to him. She tentatively stood up, the boat rocking with the movement, and she let out a squeal, her face filled with fright. To calm her, the gondolier tried to steady the boat, but she mistook that as a sign to step forwards and in doing so, she upset the balance of the boat entirely, with it now swinging violently from side to side.

'Dottie, stop!' Enid yelled, holding onto the sides in an effort to keep it steady. 'You're going to tip us into the canal!'

'Help!' Dottie yelled back, trying to steady herself but finding that her legs were shaking and she couldn't find her footing.

She stumbled and took a step forwards, but thankfully the gondolier grabbed at her arm and steadied her with one hand while gesturing to the other gondoliers around him to help. They ran over and in a single moment, three men had lifted Dottie from the gondola and onto dry land as if she were as light as an amaretti biscuit wrapper. At which point she burst into tears. Shirley, Olive and Mildred ran to her and guided her to a nearby wooden bench.

With the gondola now steadied, both Rosie and Enid were helped out. With assurances from Rosie that Dottie was OK, the gondoliers walked away to their gondola hut next to the small pier.

'Dottie, are you all right?' Rosie asked, kneeling beside the bench.

Dottie nodded, her watery eyes glistening with fresh tears and her bottom lip trembling, indicating that she clearly wasn't. Shirley dipped into her bag again and drew out another miniature bottle, unscrewed the cap and handed it to Dottie.

'Have you completely raided your minibar, perchance?' Olive asked, rolling her eyes.

'So what if I have? I don't see you offering anything to help here,' Shirley said, wrapping Dottie's fingers around the bottle and raising it to her lips to drink.

Dottie tentatively took a sip, but Shirley tilted the bottle upwards and Dottie ended up swigging the contents in one big gulp.

Seconds later, Dottie exhaled and a weak smile appeared on her pale face. Shirley looked to Olive as if to say 'I told you so' and threw the now-empty bottle in a nearby bin.

Rosie didn't entirely agree with the daytime drinking, but she wasn't qualified in adult supervision either, so she couldn't think what else to say. So she turned to Enid for back-up. Enid stepped forwards between the two ladies.

'Now I don't know about you, but that ride has totally wiped me out. How about we head back to the hotel for a nap?'

'Dottie? I feel a little unsteady after all that toing and froing. I don't suppose you could let me lean on you for the walk back, could I?'

Dottie jumped up, ever the good Samaritan, and took her arm. 'Of course, Enid. These pathways are a little unsteady and don't get me started on the bridges.' She walked away from Shirley and continued, 'Did you know there are around four hundred bridges in Venice? Imagine, four hundred! My hips ache at the thought . . .'

The others followed behind, the lure of a nap exceeding any desire to continue bickering. Rosie trailed at the back, watching the ladies as they made their way to the hotel, wondering again how she ever got into this strange and surreal situation.

Chapter Twenty-four

Flinging herself onto her hotel bed, Rosie found her eyes grow heavy with tiredness. Leaning over to pull a pillow closer to her, she fell asleep almost instantly and slept for over an hour.

When she awoke, she was shocked to find that the sky outside the open curtains was now displaying a sun low in the sky, the earlier blue replaced with a pale haze, indicating late afternoon. She stretched out in the bed, feeling the delicious rush that only a good full-bodied stretch could do, and then sat up. Reaching for her phone, she saw she still had a few more hours yet until the concert. With the draw of the huge bathtub too sumptuous to ignore, she climbed out of bed to run herself a bubble bath.

Watching as the hot water poured from its gold tap and the level of bubbles grew higher, she hummed to herself as she removed her clothes and got ready to climb in. Her phone pinged at her from the bedroom, so she went to grab it before returning to the bathroom and slipping into the best bath she had ever had. Once submerged, she opened her phone to see an email reply from Audrey.

Rosie laughed as Audrey made light of the fact that Rosie was being compensated to enjoy an all-expenses-paid holiday, eat pizza and gaze at hot Italian men while luxuriating in a five-star hotel. To prove her correct, Rosie lifted her phone skywards and then took a selfie of her in the bath, surrounded by bubbles. Staring at it, she was shocked to see how relaxed she looked and her eyes were crinkled as if from laughing.

She replied to Audrey, attaching the photo, and at the last minute, she decided to copy Bee in on the email, as she wanted to show her that she was indeed making the most of the situation. Pressing Send, she dropped the phone onto the bathmat beside her and slipped even further down into the bath so that just her face was visible. Breathing a deep, contented sigh, she closed her eyes and decided that coming to Venice was exactly what she needed, without her even realising.

After an extremely long bath, Rosie felt re-energised. She was scrubbed clean and had used every bath product available to her in the room. Her skin was crinkled and her muscles totally relaxed, and as she climbed out of the bath and wrapped herself in the largest towel she'd ever seen, she began to hum to herself, looking forward to the evening ahead.

'Today has been a good day,' she said to the room as she got dressed, smiling at the view from the balcony.

Having dried her hair and applied make-up, she found she even had time to sit on her small balcony with a glass of wine taken from the minibar and watch as the sun set for the day. Being on the top floor, she was able to observe the terracotta roof tiles of the buildings glowing with an orange hue that made it feel like Venice had its own spotlight. There were no high-rise buildings or department stores here; the tallest buildings were the spires of churches or the domes of cathedrals. It felt like Rosie had taken a step back in time by a century and she could easily imagine Venice looking much the same then, apart from the motorboats and electricity lines.

Aside from the matching rooftop terracotta tiles, each building looked unique in its design and varying colours. Rosie noted the ornate, carved friezes and delicate stonework that gave each building character and the sheer number of archways that seemed to have been factored in to each building. Frontages were painted yellow, cream, blue or even orange, and windows varied in size, from large balcony doors leading out onto a veranda, to small shuttered windows that blocked any sign of life. On the buildings that still had bare brickwork, Rosie could see even from afar that the exposed brick had crumbled on corners and in weak spots. But this only added to its charm, the cracks offering stories and tales of times gone by.

Rosie was surprised to see little to no greenery. Maybe the odd tree, but it looked like Venice had squeezed out any sign of wildlife in favour of buildings. But that didn't detract from its beauty. Despite her reluctance to come here, she couldn't help but feel awed by the grandeur of the city. Sitting on the balcony, hearing the comforting buzz of small boats passing by, smells of Italian cooking wafting up to greet her, she felt herself relax for the first time in a long time.

Rosie finished the final dregs of her wine, slipped on her shoes and grabbed her bag, realising her phone was still on the bathroom floor from earlier. She grabbed it, closing the door to her room and making her way towards the lift to take her down to the lobby. It was time to meet everyone downstairs for their evening concert at the Teatro La Fenice.

According to her phone, the theatre was only a four-minute walk from their hotel, but even so, she had advised everyone to gather in the lobby with enough time to have dinner at the hotel restaurant and then walk to the theatre. But she suspected full tummies would only slow their pace, so after a quick dinner of lasagne, they were hustled out onto the street, wrapped up warm, en route to the theatre.

The evening was chilly but clear and it was a lovely walk down narrow alleys, crossing squares full of restaurants and diners. The restaurants all had outdoor heaters that blasted warm air onto their diners, adding to the amber glow over the city. Rosie walked at a companiable pace beside Horace, allowing him to chat away about the many concerts he'd experienced in his lifetime. Hearing him chatter on felt like listening to a storyteller weave his tale to his audience. His deep baritone added depth to his words and there was an almost hypnotic quality to his voice.

By the time they reached the Teatro La Fenice, the entire party had flushed cheeks and bright eyes. They found themselves at the back of a long queue, but Rosie mentally thanked Mrs Winthorpe-Smythe again as she realised the tickets were fast-track and required no queueing. She wanted to believe that

Mrs Winthorpe-Smythe had altruistically purchased the more expensive tickets to ensure her party weren't inconvenienced by queueing, but she knew it was more likely that she insisted on only the best for herself.

As they were led into the warmth of the lobby and into the theatre itself, Rosie couldn't help but gaze in awe at her surroundings. With lavish décor and elaborate gold detailing, it was a building that was designed to impress. The theatre was decorated entirely in gold with a domed ceiling of powder blue and delicate angels and cherubs painted on, their images captured mid-flight. There was row upon row of plush red velvet seats, all facing forwards towards the stage. An usher led them down the middle aisle to their seats and Rosie admired the identical lines of gold theatre boxes that wrapped around the periphery of the theatre and rose to meet the ceiling.

They moved closer towards the stage and she found herself gazing up at the heavy, closed black curtains onstage that contrasted against the bright red and greens of the huge garland of fresh poinsettias that ran along the front of the stage. It turned out their seats were in the front row, and again, Rosie sent a silent thanks to Mrs Winthorpe-Smythe as their entire party took their seats in the whole left side of the row. The smell of the flowers was powerful and from behind the stage curtain, she could hear the movement of chairs and the tuning of various string instruments.

Her phone pinged in her back pocket and she pulled it out to find a message from Bee:

So? Fallen in love with a sexy gondolier yet? Managed to keep the OAPs alive? Bought me some authentic Italian grappa? Reply to let me know you're alive! Missing you x

Rosie smiled and took a quick selfie of herself with the impressive theatre visible behind her. She sent it with a line of smiling emojis and before she had time to write a second reply asking why she hadn't responded to her earlier email of her in the bath, the lights flashed on and off, indicating that the performance was about to begin. She slipped the phone onto silent and popped it into her bag. Looking around her, she was surprised to see how quickly the theatre had filled, with people taking their seats and the gold boxes full of excited faces.

The lights dimmed and a hush fell upon the room. Rosie's eyes followed the curtain as they pulled apart to reveal a smartly dressed group seated on metal chairs. There was a string quartet, each with their instrument in hand, and a pianist seated behind a shiny black grand piano – three males and two females, dressed in smart black outfits, the only splash of colour being the men's red ties and the women's red ribbons in their hair. They stood up in unison and took a bow at the audience before taking their seats yet again. There was a silence as if the audience had taken an in-breath and then the quintet began to play.

Rosie felt the hairs on the back of her forearms rise with emotion. The music blended with the acoustics and the setting was like nothing she had experienced before. Plus, with the chandeliers dimmed, so that the only light was from the spotlights that fell upon each of the five musicians, and the silence from the audience, her senses were heightened to focus only on what she could hear. And the sound was breathtaking.

She knew neither the name of what was being played, nor the composer, but it didn't matter. The sweet sound of the string instruments sewing together with the deep baritone of the double bass, all melting into the chorus of the piano was like an epiphany. The surround sound reverberating around her from every angle was just all-encompassing and before she knew it, the musicians stood up to signal the end of their composition.

The applause felt like a thunderous earthquake, but Rosie joined in, feeling that simply clapping was not enough to convey how moved she had been. The musicians took a bow before gesturing towards the left side of the stage in unison, drawing the eye to a sixth spotlight that was now pointing at a beautiful woman, dressed in a silky black ballgown, her dark hair piled on top of her head and fastened with a large poinsettia. She was smiling and took a deep curtsey, her intricate black corset staying put but her ballooning skirt billowing out onto the stage as she did so. It reminded Rosie of her grandmother's collection of porcelain figurines that used to sit on her mantelpiece. Rosie would stare at those figurines wondering if there really were women out there with that much poise and beauty. It turns out there were.

The woman stepped forwards and made her way towards the centre of the stage in front of the musicians, where a microphone stand had appeared from nowhere. She turned to the quintet and gave them a deep bow, which they acknowledged with a nod. As she turned back towards the audience, Rosie was close enough to take in her petite features. Her wide gown showed off her slim waist and full chest and Rosie could spot tiny red flowers sewn into the fabric, with the corset tied at the back with a lace the colour of the tiny flowers and her hair accessory. Her skin was warm olive and her cheekbones accentuated her almond-shaped eyes, which were emphasised by long lashes and heavy make-up. Her pink lips were plump and when she smiled, she showed a row of beautiful straight teeth. Rosie felt both mesmerised and inferior in her presence. This woman epitomised beauty.

And then she began to sing.

If Rosie had thought the quintet had a touch of brilliance to them, this woman took them to a new stratosphere. Her voice was powerful yet soft. Both soulful and haunting. She had the ability to bring the audience with her to her crescendo, their breaths held – and then back down again with an elongated note that left them all captured in her grasp. Her melodious voice reverberated around the room, capturing the ears of everyone there.

The musicians accompanied her, but their lyrical notes merely acted as a background noise, accentuating her voice.

As she sang, the music moved through her whole body, her arms moving in time with the lyrics, telling their own story, her facial expressions narrating the tale as she went.

Drawing her eyes away from the singer momentarily, Rosie glanced to her left to see the expressions of the rest of her group. They, too, were mesmerised, their ageing faces made youthful by the experience.

As the performer finished each song, there was a silence from the audience, a united hope that this wasn't the end and that she would continue. With each new song, the atmosphere grew more still, the audience exposed to emotions that could only be experienced in a setting such as this. But after an hour, her performance ended with the elongated final note of a set that had captivated everyone's attention.

Lifting a hand to her cheek, Rosie was surprised to find tears. The room fell silent and the atmosphere seemed to have frozen in time while the audience brought themselves back into the real world. Seconds later, the applause erupted and everyone was suddenly on their feet, giving the singer the praise that was warranted. She took a deep bow, looking bashful, and only moments later she had exited the stage, leaving the audience wanting more.

The clapping continued as the quintet took their bows and left the stage, and then the concert was over. Rosie collapsed back into her seat, spent. Her emotions were high and now that people began to empty out of the theatre, she took a moment to regain her composure. She looked down to find that Horace was patting her hand. His eyes matched hers, shiny and glazed over. They didn't speak, but they silently communicated their joy from the performance and she knew that he had been as moved as her. At this very moment, she was grateful to Mrs Winthorpe-Smythe for preferring to ski rather than experience this. It had given Rosie an opportunity to experience something she would never forget.

As they began their short walk back to the hotel, their excited chatter causing puffs of ice-cold air to rise into the starry night, she let the others walk ahead and took a moment to stare skywards. The stars were so clear and bright.

Rosie realised that maybe, just maybe, if she could experience joy through music as she had tonight, and fall under the spell of Venice's charms, then perhaps she might be able to open her heart up to the possibility of more.

Chapter Twenty-five

When Rosie climbed into bed later that evening, she found herself luxuriating in the huge hotel bed, stretching out like a cat who wanted its tummy rubbed. She felt different today. Relaxed. Happy. She wasn't needed by anyone, she didn't need to go to work, clean the house, take out the bins . . . nothing. She was free to explore Venice as she wished, providing she followed around a group of OAPs and tried not to lose any of them.

Wanting to set an alarm for the morning so that she could have yet another glorious bath, she realised her phone was still in her backpack. Reaching over for her bag on the floor next to the bed, she noticed that she had unread emails. Opening the app, she jolted as she saw two: one from Audrey and one from Benjamin. She shook her head, unsure why he'd be emailing her when she wasn't in the office, but in the spirit of goodwill, she decided to open it and tolerate whatever it was he had to say. She began to read:

Rosie,
Looking HOT! Had second thoughts, eh?! Once you've tried a bite of Benjamin, you've found you want more?! Wishing I was in there with you. You look tasty. Send me another and I might return the favour . . .

'What on earth . . .?' she said to herself. 'What is he talking about?'

But then she saw it . . . He was replying to an email she had sent earlier that day. When she was in the bathtub.

'Oh, no, no, no . . .' she said, scrolling up to see the original email. 'No, no, no,' she repeated.

She opened the attachment again, viewing it differently this time. Before, when sending it to just Audrey and Bee, she saw the opulence of the bathtub, with its gold taps, expensive tiling around the bath, the luxurious size of the bathroom visible behind her. What she now saw, through Benjamin's eyes, was the bubbles barely concealing her breasts and body, her mouth curved suggestively in a smile.

'How did this happen?' she whispered to the empty room.

Rosie looked in her sent box. Yes, she had sent it to Audrey, that email address was correct. But she'd copied Bee in, she remembered doing it. Then it struck her. She had typed 'BE' into the 'to' part and selected Bee's address from the drop-down, but her hands had been wet from the bath and the steamy atmosphere meant that she could have easily selected Benjamin's name instead of Bee. They were both so similar. And sure enough, there it was, Benjamin's work email address in the second address line.

'Shit,' she said, panic rising in her chest like ice particles.

Damage control was needed, and it was needed now. She rang Audrey's number and was surprised to hear her pick up on the first ring. It was late.

'Rosie, what have you done?!'

Audrey's voice was strained and she could hear the anxiety in her tone, even over a thousand miles away.

'Why did you copy *him* in?'

Rosie groaned, leaning her head against the headboard, and closed her eyes.

'I didn't mean to! It was meant to be Bee, not him. Oh, shit, Audrey, what am I going to do? He's responded, too. You can imagine how . . .'

Rosie tailed off, not wanting to repeat what he had said. Audrey paused, which was never a good sign, and Rosie could feel the beginnings of a headache pounding at her temples.

'Don't leave it. Sort it now, I think. Email back and just be short and smart. Something like: "Apologies, Benjamin, you were not the intended recipient. Please ignore and

consider our relationship as nothing more than work-based."
Something like that. Clear the air, but don't invite further
conversations.'

Rosie nodded along, even though she knew Audrey couldn't
see her. That made sense. She just needed to nip it in the bud
and do it now.

'You're right, you're totally right. I'll do it now.'

They said their goodbyes and Rosie typed out a quick
response to Benjamin's reply, stating almost word for word
what Audrey said to say. Pressing Send, she took a few deep
breaths and considered her next option. And quickly realised
she didn't have one. She was over a thousand miles away from
the office and it was a Saturday night. All she could hope was
that she had curbed any further responses from Benjamin by
her stern response.

Rolling over onto her side, she sighed loudly. Any buzz
from earlier was now gone and instead, she felt stupid, worried
and more alone than she had felt in a very long time.

Rosie somehow managed to sleep, but she wasn't sure how.

When she awoke, she felt exhausted. She'd tossed and turned
until she finally fell into fitful sleep around 3am. Remembering
the events of last night, she hastily rolled over to check her
phone, sighing with a mix of relief as she noted there was
no response from Benjamin. Taking that as a good sign, she
decided to get on with the day and assume the matter was
resolved. Audrey was quiet, too, with no further contact or
messages from her.

She got dressed in a daze and decided that a hearty breakfast
would cure all anxieties. She made her way down to the ground
floor, her stomach rumbling in anticipation of more Italian
pastries. At this rate, she'd be going home a stone heavier.

As she walked into the restaurant, she spotted the whole
group, already seated, and by the looks of it, having already eaten
their breakfast. Shirley noticed her first and alerted the others.

'She's here! She's finally here, let's go!'

The group pushed back their chairs and stood up with gusto, their movements appearing fast for a group of mostly septuagenarians. They came towards her en masse and gathered around her, hands leading her back through the restaurant doors and towards the lobby.

'She doesn't have her coat . . .'

'Here, toss her my scarf.'

'Someone hand her that pastry.'

She could feel herself being pulled outside the hotel as if she were caught up in a wave, her own movements making no difference to her direction of travel.

'If we walk quickly, we should make it.'

'It started ten minutes ago – we'll have missed the start.'

'Edwardo, the hotel manager, said it would be fine if we headed towards the Basilica di Santa Maria della Salute. We'll get a good view from there.'

'What is going on?!' Rosie exclaimed, trying to stop them from charging forwards. 'Where are we going?'

She managed to stop beside a narrow bridge and turned towards them, noticing their faces were flushed and excited. Olive spoke first.

'Well, I couldn't sleep in this morning, so I came down to breakfast early and sat alone. I ended up overhearing the table next to me, also from the UK, and they were talking about this event involving *Babbi Natale* that was happening today and that there would be thousands of them. Thousands of what, I wondered to myself, so I leant over a bit more to listen in and—'

'Get to the point, Olive,' someone shouted from the back of the group.

Olive glared over her shoulder and continued, 'It turns out there is this event that happens once a year, on the Sunday before Christmas Day, where up to a thousand Father Christmases' run and travel through Venice! For fun! Just imagine!' she chuckled.

Norman continued, 'It turns out it's a huge event, with people of all ages joining in—'

'So, we collectively decided to try to find them and see what all the fuss is about,' someone else chimed in.

'Just imagine, all those men . . .' Enid said.

'And women, and children,' Olive chimed in. 'It's open to anyone.'

'So, when you didn't turn up to breakfast, we decided to take matters into our own hands,' Norman said, nudging Olive, and she nodded, pulling from her large handbag a napkin concealing a bulky object and a takeaway coffee cup, its contents escaping as steam from the lid. 'Two chocolate pastries and one milky coffee.'

Rosie took them both from Olive, feeling a little overwhelmed by the influx of information, but her stomach growled in pleasure from the flakes of pastry that poked out of the napkin. She greedily took a large bite as everyone waited for her to respond.

She thought about the safety implications of people charging through the street and potentially knocking into one of her group, then thought of the medical list that now sat locked away in the safe, providing health details on each of them. Her practical mind told her that it probably wasn't a sensible idea and the race was fraught with obstacles, but then she looked at the ten enthusiastic faces that had circled her. Their eyes sparkled and their excitement was tangible.

Without pausing, she swallowed her delicious chunk of pastry and said loudly, 'Which way do we head to find these Santas, then?'

Chapter Twenty-six

The skies were a perfect azure blue as they made their way around St Mark's Square and towards the waterfront. The water was a clear blue-green and gondolas lined the dock, their patient gondoliers dressed in matching black-and-white outfits waiting beside them. Turning right at Olive's instructions, they ran parallel to the water, past a row of stalls selling Italian tourist items and wares that they had seen yesterday. Rosie thought of her mask tucked in her suitcase already.

They moved as a pack, albeit slowly, past the various water taxi ranks and piers, until they came to the edge of the land and had to take a sharp right. In doing so, they found themselves looking down the Grand Canal, with the Peggy Guggenheim Museum visible, along with a plethora of boats. Being slightly blinded by the sun, they slowed their pace, with Rosie stopping to pop on her sunglasses. Once on, out of the edge of her vision, she noticed she was standing beside a brick building with frosted windows and a sign stating Harry's Bar.

'Harry's Bar, well I never,' said Walter, chuckling to himself.

'Who's Harry?' Rosie asked.

Walter indicated for her to step forwards to take in the heavy wooden doors that appeared to work like revolving doors found in an old-fashioned department store.

'Harry Pickering, the man who provided the advance for the legendary chef Giuseppe Cipriani to create what is known as the legendary Bellini cocktail, my dear. Ever had a Bellini? Peaches and Prosecco – a total delight.'

Rosie was shocked. This little nondescript corner of a building housed the creation of a world-renowned drink. She loved a Bellini; it was her go-to choice of cocktail.

Walter continued, 'There is even a plaque inside with the words Harry's Table, situated beside the bar. Cipriani dedicated the bar to Harry.'

'Wow,' was all Rosie could manage, looking at the narrow dark doors and staring down the dark alleyway that led to its entrance. 'How do you know all this?' she asked as they continued past the bar and towards what appeared to be a dock.

'Harry Pickering was a great man. Very selfless and incredibly generous. He often talked of Guiseppe with a great fondness . . .'

He tailed off as he followed the others, leaving Rosie staring at him in disbelief. Had Walter met the man who invented the Bellini? Or was he winding her up? She took another look at the bar and decided there and then that she had to try at least one Bellini while in Venice, if just so she could tell Bee.

Thinking of Bee, she realised she hadn't checked her phone since the panicked reply to Benjamin, so she whipped out her phone. No surprises, there was an email from both him and Audrey, with another from Bee, but she ignored that. She read Benjamin's first:

From: BenjaminWStacey@wanderlustwishes.com
Sent: Sunday, 21 December 2024, 10:34:25 am
Subject: Complaint

Dear Ms Redbrush,

Based on our earlier communications that have taken place outside of office hours, I feel it only appropriate to inform you that I have put in a formal complaint to our HR department.

Regretfully, your inappropriate and sexually orientated photograph was sent to my work email address, addressed to myself. This email breaches our company's terms and conditions and can be considered both improper and concerning. Moreover,

I also consider it a form of sexual harassment towards myself, receiving photographs that are both unprovoked and distasteful.

I can confirm that this decision was not taken lightly. But in view of the distress this has caused me and in following my due diligence as an employee of Wanderlust Wishes Ltd, I feel this is the only option available at this time. Having spoken to a HR representative, they have informed me that a formal meeting date will be set once you return to the country. You are obliged to attend this meeting.

Please remember that while you are in Venice, you are still a representative of Wanderlust Wishes Ltd and therefore, I must request that you keep your demeanour and attitude professional, so as not to tarnish the reputation of the company further.

For your information, I have copied Human Resources into this email so that they can advise both parties going forwards.

Regards,
Benjamin Stacey
Branch Manager — Wanderlust Wishes Ltd

'What the actual fu—' Rosie began but was interrupted by the shrill shouting of Enid.

Rosie looked up to see Enid pointing behind her and the rest of the group were turning, too.

'There they are! The Santas! And they are coming our way!' Enid was so excited that she was almost hopping on the spot, pink spots on her cheeks.

Rosie turned and saw them, gasping. A regatta of gondolas was heading their way, along with a fleet of various small boats, and they all shared the same thing in common: they were all stacked with people dressed as Father Christmas, their red jackets, long white beards and red-and-white hats contrasting against the vivid blue sky. Rosie also took in the sheer numbers of people now gathered along every available walkway or pier, all there to catch the spectacle as it passed by.

She was jostled as the crowds tried to make their way forwards and she tried to find the group through the sea of heads, remembering her responsibility to them. She noticed Horace's towering stature and tried to meander her way in his direction, but the crowds were thickening as the regatta got closer and she was getting hemmed in. The email would have to wait until later – she had more pressing concerns.

She could hear festive music playing from somewhere – a Michael Bublé track, which she was sure was not particularly Venetian, but it sure did the trick. People were clapping and cheering, their faces beaming at the sight of hundreds of Santas floating down the Grand Canal. The crowds surged, their excitement evident.

Rosie glimpsed a flash of pillar-box red as she stood on tiptoe to locate the group of white-haired OAPs. Instead, she saw the first gondola pass, its passengers rowing with precision and ease despite their costumes. There were both male and female Santas, and the gondola had been festooned with tinsel, lights and what appeared to be cardboard reindeer cut-outs tied to the front. The motion of the gondola on the water gave the impression that the reindeer were prancing up and down as they moved forwards.

Another gondola passed by, then another, then another, all with various festive music playing or the Santas singing, and each seemed to be better than the last. Even the small boats were decorated, their bows holding snowmen, tinsel, even a dragon's head. There were boats filled with elves, their bright green-and-red outfits contrasting against the pastel-coloured buildings behind them. Rosie could even see Elvin the Elf ears poking out under their Elvin hats. They were all smiling, waving and rowing their way along the Grand Canal and every boat looked to be having fun.

Rosie pushed her way forwards a little more, her anxiety causing a pulsing in her temples, when she finally spotted a group of white-haired adults near the water's edge. Sighing with relief, she began pressing forwards, making her way towards them.

'Rosie! You're here! We can get on now,' Winnie called out, gesturing at her.

They were standing in a queue at a ferry dock and there was a small wooden boat with cushioned wooden seats that could seat about a dozen. They started climbing aboard with relative ease and excitement before Rosie even had a chance to ask why. She wanted to pause a second, wanted to collect her thoughts, but she was bustled onto the boat, the last to board.

As soon as she was in the final unoccupied seat, the boatman pushed off from the dock and started the small motor, its little engine chugging into life. They began their crossing of the Grand Canal, travelling horizontally towards a large domed building.

'The Basilica di Santa Maria della Salute,' the boatman said, gesturing towards the approaching church. 'The Basilica of St Mary of Health.'

Rosie took in the sight of the huge domed ceiling and impressive grey stonework that seemed to stretch towards the sky.

There were large archways, colossal pillars and grand doors that seemed large enough to welcome the whole city. But the Grand Canal was busy and it took all of Rosie's grip strength not to lose her balance. There was no way she could respond to Benjamin's email just yet. Her phone would end up at the bottom of the canal at the rate the gondola was swaying this way and that. It also meant, though, that she could take a moment to appreciate the beauty of the city around her.

'It's stunning,' Rosie said aloud, earning a smile from the boatman.

'Si. Bellissima,' he said, doffing his cap to both her and the church.

It only took them a few minutes to cross the Grand Canal from one side to another and before she knew it, the vessel had slowed and was pulling into a wooden dock similar to the other side. She pulled out her bag and paid for the group in cash while the others waited on the dock for her, doing a double-take as a flash of red and white appeared to her left. There was a wide walkway between the church and the dock, and it appeared that the race wasn't only taking place on the water.

There were runners of every age and sex along a route that headed in the direction of the Rialto Bridge, even children dressed as elves and little babies being pushed along in prams and pushchairs. Everyone was smiling and cheering as the throng of runners edged forwards. Some were walking and there was definitely an air of non-competitiveness to the race. It was just as busy as the other side of the canal, with the runners at least three-people deep.

The group stood there cheering them on and Rosie decided to use this moment to reread the message from Benjamin and try to respond. She scrolled back through her phone, trying to locate the lewd messages he had sent her the day after the party, thinking she could fight fire with fire. With a gasp, she scanned the message thread back to that day only to see the words, *Benjamin deleted this message.* He was manipulating the whole situation to suit him. Without realising, she allowed the crowds to edge her forwards until she was at the front, directly adjacent to the runners as they passed by.

Looking up quickly to get her bearings, she noticed that her group had somehow crossed over to the other side of the walkway and were now facing her, with a steady flow of runners passing between them. She couldn't lose her job. She loved her job. She had to make sure that she was the optimal employee. Which meant not losing her entire group in the middle of a Venetian version of a Santa Grand Prix. She looked to see if there was a clear gap for her to cross over to join them, but there didn't seem to be a break in the Santa dash. Standing on tiptoe to try to look over the sea of red hats, she thought she saw a small gap, so calculating her moment, she went to dash across.

Just as she took a step out, her phone rang in her hand and she panicked, thinking it might be Benjamin, and looked down at the screen. A moment later, the crowd gasped and she looked up just in time to see a bulky form appear from nowhere and plough straight into her. Time slowed as the pavement rose to meet her.

'Shit! Ow, shit. What are you doing?' an angry voice yelled as a heavy body toppled on her, forcing her to the ground.

Her shoulder met the stone walkway and she lifted her free arm over her head in an effort not to get trampled.

'Arghhh!' she screamed, a shooting pain stretching across her hip and shoulder.

She could feel the thunderous vibrations of hundreds of runners' feet as they stamped to their own beat and for a horrid moment, she visualised getting trampled. Fear crept across her chest as if her lungs had inhaled ice. Before she had time to collect her thoughts, the body rose off her and she curled up into a ball, her arms tucked up and over her hair to protect her head. She couldn't move. She felt frozen, terrified. She knew she was going to be trampled to death. A thought of Benjamin holding a newspaper cutting of her flattened, dead body while laughing maniacally flashed through her mind. As she exhaled a sob, she felt her body being lifted and carried roughly through the crowd by strong, warm arms, until she was lowered onto what felt like a cool, hard surface. As the arms pulled away from her, she instinctively felt a desire to grab them to hold on for a little longer.

'Seriously, what do you think you were doing?' The voice was male and annoyed.

Opening her eyes, she looked up at outline of a man, his features hidden by the shade. He was dressed neither as Father Christmas, nor an elf, but was in normal running gear, with a black hoodie pulled up over his head.

'You need to get up. Now. You're going to get trampled on.'

'OK, OK,' Rosie said, rolling over onto her knees in an effort to stand.

A crowd had gathered to help her and the steady flow of runners had slowed as they tried to gauge what was going on. She felt an arm close around her elbow from behind and help to pull her up. Once on her feet, she turned to thank the stranger assisting her but found herself staring into the brightest green eyes she had ever seen. Right at this moment, they were narrowed in annoyance and pain, with large flame-red bushy eyebrows that were almost joined in anger.

'Are you hurt?'

The voice and the startling eyes belonged to the runner who had bulldozed into her only moments earlier and she flushed with shame.

'Do you speak English? Are you hurt? *Sei ferito*? *Hai sbattuto la testa*?'

Rosie noted the Italian – it seemed fluent and spoken with ease. She shook her head, finding that when she rotated her shoulder, despite it feeling sore, the pain wasn't too bad. But her hip was aching. Looking down, she noticed her warm coat had torn slightly and white padding was trying to escape.

'Aw, man! My coat! I love this coat!'

She touched the vertical tear and tried to push the wadding back in. She put her hands in her pocket to see if the rips passed all the way through, but instead of a rip, her left hand curled around a cold, hard, thin rectangle.

Her phone.

She still had her phone.

Pulling it from her pocket and checking it still worked, despite her body weight crushing it, she looked at it as if it were a precious diamond. She couldn't believe it. She clutched it to her chest, cradling it as you would a newborn.

'So, you are English,' he said, rolling his eyes. 'At least it protected you when you fell. But is there a reason why you thought crossing the path of a competitive running event would be a good idea?'

His voice was sarcastic and Rosie looked over at him, her brow creased. He was looking down at his knees, which were both bleeding, the skin scraped away and the knees scuffed. There was also a large rip in his running shorts, which she assumed occurred when he fell. At this point, she did feel guilty.

'Yikes, sorry. I didn't realise you were hurt.'

'Yes, well, that happens when you get tripped up by a tourist,' he said, checking his watch, his brow still furrowed.

Another expletive was muttered and he whipped back his hood, revealing thick flame-red wavy hair that made him look like some sort of Viking warrior.

'I said sorry,' Rosie answered, aware of the crowds around them and noticing that her group was nowhere to be found.

'Just steer clear of the runners, yeah?'

She went to reply, but a bright flash momentarily blinded her and she turned to find the source of the flash. She found herself staring at an enamoured Chinese couple taking photographs of her, clearly thinking she was part of the race. She held a hand over her face, shaking her head to indicate no more photographs, and turned back to the runner. But he had disappeared back into the throng of runners, his flame-red hair and grumpy temperament gone with him. Rosie sighed and moved away from the crowd and towards the dock, her arm holding her ripped coat and her mind holding her largely bruised ego.

Chapter Twenty-seven

'Rosie! There you are, dear! We couldn't fathom where you had got to!'

Rosie spun around from her position on the dock to find the whole gang looking down at her. She had decided it was safer to sit on the ground and hang her legs over the side to watch the various gondolas and boats stream pass. No one could bump into her if she stayed out of the way. The passengers aboard the boats were all united in festive cheer, their outfits and singing both loud and bright.

'Oh, my dear, are you hurt?'

It was Winnie who noticed Rosie's torn coat and, like a tidal wave, they collectively rushed forwards in concern, hands reaching out and soft words being spoken. Rosie went to tell them she was OK but felt a sudden rise of emotion and her eyes filled with tears, causing even more questions and concern.

'What's wrong?'

'Have you been mugged?'

'What did they take?'

'Someone, go get help . . .'

Rosie managed to find her voice in time before Walter charged off in the search for help.

'It's OK, I'm OK. I just tripped. No harm done other than feeling foolish.'

She smiled a watery smile, wishing she was anywhere else at this point and desperately wanting to call Bee. But the pensioners were not fools.

'You tripped? How? And why is your coat torn?' asked Horace.

They were now talking among themselves, their worried voices rising, and Rosie realised she needed to stop an all-out panic.

'Listen!' Her voice rose.

Surprisingly, they fell silent and Rosie told them her sorry tale, omitting the rudeness of her red-haired runner.

'So, it was my fault, OK? I'm fine – no bruises, no cuts. Just a damaged coat that needs to visit a seamstress.' She shrugged, standing up to prove her point.

Her hip argued otherwise as a shooting pain travelled down her left leg, but she didn't let her smile falter.

Mildred stepped forwards, saluting her.

'A seamstress at your service.'

'One of the best, too,' Enid said while the others nodded in agreement.

'From the age of fifteen,' Mildred said, 'I worked as a seamstress making outfits of a quality you just don't see today. Our clothes were fit for royalty, even worn by royalty! Did you know they had weights sewn into the bottom to ensure they wouldn't shift in a gust of wind?'

Rosie shook her head. 'I did not know that.' She was amazed. This old woman with the wrist strap, thinning hair and orthopaedic shoes was once a young, brave woman with a talent worthy of royal approval. 'I'd be very grateful, thank you,' she said, smiling at her.

At that moment, with the sunshine beaming down on them, the relationship shifted in the group. Rosie felt accepted, one of them.

Staring down at the ring on her finger – the globe ring that reminded her there was a big old world out there waiting to be explored – she smiled and said, 'Right, now who's up for a bit of art at the Guggenheim, then?'

Four lost pensioners, three warnings for touching statues, two hours and one very long visit to the gift shop later, Rosie stepped back out into the afternoon sunshine, revelling in the fresh air that came from a city with no vehicles or roads. The freshness filled Rosie's lungs and revitalised her.

She had originally intended on staying as a group as they walked around, but after half an hour of trying to herd them like sheep, and with Enid repeatedly trying to get a close-up of the male statues, she decided to let everyone split up, with an agreement to meet in the gift shop at an allotted time. Remarkably, they all turned up, but it was another half an hour before she managed to encourage them towards the exit. Which was then scuppered by Walter spotting the sign for the toilets – and then she lost them all again to the joys of weakening bladders, dodgy bowels and haemorrhoids.

Which is why she found herself outside, alone, staring at the Italian buildings opposite, their crumbling façades and terracotta roof tiles almost familiar to Rosie now. The water sparkled in the Grand Canal and she knew the Rialto Bridge was only a touch further on. She knew she should deal with the email from Benjamin, but she couldn't bring herself to pull out her phone and read the message again. It felt too big a problem, yet it also felt too distant, as if that whole part of her existence was a previous life that she didn't need to worry about when she was staring at such beauty.

'Rosie?'

She turned at her name and found Horace walking towards her.

'Would you like to accompany me on a little walk? I've told the others to wait at the dock for the next boat and we will join them imminently. There's something I would like to do.'

He was smiling, but he seemed melancholy. It was clear she wasn't the only one struggling with today.

'Sure,' Rosie said, remembering with guilt that Horace had told her that Sunday was the anniversary of his wife's passing and she had forgotten. It put her issues into perspective. 'Where would you like to go?'

'It's not far,' he said, turning to walk left, parallel to the canal.

They walked in companiable silence for a minute or two until he turned left again, heading down a narrow alley, the brick buildings blocking out the daylight. It smelt musky and damp, with a faint hint of sewage emanating from what she assumed was stagnant canal water. Horace turned right, down another narrow alley, and suddenly a large square appeared, the daylight sharp and bright as their eyes adjusted.

Rosie took in the pretty open space, with a scattering of restaurants around its edge, brimming with customers, a beautiful stone fountain in the centre, its centrepiece a Romanesque woman dressed in a tunic and holding a large ceramic jug on her shoulder. Water was pouring from the lip of the jug into the shallow pool below. There were people milling around and a strong smell of garlic and wine in the air.

Horace continued forwards, heading towards the fountain. Rosie followed behind, enjoying the relaxed atmosphere of the small square and its occupants. Horace stopped at the fountain and reached out a hand onto the stone seat that ran around its entirety at its base. He turned to smile at Rosie, who stepped forwards and lifted onto tiptoes to climb onto the seat.

The stone was cold but smooth from years of human touch. She ran her hand over it and noticed the scratches and indentations from a hundred lifetimes of weather damage and use. Looking in at the water, she noticed the base covered with a layer of shiny brass and silver coins, each one no doubt a wish or hope of good things to come. She touched the water with her fingertips and noticed it was as cold as ice.

Horace slowly walked around the fountain, his head down as he ran his own hand across the stone. He stopped, moved his face closer to the water feature, and smiled.

'It's still here.'

Her interest piqued, Rosie asked, 'What is?'

'Come. Look,' he said, watching her, his fragile face animated. 'After all these years, it's still here.'

Rosie jumped down from the seat and walked around to where he was standing. There was nobody else nearby, so she didn't feel subconscious bending over to look closely where his hand was pointing.

It had faded over time, that much was clear, but it was still obvious. It was a small carving in the stone, just as the stone seat met the wall, of what looked like a simple flower head, its singular stem and multiple petals around a small circular centre.

'My blue-eyed, beautiful daisy queen,' Horace said, rubbing a fingertip over the carving.

'Did you do that?' Rosie asked, looking down at the intricate petals, their lines thin and strong.

It did not look like the work of a man with a sharp compass point or as if it had been scraped on with a key.

Horace nodded. 'Many, many years ago, I was training to be a stonemason and was lucky enough to travel as an apprentice with a large stonemasonry company that had a base out here in Italy. I spent one fantastic summer out here, in Venice, and it was while I was here that I met and fell in love with Evie.' He chuckled at some silent memory. 'She was travelling with her parents on a family holiday, having just finished college, and they had decided to stop in Venice for a few weeks while her father recuperated from a chest infection.

'They rented an apartment and ended up staying for almost a month.' He turned and pointed to a four-storey stone building above one of the restaurants to their left, gesturing to the top floor. 'And while her father remained in bed, nursed by her mother, Evie used to sit at that restaurant' – he gestured now to a restaurant adjacent to the building – 'which was but a simple café back in the day. It was there she used to write her journal. All the while, I was installing a large fountain in the centre of this very same square, so I spent a good few weeks creating what you now see before you.' He patted the stone fountain affectionately.

'I noticed her way before she ever took notice of me,' he continued. 'How could I not?! The beautiful young woman in the pale blue dress and hair the colour of marigolds. I couldn't take my eyes off her.

'Needless to say, I was particularly slow working on this project, with my mind elsewhere!' He looked across at the restaurant that had replaced the café, his eyes caught in images from decades before. 'I couldn't believe that any woman as beautiful as her would ever set eyes on someone as lowly as me. But she did. And those eyes mesmerised me every day for forty years. I was one lucky man.' He stroked the flower outline again, tracing the lines.

'It's crass, I know, but I wanted to show her that what we had was not fleeting, it wasn't a summer fling. I loved her with all of my soul and this scratching was a sign of my dedication.

'I remember how cross my stonemason senior was when he noticed the carving. He docked a week's wages from my pay for my vandalism, but it was worth it. We were married just two months later once we'd both returned to England. I always wondered if it was still here.'

He pulled out a brown velvet pouch from his inside jacket pocket and placed it on the stone seat. Sitting down beside it, he pulled the thin rope on either side of the pouch and pulled out a smooth stone, no bigger than a simple pebble one might find on a beach. It had been varnished, though, and its whitish-amber surface almost shone in the afternoon light.

Rosie sat down on the other side of the pouch and touched the stone with the tip of her finger, feeling the cool smoothness that felt almost like glass.

'I made this just in case I returned and found that the fountain was no more. Turn it over,' Horace said quietly, and she did so, picking it up and flipping it over in the palm of her hand.

She gasped as she took in the delicate engraving on the stone, underneath the varnish. It was an intricate carving of a daisy flower, with details drawn onto each petal that would have been hard to replicate, even on paper. Underneath the flower was a date.

'The date of our wedding,' he answered for her, smiling. 'The greatest day.' He looked off into the direction of the café-cum-restaurant. 'I haven't been back here since she died.' He paused, his face turned away from Rosie, but she could hear the emotion in his voice. 'And I never thought I would get the opportunity to visit here again. I'm so glad I got to come back.' His last words were almost a whisper and when he did turn back to her, there were clear tears on his cheeks, his eyes glistening. 'Thank you, my dear. For accompanying an old man back to fulfil a dream of his. You've given me peace.'

She went to argue but found her throat tight and her own eyes threatening tears. Instead, she stretched out her arm to him, opening her palm to reveal the stone. He hesitated and then took it from her, his own fingers cold and aged. He closed his fingers around the stone and shut his eyes.

Rosie felt it only fair to give him a moment to himself, so she quietly stood up and walked slowly away, back in the direction they had come. After about twenty paces, she turned to find him still in that same position, so she said nothing and waited.

A minute later, his eyes opened again and he searched for Rosie. She raised her hand and waved, catching his eye. He stood up with a little difficulty but steadied himself with a hand on the seat before turning to walk towards her. Just as he passed the fountain, he turned and with a gentle movement, threw the stone into the fountain, the splash of water evident from where Rosie stood. Turning back towards her, he joined her without a sound.

Side by side, they began the walk back to the pier – a young woman fighting back tears and wishing that she might experience that strength of love one day, and an old man walking beside her, his back straight, his white hair combed over and with a peaceful, restful smile across his lined face.

Chapter Twenty-eight

Rosie and Horace arrived back at the pier to find everyone waiting for them, their eyes matching in concern.

'So, did you find it?' Norman asked, his forehead crinkled so fiercely that he reminded Rosie of a cuddly basset hound puppy.

'Was it still there?' Albert asked, his pale face searching Horace's for clues.

'Are you OK?' Shirley said, her normally serious face softened by concern.

Horace held out both arms in front of him to reassure them. 'I'm fine, I'm fine. Rosie was with me the whole time and yes, it was there. And yes, I did get to do it.'

It was clear that they all knew what 'it' was and they all walked united towards him and embraced in a group hug, creaking joints and all. Rosie felt the tears threaten again until an arm tugged at hers and she was pulled into the hug. It was awkward, uncomfortable, yet uniquely reassuring. She could feel the emotion and support, and it reminded her of her parents' hugs, with her enveloped in their joint love.

Seconds later, a yell broke their moment and Rosie looked over her shoulder to find a boatman calling at them from the dock, indicating by tapping his watch that he was on a schedule.

'Oh, the return boat is here!' Rosie exclaimed, ushering them with difficulty out of their hug and towards the black boat that was swaying up and down in the busy waters. 'C'mon, we need to get on.'

The sun was setting and she didn't fancy waiting for the next boat or walking them back in the dark to their hotel. She could see that they were all tired from their excursion.

She gently guided them towards the end of the dock, where the boatman had tied a thick rope around the large wooden bollard that protruded out of the water and into the sky. Rosie looked down into the water and was surprised to see that she couldn't see the bottom. The water was clear yet very deep and, without the sunlight, it was darkening by the minute.

'On you get, everyone,' said Rosie.

Shirley was first on, stepping with confidence onto the large gondola and taking a seat as directed by the boat driver. Next was Olive, Albert and Walter, their hands and arms being held as they took the step from dock to boat. Then Winnie and Mildred, followed by Norman, Horace and Enid, leaving Rosie and Dottie still on the dock. The water traffic had increased on the Grand Canal, Rosie likening it to a watery rush hour.

'On you go, Dottie. I'm right behind you.'

But Dottie didn't look convinced.

'I don't think I can. Look how choppy the canal is right now. Maybe it would be best to wait a little until it calms down . . .' She tailed off, looking at the water as it clipped the boat, causing small crests of white froth to gather beneath the dock.

'There's no need to wait, Dottie. It's perfectly safe.'

'But what about weight distribution? And tide levels? Perhaps the gondolier hasn't considered wind speed today or checked for leaks.'

Rosie could see she was beginning to spiral, so she gently nudged Dottie forwards as inconspicuously as she could, mindful that the gondolier was looking more agitated as the seconds ticked past.

'I'm sure there are strict protocols he has to follow. It's perfectly safe.'

Rosie was acutely aware of how desperately tired she was now feeling also. From the rollercoaster of emotions of hearing she was suspended, getting mowed down by a runner and chasing OAPs around a museum to feeling her heart ache for an old widower who'd lost his true love, she was shattered.

'Please, Dottie. Let's not think about it and just climb in. It's only a short journey across the canal. You can see the other side!'

She watched as Dottie looked over to the opposite dock, clearly conflicted.

'This feels different. Something isn't right.'

Dottie's feet began to shuffle backwards, away from the gondola, and Rosie positioned herself behind her so that she couldn't move any further. A couple of tourists, their cameras hanging from thick straps around their necks like medals and their hands full of shopping bags, walked onto the same wooden dock, their eyes darting towards the last few empty seats on the boat. Rosie knew it was now or never.

'Dottie, I'm getting on. You can stay here if you like, but it'll mean travelling back in the dark. And alone. It's your choice.'

Letting go of her, she swerved in front of her on the dock and took the hand of the irritable gondolier, allowing him to lead her onto the vessel and into a seat. She felt slightly guilty, but she remembered the tough-love technique. Sometimes, leaving a worse option on the table means they'll re-evaluate their original thought. She looked back at Dottie, indicating to the empty seat opposite.

'Coming?'

Dottie looked pained, like she had bad acid reflux. She had also spotted the two tourists stomping down the dock, their bags weighing them down, and her eyes kept darting from them to the boat. The others began calling her.

'C'mon, Dot. Just get your arse on board.'

'You've been so brave over the last few days! You can do this.'

'Stop being such a wimp, honestly . . .'

Rosie looked over to see Shirley tutting in annoyance, clearly not empathetic to Dottie's predicament.

The couple had now reached the boat and were attempting to bypass Dottie, their efforts in broken Italian to sweet talk the gondolier having no effect. But as the male tourist tried to access his backpack, he whipped it around to his friend, unwittingly walloping into Dottie's side, causing her to become unsteady. She let out a yelp and the tourist turned with a look of pure apology.

But it had caused Dottie to panic and, in doing so, she lunged forwards into the arms of the unsuspecting gondolier, who was not anticipating an eight-stone septuagenarian to launch herself at him. Ever the professional, he caught her with barely a wobble of the boat and in a single movement, he had her seated in the last occupied seat and had untied the rope.

Pushing away from the dock, Rosie leant forwards and touched Dottie's knee.

'Well done! That was very brave.'

But Dottie was barely listening. The sky had turned from a pinky-orange to a dark blue, which meant that the canal water was no longer the inviting bluey-green of earlier but now more of a huge, dark, moving mass, which was slightly sinister. Dottie's eyes were darting both ways at the traffic passing them from both ways.

Lights had been switched on as a safety measure, but the gondola was low in the water and the lights only blinded them. The gondolier was a professional, but even he couldn't control the science of waves and their motions. The boat was swaying from side to side, its occupants moving with it. Most of the water traffic was moving up and down the canal, rather than across it, so they were cutting into the wake of large boats and vessels.

'Dottie? Look at me, you're fine. We're fine,' Rosie said, trying again, leaning over and grabbing one of Dottie's shaking hands.

As she did so, her backpack swung around to her front and she found herself removing it from both shoulders and placing it on her lap, which made it even more awkward to hold Dottie's hand. But Dottie now had an iron grip on Rosie and there was no way she was letting go.

As the gondola reached almost halfway, they found themselves in the path of two large water buses, coming from both ways, and aimed straight for one another. The lights were blinding. Dottie started squirming in her seat, looking over Rosie's head at the approaching water bus.

'It's heading straight for us!' she yelled, looking up at the gondolier for reassurance.

But he was focused on the water bus behind him and was trying to steer out of a particularly strong current.

'Rosie, it's heading straight for us!'

'Shush,' Rosie said, trying to calm her.

The others began grumbling and shifting in their seats, the tiny movements causing more disruption to the gondola's balance.

'We're going to tip over! We're going to drown!' Dottie shouted, clearly having passed into the stage of complete panic.

'Dottie, stop! We're fine,' Rosie said, shifting further forwards to grab both of her hands but realising she couldn't reach with her backpack in the way.

She decided to put the backpack behind her so that she could shuffle forwards without upsetting the momentum of the vessel.

'Dottie, look at me. We're OK.'

The gondola was swaying quite a bit at this point and all of a sudden, one of the water buses pressed their horn, causing a large blare to emit from its speakers. This had a multitude of effects and, to Rosie, they all seemed to happen in slow motion.

First, the gondolier shouted out to the water bus, clearly some obscenity in Italian, to warn them of their presence.

Secondly, Dottie, mistaking the gondolier's shouts of protest as a panicked cry for help, tried to stand up, making the boat rock furiously. In response, Rosie jumped to her feet in an attempt to steady Dottie, but in doing so, Dottie tumbled forwards into Rosie, causing them both to fall back with a loud thump onto the seat behind Rosie.

Chaos broke out on the gondola. The gondolier screamed at them both to stay still while he steadied his vessel with his oars. Out of the corner of her eye, Rosie could see a vein in his forehead flex with the strength it took for him not to let them tip over. His arms bulged and she could hear voices calling over to them from what she assumed was the approaching dock, panicked and shrill.

Rosie's back screamed in pain with the weight of Dottie on top of her, the hard wood of the side of the boat cutting into her back. She tried to move slightly, to relieve the pain, but this only resulted in a loud rip from her coat.

'Shit,' she groaned, closing her eyes and putting all of her energy into holding Dottie tight.

There were other arms holding Dottie down, too, and as the water buses manoeuvred around them, the gondola finally found its balance and began moving towards the dock again.

Rosie tried to shift but found she couldn't. The weight of Dottie's body tentatively relaxed into her as the gondola steadied, so she simply held her position, her eyes closed, until the Italian voices came closer. With a gentle bump, she knew they were at the dock. The gondolier was furious, yelling in Italian with the other gondoliers on the dock. With a multitude of strong arms and leaning bodies, each of the passengers were shifted up and out of the vessel.

Finally, Rosie opened her eyes again and found it was just her and Dottie left. Her back was in agony now, as if a knife were stabbing into her ribs from behind, and so gently, she tried to get Dottie to sit up.

'Dottie, we're here. It's OK, we're here.' She spoke quietly into Dottie's ear, her grey hair smelling of hairspray and Parma violets. 'You're safe.'

She could hear sniffles coming from Dottie, but her body shifted its weight ever so slightly away from her and the relief was immense. The gondolier climbed onboard to assist, lifting a now frail Dottie onto her feet by placing both arms under her armpits and lifting her into an upright position. It was clear that Dottie was shaken, her legs wobbly and her face ashen.

Another gondolier climbed gently into the boat and collectively they navigated her to the side of the boat where the steps were. Other gondoliers helped to lift her out and onto a nearby bench.

Rosie leant forwards to stretch out her back, hearing yet another ripping sound as she did so. She groaned and reached around with an arm to feel the damage. Under both armpits, she could now feel that the fabric of her coat had torn and yet more padding was trying to escape.

'*Signora*, are you OK? *Sei ferito*? Are you hurt?'

That was the second time today that someone had asked if she was hurt and if it wasn't for the screaming ache across her shoulder blades, she might have laughed. Instead, she shook her head. Looking up into the gondolier's face, she saw that his eyes were full of concern and any anger from before had disappeared.

'They have called for *medico assistenza*, er, medical help,' he said, pointing towards the dock, where a large crowd had now gathered. 'Here, let me help you off the gondola and onto dry land.'

His large, calloused hands were incredibly gentle as he gripped her hand and elbow and helped her onto her feet. Pain spread from her shoulder blades through to her chest and she couldn't help but wince as she took a few steps forwards. The boat was being held steady by a group of gondoliers now, so she could walk without any tilting. As she took her first step to leave the boat, she suddenly remembered her backpack and turned to ask the gondolier to grab it for her, but her seat was empty. As was the gondola floor and the seats next to hers. She only saw dark, stained wood.

'My backpack!' she exclaimed. 'My bag! Where is it?'

A flash of terror ripped through her chest, adding more pain to her already aching body. She tried to go back, but the gondolier was behind her, helping her out of the boat.

'I need my bag. Where is it?'

He turned back to look but shook his head. 'Perhaps one of your group took it. Exit the gondola and I will search,' he said, gesturing for her to step up onto the dock and into the waiting arms of two gondoliers wearing matching black-and-white T-shirts.

She did so but immediately turned around to look at the boat again. True to his word, the driver stepped back into the base of the boat and dropped to his knees, checking under the seats to see if her bag had rolled under them and somehow been hidden.

It was clear each seat was empty, apart from a few splashes of canal water from their choppy journey over. He stood back up and shrugged his shoulders, indicating there was nothing.

'It must be there, I had it behind me. On the seat behind me . . .'

Her voice faded away when she remembered shoving it behind her to assist Dottie. Then how when Dottie fell onto her, she jolted back, feeling a shift of something moving behind her and then hard wood.

'Oh, no, no, no,' she said, her hand rising to her mouth. 'This can't be happening. Please don't let me have lost my bag.'

Her voice had risen into almost a wail, causing a few of her group to step forwards.

'What's the matter?' Shirley said, flagged by Olive and Walter.

'My bag, my bag is gone. It was on the seat behind me, but it must have slipped off the seat over the side . . .' She couldn't finish her sentence. Her heart was racing and she could feel bile rise in her throat. 'My bag, I need my bag.'

'Shh,' Shirley said, trying to calm her. 'It's OK, it's OK.'

She took Rosie into a hug while Walter stepped forwards to talk to the driver. Their voices were muted, but it was clear by their lowered tone that the outlook wasn't positive.

'We have to find it,' Rosie cried. 'My passport, my things, all the money, it was all in there . . .'

The realisation of having lost everything hit her and she could feel the frustrations of the day overwhelm her like a wave. Tears threatened, but this time she didn't try to stop them, instead releasing them onto Shirley's shoulder. Tears for her suspension, her embarrassment and now her failure even to look after a group of old-age pensioners on a short holiday.

All the while, the world continued around her – questions asked, gondoliers assessing the waters, medics arriving and caring for Dottie, concerned hands placed on Rosie's shoulder.

Things that all took place in a haze while Rosie cried. A policeman arrived to see what all the kerfuffle was about, but upon hearing about the lost bag, he simply shook his head in sympathy and walked on.

After finding the tears were all but spent, Rosie stepped back from Shirley and wiped her runny nose on the sleeve of her coat. It was torn and ruined anyway. She was aware that she probably had mascara running down her cheeks and eyeliner smudged everywhere, but she didn't care. She just wanted to have her bag back.

She reached into her pocket for her phone and found an empty space. Her phone was missing, too. In a flash, she remembered shoving it into her backpack before boarding the boat.

All was lost. Without a phone, she was stranded. Without a phone, she couldn't reach out to Bee, to Audrey, check her emails, ask for help, anything. And without a purse, she couldn't buy a replacement. Panic crashed over her like a wave.

An Italian medic walked over to her, asking in good English if she needed any assistance, but she shook her head. The pain in her back was intense and her hip ached, but she couldn't trust herself to speak.

'Rosie?' a quiet voice asked.

She looked over to see Horace standing beside her, looking uncomfortable.

'Yes?' she croaked, noting the concern in his face.

'I am so glad you're OK and not too badly hurt.'

Rosie could sense he was stalling.

'Thank you,' she said, waiting for him to continue.

He shifted from one foot to another before speaking.

'Um, I don't suppose that all of our passports were in your backpack, were they?'

It was clear he was speaking for the whole group, as they all hushed to listen to her answer. An image of the tiny safe in her room crammed full of the pile of passports and a bit of the money flashed into her mind.

'No, they weren't. They're at the hotel,' she said, and the relief that swept around the group was palpable.

'Oh, thank goodness,' Horace said before realising his faux pas. 'I mean, I am so sorry for you and your no doubt precious belongings . . .'

Rosie nodded, feeling light relief that she'd at least had the foresight to protect their belongings. If only she'd ensured the same amount of protection for her own stuff. She smiled weakly and tried to regain some composure. She walked over to the gondolier, searching his face for clues.

'Is there any chance my bag might get washed up somewhere?' she asked, holding onto her last thread of hope.

But his face said it all – it was a no.

'The canal is very deep,' he replied, his accent strong. 'Something heavy like a bag would sink to the bottom. My friend, I think your bag is lost.' He placed a hand on her shoulder and gave it a little squeeze. '*Signora*, I am so sorry.'

And that was it. Rosie's last thread of hope sank to join her backpack. She was without her passport, without her purse and without her phone. Rosie Redbrush was now stranded, without any hope of getting home in time for Christmas. And she had no idea what to do next.

Chapter Twenty-nine

An hour later, Rosie was in the lobby of their hotel trying to cancel all of her cards and notify her bank of the situation. Sadly, she had completely forgotten to take out any holiday insurance due to the last-minute decision for her to go, which she knew, as a travel agent, was a massive oversight. By having no insurance, she was alone in trying to sort everything.

The others had each gone to their rooms for a rest. It had been a long day for everyone, and Rosie had insisted that she was fine to sort it alone and that she would meet everyone downstairs for dinner in a couple of hours. But sitting there with nothing but a badly ripped coat, she had never felt more alone.

'*Signora?*'

The female receptionist had been so helpful, but even she had her limits.

'Unfortunately, there is no British Embassy here in Venice. The nearest one to us would be in Milan.'

'Milan? How far is Milan from here?'

In her experience, having sent hundreds of people to Italy on holiday, she knew that there was a fair distance between the two locations, but in her hazy and fragile state, she couldn't think straight.

The receptionist looked pained before speaking.

'From here by car, approximately two hundred and seventy kilometres,' she said softly. 'But we have a good train service that goes directly to Milan, or you can hire a car and drive yourself—'

'My driving licence is currently at the bottom of the canal,' Rosie moaned, leaning forwards and burying her head in her hands.

'Um, no problem,' the receptionist said. 'We can sort travel arrangements via train for you.'

She remained positive, but Rosie felt nothing but negative.

'But how would I pay for train tickets? My purse and money were also in my backpack.'

'Can anyone in your group booking assist you?'

How could she ask a bunch of old-age pensioners to lend her any money? How embarrassing. She shrugged at the receptionist, returning her head to her hands. This was all such a nightmare. She needed Bee.

'Would I be able to make a call?'

The kind receptionist nodded, indicating for her to come around to her side of the desk, and handed her one of the reception phones. Summoning up all of her core memory strength, she rang Bee. She answered on the third ring.

'Hey! Hold on one minute . . .' The phone receiver was noisily placed on a surface and Rosie waited, assuming she was dealing with the children.

'Hey, babe! Sorry, one of the twins had done a huge poo and it had spread all over—'

'No time,' Rosie interjected. 'I need help.'

'Are you OK?' Bee said, sensing the mood. 'What's happened, are you hurt?'

'No, not hurt, but I'm stuck. My backpack is at the bottom of the canal and I have no passport to get home, no purse and therefore no identification. Oh, and no phone. I only have a bit of cash on me and no insurance. Help!'

She blurted it out so quickly that she wondered if Bee had heard it all. There was a brief silence, then a loud yell from Bee.

'Nav! Take over – *now*!'

There was a shuffle and a few muted questions as Bee clearly had a short, whispered conversation with her husband. Then she was back on the phone.

'Right, we can sort this,' she said, and Rosie swore that she heard Bee metaphorically roll up her sleeves. 'I can transfer some money over to you, no problem. How much do you need?'

'That won't help. I don't have my phone to pay contactless.'

'Shit.'

'But I need to get to Milan, apparently. That's where the British Embassy is.'

'What if I book the train tickets for you? I could send them to the hotel email address for them to print?'

Rosie paused, thinking. 'That might work actually—,' at which point she pulled the phone away from her ear as an ear-piercing scream hit her eardrum, followed by the panicked shout of Bee, 'what's happened, Nav? Who's hurt?' A pause as Bee waited and some muffled yells were just audible.

'Shit.' Bee said again, 'It's Aanya, Nav's mum. She's fallen over in the garden, apparently.' There was a rustle as Bee began moving but continued talking. 'But Rosie, even if I manage to book a ticket, how will I know how long you'll be there for? What ticket should I get?'

'I don't know,' Rosie wailed, trying not to cry.

'And what about your group?' Bee continued. 'Are they going to travel with you to Milan?'

Rosie paused for a second. Travelling hundreds of miles with ten elderly people, all with differing ailments? No chance.

'Definitely not. They can fly home the day after tomorrow, as agreed.'

'So, you're going to travel alone?' Bee said, her voice rising at the question.

For the first time, Rosie detected a little doubt in Bee's tone. 'Around Italy?'

'Yep. It'll be fine,' Rosie said, not allowing herself to worry. She had to do it, else she'd be stuck in Italy forever. 'Oh, and I ripped my coat, so I could do with replacing them. It's so cold here.'

'You've ripped your coat? Rosie! What is going on? Were you attacked? Are you hurt?'

'A separate incident. Don't worry, I'm fine. I just need a new coat. Oh, and Benjamin has made a complaint against me for sending him a sexy selfie...' A sob escaped her as her worries tumbled out, one after another.

'OK, now I'm officially worried. Rosie, do you want me to fly out? I can leave the kids with Nav for a few days. He doesn't need to go on that conference—oh shit, Aanya's ankle looks pretty busted.' It was clear by the voices and the sound of traffic that she was now outside. Rosie could hear a woman sobbing, children crying and Nav on the phone to what sounded like a paramedic.

'Bee! Aanya sounds bad, go deal with that. I'm fine. And I can sort this myself. You just stay put,' Rosie argued, her stomach sinking.

She was aware the receptionist was listening to her every word. She ended the call quickly, telling Bee to ring Audrey for all the gory details and promising to ring back again when she had a plan. Thanking the receptionist, she glanced at the large screen, which was open for bookings.

She turned to the receptionist again and asked, 'Would I just be able to send a couple of emails real quick? I promise I'll be a few minutes, max.'

The receptionist looked at her pityingly. Checking her own phone, she said, 'I'm due my break now, anyway. Go ahead. I'll be back in fifteen minutes. Rosita will help you if you need anything else.'

She spoke quickly in Italian to her colleague and disappeared, leaving Rosie to log into her emails. Typing quickly, she sent an email to Audrey:

Audrey, help! My backpack is at the bottom of the canal. No passport, no purse, no phone and no driving licence. All ten passports accounted for regarding the other ten members of the party. No insurance. Can you help? Ask Benjamin for assistance, please?!

She pressed Send and then spent the next few minutes biting her cuticles and hopping from one foot to another. Finally, after refreshing the screen for what felt like the millionth time, an email appeared from Audrey:

Oh, no! Oh, Rosie! I've just spoken to Benjamin and he's saying that he won't action anything as you're under investigation for sexual harrassment?! What is going on? What's happened? Are you safe?

If you are under investigation, then the company won't help, which means I can't organise emergency travel money for you, as they will have frozen your account. CALL ME!

But Rosie couldn't remember Audrey's mobile number. She barely remembered her own. She tried calling her work phone but no one answered, and she realised it was Sunday and no one would be in the office. The receptionist returned from her break, so Rosie admitted defeat. The hotel had been so helpful, but a coachload of new guests had just arrived and she realised she was in the way. Thanking the receptionist, she headed out of the lobby and towards the stairs to walk up to her room. The lifts were busy with arriving guests.

After puffing her way up copious steps, she eventually reached her room, unlocking the door with the new key card that she had been given downstairs. Approaching her bed, she noticed her charger was still plugged in on her bedside table. A fat lot of good that was going to do. She threw herself onto the bed.

If Audrey searched for the booking on their internal system, she'd find the original booking for Mrs Winthorpe-Smythe. That made her feel a smidgen better, but not much. Dragging herself up from her bed, her whole body now aching, she headed straight to the minibar. Downing one mini-bottle in seconds, she grabbed a second and third before heading straight for the queen-size bed. Climbing into bed in her clothes, her weary body ached to relax.

An hour later, she felt ever so drunk. She slid down further into the bed, pulling the covers right up to her chin, and felt her eyes grow heavy. She should get up and change. She'd agreed to meet the others for dinner in the hotel restaurant and she needed to send those emails, letting everyone know she was OK. And she was technically still on duty.

She should drink some water to rehydrate, she thought, her throat already parched. She should have taken painkillers for her aching hip. But she did none of these things. She simply let her eyelids close and fell into the deepest sleep, her body and mind exhausted.

Chapter Thirty

'Do you think she's dead?'

'No, I can see her breathing.'

'And dribbling, too.'

'Poke her gently – don't startle her.'

Voices floated into her mind, hazy and distant, but Rosie felt so relaxed that she ignored them, instead enjoying the dream she was having of locking Benjamin in a windowless room with only spiders for company.

'Rosie? Rosie, sweetheart, are you OK?'

Rosie moaned, her dream beginning to fade like fog in a tunnel. She didn't want to wake. But these voices were insistent, and now she could feel herself being poked.

'She spoke! She's alive!' a woman's voice proclaimed.

'Of course she's alive. She's clearly passed out from all the drink.'

Rosie heard a clink at the sound of what appeared to be multiple glass items. She attempted to roll over, but her head thumped hard, resisting the movement. She groaned again.

'Rosie, wake up, dear girl.'

This time the voice was different – female.

'Or else they are going to call for a doctor.'

A doctor? Rosie thought. *Who needs a doctor?*

Intrigue got the better of her and she opened her eyes, searching for a familiar sight. Instead, she found herself staring up at two pairs of concerned eyes and there was a strong smell of lavender. The eyes crinkled as the faces smiled and she took a moment to find her memory. A hotel room. Mildred and Shirley. Italy. Venice.

Lost backpack.

Rosie moaned again, this time from the realisation hitting.

'Get her some water. She's clearly not well,' said Winnie.

A kerfuffle broke out as they both tried to find the water and glasses. They exited the bedroom together, allowing Rosie a modicum of privacy to attempt to sit upright. She was now aware that she was still in her clothes from yesterday and that she was sprawled out like an overheated squirrel.

Moving slowly, her attention was drawn to the ache in her hip, knees and back, but she managed to scrape herself into a relatively upright position. Looking down, her vest had lowered massively in her sleep and she was displaying far more chest than she anticipated.

Mildred and Shirley reappeared just as she hoisted her vest back up over her bra, her face flushed red.

'Oh, don't hide them on our account,' Mildred said, waving away her concerns. 'We've seen it all in our time.'

But Rosie pulled up the covers anyway and accepted the large glass of water from Mildred's hand without a word. She gulped down the cold water, aware how parched her throat was. It was the loveliest water she had ever tasted. She finished the glass and Shirley took it from her and disappeared, no doubt heading for a refill.

'Right, young lady. Here is the plan. You are going to get up and get dressed. You have a train to catch.' She looked at her wristwatch. 'You have two hours to sober up, eat something and catch the 8.52am train to Milan.'

'What?' Rosie said, her brain simply unable to keep up with the speed of Mildred's dialogue.

'My dear girl, say pardon, not what.' Shirley had returned to the bedroom with a fresh glass of water.

Rosie mumbled her apology as she accepted the second glass.

Mildred continued, 'We have booked you a train ticket to Milan. For today. It arrives in Milan at just after half-past eleven. We have also managed to secure you a midday appointment at the British Consulate office in Milan to sort out your passport problem and we've given you money for a taxi straight there, you'll have enough time. There was a fee to pay to the Consulate so we asked the nice hotel manager Edwardo, to pay it for us online and to charge it to Mrs Winthorpe-Smythe. He has her credit card details on the system apparently. You might need a passport photo too, but we've been told by Edwardo that there is a photo booth at the train station. We'll give you the cash to cover those costs, too.' Mildred had pulled out a notepad and was checking her list, tapping the paper with her fingernail. 'It's only a return day-trip, mind – we need you back tonight to help us celebrate our last night together. We did want to come with you, but our insurance only covers us if we stay within a ten-mile radius of Venice. With all of our ailments, we are a right problematic bunch.

'So, come on – rise and shine!' She tapped the bedding as if it would activate Rosie into action.

'But who paid for the train? I don't have my purse,' Rosie asked, but they blew away her question with a waft of their hands.

'It's all settled. Don't worry. And some euros for your trip,' Mildred said, handing over an envelope to Rosie, which was bulky.

'But—'

'No buts, just get up,' said Mildred briskly. 'Dottie is feeling terrible enough about yesterday and if you don't appear downstairs for breakfast in the next thirty minutes, I honestly think that woman is going to grab a snorkel and deep-dive for that backpack herself.'

They all giggled at the image and Rosie felt herself glow at the kindness of these women.

'Thank you. I will repay you when I can—'

'Hush, now. We're friends, and friends help each other out,' said Shirley,

And with a short pat to Rosie's lower leg, both Mildred and Shirley rose to leave.

'We'll give you thirty minutes. If you're not down in the restaurant by then, I have permission to throw a champagne bucket of ice over you,' Mildred warned, giving her a cheeky wink.

Seconds later, they were gone, leaving Rosie clutching both a glass of water and her thumping forehead.

True to her word, Rosie managed to get down to the restaurant within thirty minutes and she took her seat next to Horace. Dottie was sitting opposite and looked terrible, her already sunken eyes purple around the edges and her bottom lip red from repeatedly biting it from anxiety.

Rosie accepted the large coffee that was poured for her and even her hangover couldn't stop her from reaching for one of the delicious croissants that she had grown accustomed to.

Dottie waited for her to take a few sips of her coffee before blurting out, 'Oh, I'm so sorry, Rosie. It's all my fault. I am such an idiot.'

But Rosie held up her hand to stop her. 'You are in no way an idiot. I put the backpack behind me on the low seat, you weren't to know that. And I was the one who didn't store her passport along with the others. I should have placed my bag on the floor between us and kept any valuables in the safe. I'm just glad I didn't lose all of our passports . . .'

But Dottie was still shaking her head and wringing her hands anxiously.

'Dottie, please. If you feel guilty, then I'll feel guilty, and where will that get us, hey?' She stretched her left arm out across the table and placed it over Dottie's, looking her in the eyes. 'Life is strange. It has thrown us together for reasons unknown, yet I believe that out of every bad situation comes a bit of good. So, let's see what good comes my way, yes?'

Dottie nodded, her shoulders dropping and a small smile forming. 'That's a nice thought.'

'It's what my mum always used to say when things didn't go to plan,' Rosie said, letting go of her hand and taking another sip of coffee.

'Then your mum is a wise woman indeed,' Dottie replied.

'Was a wise woman,' Rosie corrected, looking down at her plate.

'I'm so sorry, Rosie,' Dottie said. 'I didn't know.'

'It was a long time ago, don't worry,' Rosie said, used to answering these questions, used to reassuring the person asking that she was OK.

'No matter how long ago it happened, it is still a part of you that has gone, a part of you that will remain unanswered,' Dottie said, and Rosie looked up at her, her own eyes glazing over with tears.

She didn't answer, she couldn't. She just smiled and nodded.

This trip had been so much more than she ever anticipated. Yet despite the anguish, the bruises and the lost backpack, a part of Rosie felt grateful that she had come.

Chapter Thirty-one

Rosie hadn't had time to email anyone before she had been ushered out to a waiting water taxi. She had hoped to call the office to try to get hold of Audrey, but after two cups of coffee, the time for her departure was upon her.

Feeling naked without her backpack and with only a torn coat to her name, she boarded the already paid-for water taxi and waved to her new friends as the engine roared into life and headed down the narrow canal in the direction of the train station. It was only a twenty-minute taxi ride in total, but as Rosie took in the views, the city began to feel familiar to her. The way the water lapped almost to the doors of the buildings and how washing hung from windows offered a splash of colour in an otherwise brick-coloured world.

The way the buildings crumbled and appeared neglected only added charm to a city that had centuries of history behind it. Each broken windowpane, each crack in the walls hinted at a story untold. Rosie tried to take it all in. She wanted to live in the moment, not stress about what was coming next.

After what felt like only seconds, the water taxi approached the station's docking area. It was busy with water traffic, including ferries and other smaller boats. Rosie looked over at the shallow steps that led up to the train station, its single-storey building elongated lengthways instead of in height. It had a thick, flat roof that was mostly plain bar a concrete motif carved into the stonework. The modern style of the building contrasted against the typical Venetian style of those surrounding it, but, despite its size, it didn't appear imposing. But it was very busy, with crowds arriving and departing via the grey steps through the opening of the station, its darkness hiding what lay behind the numerous glass doors.

Thanking the taxi driver, she unconsciously looked for her backpack on the seat beside her as she got up to climb out of the boat, remembering with a jolt that she was travelling with nothing.

She made her way up the many steps towards the station, glancing across at the people around her coming and going, all with purpose. There was an air of sophistication emanating from the commuters, their smart suits and designer outfits screaming style and money. Rosie subconsciously wrapped her ripped coat around her core a little more tightly, wishing she'd had the foresight to spend more time on her make-up this morning. She felt slobby and unkempt.

As she pushed through the glass doors of the station, the hustle and bustle hit her like a rush of wind to her face. She looked down at her return ticket, feeling like a character out of the 1980s, with a paper version clasped in her hand. One of the group had purchased a small purse from one of the tourist stands in St Mark's Square and very kindly handed it to her, stuffed with euros from a quick collection around the breakfast table that morning, so she had real cash, an actual printed ticket and a folding paper tourist's guide for Milan in her pocket. Nothing else. She missed the ease of having a phone and having instant access to the world, simply at the press of a button.

She glanced up at the departure board that hovered above her, flickering and changing as it constantly updated. She noted both her allocated train, its designated platform, and a small photo booth beneath. Heading for the booth, she threw her shoulders back in an effort to look confident. She was a woman on a mission. She was eager to get to Milan and sort out the chaos that was her life.

After an uneventful and surprisingly comfy train ride to Milan, Rosie found herself suddenly stepping off the train onto another busy platform. The entire carriage had been absorbed in their devices, their heads down looking at phone screens, typing furiously on laptops or watching some inane YouTube video. No one stopped to stare at the landscape whizzing by or to take a moment to savour the quiet. Too lost in their own thoughts and addicted to their media.

Rosie would normally have been the same, but without a phone or a device, she had found herself enjoying the passing countryside and taking in a country so unfamiliar to her. People swarmed around her like insects and she decided to walk quickly and determinedly out of the station and into the open air.

She couldn't help but look up at the curved ceiling of wrought iron and steel, the greying sky threatening rain. It felt a lot cooler in Milan than it did in Venice and Rosie shoved her hands into her pockets. Riding up the escalator, she gasped at the impressiveness of the station. It was a huge stone building, with a height that was reminiscent of a cathedral, with an arching roof and commemorative motifs and murals tiled into the walls. The juxtaposition between old and new was obvious, with huge, opulent chandeliers lighting up the Five Guys, Starbucks and a Sephora, among other shops and services. She felt tiny amid such grandeur.

Searching for the exit, she ended up simply following the throng out through the swooshing doors and into the daylight. The station abutted a large, open area, its imposing stone columns looking out onto a huge Christmas tree that stood proud in a rectangular area of grass to her right. There were roads and traffic, and small pockets of greenery and trees lining parking spaces. The Christmas tree, the tallest by far, held a large star atop its branches and large baubles reflected its surroundings. Taxis, trams and cars moved in and out of parking spaces and travelled both ways in front of her. It was a busy area, with horns beeping, traffic moving and people hurrying around as if knowing there was a storm coming.

Matching white taxis were lined up opposite the station and Rosie joined the end of the short line, hoping the distance from the station to the British Embassy wasn't far. Mostly because she didn't want to use up all of her euros in one go. Checking in her purse for the piece of paper bearing her directions, supplied very kindly by the reception staff back at the hotel, she finally climbed into the back of a taxi.

'British Consulate General, *grazie*,' she said, leaning back into the seat, hoping the driver wouldn't begin talking to her in Italian. She had reached her limit with her language abilities.

Closing her eyes, she leant her head back, just as the pitter-patter of rain was audible on the roof of the vehicle. She should take in the sights, appreciate another European city that she could now mark off her list, but instead she dosed off, her frown lines relaxing as she fell into an exhausted sleep, unaware of the busy city traffic; unaware of the time ticking on by.

'British Consulate General,' the driver stated, slowing the taxi to a halt and waking Rosie with a jolt.

She looked out of the window, now wet with raindrops, to find that they had stopped in a city road that seemed no different from any other: motorbikes lined up in front of a typical bland office block and a dead end crammed with parked cars trying to turn around. There were a few trees dotted around, but they were lost in a sea of pale buildings and shop fronts.

'Oh, um, *quanta costa*?' she asked, reading the line from her sheet, mentally thanking the kind hotel staff for popping down some necessary Italian phrases.

He smiled kindly, taking in her tired eyes, pale face and dirty, ripped coat. He looked up at the imposing building beside them and back at her as if trying to work out her purpose.

'*Niente*,' he said, waving away the charge by resetting the counter on his dashboard to zero and gesturing for her to exit the car.

Rosie wasn't sure what he meant, so she opened her purse and began pulling out notes.

'No. *Niente*.' He placed a hand over his heart and tapped it, giving her a grandfatherly smile.

She took in his trimmed and tidy grey beard and crisply ironed shirt and the large gold ring on his wedding finger. She tried to pass him a couple of notes, but he simply pushed her hand away, shooing her out. She swallowed hard, tears threatening at his kindness. He clearly thought she was in some kind of trouble, which, she realised, she was.

'*Grazie*,' she said, opening the taxi door and climbing out, grateful at that moment that she didn't speak Italian, as she didn't think she'd be able to talk with the huge lump in her throat.

As the car moved away to turn around, she took a deep breath and released it, looking upwards towards the skies that were now producing a fine mist rather than a heavy downpour. The clouds were a depressing shade of grey. She then turned to look at the British Consulate General building behind her, noticing that right at the top of the stone edifice was the British flag that hung above a large 'British Consulate' sign, which was proudly facing outwards.

Walking up to the building, she felt a jolt of excitement. Hopefully, by the end of the day, she'd have a new passport in her hands and she could get home in time for Christmas.

'Positive thoughts,' she said aloud to herself as she took a deep breath before pulling the cool metal handle of one of the large glass doors.

But it didn't budge.

She moved her hand and tried the other door, pulling hard, but it was stuck like glue. Locked, she realised.

She pressed her face against the glass to look inside and saw that all the lights were on, but there were no souls to be spotted. She tried the doors again, but they resisted. She scanned the doors for a clue but there was no sign stating it was closed. Looking to her left, there was a wall plaque stating its opening times. Its office hours were Monday to Friday, 9.15am to 12.15pm and then 2.15pm to 4.15pm. It appeared that they closed for lunch. Every day. Checking her wristwatch, she saw it was 12.25pm. She wasn't getting in there any time soon.

'Shit.'

It was far later than she thought. The traffic must have been bad or she queued for longer than expected to get one. Either way, she had missed her appointment and would now have to wait for the Consulate to re-open. Glancing left and right, couldn't see a café anywhere close by and the rain had come back with a vengeance now, beating down onto the dirty tarmac like rainwater from a watering can. Feeling the growlings of hunger, she decided to risk it and headed off towards what looked like a small square ahead of her. Ten minutes later, she was soaked through and still hungry. She hadn't found a café or even a mini-market in which to purchase an umbrella. Not that she really wanted to dip into her limited cash.

Before she realised, she was lost, her sodden feet splashing through puddle after puddle in the hope of finding somewhere warm and dry. But when she turned back for a familiar sight, she couldn't see which road was the way back. She felt like Dorothy without the ruby slippers, or Hansel and Gretel without the trail of breadcrumbs to help her get home. Well, not home, but at least back to the consulate.

She found herself at a huge roundabout, with traffic swirling around it, including bright yellow trams that contrasted against the drab grey buildings towering over her as she tried to find her bearings. She saw multiple signposts and recognised none of them.

Swallowing down the beginnings of fear in her chest, she decided to bite the bullet and hail a taxi to take her back. But that proved easier said than done. With the driving rain and cold wind now whistling around her, she could see multiple white taxis in the maelstrom of traffic, but she couldn't see any with an available light. The cold wind whipped her hair up and around her face and through the gaps in her coat, making her shiver. She felt miserable.

Until, through the rain, she saw it.

A white light box, lit up in the distance.

She took a step towards the pavement edge, raising a hand and sighing as she heard her coat rip even further with the movement. She wriggled her fingers and drew herself up onto tiptoes, noticing that the taxi was approaching her exit from the roundabout. She beamed at the car, hoping her intention was clear. However, what she didn't see was the huge truck travelling towards her from the other direction. And what she hadn't considered was the fact that drivers drove on the right-hand side in Italy.

With her eyes firmly focused on the moving white taxi, she failed to see the truck or notice the huge puddle that had formed from a blocked rainwater drain beside the curb. Only when a wave of freezing, dirty brownish drain water rose up to meet her did she realise her error.

It was like being hit by a frozen pane of ice. She screamed out, her voice carried away by the rumbling engine of the truck as it passed her, and looked down to find the water dripping off her like a melting ice sculpture. She was drenched. The coat had changed to a shade darker and was now sodden to the point where it weighed her down. Her hair was flat to her face, limp and soaked. And any make-up that she had applied that morning at the hotel was either now completely washed away or was halfway down her face.

'Are you kidding me?!' Rosie shouted to the retreating truck, but it continued along its way, seemingly oblivious.

She tried to wipe off as much of the residual water as she could from down her front, but it was no use. She was soaked through.

A horn beeping made her look up. The taxi she had been gesturing to had stopped across the road from her and the driver was staring at her with an obvious look of pity. He gestured for her to come over. After crossing the road away from the large lake of water and stepping onto the opposite pavement, she opened the passenger door. The driver was a woman, mid-fifties, with long, straight dark hair tied into a knot on top of her head. Her cheeks were rosy and she had freckles covering both cheeks and her delicate nose.

'Do you speak English?' Rosie asked, wiping her face of fresh rain.

The woman smiled. 'Of course! My son-in-law is from Brighton,' she said, gesturing for her to climb in.

'But I am wet through – I'll soak your seat,' Rosie said, gesturing to her dripping hair and soggy appearance.

'The back seats are plastic-covered. I've been in this trade too long not to prepare for the worst,' the woman said, her accent strong but her grasp of the English language clearly very good. 'Hop in.'

Rosie did as she was told and gratefully climbed into the back of the car, the plastic covering squeaking and sliding underneath her as she shuffled into the seat.

'Where to?' the driver asked, looking back at her and smiling in a motherly fashion.

'The British Consulate General, please,' Rosie asked, hoping she wasn't going to have to dip into her cash too much to pay for this additional journey. She had no idea how far she had walked.

'Are you joking?' the driver asked.

'No,' Rosie replied, looking confused. 'Why?'

'You'll see,' the woman said, chuckling, as she pushed the gearstick into first and began weaving into the city traffic.

She made her way towards the huge roundabout but joined it only for a moment before she came off at the first exit. She travelled on for another thirty seconds or so before taking a right and then another right, coming to a stop at a dead end.

'The British Consulate General,' she stated, pointing at the now-familiar building.

'But it is so close!' Rosie felt stupid. She had walked for over an hour, yet it appeared she had walked almost in circles.

'You seem lost in more ways than one,' the driver said astutely.

'You could say that,' Rosie said, pulling out her purse to get some cash.

'No,' the woman said. 'Save your money. No charge. You look like you need to find your way home.'

'Thank you,' Rosie said, smiling gratefully and feeling so foolish.

The woman was right. She needed to find her way home and she hoped and prayed that there was someone in the building next to them with the kindness, compassion and ability to get her back home quickly – hopefully with a freshly printed passport.

Chapter Thirty-two

'Next!'

Rosie had been fortunate enough that despite missing her own appointment time, a cancellation meant that an available slot had become available at two-thirty. But she had been waiting in a plastic chair for several minutes so far, and she was damp, frizzy, and really thirsty. Normally, she'd have whiled away the time by browsing on her phone, but with no distraction, she'd just had to stare at the huge clock above a wall of shelving covered in large leather-backed books as it ticked away the seconds. Above the clock was a huge British flag attached to a shiny metal pole. While waiting, she'd had the time to observe every part of the building, with its open-plan office, shiny wooden parquet flooring and four individual plastic pods that had the ability either to be clear Perspex or private.

Each held a desk, an employee in a suit and a chair for a visitor. When the next caller entered a booth, the pod then switched to a privacy screen for the duration of the meeting. Rosie had been watching each pod and as yet, Pod 4 hadn't been used, or else the meeting in there had been going on far longer than the other pods.

'Next!'

The queue shifted forwards, with Rosie now next in line. The man in front of her headed into Pod 2 and she waited, anticipating the next call. But another ten minutes passed and she could feel her bladder beginning to complain. The lady seated next to her shushed her and she realised she had been tapping her foot on the floor.

'Sorry,' she said, turning around to apologise.

The woman was smartly dressed, with a designer pull-along suitcase and matching oversized handbag. She had a silk scarf beautifully tied at an angle around her neck, and her black dress and camel-coloured coat screamed expensive. Rosie saw her own reflection in the dark glasses and blanched. She looked terrible.

'Next!' a male voice called.

Rosie turned to see the number above Pod 4 lit up and a suited man standing beside the pod. A man with thick flame-red wavy hair that he tried to tuck behind each ear, but it simply sprang back out again. He gestured at her from a distance and then disappeared into his pod, and she followed, her trainers squeaking slightly from still being wet. She tried to smooth down her coat and brush her fingers through her hair, but all that resulted in was her fingers getting jammed in the knotty, lanky birds' nest that once resembled her hair.

Walking inside the pod, she saw him flick a switch and the pod's transparency disappeared, making the pod feel smaller. She took a seat opposite the man's desk, taking in his bushy eyebrows and deep furrowed frown lines as he moved to sit in his seat behind the desk.

He seemed familiar, she thought, as she tried to sit up straight and look like a decent human being. He cleared his throat and wished her a good afternoon, without making eye contact. As he went to sit down behind his desk, she noticed him wince in pain and adjust his suit trousers away from his knee with a large hand. A hand that was also grazed as if he had fallen over and . . .

'I know you,' she said, pointing at him. 'You're the guy in Venice, the guy running in the Santa race yesterday.'

She scanned his face, taking in the bright green eyes, and watched as he looked up at her for the first time. He looked over her outfit, took in the state of her hair and make-up, and then noticed the rip beside the side pocket of her coat. His face clouded and she realised that recognition had taken place. And he did not look best pleased.

'And you're the non-runner who knocked me down, ruining any opportunity for a personal best,' he said. 'Not to mention taking me out of my training schedule for my next half-marathon.'

'I'm really sorry,' Rosie said, flushing. 'It was a total accident.' She looked down at her hands pressed together in her lap.

'Not to mention that the fall activated my old knee injury again, leaving it swollen like a grapefruit.'

'Again, really sorry,' Rosie said, wondering how a knee could look like a grapefruit and almost feeling tempted to ask.

'And yet, as luck would have it, here you are, in my office. I hope you're not here to physically attack me again?' He turned away from her and focused on his computer screen.

She laughed, assuming it was a light-hearted joke, but he didn't smile. So she stopped laughing and said seriously, 'No, of course not! I don't hurt people as a hobby,' she said, feeling slighted. This was not how she intended this meeting to go. 'I need professional help, please.'

'That's obvious,' he muttered, his eyes still firmly on his screen, but she chose to ignore it.

'I've lost my passport, purse and phone, and my scheduled flight home is tomorrow, which I really want to be on. I don't want to be stuck here for Christmas. I've paid the fee and I have replacement passport photos too.' She could feel sweat on her upper brow and realised how much she needed his help. 'Could you please just issue me with a replacement passport so I can leave, and then we don't need to cross paths again?'

She realised her faux pas. 'I meant figuratively, not literally.'

He clicked his computer mouse multiple times, not even glancing in her direction.

'When did the incident occur?'

'Yesterday afternoon. In Venice.'

'And how did you happen to lose your belongings? Were you attacked, mugged, held at gunpoint or a victim of pickpocketing?'

'None of those things. My bag fell into the canal. And then sank.'

'Your bag fell into the canal,' he repeated, typing the information into his computer. 'How did the accident occur? Were you a victim of tidal currents? Or overcrowding on one of the water buses?'

'None of the above,' she quipped. 'An old lady fell on top of me in a gondola and I knocked my backpack into the canal.'

He stopped typing for a second to look at her. 'You knocked your own backpack into the canal,' he said, his face deadpan, 'after an old lady jumped on you while on a gondola.'

'Well, she didn't jump. She fell,' Rosie corrected.

But he continued, 'And this was all after bounding into an organised race and taking out one of the semi-professional runners? You had a busy day.' He gave her a look and then turned his attention back to typing. 'To process the application for an emergency travel document, I will ideally need the police record number. Which police station filed the report?'

'Police station? Report?' Rosie said, looking confused.

'Just the number or reference and I'll be able to drag the details up on our system.'

There was a pause before Rosie spoke again, quietly. 'I never filed a report. I never reported anything. I remember seeing a policeman, but I assumed he was seeing if I was hurt, so I didn't mention anything.' She realised how lame this sounded, how naive she had been.

'You didn't file a report? There is no record of the incident occurring?' he said, pausing from completing his own report. 'Then I'm afraid I cannot help you here.' He stood up. 'On behalf of the British Consulate here in Milan, may I thank you for your visit and good luck in your endeavours.' He gestured for her to leave and pressed the button on the wall panel, activating the privacy screen so that it became transparent again.

'Whoa, wait!' Rosie said, jumping up to stop him. 'You have to help me.'

'I don't have to do anything,' he said, correcting her.

'You're the British Consulate and I am a British national. You have a responsibility to help any citizens who are lost, distressed and unable to travel. I fall under all three categories.' She held up three fingers, the hole in her coat opening, revealing her jumper. 'You have to help me.'

He shook his head, his demeanour unchanged. 'I cannot help you without a police report. Get me one of them and then the British Consulate can help you further. We look forward to seeing you again soon once you have the correct information.' He gestured more forcefully for her to leave. 'I recommend you return on either a Wednesday or a Sunday.'

'Why? Is that so I can come back to see you directly?' Rosie asked.

'No, it's because I don't work on those days and therefore I don't need to worry that you'll rugby-tackle me to the floor without warning.'

He held out a hand to shake hers in a gesture of goodbye. A tiny smile met his lips and it drew attention to a deep dimple in his left cheek. Annoyingly, it was incredibly endearing.

'Please, you need to help me. I want to go home.'

She knew she was begging, but she couldn't imagine having to go back to Venice without a valid passport in her hand. She didn't shake his hand. She didn't want him to throw her out. Their eyes locked and he sighed, his head dropping.

'Look, you don't need to travel back to Venice. It's not ideal, but you can file a police report here in Milan. Especially as you are currently destitute. There is a police station a five-minute walk away from here and they can complete a report fairly quickly. Let me give you the directions.'

He returned to his desk and pulled out a small card. Turning it over, he scribbled on the back of it and handed it to her. She noticed it was his business card and when she flipped it over, he had written down directions in small, tidy handwriting.

'Thank you,' she said feebly, suddenly feeling immensely tired. His expression changed and softened.

'Look, we are open until 4pm. If you head over there now, you might just be able to get back here in time for us to begin the process of your emergency travel documents. But you'll need to hurry,' he said, checking his wristwatch and tapping it gently.

A rush of relief washed over her and she took his hand in hers, shaking it.

'Thank you, um . . .' She looked down at the business card and noted his name. 'Fox?'

He flushed a little at the mention of his first name. 'Fox, it's short for Foxton,' he said. 'My parents clearly hated me.'

It was a joke and it helped to break the tension. Rosie laughed and then turned to leave.

'Thank you, Fox,' she said. 'I'll be back soon.'

Chapter Thirty-three

Rosie almost ran to the police station after noting the time on the huge clock in the British Consulate foyer. She had less than an hour to get there, file a report and ask for it to be printed before running back to the consulate.

Thankfully, the police station was quiet and she was seen straight away. The female officer spoke fluent English, having spent two years studying there, and the report was competed with an ease that did not reflect the luck of Rosie's day so far. The police officer even allowed her to use the station bathroom, as she was desperate. The only hiccough was the fact that there was a printer issue and it took the officer a while to realise the error.

This meant that she found herself running back through the streets of Milan, splashing through deep puddles, clasping a printout of the report in her hands. Thankfully, the rain had stopped and her journey back was relatively dry, though her trainers were now covered in dirty splashes. But the traffic was heavier and the pavements were crammed with people, which meant she had to meander around groups of tourists, young children and shoppers, all with time to spare. She reached the street for the British Consulate General and forced herself on, her panting loud and her chest straining with pain and the lack of oxygen.

Slowing to pass a queue at the bus stop, she saw Fox up ahead, walking out of the building, with a group of colleagues. He looked totally different outside of the office and was smiling.

'Fox!' she shouted without thinking and ran towards him, almost tripping and falling headfirst into his arms.

Thankfully, he stopped her falling face first into the pavement.

'Shit!'

'You? Again?' he said, lifting her back into a standing position with ease.

She had grasped his left arm and was surprised at how muscly it felt, even over a coat and suit.

'You're starting to make a habit of this,' he said, waving away his colleagues, letting them know she was OK. 'Should I be concerned that you're actually trying to take me down?'

It was another quip, but Rosie was grateful for it.

'I'm so sorry,' she said, trying to catch her breath. She had sweat on her face and felt it sliding down her spine. If it was possible for him to see her in a worse light than an hour earlier, she had successfully completed that challenge. 'But look,' she said, holding up the now-crumpled form. 'I have the report. Can you get me my passport now? Please?'

He looked uncomfortable. 'We're closed. We closed ten minutes ago. I'm so sorry, but the office is locked up for the night.' He did genuinely look sorry. 'But if you come back in the morning, I can make sure you're first to be seen?'

'In the morning?' Rosie said, wiping her hair out of her face. 'But I have a return ticket to Venice tonight! I can't stay here! I can't go back empty-handed.' Her eyes filled with tears and she felt depleted. Hungry, tired, dirty, alone – she had reached her limit.

'Look, shush. Calm down a little. Um . . .'

'Rosie,' she said, wiping her nose on her sleeve. 'My name is Rosie Redbrush.' A hiccough escaped.

'Look, Rosie. Let me help.' He took the report from her and smoothed it against his chest before folding it neatly and placing it in his jacket pocket. 'I know of a little hotel just around the corner from my place. The owners are friends of mine. I'm sure they can squeeze you in for one night and then we'll process your application first thing.'

'But I don't have much money. I just have a bit of cash—'

'Don't worry about the money. As I say, it's a friend of a friend and a small hotel. Just don't empty the minibar or order Wagyu beef for dinner. Oh, and leave them a blinding review on Tripadvisor.'

'I don't know . . .' she said, thinking about her paid return train ticket and her group back in Venice.

The idea of staying in a strange city and being led to an unknown hotel by a total stranger set off a beacon alarm in her head. As if reading her mind, he pulled out his phone and typed away before turning his screen to her.

'This is the hotel. It's a seven-minute walk from here and is available on most major hotel booking sites. Take a look . . .' He handed her his phone and rummaged in his coat pocket, pulling out his large and expensive-looking wallet. Flipping it open, he scanned the cards before pulling out his driving licence. 'And here's my driving licence. It shows my name, address and proof of who I am. If you're concerned about walking with a stranger to an unknown hotel, then keep hold of the licence until you're safely inside the hotel.'

Rosie scanned the driving licence, taking in his photograph. It was actually extremely flattering, which made her slightly grateful that her own licence now lay at the bottom of the canal and she didn't have to show him her photo. She had had it taken when she had just got over a bad case of conjunctivitis and her eyes were still red, and her face blotchy as a reaction to the antibiotics. To compare, he looked like a sexy model from a male charity calendar and she looked like the *before* photo in a make-over show.

She looked at the website for the hotel and saw it was a real website. Clicking on the directions button on the website, it opened an app in his phone and brought up a real-time map. He was right, the time indicated their arrival in eight minutes.

Making a snap decision, she handed the phone back to him and smiled. 'OK, thank you. I would really appreciate that.'

'Cool,' he said, looking slightly worried himself.

A strange, dirty, sweaty mess of a woman who had attacked him twice in two days was clearly not a regular occurrence for him. She suspected he offered to help her before he really thought it through. But he was clearly a gentleman and he threw his arm out in the direction of the busy traffic, back the way she had just come.

'Let me lead the way and we'll have you there in no time.'

And just like that, Rosie began to walk side by side with a total stranger, in a new and unknown city, and with no documents to prove who she was or whether or not she was telling the truth. It felt surreal, and scary, and unknown. But a tiny part of her, she realised as she began to make conversation with Fox, was enjoying the rush of excitement that came from stepping outside of her comfort zone and living her life, as Bee told her to: in the moment.

Chapter Thirty-four

'So, what brings you to Milan, then?'

Rosie felt uncomfortable walking beside him, so decided to make the time pass quickly with questions.

'I work here,' he answered directly, his eyes facing forwards.

'How long have you worked here?'

'Almost two and a half years now.'

'And do you like living in Italy?'

'It's no different to any other city, really. Same grubby buildings, same piles of rubbish,' he said, gesturing to the stacks of black bin bags on the pavement beside them, 'same bills to pay. It's just the currency that has changed.'

'You surely can't mean that!' Rosie said, looking at the beautiful buildings and enjoying the vibrant atmosphere as they passed a busy section of cafés and shops. 'Italy is beautiful.'

'You get used to it,' he answered flatly, his stride never slowing.

Rosie could smell the fresh coffee and delicious aromas of pastry goods hanging in the air, inviting her to stop.

But Fox didn't let up on his pace. He seemed to be a focused man and despite her stomach begging her to stop, she kept to his side as they trailed the streets of Milan. He didn't seem keen to engage in further questions, nor did he seem interested in her life history, so they continued in silence.

After a few more minutes, Fox slowed to a friendlier pace, having appeared to have forgotten Rosie even existed. His polite conversational skills were clearly only for work-related purposes, between working hours. But it gave Rosie time to look around her.

The buildings were still high, but this area seemed more residential, with pockets of greenery here and there, and little squares that housed small shops and cafés. They passed a small playground, where there were a handful of toddlers running around while their mothers talked and drank from flasks, no doubt making the most of the daylight before it disappeared into the night. The sound of childish laughter and play made Rosie smile. She missed Bee's kids. Her heart ached for home and with this focus, she upped her pace.

Fox changed direction and walked through a narrow alley, its mossy stone buildings either side smelling dank and dirty. She felt slightly unnerved by being alone with a strange man, with no artificial light illuminating their path and the daylight almost gone. Fox was striding ahead, his shadow never faltering, so she slowed her pace a little, hoping this wasn't a foolish adventure.

But then the alley opened into another slightly larger courtyard and the building ahead was so pretty that Rosie let out a little gasp. It was four storeys high and painted the colour of burnt orange. Each floor housed a row of four small balconies, painted either gold or sage green, and each with matching rectangular window boxes, full of the brightest flowers and a small, ornate table and chairs.

On the ground floor, stood centrally, was a set of closed deep-mahogany double doors, with a Christmas wreath on each one, which was huge, festooned with what appeared to be dried fruits and ribbon.

As they approached the building, Rosie noticed the frieze painted on the building's frontage, above the top floor where the roof peaked at its highest. The mural was delicately painted and depicted an image of the Italian countryside, with a farmhouse, fields and a pathway lined with cypress trees. Above the image, hand-painted gold words had been enscribed with precision, the cursive scrawl spelling out *Il Posto Tranquillo*.

'Is that the hotel?' Rosie asked, really hoping it was.

Fox nodded, a small smile on his face. 'Yes, we've arrived.'

'*Il Posto Tranquillo*,' Rosie said, wincing at her poor attempt at Italian. 'What does it mean?'

'Loosely translated, it means "A Quiet Place",' Fox said, walking towards it, his footsteps loud and echoing on the cold stone of the courtyard.

There was no one else around. Rosie thought the name fitted beautifully with its surroundings. She could barely hear the noise of the city here.

'A quiet place,' Rosie repeated, nodding. 'Good name.'

'I think so,' Fox said, turning to look at her with what was the first genuine smile she had seen.

Annoyingly, it made him very attractive, with his straight teeth and deep dimple reappearing.

'It's what everyone needs at some point,' he added.

Looking over his shoulder, she noticed a large wooden structure positioned in front of a tall building on one side of the courtyard. It was basic in its build, with simple wooden beams and a straw roof. She wondered if it was for selling wares or typical Italian trinkets. In the evening darkness she couldn't see inside the structure, just shadows. There were lanterns sporadically hanging from the front beam, but they were unlit and the whole place appeared abandoned. She turned her attention back towards the hotel.

They had reached the double doors at this point and Fox pushed one open, then stepped back to let her enter first. She was shocked. Not many men these days still upheld traditional standards and she could feel her cheeks flushing as she walked under his arm to enter the building.

The entrance hall was dim, but it didn't matter, as it was lit by the most gorgeous Christmas tree to Rosie's right. She could smell the pine and cinnamon sticks that were tied to its branches, and a citrusy aroma of dried clementines hanging from ribbon. The lights were a warm yellow, and the whole tree looked understated and traditional. Rosie noticed that underneath the tree were piles of brown paper packages, with festive ribbon that varied with each present.

She wanted to take a photo but was aware of Fox standing just beside her and felt like he would not appreciate the touristy move. Instead, she looked left to a long mahogany reception desk that ran along almost the whole side of the entrance hall. Behind the desk was a wall of cubbyholes, some with post visible, others with just a large golden key linked to a red velvet cord and tassel that hung from each for easy access.

The reception desk was empty, but opposite the desk was a large table containing a carafe of red wine and a basketful of pastries, their golden exterior flaky and fresh. Wine glasses stood beside it, along with small dessert plates. Rosie's mouth watered at the sight; she hadn't eaten all day. At the end of the entrance hall was a single lift, its metal grill doors closed, but she could see through them to the open recess of the lift itself.

The entire place was charming. And quiet. She felt herself breathe out, watching as Fox moved around her towards the table, where he poured himself a large glass of wine. He turned to her, his face questioning, the carafe still held in his hand.

'Would you like one? It's complimentary.'

Rosie nodded eagerly, stepping forwards to take a now-full glass from the table. She pointed at the pastries.

'Are these free, too?' she whispered but wasn't sure why.

It felt less of a hotel and more like they were trespassing in someone's private abode. He nodded and took the top one for himself and took a large bite. Feeling bolstered by him, she did the same, rejoicing that it was just as gorgeous as the Venetian ones but with the added delight of being filled with apricot jam.

Fox moved across to the reception desk and tapped gently on the gold metal bell that was placed on top of a large red hardback book. The sound echoed and Rosie looked around the room for a door or staircase but couldn't spot either. Dark wooden panelling covered every wall. They waited.

Rosie finished her pastry and took a sip of the wine. It was rich and fruity and paired deliciously with the apricot jam. She greedily took a large swig and was about to grab a second pastry when at the sound of distant footsteps on a heavy floor stopped her. She looked around but found no trace of anyone.

Then, as if by magic, part of the wall panelling to her right slid open, revealing a curvaceous older woman, dressed in a long flowing black skirt and white blouse and with the smartest grey bob Rosie had ever seen. It didn't move as she walked, its shine accentuated by the twinkling lights of the Christmas tree. The woman spotted Fox and embraced him in a warm tight hug. Rosie noticed that he didn't refuse it.

'*La mia piccola volpe rossa!*' she said, her voice gravelly and delighted. 'My little fox! How long has it been? I have missed you!' She pushed back his face with both hands and stared at him before kissing him on both cheeks. 'Ah, you are too gaunt. You do not care for yourself. Eat! Eat!' She gestured to the basket and in doing so noticed Rosie standing behind Fox. 'Oh! And you have brought us a guest?'

'Oh, yes, sorry. Alessia, this is Rosie. Rosie, meet Alessia. Alessia is the owner of this hotel.'

Rosie stepped forwards to shake her hand but instead was enveloped in a hug so welcoming that she wanted to stay that way forever. Alessia smelt of cinnamon and soap and Rosie was instantly transported back to Jonah's Café and his cookies. She suddenly felt hugely homesick.

Alessia pulled back and turned her attentions back to Fox, who had cleared his throat.

'Alessia, we are in need of a room for the night. Do you think you could accommodate Rosie tonight? She's had a spot of bad luck and has lost both her passport and all of her money. I don't suppose you could put her up for the night, could you? As a special favour to me?'

His hand was resting on Alessia's arm affectionately and Rosie blushed, feeling foolish for being someone so needy. Watching Alessia's face change from happiness to concern only exacerbated this feeling.

'Oh, *mio caro*, my dear, we are fully booked! For tonight is the beginning of the *presepi viventi*! I am so sorry.' She genuinely looked upset, grabbing both of Rosie's hands in hers and squeezing them.

'It's fine, please don't worry—' Rosie tried to interject, but Alessia didn't give her a chance.

'Any other night, I could have found you a room, but *presepi viventi* is very important for our heritage and families, as you well know, Fox. It is a time for tradition and for showing our faith for everyone to see. But Gabriella said you couldn't make it, Fox. That you were out of town?' She looked at him questioningly, but Rosie noticed he wouldn't catch her eye.

'Well, yes, I was, but circumstances have now changed.'

'So you can participate now? Oh, *fantastica*!' She clapped her hands together in glee, ran around the reception desk and picked up the phone. 'Does Gabriella know?'

Before he even had a moment to reply, she had begun dialling, holding up a finger to her lips, indicating for them to stay quiet.

He looked awkward, his eyes darting from Rosie to Alessia. If she had felt uncomfortable before, then she was now at a whole new level of unease. Not only was she standing in a hotel without any rooms, but she was also stuck with a stranger who couldn't help. She shuffled a little, hoping to make a discreet exit, and wondered if she'd have time to make it back to the train station and use her return ticket back to Venice. She could attempt to sort out this whole fiasco tomorrow.

'Well, thank you for offering to help, but I had better get going.' She whispered it to Fox, edging even closer to the door.

'Where will you go?' he said, his eyes darting between Rosie and Alessia, distracted by the tirade of Italian flowing from Alessia's mouth.

'Oh, don't you worry about me. I'll be fine.' She tried to fake a smile but found it harder than she anticipated. Instead, her lip began to wobble. She held up a hand to wave her thanks.

'No, you can't just head off with no money, no ID, no knowledge of a city as large as this . . .' he whispered back, following her towards the door.

She wafted away his concerns and reached out for the door handle, wanting to get away from him. But they both turned towards Alessia as her voice rose to a squeal and she slapped a hand down onto the counter excitedly.

She beckoned them over and Fox turned back, whispering, 'Hold on, don't go,' before approaching Alessia as she finished her call, returning the receiver to its cradle.

'Fox! That was Gabriella!' Her face was animated, making her look much younger than her years. 'She has been asked to join the Venice Symphony tonight as their lead singer! At the Teatro La Fenice, too! *La mia bellissima diva!*' She kept clapping her hands in glee and pressing them against her flushed cheeks. 'Fox, can you believe it? Our Gabriella.'

'Yes, well, um, that's amazing,' Fox said, his smile stretched across his face like a tight elastic band. 'But wasn't she meant to be Mary in the opening night of *presepi viventi* tonight?'

Alessia's face turned from happy to panic in an instant. 'Oh, no, you're right. She is meant to be our *Vergine Maria*! Where can I find another Maria at short notice?'

Rosie held up a finger and cleared her throat. 'So, it seems like you have a lot on your plate right now, so I'll just head off, but thank you for the pastry.'

Her voice triggered both Fox and Alessia to turn and look at her. Alessia's gaze was oddly unsettling.

'OK, bye, then,' said Rosie awkwardly.

She turned to leave, but Alessia called out.

'Wait! I can help. I have a room you can stay in.'

Rosie turned back. 'I thought you were full?'

'Yes, we were. But with my daughter no longer coming, you can stay in her room. For free. With dinner and breakfast included.' She smiled, gesturing for Rosie to come forwards.

'Oh, that's so kind of you, thank you,' Rosie said, relief flooding through her at the thought of not having to walk in the dark alone.

'As long as you take the place of Maria tonight,' Alessia interrupted, her smile strong.

'Maria?' Rosie asked, really confused at what she was asking. 'I don't understand.'

'Alessia, I don't think that is very fair,' Fox said, looking uncomfortable.

'Fair? She gets to stay here for free. All I ask is that she spend an hour of her evening taking part in our very important tradition.'

'But everyone will be there. It's the *presepi viventi*. She hasn't prepared—'

'I could dress her and Sofia could do her hair.'

'She doesn't speak Italian.'

'I sense Italian in her. Look at that beautiful face. Italian heritage!'

'Alessia, please—'

'Sorry, sorry,' Rosie said, stepping between them. 'What is a *presepi viventi*?'

Fox turned to look at her.

'It's a live-action nativity. It's an Italian Christmas tradition. People dress up and hold their poses while people come to visit a recreation of the birth of Jesus Christ.'

'Live-action? You mean, like actors?'

'No, not like actors,' Alessia said, walking around the desk and putting an arm around Rosie's shoulders, drawing her away from the doors and towards the lift. 'Just wonderful kind people. Like you . . .'

As the lift dinged its arrival on the ground floor and the metallic doors squealed open, Rosie suddenly felt like she had been cajoled into something that she had not agreed to and was in no way prepared for.

Chapter Thirty-five

'I don't know how I got roped into this.'

Rosie looked over at Fox, who was standing to her left, his voice muffled by his clip-on, chest-length fake beard and his red hair covered by a stripey blue-and-white tea towel. He stood stiffly beside two other shepherds dressed in similar gowns, both hands leaning on his staff. His brow was furrowed and she would have found the situation laughable, but she was equally wondering how she had ended up standing in as the Virgin Mary.

The last two hours had gone by in a blur, with a group of Italian women gabbling incoherently while pruning, blow-drying and transforming Rosie from a bedraggled, tired mess and into a clean and respectable woman in her thirties. They'd even given her hair a trim and used some huge device to add large waves, giving it some much-needed volume, while simultaneously plying her with more glasses of sweet wine and pastries.

It had actually been nice feeling looked after. Following the initial blatant blackmailing by Alessia, Rosie had been marginally compensated by being shown into a large, opulent bedroom before being instructed to shower, change and wait for the others to arrive. It had given Rosie a moment to take in her surroundings.

The room was clearly not a hotel room for guests. There were personalised posters on the walls of Italian boy bands and the bedding had a patchwork quilt that looked like it had been handmade. The curtains were thick velvet and the carpet was plush, Rosie's toes sinking deep into the thread.

There was a large moon-shaped dressing table covered with cosmetics, perfume bottles and numerous picture frames, all showing snapshots of groups of girls at various ages, their arms wrapped around each other, a moment forever captured. One girl was in all of them. A teenager with long, dark hair and clear skin, with the loveliest of smiles. Gabriella.

Rosie turned away from the dressing table and headed over to the large double bed. Above it was a rectangular cork noticeboard full of overlapping Polaroid images, along with concert ticket stubs, stickers and scrawled notes. It felt personal, like reading a person's diary without their permission, so Rosie went to turn away. Before she did so, she noticed a number of photos of Fox, smiling and casual. In each one his arm was wrapped around Gabriella's shoulders. Rosie looked away, feeling like an intruder.

She found herself staring back at her own image, the entire wall opposite being built-in mirrored wardrobes. Her eyes were drawn to her left, where another wall held three large shelves full of trophies and medals. She walked over to take a closer look, inspecting each one, noting the first-place number on each one, despite not understanding the inscribed Italian. Some trophies were in other languages, too, the images depicting the outline of someone singing or a microphone. Gabriella was clearly a talented singer, as they were for numerous singing competitions and awards.

Her moment of quiet was soon disrupted by a gaggle of women entering the room and the next few hours whizzed by before she was ushered outside into the cold and into position in the manger. She shifted slightly as a fly landed on her nose, shaking it off with the tiniest of movements. The fly moved on and she took her position again, her face angled towards the manger. Out of the corner of her left eye, she could see that a crowd had formed and she could hear their conversations over the Christmas music, which was echoing around the courtyard from the small choir in the corner.

Rosie looked down at the manger and found two large, innocent eyes staring back at her. The eyes blinked and two pudgy little fists rose in greeting, along with a toothless smile. Rosie smiled back. But they weren't alone in the make-shift manger – there was a whole living, breathing cast of the nativity squished in around her as they all stood on a straw-covered floor. Rosie was seated on an actual bale of hay, her blue gown reaching the floor, with three shepherds, three kings, a Joseph and an actual sheep and donkey in a pen in the corner.

Alessia was dressed as one of the three kings, her velvety red robe tied like a cap around her neck. She was wearing a crown that glistened against the lanterns, which now burnt with real candles. In her hands was a cardboard box designed to look like a large bar of gold.

They had been in position for ten minutes now and already Rosie could feel her back aching from holding her pose. She felt sorry for the others who were standing. When Alessia had informed her it would only be for an hour before the next shift took over, she thought it would pass in a blur. But actually, staying still, with no distractions, appeared to have the magic ability of slowing time to a gentle crawl.

She looked down at the baby again. It was distracted by the slight sway of the lanterns and stayed wide-eyed as the light cast shadows on the roof structure above them. Rosie decided that if a baby could hold its attention for the duration of its debut show, then so could she.

One of the cast sneezed, causing others to jump, and the audience collectively chuckled, the fourth wall broken for a moment before positions were resumed. For the umpteenth time, she wondered how on earth she had got herself into this situation. Just over a week before, she had been munching on Jonah's cookies and wondering how she was going to meet her quarterly quota. Only days later, she was essentially a nomad stuck in a strange country where she had never felt more alone. Or braver, she realised. She had been forced into a situation, yet, instead of crumbling and passively waiting for help, she had pulled up her big-girl pants (or zipped up her now-ineffective and damaged coat) and travelled alone to Milan. Her spine straightened at the thought and she decided that she ought to honour her part in the nativity, so she spent the next fifty minutes being the best Mary she was capable of.

As a nearby clock chimed to mark the end of her shift, Alessia stepped down from her post and so, with a quick wave at the most well-behaved baby she had ever met, Rosie returned to Gabriella's room so that her robes could be removed and passed to the next Mary. Warming her toes by slipping on her now freshly laundered and still-warm socks and jeans (this hotel was going to get an incredibly good Tripadvisor review when she finally made it back home), Rosie heard her tummy growl.

Knowing it was just a bed and breakfast, she realised that unless she wanted to go to bed hungry, she was going to have to go out and find somewhere to eat. It turned out there was a limit to how many Italian pastries and glasses of red wine one woman could eat in a twelve-hour period, so she pulled on her warm, clean clothes and headed out of the room, grabbing her coat as she did so, to find Fox waiting outside in the corridor. He was now dressed in casual clothes and had one foot resting against the wall as he leant against it. He was wearing jeans and big tan ankle boots with the laces loosely hanging at their sides, a navy T-shirt that was crisply ironed and a stripey red-and-navy overshirt that reminded her of something a lumberjack would wear. Plus, it contrasted awesomely against his wild curls. He looked like a model in an American catalogue that sold farm equipment. But in a sexy, dishevelled, throw-you-over-one-shoulder way that Rosie found oddly unsettling.

'Oh! You shocked me!' she exclaimed, pulling her door to and placing a hand on her chest.

'Sorry,' he said, not looking in the least bit sorry. 'I was told to wait here for you until you were dressed.' He dropped his leg down and shoved both hands in his jeans pockets.

'By whom? And why?' Rosie asked, feeling slightly like a disobedient teenager who required babysitting.

'Alessia said that you needed to eat something and that she was far too caught up in the nativity events tonight to cook. Said I was to take you out somewhere. To eat. Together.'

He spoke the words as if to convince himself it was a good idea to take her out. She felt slightly affronted by his clear lack of enthusiasm, but then she remembered that she was the girl who knocked him out of a race, injured him, then turned up like a crazy person in another city demanding his help. To be honest, she was surprised he hadn't run in the other direction. Except that he couldn't run. Because of her. She smiled awkwardly.

'Well, that's very kind of her, but don't feel you have to. If you could just lead me to the nearest supermarket or café, I'm sure I'll find something to eat.'

'I'm sure you would,' he said, pushing off from the wall and taking her battered coat from her before helping her into it.

It was a very gentlemanly gesture and she found it oddly intimate.

'But I have been given strict instructions and the consequences of not doing so would be dire.' He looked serious.

'Alessia?'

'Alessia,' he answered, closing his eyes and nodding slowly. 'You have no idea the power that woman elicits in this town. The last person to disobey an order from her was seen being shipped off to the docks the very next day. Never to be seen or heard from again.'

He was talking in a serious tone, but when she looked up at him, there was the tiniest smile playing on his lips and she laughed.

'You cracked a joke . . .'

'I did.'

'You have a sense of humour, then.'

'I do. Only sporadically, and I save it for only a very few people.'

'Then I am honoured,' she said, taking a bow as they made their way into the rickety lift that shook into motion and started to descend.

He chuckled, his eyes turned ahead as the hotel floors visibly passed by. Reaching the ground floor, they could hear the choir still singing and a blast of cold air met them as they made their way outside. Alessia was there in a flash.

'Rosie! Dear Rosie. You are a natural! The comments I've had on your Mary have been *eccellente*. What an opening!'

She was flushed and had clearly already started on the wine as her eyes were glazed and she was swaying slightly.

'I mean, you're an amateur compared to my Gabriella, but still, there is potential. With time and effort, you could potentially blossom from a plain English rose into a beautiful colourful *orchidea*!' Alessia chuckled, clapping her hands together gleefully.

'Er, thank you . . . I think?' Rosie said, feeling both insulted and complimented in the same sentence.

Fox was right, Alessia really was a force.

Rosie looked to him and he just rolled his eyes and mouthed, 'She's drunk.'

Alessia continued, 'It's such a shame Gabriella isn't here to witness all this . . .' She swept out her left arm with gusto, spilling the contents of her wine glass onto the stone court-yard, luckily missing everybody. 'Isn't it, Fox? We miss our little Gabriella so much, don't we?' She hiccoughed loudly and looked close to tears. 'Especially you, Fox.' She raised her free hand to his cheek and stroked it softly. 'Now, when are you going to make an honest woman—'

'Let's go,' Fox said, grabbing Rosie's elbow and yanking her away from Alessia with force.

She stumbled when turning and struggled to keep pace with him, but he didn't let go, his stride long and fast as they made their way across the courtyard towards the alley. Rosie could hear Alessia laughing raucously, clearly having moved on to the next person in the crowd. Rosie couldn't help but giggle to herself as Fox led her down the alley and out into a larger square.

Just seconds later, they were standing outside a traditional Italian pizzeria, its interior spilling out onto the pavement but protected by a plastic-covered gazebo. An orange hue lit the square around them from the large patio heaters, which had been placed inside the gazebo to keep its diners warm. Rosie looked up to see the large sign naming the restaurant, Georgiana's Pizzeria, with two large Italian flags proudly situated at each end. The restaurant looked cosy and elegant, and when Fox opened the door to enter, the most amazing waft of garlic, herbs and wine met Rosie's senses and she suddenly felt ravenous.

A waiter in a white shirt, black bow tie and trousers approached Fox with a huge grin on his face and enveloped him in his arms. Despite Fox towering over him in height, this man still managed to embrace him fully, his words tumbling out of him. Fox replied fluently, the Italian rolling off his lips naturally and in a relaxed manner.

Rosie stood there feeling like a third wheel. She shifted from one foot to another until the waiter noticed her and took her hand, kissing the back of it.

'Apologies, Rosie, this is Sylvan. He is the head of house and husband of Georgiana, the chef. Sylvan, this is Rosie. Rosie is from out of town, just here for one night.'

'Welcome, welcome,' Sylvan said, smiling warmly. 'Come, come, your table, *Compositore* Fox.'

'*Compositore* Fox?' Rosie whispered as they were led to a secluded plush leather booth at the back of the restaurant.

A metal *Riservato* sign was sitting on the table, which was whisked away as soon as Sylvan reached it. They sat, and Sylvan disappeared in a puff of aftershave and tiny nods.

'It's a nickname,' Fox replied, his eyes drawn to the specials board.

It was easier carving a diamond from a piece of coal than it was extracting any personal information from him. She rolled her eyes.

'That much I gathered. What does it mean?'

'I forget,' he said, smiling stiffly at Sylvan as he returned to their table with a bottle of red wine.

The man began pouring without waiting, Rosie assuming this was a regular haunt for Fox. They continued talking in Italian while Rosie took a moment to take in her surroundings. There were empty wine bottles hanging upside down and covering the whole ceiling of the restaurant, and each table appeared to have a clear vaseful of bottle corks. The walls were full of photographs over the years, some ageing and yellow, some even black and white, but all contained images of families eating and laughing, the restaurant being the backdrop in every photo. The place felt warm and inviting.

'Rosie, are you happy for me to order? Sylvan will bring out a selection of dishes if so.'

Rosie nodded, taking a sip of the most delicious red wine she had ever tasted. Bearing in mind this was her third glass of red today, she knew that at some point she would have to switch to water. Sylvan disappeared, leaving them both alone.

Silence descended on the booth and Rosie twiddled the ring on her finger round and round as a distraction. She looked down to watch the metal Earth map spin around as she did so. Fox took a large gulp of his wine and looked anywhere but her. She wondered if she should escape to the bathroom and stay there until the food arrived, but her thoughts were interrupted by the nearby but muffled sound of a mobile phone ringing.

Fox opened his coat pocket and pulled out his phone, with the screen facing him. His face lit up with the blue light and Rosie could clearly see his features change to irritated. He ended the call without answering and placed it on the table between them. Rosie suddenly had an idea.

'Say, would it be OK for me to just check my emails on your phone quickly? I haven't been able to check anything since yesterday.'

The notion of being back online with the world and being contactable made her heart race. Was her job still secure? Had Benjamin been hit with the morality stick? Were the group in Venice OK? Fox looked dubious but nodded curtly before unlocking the screen and handing his phone over. The first thing Rosie noted was that he had a row of three guitars as his screensaver: two electric and one a standard but pretty battered one. She could feel his eyes on her so didn't query it, quickly logging into her email account and scanning the unread emails.

Sifting through the spam and junk emails, she noticed four that were marked as urgent and flagged accordingly. The first was from the Grandioso Canale Vista Hotel:

From: MariaConstinable@grandiosocanalevistahotelgroup.com
Sent: Monday, 22 December 2024, 20:55:12 pm
Subject: Reservation Booking — CH54481541 — Mrs Winthorpe-Smythe — Party of Eleven

Dear Ms Redbrush,

First, I hope your appointment at the British Consulate General was a success and that your delay in returning to our hotel is simply because of a choice to explore the wonderful city of Milan while you were there.

However, your group have informed us that you were due to travel back on the 16:00 train direct from Milan to Venice but that you have not returned. Please can you confirm at your earliest convenience that you are well and that we should not be concerned. The safety of our guests is of the utmost importance to the staff here at the Grandioso Canale Vista.

Secondly, a polite reminder that all guests must vacate their rooms on the day of departure by 11am. I note that your possessions are still in your room and we are fully booked tomorrow evening, so we will require the room key to be returned to us once checked out. There is a late check-out fee for those guests who are unable to vacate within the specified time.

Once again, if we can be of any assistance, then please do not hesitate to contact us. A member of staff is on the desk 24/7.

Best wishes and season's greetings,
Maria Constinable

Deputy Manager at the Grandioso Canale Vista

Rosie scoffed. They didn't seem too concerned about her welfare; they seemed more concerned about turning the bedding over to the next paying customer. She replied quickly, stating her situation, and asking for them to clear the room of her possessions and to keep them in storage. She knew it wasn't much. A suitcase full of clothes and a book from the bedside table. She then proceeded to tell them to empty the safe in her room and return the contents to Mildred. It was the group's passports, medical details and extra money that was set aside for emergencies. At least then she had given them back their options and their means to travel home. Whether she was with them or not.

She added a plea to Maria to organise transportation for them all to the airport, at whatever cost. She also asked them to contact Mrs Winthorpe-Smythe on her behalf to pay for any extra costs of transportation. She stated that the details should all be with the passports and tickets, locked away in a safe that was nowhere near the canal or in danger of being waterlogged.

Trying not to think about the group and how worried they must be, she moved on to the next couple of emails: one from Bee and one from Audrey. Bee's email had a slightly hysterical tone to it. It was full of questions and concerns, ending with a panicked question as to whether or not she should fly out to rescue her as she considered this to be a state of emergency. Despite the worried tone, Rosie couldn't help but chuckle. Bee was theatrical to say the least, but it was nice to feel loved.

She replied quickly, saying she had a place to stay in Milan until tomorrow, when a new passport would be issued. She quoted the name of the hotel and told Bee to contact her there if she needed to, but that she was fine and being taken care of by a member of the consulate. She didn't say anything more, though. If she said she was currently being wined and dined by a good-looking man, she'd never hear the end of it.

The second email from Audrey had a tone of concern, too, but was more practical. She had listed a number of places to stay in Milan, along with contact details and maps. She had also sent a screenshot of various flights departing over the next few days, informing her that she had been put on standby for any flight returning to City airport over the next few days.

Audrey then rambled on angrily about how she had 'accidentally' scratched Benjamin's pride and joy, his car, while getting past it with her wheelchair. She was emphatic as to how it was accidental, as was the fact that twice now, she had found herself dishing hot sauce into Benjamin's tea. This was particularly embarrassing for him, she continued, when the second time gave him a shocking case of diarrhoea during a very important face-to-face meeting with the company directors, marking both his card with his employers and his trousers. Rosie couldn't help but giggle at the visual of Benjamin shitting his pants while trying to act aloof. Good ol' Audrey.

Rosie responded quickly, as a few small dishes were placed on their table by Sylvan: bread, olives, mozzarella balls and garlic cloves in olive oil. She noticed that Fox dug in greedily. As the smells rose towards her, she typed faster, informing Audrey of her current situation and asking her to contact Mrs Winthorpe-Smythe as a matter of urgency to inform her of the situation. She also remembered to tell her that Mrs Winthorpe-Smythe was skiing, and not caring for her convalescent sister.

The final email was from Wanderlust Wishes HR Department, requesting that on her return from Venice, she travel to head office for a meeting. They had set a time and date for 29 December. What a great post-Christmas bonus, Rosie thought.

Tears threatened, so she took another gulp of her wine. She loved her job. It brought her joy and comfort and gave her a life she was accustomed to. She couldn't let Benjamin take it all away from her. A tear escaped and rolled down her cheek and to hide it she took another large gulp. She sniffed deeply and felt Fox's eyes on her. She didn't want to cry in front of a stranger, let alone a tall, handsome and moody one. She accepted the meeting invitation, closed her email and slid the phone across the table towards Fox. She then rummaged in one of the deep inside pockets of her coat as a delay tactic for her to get control of her emotions, her eyes cast down as she pulled out Fox's driving licence and slid that across the table too. She had noted his details down onto a hotel notepad in her room earlier.

'Thank you,' she said, a slight crack in her voice.

She didn't look at him. Instead, she focused on the tapas-style dishes in front of her, picking up a piece of bread and tearing it into little pieces on her napkin. Sylvan appeared again and topped up both of their wine glasses, with Fox thanking him. Rosie stayed silent, not trusting herself.

'Rosie, are you all right?'

'I'm fine,' she said, grabbing another piece of bread and tearing that into tiny pieces. She now had a mound gathering in front of her.

'Are you sure? You're ripping into that bread like it has personally offended you.'

Rosie dropped the rest of the bread onto her side plate and brushed the crumbs from her fingers. She exhaled, but it sounded part-whine, part-sob.

'It's OK, we don't need to talk. Actually, I'm quite happy not talking, if I'm honest . . .' He tailed off, taking his own chunk of bread and dipping it in the olive oil.

'In a nutshell,' Rosie began, finally meeting his gaze, 'my boss and I made out at the Christmas work party — my first mistake. In my defence, I was very drunk and lonely, and he is a man with no moral compass and a penchant for anything in a skirt. Then, I got blackmailed into a work assignment abroad and agreed to it with no prior experience — a second major mistake.' She held up two fingers to show she was counting and took a large gulp of wine. 'Then I sent the same male boss a naked bath selfie, which was, again, a huge mistake. Not because I regretted sending it, but because I meant to send it, in a totally nonsexual way, to my best friend. Not my boss.' A third finger went up. 'Then I got suspended for workplace sexual harassment because of said boss being pissed off that I wouldn't sleep with him; another mistake.'

Her words jumbled out quickly and without thought.

'And then I lost my favourite backpack to the Venetian depths, along with my identity, important documents and phone. All because an old women toppled on me on a gondola; even though she'd warned me that she feared the water. Even though we'd nearly fallen into the water a day earlier.' She sighed. 'I should have listened, which, in hindsight, was—'

'A huge mistake,' Fox finished for her, repeating her phrase back at her. 'It sounds like you've not had the best week.'

'You could say that,' she said, rolling her eyes and leaning into the booth, resting her head back.

The bottles hanging from the ceiling glistened and sparkled in the candlelight from the diners' tables. They also appeared to have multiplied since she last looked. Weird.

'It also sounds like your boss is a bit of a prick and that you were clearly taken advantage of.' He shrugged as if it were as simple as that, a black-and-white conundrum with a simple answer.

'You could also say that, but that still doesn't change the fact that I am currently suspended and I am effectively a nomad.' She tried an olive and realised it tasted earthy, salty and simply delicious. 'That's until you come in, hopefully. You're my . . .' She paused to think before exclaiming, 'POOH!'

'POOH?' he said, looking around to see if anyone else was listening.

'POOH!' she repeated. 'My Passport Out of Here!' She giggled, finding herself hilarious.

'Ah, I see,' he said, smiling. 'Very funny. But perhaps just call me Fox.'

Sylvan appeared with a selection of pasta dishes with serving spoons, all steaming, a mix of tomato-based and creamy recipes, piled high with clams, prawns, mince and a selection of salads. The amount could feed the entire restaurant and she couldn't wait to dig in.

Sylvan placed a bowl in front of each of them and left them to it, with Fox graciously serving her first. She pointed at two dishes and he gave her a helping of each before serving himself. She took a bite and moaned; it was delicious. They both ate in silence for a few minutes, savouring the food and washing it down with sips of wine. Rosie's head was spinning a little, but it was nice to feel a little light-headed and not carry the weight of the world on her shoulders.

Their silence was interrupted by the sound of Fox's phone ringing, its vibrations causing it to tremble across the table between them, face up. Rosie noticed the blue screen displaying the caller. It said Gabrielle and the profile picture was of a beautiful dark-haired woman standing onstage holding three huge bouquets of flowers and blowing a kiss into what Rosie assumed was the audience. It looked oddly familiar.

Fox paused from eating and looked at the phone. Sighing, he answered it, speaking in fluent Italian, his forehead creasing again and his tone indicating frustration. Rosie tried to distract herself with the food, so as not to show she was listening, but without a phone to scroll or a bag to rifle through, she was left with sprinkling parmesan onto her already cheese-covered pasta.

The call continued for a few more minutes, enough time for Rosie to down the contents of her glass, and then the call appeared to end abruptly, with Fox putting the phone back into his pocket rather than on the table. Without comment, he continued eating from his plate, his eyes down.

'Throwing it back, are you OK?' Rosie asked.

'I'm fine,' Fox replied curtly with a cursory smile.

'I couldn't help but see the caller ID. Is that Alessia's Gabriella? As in whose room I'm sleeping in tonight?'

Fox said nothing, but after a pause, he nodded.

'Is she a singer or in a band?' Rosie prodded, the wine giving her a confidence she didn't normally have. He gave her a look, so she quickly followed it up with a nonchalant shrug. 'It's just that I noticed all the trophies in her room, so I assumed she'd made a career of it.'

This seemed to placate him and he nodded.

'She's an opera singer, actually. An extremely talented one, too. I watched her perform on Saturday night, the night before you and I ran into one another. Literally.'

Shapes began to fall into place in her memory like a virtual game of Tetris. An opera singer, in Venice, on Saturday night . . .

'Where did she perform?' Rosie asked.

'At the Teatro La Fenice. It's a beautiful building, actually. The architecture is awesome.'

'I know, I was there,' Rosie said quietly, blushing, but she wasn't sure why.

'You were there on Saturday night? This Saturday night just gone?'

Fox looked shocked, but then so would she if she found the person who assaulted her in the street was also stalking her the night before.

'Yep. Booked on my behalf for our travelling group. I had no input.' She crossed her hands to emphasise her point and continued, 'But we did have front-row seats. She was phenomenal.' Rosie thought back to the singer onstage, her graceful presence, her voice, the way she blushed when applauded, how she seemed to direct her attention to one person in the audience . . . 'Wait, if you were there, did she wave to you at the end of the night? From the stage?'

Fox looked uncomfortable and cleared his throat. 'Possibly. But it was a packed auditorium, so it could have been anyone, really . . .' He tailed off and focused on the remnants on his plate, pushing pieces of pasta around like he were sifting for gold.

Rosie could sense there was a tome of a background story there, but she was a stranger to him, so she didn't question him further. They continued eating in silence until she could eat no more. She leant back into her booth to stretch out her stomach. Italy had not been kind to her waistline.

She watched as a group of four men arrived, clearly part of a band, and began setting up their instruments in the far corner of the restaurant. Sylvan appeared as if from nowhere to clear their plates and she thanked him gratefully. Moments later, a selection of desserts was laid out between them, with Rosie recognising most as typical Italian desserts. Tiramisu, panna cotta, figs in honey and a selection of biscotti. He then placed a bottle of grappa in the centre of their booth with two shot glasses.

'*Saluti!*' he shouted, as other voices chimed in.

Fox poured a shot into each glass and tapped his against hers. '*Saluti.*'

'To past mistakes,' Rosie said, downing the contents of the glass in one.

It burnt her throat with an intensity that made her eyes water. She watched through glassy eyes as he topped up both of their glasses and held his aloft.

'And past relationships,' he said, tipping his head back and swallowing it in one go.

She mirrored his actions and squeezed her eyes shut tight as the burning made its way down to her stomach. She wanted to ask more questions but didn't. Instead, she tapped her glass for a top-up, to which he duly complied. This time, she made the toast.

'To random strangers who knock you off your feet . . .'

With this, he laughed – a proper chortle – and continued the toast.

'And to random evenings involving a manger, a stable and a stranger visiting a new city in need of a bed for the night.'

His eyes glinted and they both laughed, clinking glasses and downing their third shot in a matter of minutes.

'Cheers!' Rosie said, plonking her glass on the table upside down.

The desserts looked delicious and she picked up a spoon to dive in.

Chapter Thirty-six

The rest of the evening passed in a hazy, drunken blur. Rosie remembered drinking more shots at some point and finding that her feet were itching to dance. The band encouraged it and at one point, Fox disappeared, only to be found playing a guitar with the band and singing along in Italian. He had a beautiful voice, she noticed, and lit up when he played. She danced with random waiters and hugged passers-by. At some point, the restaurant had emptied out, and both she and Fox found themselves drinking with Sylvan, his wife, the waiting staff and the band. Time seemed to fade and whether it was minutes or hours passing, she really couldn't tell. Or care.

Once Sylvan and Georgiana had effectively thrown them out, Fox and Rosie found themselves wandering the almost-empty streets, their tiredness evaporating with the cold air and their bodies remaining warm from the drink.

They walked without purpose, rambling through the city streets, hopping on and off the yellow wooden trams that whizzed them around the city with abandon. Fox's lips loosened as the alcohol coursed around his body. He shared stories about his childhood, growing up in the countryside, isolated with just his two brothers, parents and grandparents. He talked of how his parents feared the city life, preferring to stay close to their little hamlet, choosing familiarity over travel and the mundane over excitement. But Fox had always had itchy feet, even from a young age, when he used to hike up the tallest hill in their district and look out far into the distance, wishing he could just pack up and leave.

'My favourite book was *The Hobbit*,' he said as they hopped off a tram and found themselves meandering the narrow streets, walking without purpose. 'I wanted to pack a bag and just travel the world. I felt trapped. Bilbo Baggins inspired me.'

'Who?' Rosie asked, finding a lamp post and swinging around it drunkenly, imagining she was Gene Kelly in *Singin' in the Rain*.

'Bilbo Baggins! The main character from *The Hobbit!*' he exclaimed.

'Wow,' Rosie said, stopping her swinging and looking at him.

'I know, right?'

'No, I mean, wow. You really are a total geek!'

She started laughing and he looked affronted before laughing himself.

'Nothing wrong with being a geek. All the best people are.'

He shrugged and looked up at a signpost above his head. His face broke into a grin and he grabbed her hand and pulled her along behind for a few paces until he stopped abruptly and she barrelled into him drunkenly.

'Hey!' she said, finding her feet. 'What's that all about?'

She looked down to see he was still holding her hand. It felt nice. Her hand fitted like a jigsaw piece into his. He looked at her, their eyes meeting.

'Turn around,' he said, nodding over her head.

Rosie turned and gasped. In front of them was a large open area bathed in darkness.

It was similar in design and shape to St Mark's Square, complete with a huge Christmas tree that stood proud in front of them. It was unlit owing to the late hour, but it was easy to imagine its beauty when illuminated. Behind it stood an enormous and spectacular cathedral, its many spires pointing up towards the heavens, its gothic architecture contrasting vividly against the buildings that it dwarfed.

'What building is that?' She took a few steps towards the square, still holding his hand.

'It's the Duomo di Milano,' Fox said, walking beside her.

Even in the darkness, the building was a spectacular structure, the moonlight casting it in its own starry spotlight on the many spires and impressive statues.

'The Cathedral of Milan.' Fox gazed up at it in wonder. 'Built in the thirteenth century, it took approximately six hundred years to construct and is one of the largest cathedrals in the whole of Europe.'

They walked towards the multiple doors to the cathedral, looking skywards at the stained-glass windows that no doubt transformed into a spectacular light display in the sunshine. Now, though, the windows were dark and the cathedral quiet. But Rosie didn't mind. They were only two people around, and she felt in awe of the beauty and atmosphere that emanated from the building.

'Wow,' was Rosie's response, which seemed far too small a word for such a momentous building.

They walked up towards the cathedral and turned to the right to walk parallel with it. Neither spoke – both just took in the detailed carvings and design, still holding hands, until finally they passed it and headed back into the sights of the city streets, which Rosie had come to expect of any European city. Their conversation picked up again and they fell into a natural rhythm, walking and talking, with no destination in mind.

Without realising, they found themselves approaching the central train station and Rosie was delighted to have found a building she recognised. Rosie was both incredibly drunk and incredibly tired, but she felt free. And she realised with an intoxicated jolt that she hadn't felt that way in a long time. Hazily looking at the ring on her finger, she nodded, pulling Fox by the hand towards the nearest counter. She had lived her entire life in a radius of only fifty miles and, like a bird learning to fly, it was time for her to soar.

Chapter Thirty-seven

Rosie opened one eye and then immediately closed it. The sunlight was painfully bright. She moaned and tried to adjust her position but found that her whole body ached as if she had slept on a hard surface all night. Noise began to infiltrate her exposed ear and she could hear an intercom blasting out Italian alongside various sounds that reminded Rosie of a doorbell. It was cold, a little breezy, and it smelt like grime and dirty bins.

Something was digging into her back and when she raised an arm to try to move it, she found herself touching not a comfy pillow or a squished duvet, but instead what felt like crackly dry newspaper.

'Rosie? Can you hear me?'

Rosie tried to answer, but her mouth felt like it was full of sand and only a grunt escaped her lips. *What on earth is going on?* She rolled onto her back and tried opening her eyes again. She found herself staring at an unfamiliar high ceiling divided into rows of glass compartments, with a blinding white sky above.

The side of her face ached. A cold wind was blowing around her and she shivered. Was she on the floor? Or a bench? Where was she?

The notion of lying on some dirty, bacteria-infested public floor somewhere was enough to rouse her. She tried to sit up but only managed to make it onto her elbows before a headache ripped across her forehead as if it were caught in a vice that was being slowly tightened.

'Take your time.'

A familiar male voice spoke to her from close by and then she felt unwanted hands sliding under her armpits and lifting her upright into a seating position with surprising ease. Nausea pulsated over her and she closed her eyes again just as a hot styrofoam cup was pressed into her hand. Taking a deep in-breath, she jumped as a loud whistle blew, almost perforating her eardrums, and she opened her eyes in shock. Fox was kneeling on the floor in front of her and she quickly took in her surroundings, horrified.

She was sitting on a cold, metal bench in a busy train station, people walking with purpose, some dragging pull-along suit-cases, or lugging bags and pushing prams with sleeping babies inside. The shiny floor beneath her feet was a long concourse elongated by black-and-white stripes, with a large ticket office to her left and a row of what looked like shops and places to eat. There were multiple yellow and black boards detailing train information and numbered boxes for platforms. It was noisy, chaotic – far too much for her to deal with. She had absolutely no idea where she was or how she'd got there. She tried to stand, but her legs were weak and the soles of her feet were sore, yet she had no idea why. She drew her eyes back to Fox.

'Where are we?' she whispered, her voice cracked and quiet.

Fox looked pained and just as he went to speak, another whistle sounded and the chugging of a train pulling away from the station became evident. He stood up, wincing as he looked up at one of the many information boards. Rosie tried to take a sip of coffee, but the hot, bitter liquid touching her tongue was too harsh and she almost gagged. She took a few deep breaths to try to loosen her tightening throat.

'Fox, where are we?' she whispered again, feeling both disorientated and now a bit frightened.

Fox turned to look at her and then joined her on the metal bench, moving the rolled-up newspaper from behind her. So that was what was digging into her back, then. He sighed, stood up again and turned towards a sign.

'We are in Firenze Santa Maria Novella.'

She turned to looked up at him and took in his pained face, red-rimmed eyes and the slightly greenish tinge to his pale skin.

He looked like she felt. Someone bumped into him, rushing towards a platform, and he had to steady himself.

'And is that part of the Milan Central Station?' she asked, looking around for a familiar sight from when she arrived yesterday.

But everything appeared new to her. This station appeared smaller and with a more modern appearance, holding no resemblance to the Milan train station.

Fox shook his head sadly.

Panic started to rise like a roaring fire from her feet upwards and she could feel a cold sweat coming on. She was lost.

'Then a station near Milan?'

Fox shook his head again. He cleared his throat before saying quietly, 'Not quite. A train station in Florence.'

Rosie paused, her hung-over state meaning information trickled through like amber running down a tree trunk. She put a hand to her forehead and massaged it.

'Sorry, Florence? Like Florence, Tuscany? Like nowhere near Milan?'

Fox shrugged, looking hopeless, running his fingers through his thick and now very messy curls as he looked around him in shock.

'I don't even remember how we got here. Do you?' asked Fox.

Rosie tried to think back to last night. The memories were blurry, like looking out of a car window in torrential rain; none of the hazy images clarified anything.

'I really don't,' she said. 'How much did we drink last night?'

'Clearly, too much.'

He looked dishevelled, like he'd slept in his clothes, which, she realised a moment later, he had. She looked down at her own clothes, noting that her jeans were covered in mud and what looked like oil stains. She reached around for her phone, remembering with a jolt that she had nothing on her – no phone, no purse, no money.

'What time is it?' she asked.

'Just after midday,' he said, pointing to a large square clock hung on the wall behind him.

'Lunchtime? How can that be?' Where had the hours gone?

'Well, according to the ticket in my pocket, we ended up on a train this morning at 5.15am.'

Rosie couldn't believe it. Did they walk around Milan city for hours? What time did they leave the restaurant? It was all a blur. He held out the ticket to show her and she noticed the date first.

'Wait! My passport! We need to get back to Milan. Now. I fly home tomorrow.'

She knew she was wailing, but she felt horrified. Not only was she now at risk of missing her flight, but she was also at risk of not getting replacement travel documents. She tried to stand, but as she did so, a wave of bile rose in her throat and she turned to her left and violently threw up in the open litter bin beside the bench. She could feel Fox rubbing her back whilst she heaved but had to wait until the heaving stopped before she thanked him. She collapsed back onto the bench and wiped her mouth with the sleeve of her coat.

'Sorry,' she muttered, not daring to make eye contact with Fox. She felt wretched.

'Don't worry at all,' he said, clearing his throat. 'I've seen worse.'

She took some deep breaths, trying to regain some composure before she asked in a painful, hoarse whisper.

'When is the next train back?'

Fox was silent. The silence was ominous and caused enough concern that Rosie dragged her eyes up to look up at him. He cleared his throat.

'The next train is hopefully scheduled to leave at quarter past two.'

'Okay, let's catch that one, then.' Rosie answered, ever hopeful. But his face winced as if in pain.

'But it won't get us into Milan until after five. Which is after the consulate has closed. And it doesn't open again until after Christmas.'

She put her head in her hands, wanting to cry but feeling so dehydrated that her tear ducts were bone dry. Questions swarmed around her mind like hundreds of DNA strands swirling inside her brain.

'Can I use your phone just for a second, please?' she croaked.

'I would normally say yes, but it has gone completely flat. I managed to make a couple of phone calls about twenty minutes ago and that appeared to drain whatever battery life remained.'

Rosie groaned. She felt truly awful. Physically and emotionally.

'So,' Fox said, trying to lighten the mood by smiling but then wincing as if it hurt. 'Do you want the good news, the relatively bad news or the very bad news?'

'Surprise me,' she said, attempting the coffee again, which, now cooled, seemed a little more palatable.

'OK, so let's start with the relatively bad.' He clapped his hands as if he were about to put on a show. 'There was a train that could have got us to Milan in time, but we just missed it. By about fifteen minutes. And the next couple of trains have been delayed due to a fallen tree branch on the line.'

Rosie's face must have looked horrified, as Fox quickly clapped his hands together and continued, not wanting to break his flow.

'The very bad news is that we clearly won't make it back to the embassy today, not without some sort of transportation to take us. All the airport cars have been rented due to the delays and the coach takes about five hours, which again puts us way past closing time at the embassy.'

'Are you actually kidding me?' Rosie interrupted, feeling very sick.

'Ah, but let me finish,' he said, and her last thread of hope ignited, assuming he was now going to deliver the good news. 'After today, the embassy closes for the Christmas holidays and doesn't reopen until Monday, 29 December. So, you're effectively now stuck in Italy for Christmas.'

Rosie's thread of hope extinguished in a single puff and she felt exasperated. 'Was that meant to be the good news?'

'Oh no, that was a continuation of the very bad news. The good news,' he said, checking the clock behind him again and smiling, 'is that my sister happens to live in Florence and just before my phone died, I made a quick phone call to her, explaining the pickle we had got ourselves into, and she very kindly agreed to host us both for Christmas. So, silver linings, eh? She's on her way to meet us now. She should be here any minute.'

He looked almost cheerful, but all she could feel was desperation.

'I'm really stuck here for Christmas? In Italy?'

Her voice was barely audible, her energy leaving her body like air escaping from a balloon. She felt overwhelmed. Weak. Vulnerable.

She tried to stand up, to escape the train station, to escape her situation. But as she went to take a step to run, her vision swam and she found herself falling to the ground, her whole world going black.

Chapter Thirty-eight

For the second time that day, Rosie opened her eyes, having no idea where she was. She tried to move, but her body felt heavy, as if it were full of cement.

'She's awake!'

Rosie recognised that voice – it was Fox.

She opened her eyes gingerly and found Fox's face directly over hers, his concern evident. He then proceeded to speak in Italian to other bodies in the room and everything came flooding back. Florence, the embassy, Christmas. Fox turned back to her and helped her to sit up, thrusting an Italian brand of chocolate bar into her hands.

'Eat,' he instructed, and her stomach rumbled at the sugary treat.

She didn't need telling twice, ripping into the chocolate bar and taking a big bite. It tasted amazing and she quickly devoured the whole thing. Looking around the room, she noticed she was in a first-aid room and was lying on a medical bed. There was a desk ahead of her with a man seated and writing, clearly listening to Fox as he reeled off what she assumed was her reason for fainting.

Seconds later, the door opened and a beautiful woman walked in, her long amber hair cascading down her back and past her shoulders. It was very thick and shiny, like she'd just come straight from a glossy hair advert. But it was her face that Rosie couldn't help but stare at. Her eyes were almost olive in colour, with thick bushy eyebrows and cheekbones that were high and soft. There was a blush to her cheeks that indicated health and outdoor living, and her entire face was etched with freckles. Her lips were plump but naked and Rosie noted that she appeared to be free of make-up.

The woman strode over to Fox and hugged him with the ferocity that made Rosie assume she was his sister. And standing together, she could see a similarity not just in colouring, but in their facial structure and attractiveness. Fox turned to Rosie and she blushed, realising she had been staring at them both.

'Rosie, meet Tabitha. Tabitha, this is Rosie.' Fox introduced them and looked at his sister fondly.

'Nice to meet you, Rosie,' she said, smiling warmly. 'Sorry to hear of your troubles, though. Fox told me about them on the phone. And I hear, owing to his pure idiocy, that you are now forced to spend your Christmas with his ugly arse!'

Fox punched her in the arm affectionately.

'Which seems like the ultimate punishment for any woman.'

That earnt her a sibling headlock, with Fox running his knuckles over her head. She pushed him off her and he let go, laughing. Rosie couldn't believe the change in him, from moody and dismissive, to affectionate and playful.

'It wasn't Fox's fault,' Rosie replied. 'He didn't push my backpack into the canal or force me onto a train to come here. If anything, he found me a place to stay for the night and made sure I was fed and cared for. If it wasn't for him, I'd probably be crying in a ditch right now.'

Fox's eyebrows rose at the unexpected praise and he shot a look to Tabitha that said, *See?*

'Well, that does sound pretty gallant of him,' she said, glancing his way.

The first-aider cleared his throat and Fox spoke a couple of sentences in Italian before turning back to Rosie.

'He's asking if you need an ambulance or transportation to see a medic. I informed him that we would take care of you, but he needs your acknowledgement, too.'

Rosie nodded in the medic's direction and held up a thumb to show that she was fine. She tried standing and found that she was less shaky now she had eaten.

'If you feel well enough, we can make a move to mine, if you like?' Tabitha said. 'It's not huge and you'll have to put up with my boys running you ragged, but it's cosy. The apartment has hot water for at least three hours of the day, and if you don't mind creaking pipes and a shared bathroom, then you'll fit right in.'

'Sounds perfect,' Rosie said, warming to Tabitha, 'but I'll chip in and help in any way I can. I know I can't pay towards anything, but I'm a good cook and I'm extremely tidy.'

'Then you'll stick out like a sore thumb,' Tabitha said, laughing. 'We're messy and consider a plate of pasta with grated cheese a delicacy, so I may take you up on that offer.'

They all laughed and with Fox's hand on her elbow in case she fainted again, they made their way out of the station.

'So, we need the red line to Batoni,' Tabitha said as they waited for the next tram.

The sun had risen high into the sky by this point and Rosie had time to take in the picturesque town.

'The trams are so awesome here. They are clean, cheap and always run on time. We had planned to buy a second-hand car when we moved here two years ago but found that we just didn't need one with such an efficient public tram service.' Tabitha pointed at the incoming tram, indicating that it was theirs to catch. 'Otherwise, I would have offered it to you to drive back to Milan.'

'Wow, that's very kind of you,' Rosie said, 'and trusting! But without any documentation or ID, I wouldn't want to drive anyway.'

'Fox, what about hiring a car and you driving back?'

'I did try at the train station, but they were all out. Plus, even if I did manage to get a car and Rosie stayed at my place, she'd be alone for Christmas as I'd be here. And the embassy would still be closed.' He shrugged. 'I feel so terrible. I don't even know why we came here.' He pushed his fingers through his thick hair, some of the smaller curls springing back into place.

'I do,' Tabitha said, turning to Rosie. 'Don't you remember calling me in the early hours?'

'I called you?' Rosie said, looking over at Fox, who looked equally confused.

'Well, the call came from Fox's phone,' Tabitha said as the tram came to a stop beside them, 'but it was actually Rosie who called me.' She smiled at Rosie before she turned and quickly hopped aboard, leaving both Fox and Rosie staring at her in total shock.

'I called you?'

'Yup,' Tabitha said as the three of them took a seat and the tram sped up along its line. 'You're a fun drunk, actually. You rattled on about the importance of family and how Fox was lucky to have you . . .' Tabitha looked over at Fox and he rolled his eyes. 'You then talked about the importance of creating traditions and lasting memories, blah, blah, blah, and then the next thing I know, my big brother comes on the line saying he's turned up a day early and has brought along a guest. I put two and two together and made up the sofa bed.'

'Do you remember me doing that?' Rosie turned to Fox, who shook his head and shrugged his shoulders to indicate no.

'I do remember talking about Tabitha and the kids, and showing you photos on my phone, though.'

'Aw, you do love me!' Tabitha teased, earning a punch in the arm from him.

'Oh, Fox. I'm really sorry. And, Tabitha, I would never normally impose on anyone, let alone a total stranger.' She placed her head on the metal handrail in front of her. 'I am mortified.'

'Aw, don't be!' Tabitha said, rubbing Rosie's forearm kindly. 'It's nice to know Fox is finally having some fun after the whole Gabriella debacle.'

This earnt her a hard stare from Fox and she shut her mouth tight, her lips narrowing into thin lines. Rosie looked over at Fox in the seat next to her but found him staring at his feet. She didn't pursue the conversation further.

'Well, please let me repay the favour in any way I can. Washing, drying, cleaning, let me make it up to you.'

'Rosie, chill,' Tabitha said. 'I run an open-house policy – my husband is a reverend. We have visitors all the time. I don't like a quiet house. Our sofa bed is like a revolving door. It's forever being closed and reopened with visitors, expected and' – she pointed to Rosie – 'unexpected.'

Rosie looked to Fox, who was nodding. 'It's mayhem. But great fun.'

'And it's home,' Tabitha said, indicating that their stop was coming up and standing up in readiness.

Rosie smiled, excited at the prospect of being part of a home, a real home. Full of laughing children, chaos and family. Aside from Bee's family, she hadn't felt part of a family since her parents died. She might not make it home for Christmas, but at least she would get to experience it surrounded by love.

Chapter Thirty-nine

Tabitha was being modest when she said her place was cosy. After navigating four flights of stairs, Rosie was welcomed into a large hallway that could accommodate the many little pairs of shoes and multiple coats hung from named hooks. The flooring was wooden and the walls painted yellow, with photographs lining the wall haphazardly, like a portrait gallery, showing a timeline of a growing family.

Tabitha yelled, 'Boys! We're home!'

There was a thunderous sound of little feet charging towards them and from one of the many doors to the left came a tornado of four boys, all under the age of five, tumbling towards them. They ran at Tabitha, who with the skill of a professional acrobat managed to catch all four of them in one large hug, their bodies leaving the ground with a squeal of delight. Then one of them noticed Fox.

'Uncle Fox! Look, it's Uncle Fox!' The eldest boy broke free from Tabitha and jumped into the open arms of Fox, bypassing Rosie altogether.

She took a step back into the shadows, not wanting to impose on a family reunion. The other children dropped from their mother and joined in with the giant hug, with Fox blowing raspberries on their faces and tickling them one by one. Giggles burst from their little faces. Rosie felt unsettlingly attracted to him, seeing how good he was as an uncle.

The boys broke off when they noticed her presence.

'Who's that, Uncle Fox?' the eldest stage-whispered, staring at her nervously.

'Oh, sorry, boys,' Fox said, standing up. 'This is my friend, Rosie. She's here to spend Christmas with us.'

Rosie smiled at them, surprised at how much she wanted them to like her.

'Hi, boys, it's lovely to meet you all.'

She knew from experience with Bee's twins that you take it slow and let them warm to you instead of pushing to be friends, so she simply gave them a little wave.

'Hi, Rosie,' the eldest said, his face uncertain. 'Uncle Fox, is this your new girlfriend?'

Tabitha snorted and Fox glared at her before responding to his nephew.

'No, Teddy, Rosie is just a friend, nothing more. But she's a bit sad as she can't make it home for Christmas, so we are all going to celebrate together. Sound good?'

The boy nodded before grabbing a notepad and a pen from the narrow hallway sideboard and offering it to her, his palm flat. His expression was serious and he indicated for her to take it.

'For me?' she said and removed it from his hand. 'Do you want me to draw a picture of something?'

But he shook his head seriously.

'No, if we're quick, we might just catch him,' he said, and his younger brothers nodded solemnly.

'Catch who?' Rosie asked.

'Father Christmas, of course! Before tomorrow. It's vital. We have to tell him where you are, otherwise he won't deliver any presents to you.'

All three little heads nodded, their eyes wide.

A moment of tension passed between the adults. Rosie looked across at Fox, their eyes connecting, and she knew what she needed to do. She looked back at the little boys, changing her expression to one of theatrical concern.

'Well then, let's get writing!' She pretended to check her wristwatch. 'It's almost one hair past a freckle. The presents are probably being loaded into the sleigh as we speak! We don't have a moment to lose!'

'It's OK. Come with me,' the eldest said.

And before she knew what was happening, Rosie was being pulled along by three pairs of small hands and led away. Looking back at Fox, she saw he was smiling and for reasons unknown, she felt her heart leap a little. Without thinking, she winked at him and watched his face change to surprise. Her stomach dropped. She'd taken it too far, she'd stepped over the line, she'd . . .

Fox winked back at her, his green eyes scanning her face, and a frisson of sexual tension passed between them. But before she could delve into the meaning of the wink, she was dragged into a large kitchen and pulled towards the dining table.

'Sit, concentrate,' the eldest said. 'We've got work to do.'

Chapter Forty

A few hours later, Rosie was yawning almost on repeat. The antics from the night before, plus sleeping on a public bench, were beginning to take their toll. What she really wanted was to close her eyes and sleep.

She had spent the afternoon playing with Tabitha's boys, who she now knew as Teddy, Albie and George. She had also met Lewis, Tabitha's husband, who was one of the nicest men she had ever met. He was warm, he listened to her sorry tale and he generously told her that they would be honoured to have her spend Christmas with them.

They were seated at a heavy oak dining table that sat proud in one end of the living room and had just finished a huge vat of *pasta al pesto* with slabs of buttery garlic bread. Even the children were quiet, caught in a carbohydrate coma, and Rosie stifled another yawn-burp.

Lewis, who was grabbing another bottle of red wine from the kitchen, popped his head through the small hatch built into the wall between the kitchen and living room.

'Rosie, how rude of us. Is there anyone you would like to call or email? You're more than welcome to use my office.'

Rosie gratefully accepted, suddenly aware that Bee and Audrey were probably fraught with worry. She hadn't even thought to let them know she was safe. She let Lewis lead her to his study, a small room full of shelves, books and a huge desk that faced the door and had an office chair on wheels tucked neatly under it.

Lewis pulled out the chair and encouraged her to sit, signing in to his computer and watching as his large screen filled with a family photo of them all beside an entrance to a very pretty church. He left her alone and once the door was safely closed behind him, she picked up the phone.

Bee didn't give her a moment to speak.

'Rosie, finally! Thank goodness! Do you know how worried we've all been about you? Are you OK? Tell me you're not hurt?' Her tone was urgent and she spoke quickly, her questions rolling over one another to come out.

'I'm totally fine,' Rosie said. 'I'm safe and well. I just haven't been able to get a replacement phone yet or been near enough to one to make a call. I'm sorry I've worried you, but I promise I'm fine.'

She heard Bee take a deep breath before continuing.

'Rosie, I love you dearly, but if you make me panic like that again, I will disown you, OK?'

'OK,' Rosie said, smiling.

'And on top of that, I'll tell Jonah never to let you near another one of his famous cookies ever again, agreed?'

'Wow, you mean business,' Rosie replied.

'Agreed?' Bee repeated sternly.

'Agreed,' Rosie said, chuckling. 'Am I forgiven?'

A pause.

'Yes, OK.'

'So, tell me. Are you guys all OK?'

'Oh, we're all fine,' Bee said dismissively, 'but that's not important. Now I know that you're not lying face down in a ditch somewhere, I can move on to more pressing matters.' Rosie heard her moving away from the sound of the children before continuing, 'Are you near a computer?'

'I am, actually,' she said, touching the mouse and watching the cursor move around the screen. 'Why?'

'Audrey told me that you intended to respond to Benjamin's email on Saturday night, stating that it had been sent in error and that he was not the intended recipient,' Bee continued, ignoring her question completely. 'Did you do that? Did you send an email before receiving one from him about the complaint? Did you?' She was almost panting, her questions coming quick and fast.

'Yes, I did,' Rosie answered. 'That same night, actually. I was mortified. Can you imagine the embarrassment—'

'No time for emotions right now,' Bee said, interrupting. 'Seriously, there's no time. Can you log in to your email and forward me that reply to him, proving it was sent by mistake? And forward it to Audrey – that might be quicker. But do it now.'

'Er, OK,' Rosie said, placing the receiver between her shoulder and ear as she logged in and searched through her sent items. Bee was unusually silent while she waited and after a few moments, Rosie spoke again. 'Sent. To both of you.'

Bee didn't respond, but Rosie knew she was near her own laptop, as she could hear Bee typing hard on the keys, her long nails tap-tapping away. Rosie took the opportunity to read back through her response, thinking how long ago it felt, when in fact, it was only a few days. Reading her own words, she could see that there was no chance she could be misconstrued:

From: RosieARedbrush@rosesarered1999.com
Sent: Saturday, 20 December 2024, 10:34:25 PM
Subject: RE: Look at me!

Dear Benjamin,

That selfie was sent to you in error. Please let it be known that I would neither want to encourage nor excite you by sending photographs that may be misconstrued as a come-on.

When typing out my best friend's name, I accidentally selected yours from the drop-down box owing to the fact your name is similar to hers. The intention of the selfie was to show her my hotel room. Nothing more. Please delete the photo. Our little dalliance at the work Christmas party was a drunken mistake, nothing more. Going forwards, my thoughts towards you will remain purely professional.

Rosie

'Awesome,' Bee said, her tone relaxing. 'That's just what we need.'

Bee exhaled dramatically and Rosie could hear her tapping away again, but this time the sounds were similar to a text being written on her mobile phone.

'Do you want to tell me what's going on?' Rosie said, feeling so out of the loop.

'Not yet. First, we talk specifics. Where are you? Who are you with? Why didn't you fly home with the group and, most importantly, are you safe?'

'I'm in Florence, I'm with Fox, but not alone. I'm staying with his sister and family. I couldn't fly home as I still haven't been issued with a valid passport and yes, I feel very safe.'

There, details provided.

'Who the heck is Fox?' Bee wailed. 'Is that a man? And what the heck are you doing in Florence? Rosie, tell me everything.'

And so with a big intake of breath, Rosie proceeded to tell her everything since she'd left Venice. She included the consulate, the nativity, the restaurant, the walk to the train station . . . everything. When she found herself up to date, she stopped. There was a pause on the line and Rosie wondered if perhaps the call had disconnected.

'Hello?'

'Rosie. This is . . . unbelievable! I actually can't believe this!'

Bee sounded both surprised, concerned and a little in awe of what Rosie had faced over the last few days.

'You convinced a total stranger to take you under his wing, find lodgings for you, prove his identity so that you were never in any risk, feed you, then invite you to stay with his family for Christmas . . . all over the course of a few days . . . Rosie, who are you?'

'Well, it wasn't exactly like that,' Rosie began, but Bee didn't give her a chance to reply.

'See?' Bee told Rosie over the sound of the children's teatime, which was audible in the background. 'You're living! You're out there, exploring the world and experiencing new things!'

'Not always by choice,' Rosie tried to argue as she twizzled the ring engraved with the world around and around her finger. 'This wouldn't have happened if I hadn't made the mistake of not protecting my backpack.'

'Some of the best decisions are made from the biggest mistakes,' Bee said wisely, reminding Rosie of her mother. 'Enjoy this. And enjoy him! He sounds like a total dreamboat,' Bee continued before shushing down the phone to her children, who had clearly found her hiding space. 'However, dreamboat or not, let me know the full address, including postal code, of where you are currently staying. I want his full name and national security number, and the number you are calling from. Just, you know, in case my best friend goes off grid again and I lose my shit at the passport office for a second time, demanding they send in the military to find you. You know,' she repeated, 'just in case . . .'

Rosie laughed. It was nice speaking to Bee, it felt normal. Like she wasn't thousands of miles away. She noticed a stack of Lewis's business cards beside the large computer screen and quickly provided the details. She also gave details of the consulate in Milan, stating that Fox was an employee there. She decided against telling Bee about the Santa race in Venice and bumping into him there. She didn't think Bee could cope with any more surprising tales today.

They chatted briefly about Christmas, the children and how Bee's dreaded in-laws had finally arrived, before Bee's landline rang in the background.

'Shit, that's Audrey. Rosie, ring Audrey, will you? I can give you her mobile number if you've forgotten it. She needs to talk to you.'

Assuming it was work-related, Rosie agreed, taking note of Bee's number, along with Audrey's, on actual paper with an actual pen. The events of the last few days had taught her never to rely solely on devices ever again.

After ending the call with Bee, she checked the time and silently prayed that Audrey might still be at work. If she was lucky, she'd just catch her before she headed home for the day.

Audrey picked up on the second ring, her tone anxious. But upon hearing Rosie's voice, her manner changed and her questions flowed faster than the currents in Venice's canals.

After reassuring her that she was OK and that she was safe (again, another repeat of location details), Rosie asked, 'What about getting the group home safely tomorrow on their flight? Are they all OK?'

'They're fine. I managed to get hold of Mrs Winthorpe-Smythe and she has reluctantly agreed to be there to greet them at the airport on their arrival with a minibus and a large apology, I suspect. I'm not sure how many of them will still be residing at her care home in the new year! Oh, and the hotel is sending a couple of their employees with the group to the airport in the morning, so they won't be unaccompanied in Venice either. Mrs Winthorpe-Smythe is going to have a nice tidy bill from the hotel in the next few days, I suspect,' Audrey chuckled.

'But they're OK. That's all that matters.'

A knot released in Rosie's stomach that she didn't even realise had been there. She had been so worried and guilt-ridden, but knowing that they all travelled home without incident made a huge difference. She took a deep breath and found herself slumped back in the office chair.

Audrey asked, 'Rosie, have you spoken to Bee yet?'

'Only just. I literally just ended the call with her to phone you. She asked me to forward you an email. Have you received it?'

'Yes, I have,' she said, her voice muffled as if she had her hand over her mouth. 'Bear with me one second.'

Her tone had changed and, to Rosie, that only meant one thing: Benjamin was in the office. She stayed silent, waiting, knowing he would leave eventually. She could hear the tapping of Audrey's keyboard, implying she was working. After a moment, she heard Audrey speak.

'Goodnight, Benjamin. See you tomorrow. I hope your stomach settles eventually.'

There was another pause and then a large sigh.

'OK, he's gone . . .'

Audrey went on to tell her what had happened since they were last in touch.

'So, this morning, Bee stormed into the office, with all three kids in tow, and asked to speak to me. Benjamin has been sitting at your desk. He's done that most days since you left, as it means he can check on what I am doing. But also, I think he's been trying to find more dirt on you, the sneaky little git.' Audrey paused, a little breathless. 'Bee spotted him immediately and gave me a nod.

'She then proceeded to let all three children loose from their double buggy so they could run wild around the place, pulling all the brochures from the racks, wiping their hands down the front window and screaming blue murder. Benjamin, of course, made a hasty retreat to the privacy of his own office and firmly shut the door, allowing Bee and I to talk safely out of earshot.'

Rosie couldn't help but titter at the visual picture she was painting of Benjamin as he cowered in his office, away from any potential germs or dirt.

'It was at this point that she asked me what had happened after sending the bath selfie. On discovery of your mistake, she wanted to know how you had responded. I said I didn't know but that I had advised you to respond to his email, telling him it was sent in error. But I didn't know if you had done it, as I didn't get a chance to speak to you again. It was at that point we realised how important it was to get hold of you. And how we might be able to prove what a snivelling, conniving pig Benjamin really was.'

'How does my email response help?' Rosie asked.

'Having just scanned it now, it clearly states that you sent it in error. You asked him to delete the photo and, more importantly, you acted on this before he even had a chance to raise a complaint. Proving that he panicked and didn't want you to report him, so he turned the tables on you first.

'I'm sure there is no trace of your response anywhere on his computer, but there would be on yours. In your sent items. Now you've sent it to me, I can send it on to HR and in doing so, they'll have to re-evaluate their position on your suspension. Especially when other team members have decided to come forward now, stating, in writing, that he has not . . . how shall we say it? "Always remained professional."'

'Oh my gosh,' Rosie said, putting the dots together and realising that perhaps Audrey might be right.

Yes, she had made an error, but she tried to rectify it – and he took the opportunity to reflect the blame back on her.

'The email that I forwarded on to you should also show his initial response to me. Have you read it?'

'Hold on,' Audrey said, and Rosie waited, not wanting to read his salacious response again. 'Ew!'

'I know,' Rosie said.

'What a pig.'

'A stupid one.'

'And a very smelly one,' Audrey said, laughing.

'Eh?' Rosie said, not following.

'So, going back to this morning's visit from Bee. While the kids were running around having a blast, the morning's porridge had made its way through little Arya's system and he stopped mid-play, his fists clenched, his eyes glazing over . . .'

'I know that stance,' Rosie said, starting to giggle.

'Yup! The most enormous poo filled little Arya's nappy, and Bee was forced to change it there and then. Once changed, the poor thing was pooped out—'

'Pun intended,' Rosie interjected, and they both laughed.

'Absolutely! Anyway, Bee decided to head home in the hope that you might call. The dirty nappy sat on your desk, wrapped up in a nappy bag, its contents secured by the large knot in the bag. She went to pick it up but stopped, looking at me. A connected idea ran through us like a hive mind.

So, I said to her loudly, "Thank you so much for coming in today, Mrs Stool."

'Nice,' Rosie said, laughing.

'I know, quick thinking, right?!'

They both laughed, and Audrey continued, 'So I watched Bee leave and then I quietly moved the bag over to your desk chair and removed the nappy carefully from its bag, loosening the straps that held the "contents" in place. Laying the nappy open side up, and only gagging for a moment, I returned to my desk, where I continued to work. Ever the professional.' She sniggered. 'Benjamin eventually came back into the office after checking the place was empty.

'He complained about the smell, but I reassured him that one of the children had had their nappy changed on the floor but that the contents had been removed and only a lingering smell remained. What he didn't know was that I had sprayed a few drops of perfume onto my collar, so that all I could smell was the sweet tones of Chanel No.5.

'I watched as he made his way around your desk and pulled out the chair, without glancing down. When he sat down, the squelching sound was evident, even over at my desk, and he jumped up, turning to see what he had sat on and effectively showing me his arse covered in baby poop!

'It had smeared over his suit trousers and a little had gone on the two flaps of his suit jacket, too. He looked livid! His left hand moved to touch his trousers and became covered in gooey, slimy poo, at which point his face paled and he started heaving.

'A new customer walked into the shop and as they did so, Benjamin flew from the chair, the sticky tape from the nappy tabs firmly attached to his behind. As he ran to the stairs, it looked like he was running away with a large, bulbous, leaking haemorrhoid swinging from his behind!'

They both laughed hysterically, the image of Benjamin covered in faeces just too much. Rosie's eyes were streaming and her sides ached from laughing so much. She laughed so loudly that Fox popped his head around the door just to check if she was OK.

Which she was. With friends like Bee and Audrey, she was more than OK – she was blessed.

Chapter Forty-one

An hour later, Rosie was tucked up in the comfiest bed she'd ever laid in. It might have had something to do with the fact that her bed the night before had been a metal bench, but even so, Rosie couldn't believe that she had been welcomed into this family's home as a total stranger, yet she was treated like an old friend.

Fox had been stuck on the sofa bed for the night, despite her protestations that it should be her on the sofa as she was the unexpected guest. But he wouldn't hear of it. Even now, she could hear the springs of the old sofa groan and creak as Fox attempted to find a comfortable position.

Fox was definitely a man of many layers, she thought, as she looked out through the gap of the partially closed curtains and into the star-filled night sky. Her initial thoughts were that he was grumpy, irritable and generally just not fun to be around, but the more time she spent with him, he revealed a little more of himself. He was a musician, an uncle, an affectionate brother; he was kind, generous and willing to put his own comfort aside to help others, whether it be giving up his room for Christmas or donning a nativity outfit to stand in the cold beside a donkey.

One thing was for sure, she thought, as her eyes closed and her body grew heavy – without his help and company over the last few days, she would have been lost. In more ways than one.

Rosie fell into a deep sleep, comforted by the light of the full moon outside her window and the hope that this Christmas would be a happy one, despite its strangeness.

Rosie woke to the sound of childish laughter and for the umpteenth time in the last week, she had to think where she was. The bed was comfy and warm, and winter sunshine poured in through the gap in the curtains. The glorious smell of fresh coffee oozed under the closed door to her room.

There was a small analogue alarm clock on the bedside table and she noted that the time was ten o'clock. She couldn't remember the last time she had both slept so well and so late.

Her eyes grew wide as she realised that in an alternate reality, she would be on a plane right now, waving goodbye to the sights of Venice and heading home. She thought of her ten new friends and chuckled. She bet all her remaining euros that they were relishing in all the attention from the hotel and being treated like movie stars, their every need met.

Rosie stretched out, feeling free. There was no phone to check, no work to do, no decisions to make. It was Christmas Eve and she had no demands or prior engagements; it was both unsettling and enlivening.

She would have stayed where she was, except her tummy rumbled and her mouth watered at the smell of a delicious breakfast wafting around the apartment. She slid out of the covers, straightening her borrowed spotty cotton pyjamas, which Tabitha had given her last night, and gingerly opened the bedroom door.

The hallway was lit and there was an A4 piece of paper on the floor in front of her. Picking it up, she stared at the crayoned, childish picture of a stickman Father Christmas holding presents. There was an arrow pointing left, which she assumed was an order for her to follow, so she plodded down the hallway and found herself in the open-plan lounge, where the three boys were furrowing under the large Christmas tree beside one of the bay windows.

They were whispering between themselves and Rosie stayed silent, watching the cute scene.

'Good morning, Rosie.'

A deep, sexy voice spoke to her from behind and she turned to find Fox standing there, holding two cups of steaming coffee and wearing just a pair of what she assumed were Lewis's jogging bottoms. She glanced down to his bare chest, which was eye height to her, and she was surprised to find his physique to be incredibly muscular, with strong pecks and a six-pack that instantly made Rosie want to run her hands down it.

'Coffee?'

He held out an arm, gesturing to one of the coffee cups, and she took it gratefully, simultaneously trying to avert her eyes from the bicep that was flexing.

'Thank you,' she said shyly, suddenly aware that she was wearing a pair of mumsy pyjamas, which were buttoned up to the collar, in a very unsexy fashion.

She also realised that she had no make-up with her, no change of clothes and no way to purchase anything. Unless . . .

'So, we are on babysitting duty this morning. My sister is out doing last-minute Christmas stuff and Lewis is at church, but then I thought it might be nice to go into Florence. Make the most of the sunshine.'

He gestured to the bay windows and even she couldn't resist smiling at the vivid blue sky contrasting against the terracotta rooftops.

'That sounds good,' she said, taking a sip of the most delicious coffee she'd ever tasted.

There was a hint of spice in there and when she looked up at him, he said, 'It's cinnamon. I hope that's OK? I love cinnamon.'

'Me too,' Rosie said, taking another sip and enjoying the warm smoothness of the liquid as it warmed her insides.

'Especially in cookies,' Fox continued.

His faced turned to watch the children play with a bright green-and-red moving toy train, which looped around the Christmas tree on its circular track, blowing its horn on repeat.

'There's this amazing place not far from here that does the

most incredible cinnamon and cranberry cookies. We can head there if you like, too?'

Rosie thought of Jonah's Café and Martha's amazing cookies. She thought of how this whole trip away had started with a fight over a box of them. She chuckled.

'Sounds great.'

He turned to smile at her, a genuine smile, and she felt herself relax.

'Actually, I was going to ask you a favour,' she began, enjoying watching his left eyebrow rise with intrigue and a smile play on his lips.

'Oh, sounds interesting.'

There was a definite hint of cheek about him this morning, Rosie noticed, and she flushed at his sexy smile. His hair looked ridiculously unkempt and she felt an impulse to run her hands through it. The beginnings of stubble framed his defined jawline. She felt flustered and turned to look at the children, hiding her face behind her coffee cup.

'Um, yes, well, would it be possible to have your bank details, please?'

'My bank details? Should I be concerned?' he asked, looking at her with that same sexy half-smile. 'Is all this a ruse to fleece me of my money? Cute girl pretends to be lost to prey on innocent men, using her sexy wiles to persuade them to give it all away?'

Rosie flushed deep crimson. Not because of his jokey accusation, but because he'd called her cute. And sexy.

'Nope, the opposite, actually,' she said, sticking her tongue out at him to deflect her blushes. 'I want to give you money. My friend has transferred money into my account to help me, but up until now, I've been unable to access my account. But if I transfer some money to you via online banking, then you could withdraw the cash and I would be able to buy some necessities, like spare clothes, make-up and so on . . .'

His face changed as he pondered her request. 'Actually, that's not a bad idea. I could do with some extra clothes, too, and I've come without any of my presents for the boys, either.'

At the sound of the word 'presents', the boys' ears seemed to prick up like hyenas' and before Fox knew it, he had three sets of hands pulling at him, asking what they were getting for Christmas.

'Boys, boys, boys, calm down. If you quieten down, I'll tell you.'

They hushed instantly, their innocent faces gazing at him, their mouths tightly shut, their bodies held still.

'Well done, very good. If you don't tell your parents, I'll whisper it in your ears, but you have to come really close, as it'll be a very quiet whisper.'

They inched closer, their bodies pushed up against him, and he looked over their heads at Rosie, giving her a wink.

'Closer,' he urged, getting them even more squished into him. 'Now, cup both hands up to both ears so that you can hear everything I say.'

They did as instructed, their little hands cupped around each peachy ear, their eyes large and expectant.

'Good lads. Now, lean in . . .'

He leant down so that his head was level with theirs. The room was silent, the excitement palpable.

'Your present from me will be . . .' He tailed off, looking at each of them in turn, his face serious. '*The bear!*'

And with a roar, he scooped all three boys into his arms and let out an almighty roar. Their little faces lit up and they squealed, yelling at him to get on the ground. Fox gently lowered them and fell onto his hands and knees, letting them climb aboard his back and proceeding to stomp around the furniture, roaring and shaking, with them holding on while hysterically giggling.

Rosie was laughing, too, and as she watched them all play, she found herself starting to fall for the grumpy, stern-faced consulate employee. Despite his flaws, he was able to morph into a very sexy bear.

Chapter Forty-two

'. . . three-thirty, three-forty, three-fifty – three hundred and fifty euros,' Fox finished, counting out the notes into Rosie's flattened palm.

Rosie beamed. Finally. She folded the wad of notes and stuffed them into the back pocket of her jeans. She didn't trust her coat pockets, as a number of them were torn. And she had no intention of losing any more money on this trip.

'Thanking you.'

They were inside an Italian shopping mall, a large three-storey building consisting of floors of shops and even a food hall on the top floor. The ground floor where Fox and Rosie were standing was full of shoppers, their arms laden with shopping bags and their faces taut with stress. Despite the Christmas music blaring from large speakers and the huge hanging baubles twinkling in the overhead lights, the atmosphere was more 'no, no, no' than 'ho, ho, ho'.

'Do you want me to stay with you while you shop? Or are you comfortable shopping alone?'

Rosie appreciated the gesture, appreciated his gallantry when it came to ensuring she felt safe, but she had no intention of underwear shopping with him watching on. Especially as all the pastry-eating this week had definitely made her only pair of jeans feel a little tight.

'That's very kind, but I think I'll be fine,' she said, smiling and walking over to a map of the mall layout.

'OK, so how about we meet back here in an hour, then? Will that give you enough time to get everything you need?'

Rosie looked at the huge clock tower in the centre of the

shopping centre, stretching upwards to the top floor. It's four faces informed her of the time.

'Sure, sounds good.'

But Fox still looked a little dubious, looking around at the shoppers passing by them.

'Look, take my phone, then if there are any issues, you can at least feel safe or call for emergency help.' He pulled out his phone from his own back pocket, but Rosie held up her hand to refuse it.

'It's a shopping mall. Not Kilimanjaro. There are no major risks here, other than I might spend every penny and be left skint again.' She squeezed his arm to reassure him. It felt large and muscular. 'An hour and I'll see you back here.'

She let go and turned to leave, walking away from him towards the nearest escalator. Looking back, she found he was staring at her with a concerned look on his face. She smiled, gave him a little wave and joined the queue to climb to the next level. She was touched at his concern but had to remind herself that it was only because he was stuck with her until she got her new passport. Then, she was sure he would forget all about her. The thought made her feel instantly sad.

An hour later and true to his word, Fox was standing in the exact spot where they had parted. Rosie spotted him first and for a glorious moment, she got to observe him unnoticed. He was wearing a bright blue V-neck jumper and a new three-quarter-length wool coat, which looked expensive. In his hands were multiple bulky bags.

As women passed by, they glanced back at him and Rosie felt a rise of indignation inside of her. He was clearly an attractive man who stood out owing to his fiery hair, blazing eyes and broad physique, which screamed sexy. The new clothes only added to the appeal. He seemed totally oblivious to their glances, his eyes searching the crowd anxiously. That was, until he spotted her approaching.

His face broke out into a wide, relieved smile. Then his expression changed to one of surprise as he noticed her appearance. It looked like he considered it a good surprise, Rosie observed with another warm flush. She reached him and smiled coquettishly as he looked her up and down.

'Wow,' he said, 'that's an improvement.'

Rosie smiled. 'I don't know whether to be flattered or insulted,' she said, dropping her bags onto the floor between them.

Looking down at the palms of her hands, she could see the red lines of the handles imprinted on them. She straightened the new dress she had purchased, suddenly feeling very self-conscious.

'Definitely flattered,' he said, his eyes still observing her. 'A marked improvement on the dishevelled, drenched and highly stressed woman from the other day. You look really nice.'

He was smiling and Rosie felt at a loss for words.

'Well, thank you. Although I couldn't have looked much worse than I did, so I guess anything is an improvement.'

She exhaled hard to move a strand of hair from her face, but it blew upwards and then fell back to its original position. Fox took a step forwards and gently moved the strand out of her eyes and tucked it behind her left ear. It was intimate and their eyes locked for a second, a heat rising in Rosie's stomach, which had nothing to do with the recent purchase of a coffee.

'Thank you,' she whispered, drawing her eyes away from him and towards his shopping bags. 'I see you've been making a few purchases as well?' She nodded in the direction of his bags and he seemed to snap back into life, looking down.

'Yep, new clothes, new shoes, new underwear. Oh, and a ridiculous number of presents for everyone. And yes, before you ask, I do compensate for not seeing my nephews as much as I'd like to by buying them expensive gifts.' He shrugged as if he didn't mind, his status as the loving uncle clear.

'They're lucky to have you, by the sounds of it,' Rosie said, watching him shrug off the compliment.

'So, apart from the new dress, which, may I add, was a good purchase, did you get everything you needed?'

'I did, actually,' Rosie said, looking at the many bags full of new items, including clothing, underwear and a few extras.

It turned out Italy was fantastic for shopping. She had found some wonderful dresses, pyjamas, underwear and a beautiful midi herringbone coat that was the deep crimson of a Christmas poinsettia.

'But I'm not quite done,' she said, looking around at the various shops in their vicinity. 'There's just one more thing I need.'

'Go on,' Fox said.

'I desperately need a new backpack.'

'Yes, you do,' Fox said, stifling a laugh, 'you definitely do.' He gathered his bags, along with some of hers, as if they were filled with merely helium, and gestured for them to make a move. 'But can I request one tiny thing?'

'Sure,' said Rosie, adjusting her new scarf around her neck and walking alongside him. 'What is it?'

'That you make sure it is definitely waterproof.'

There was a beat of silence before they both burst out laughing, with Rosie play-swatting him with her remaining bags.

Chapter Forty-three

'You can't walk in with half a giant cookie in your hand.'

'Aw, but I don't want to rush it. It's sooo good!'

'Agreed. But it's about to begin and Tabitha will not be impressed if I'm late.'

Rosie looked down at her half-eaten cookie fondly, and with a huge amount of restraint, she placed it back into the paper bag and wiped her mouth to clear away any crumbs. She looked up to find Fox staring at her, his face soft.

'It's an hour's service, then you can carry on eating,' he said, taking the paper bag out of her hand and shoving it into his inside jacket pocket. 'Just in case,' he said before stepping back so that she could enter the church before him.

She could get used to being treated in such a chivalrous manner.

As they entered the warmth of the church, Rosie was enveloped in a comforting Christmassy feeling. There was a choir at the front in the stalls near the altar. They had entered via the vestibule and Rosie gasped at the beautiful nativity scene ahead. There was straw on the floor, a small picket fence, a stable built from haystacks with a makeshift palm roof and figures from the nativity all facing towards a crib. A spotlight lit the crib with a yellowy-gold haze that felt like it was being generated by moonlight. A baby Jesus was swaddled in a plain blanket and there were children standing behind the picket fence, gazing at the scene.

Turning right towards the altar, she let Fox lead the way down the aisle, noticing how packed the church was. Each pew was filled with smiling families and excited children, and Rosie quickly spotted Tabitha with the children. She shuffled the boys up the pew to give them room to sit down, but the space was tight and Rosie squished herself in between Tabitha and Fox.

Looking ahead towards the choir, she took a moment to listen to the hymn. They were singing in Italian and Rosie felt moved by the choral symphony of voices echoing around the building. She spotted Lewis beside the organ, speaking to a member of the clergy, his white robes lit by tall candles that flickered behind the altar. He was smiling as he talked, his whole demeanour relaxed.

The choir finished their hymn and Lewis stepped forwards to begin.

'*Benvenuto* and welcome to our Christmas Eve Crib Service.' He held out his arms towards the congregation, his smile wide. 'Our service today will be a mix of both Italian and English, which is mirrored in the service sheets in the seat pocket in front of you. Let us pray.'

Rosie opened her service sheet as the service began and took a moment to glance across at Fox, noticing his head bowed in reverence and his eyes closed. As the prayer finished and the congregation were asked to stand, she was startled to think how relaxed she felt in his presence. Normally, on Christmas Eve, she'd be with Bee and the family, or working until close of business. But here she was, with people she barely knew, with few possessions, and rather than feeling lost and alone, she felt included and happy.

As the organ began its opening chords for 'Away in a Manger', Rosie found herself wanting to sing loudly and she belted the lyrics out, a little tunelessly but with gusto. She noticed Fox stare at her from the corner of her eye. She turned and smiled widely, her voice cracking a little at the high notes but no longer caring. Their eyes met and he joined in, his singing now elevated to fortissimo, his deep baritone conflicting with her weaker soprano. Rosie's expression changed to one of surprise – his voice was beautiful. Deep, warm and with a gruffness that gave it an edge. The boy could sing. But rather than being embarrassed, she simply upped the volume and they spent the rest of the hymn competing, with Fox only winning because Rosie got a fit of the giggles.

The rest of the service was lovely. Lewis spoke with reverence, yet was able to speak to the children, too. His speech about the nativity reminded Rosie of her own starring role a couple of days ago, albeit briefly.

When Lewis asked the young of the congregation to come up and help re-enact the nativity with him, Rosie watched as Teddy, Albie and George solemnly joined their father near the pulpit, along with about thirty other children of various ages. With Lewis to guide them, he began his trek towards the altar, where a comical pantomime horse now stood patiently, along with a dressed-up Mary and Joseph. There was also an adult holding a large pole with an illuminated lantern above their heads and as the person moved, the characters followed, as if following a star.

The children moved around the entirety of the church, where various nativity scenes had been recreated, some with humour. Such as the inn door falling off its cardboard hinges due to the innkeeper having leant on it. Or the real-life sheep that was brought in that kept running in and out between one of the shepherd's legs, causing him almost to trip.

The children loved it, the adults loved it, and by the time they arrived at the stable at the back of the church, the figurines that Rosie had admired earlier had been removed, allowing for the nativity members to enter through the picket fence and pose for the final reading. The children gathered on the straw in the stable, their innocent eyes listening to Lewis speak, their attention captured. It was a truly immersive experience.

Half an hour later, the crib service was over and most of the congregation were gathered in the hall adjacent to the church. Children were running around, weaving past tables, giggles and childish laughter audible against the general humdrum of voices.

Rosie was seated at a large table with Tabitha and Fox and was munching on a traditional Italian Christmas biscuit, which she was told was called an anginetti. Whatever it was, it was delicious. Tabitha was clearly well known within the church community, with people stopping to chat and shake hands. Her attention was elsewhere, meaning that Fox and Rosie were left by themselves.

'So, if you hadn't abandoned your travel group, been a bit slapdash with your belongings and made some very poor choices when inebriated, what would you have been doing this Christmas Eve?' Fox said, removing his scarf and placing it on the table. 'Spending it with your family? Boyfriend?'

'Oh, I don't have any family,' Rosie said, shrugging, 'or a boyfriend. My parents died when I was young and I was an only child.'

She waited for the inevitable look of sympathy that she always received when telling her life story. Fox dutifully complied, his face full of concern.

She pre-empted his apology. 'Don't worry, you weren't to know. I'm fine, it happened a long time ago.' She smiled to prove her point. 'I would be spending Christmas like I always do, with my best friend and her family.'

Fox nodded, scanning her face, which made her blush a little. 'Well, that sounds lovely. Tell me about your best friend.'

And so Rosie did. In the strange hall, in an unknown town, in a new country, Rosie recounted her lifelong relationship with Bee, her love for her best friend evident. She talked about Nav and the children and how she considered them both like the siblings she never had. She didn't touch on her parents, though. Fox listened and it felt like all the other voices faded, his attention on her and her only.

When she finished, she returned the question.

'So, do you always spend Christmas with your sister?'

'Since she had the boys, I tend to,' he said, smiling as Albie and George ran past their table in a fit of giggles. 'My parents don't like to travel, so I go home every November to visit them in Scotland, but Christmas has always been here since Tabitha moved out to Italy.'

'Sounds like you are a good uncle,' Rosie said, wondering what it must be like to have a blood relation who you love unconditionally. 'And what about a partner? Girlfriend?'

There was the briefest of pauses. A pause so tiny but that spoke volumes.

Fox diverted his gaze from her and replied, 'Nope. No partner or girlfriend. I don't need the complication.'

Rosie nodded, unsure if this made her ridiculously happy or disappointed. Fox seemed uncomfortable and as she reached for another biscuit, he jumped out of his chair like a spring-boarding basset hound and grabbed Albie by the waist, pulling him into him. Albie threw his head back in peals of laughter as his uncle threw him over his shoulder in a fireman's lift and proceeded to stomp off in the direction of the other children. Moments later, he gently placed Albie back down, but in doing so was swarmed by excited children, all wanting to be jostled and played with.

For the first time in a while, Rosie wished she had her phone. In situations like this, distracting oneself with a phone is a great way to look busy and not alone. But with no phone and only a plateful of biscuits in front of her, she decided to head outside and walk back over to the church again.

Wrapping her new coat more tightly around her to block out the cold wind that had arrived, she nuzzled down into its collar as she walked the few steps across the road and back into the churchyard, removing the half-finished cookie from her coat pocket and continued eating. The church looked wonderful. Candles were lit in each stained-glass alcove, and the open doors made it look warm and welcoming. A few people were gathered by the door, speaking in Italian, so she decided to meander around to the side of the entrance and take a look at the churchyard.

Rosie had always loved a churchyard. People assumed she wouldn't because of the connection to her parents dying, but she actually found solace in the quietness. She found it a place of love and devotion. A place where, even though the person had gone, their imprint was powerful on their loved ones left behind, their care showing in the numerous splashes of colour in the form of flowers and plants.

Just as she turned a corner around the back of the church, she spotted an old man tending to a grave, despite the cold, despite the darkness, his back arched as he knelt over a gravestone. As she moved closer, she could hear him humming an upbeat tune. He turned at her movement and gave her a smile. He reminded her of Horace and his love for his wife. How lucky these men were to have been touched by a love so strong that it continued even after their physical separation.

She waved back and continued her stroll, turning the next corner and looking skywards at the clear and star-filled night. She found it so surreal that she was standing in Italy on Christmas Eve, about to spend Christmas with complete strangers. She was taking risks, travelling, meeting new people . . .

'Rosie?'

She heard her name called out and recognised Fox's voice in the dark. She saw him turn the corner and spot her. He sped up until he was in front of her.

'Are you OK?'

In the moonlight, she could see his face was again full of concern.

'I'm fine, why?'

'Because you just disappeared. One minute you were there and then when I returned to the table, you'd gone. I was worried that maybe I'd . . .' – he tailed off – 'maybe I'd offended you.' He ran a hand through his thick hair.

'No, no, no offence here. I just thought I would take a moment, that's all.' She smiled to show she was fine.

'OK, cool,' he said, looking around them, 'but we should probably think about heading back as Tabitha has already left with the boys and has big plans for our Christmas Eve dinner.'

'Of course, let's go.'

Rosie followed him back through the churchyard and onto the street, their silence no longer awkward but companiable.

'By the way, if we're walking back towards the tram stop, is there any chance we could just pass by that bakery again?'

She said it innocently, almost nonchalantly, but Fox laughed. 'One cookie not enough, hey?'

Rosie went to retort, but he'd already started laughing, so she shrugged and answered, 'When in Rome—'

'Please don't tell me that's next on the agenda. At this rate we'll have taken in half of Italy before the new year!'

They both laughed, continuing their walk under the stars, side by side.

Chapter Forty-four

'They're here! They're here!'

Rosie and Fox were ushered in by a flustered Tabitha, her face flushed and her apron skew-whiff. Her freckles were more prominent with her red cheeks, tendrils of hair escaping her messy bun and falling in front of her face. She almost pushed them down the hallway into the large living room, where Rosie turned to hand Tabitha a large white cake box.

'For you,' she said.

Tabitha looked shocked. She opened the lid to see a beautifully wrapped cake in gold cellophane with a gold ribbon around it. The shape clearly indicated it was a panettone.

'Oh my gosh, how wonderful. Lewis, look! How beautifully wrapped, too.'

Lewis walked over, a bottle in one hand and a bottle opener in the other. He was back in his jeans and jumper.

'That's very sweet of you, Rosie. Thank you!'

Tabitha took the box from her hands and passed it to Fox before giving Rosie the tightest hug.

As she let go, she threw her hands into the air before proclaiming, 'My salmon!'

She ran towards the kitchen, leaving Lewis chuckling as he popped the cork on the red wine.

'By the way,' he said, 'we have another guest at the dinner table this evening. A church member who has lately become a widow, her name is Agnese. Her husband, Aurelio, died about three months ago and she has no family to spend Christmas with, so Tabitha and I decided to welcome her in to join ours.'

Tabitha nodded. 'It'll be a squeeze around the table, but that's what Christmas is all about, hey?'

'Absolutely,' Fox said, nodding before taking the box into the kitchen. 'Now, how about we decant some of that delicious-looking wine, eh?'

Rosie headed to the bathroom, but as she reached the door, it opened suddenly to reveal an old grey-haired woman, dressed all in black, her face so lined it was hard to see if she was frowning or if that was just how she looked.

'Oh, sorry!' Rosie said, jumping back to let her pass.

The woman smiled and nodded curtly but made no noise as she passed by, leaving Rosie to wonder what her story was.

The dinner Tabitha had prepared was sumptuous. A whole poached salmon sat in the centre of the dining table, along with bowls of steaming pasta, buttery prawns, salad and bread. The plates were as crammed in as their diners, with the children squished up against one another to allow for the extra chairs. Rosie was seated next to Fox and their thighs touched at the lack of space. She could feel the warmth from his shoulder against hers and she found she liked it. It was a hodgepodge of a gathering, but a happy one. As the wine flowed and the food was eaten, the diners relaxed into a comfortable scene, with the children steadily getting more excited about Christmas as the evening wore on.

Dessert was brought out, a large tiramisu and a bowl of figs in syrup, along with Rosie's panettone and an array of dessert wines. Agnese was quiet for most of the meal, despite Fox's attempts to strike up a conversation in Italian. She nodded and smiled, but Rosie noticed her observing them almost as a spectator at the table, much like herself. They were outsiders observing a traditional happy family.

Fox had also changed – his demeanour was different and he laughed with his sister, bantered with Lewis and seemed genuinely relaxed. His sleeves were rolled up to his elbows, revealing wide forearms, with just the hint of a tattoo under his left arm. It looked like the tip of an arrow to Rosie, but she tried not to stare without making it obvious, subconsciously finding herself wanting to run her finger up the arrow to see where it led. He must have sensed her looking, as he turned to gaze at her, his eyes connecting with hers.

As Tabitha brought out the coffees, more wine was consumed and Lewis, who had to head back to church for midnight Mass in a few hours, was on bedtime duty.

'C'mon, boys. Time for bed.'

Despite many protestations and cries that they weren't tired or sleepy or in any way ready for bed, within fifteen minutes Lewis returned with a smile on his face, confirming all three were asleep and snoring. Rosie checked the clock on the wall and was surprised to see it was gone 9pm. Their meal had lasted hours, yet the time had flown.

'Can I help clear up, Tabitha?' Rosie asked, stifling a yawn.

'Aw, that's very sweet of you. And unlike my brother dearest, who wouldn't know a tea towel if it whacked him in the face.'

'Ah, c'mon now, Tabby-cat. Don't be mean, it's Christmas.' He stretched out in his chair, the shirt rising with his arms, revealing the waistband of his jeans.

Rosie noticed a line of hair but looked away quickly.

'Will you clean up, then? I could do with wrapping a few final presents before Lewis heads off to church.' Tabitha pushed back her chair, one eyebrow raised.

Fox copied her movement and pushed back his own chair to stand up. 'For my sister, anything.'

He took a comedic bow and there was a slight wobble to his stance. Rosie realised that they were all a little tipsy. Again.

She stood up beside him, almost knocking him to one side with her shoulder, causing them both to giggle. Tabitha rolled her eyes and invited Agnese to come and join her on the sofa, which she dutifully did without comment. Rosie noticed even Agnese seemed a little wobbly on her feet and she watched as old lady took her wine glass with her towards the sofa, much to Tabitha's obvious concern. Agnese hadn't said a word since she'd arrived, yet as she moved away from the table, she released the almightiest hiccough, which seemed to startle both her and Tabitha, who was guiding her by the elbow.

Tabitha kept her composure, but both Fox and Rosie descended into giggles, despite the glare from Tabitha. Agnese didn't seem to notice, though, and continued towards the sofa, her wine slopping around in the glass as if she were walking around a ship on rocky seas. As Tabitha lowered her into the sofa, another huge hiccough erupted like Mount Vesuvius from her innards, which set Rosie and Fox off into more hysterics.

Grabbing her hand, Fox pulled Rosie away from the table and into the small kitchen, where piles of pots, pans and dirty dishes were stacked up. To Rosie, it looked like a mammoth task. But she rolled up her sleeves, pulled her hair up into a high twist and fastened it with two chopsticks she saw resting on a top shelf . She slipped on the big yellow rubber gloves that lay over the drainer.

'I'll wash, you dry,' she commanded, nodding in the direction of the sink.

'Yes, sir!' Fox said, saluting her and searching for a tea towel.

He grabbed some kitchen roll and held it out with a questioning look. Tabitha clearly wasn't exaggerating when she said he wasn't a pro in the kitchen. Rosie pointed a rubber-gloved finger towards the back of the kitchen door, where the kitchen towel hung from a hook. He grabbed it and poised himself, ready to begin.

With Rosie washing and him drying, they found themselves staring out through the large kitchen window at the rooftops of the town. It was a very pretty sight, even at night when the Apuan Alps weren't even visible. But just knowing that they were surrounded by giants such as Monte Ceceri and Certosa made Rosie feel like she didn't want to leave. She would have loved to have the time to climb them, to feel on top of the world.

It took almost an hour to clean the entire kitchen. Probably because they kept messing around and laughing, their hands repeatedly touching, their bodies side by side. But by the time they found themselves back in the living room, they were immediately aware that they were the only ones still awake. Tabitha had fallen asleep with a present still in her lap and sticky tape covering most of her fingers, and Agnese was snoring gently, her head leaning to one side, her mouth slightly agape. The wine glass was now empty and had fallen sideways onto the sofa, but thankfully at an angle where no droplets had escaped.

Fox shushed Rosie and they tiptoed out into the hallway to alert Lewis, who was busy finishing his sermon for the next day. In a well-practised manoeuvre, he scooped up his wife in his arms and took her to their bedroom, but they were all at a loss as to what to do with Agnese. She looked so comfortable.

'What if you grab her legs and I'll take the arms and we'll carry her to the car?' Fox said, looking at Lewis.

'Down four flights of stairs?'

'You can't carry an old woman down four flights of stairs. Actually, you can't carry an old woman anywhere without her permission!' Rosie said in hushed tones. 'Look, I'll wake her, you get the door' – she pointed at Fox – 'and you get your car keys,' she said, pointing to Lewis.

They both nodded and disappeared off. Leaning down so she was eye level with the old woman, she gently began to pat her hand to attempt to rouse her.

It didn't work.

She then moved up to her shoulder, shaking her ever so gently so as not to panic her.

This time, it worked. Her eyes pinged open and she gasped at Rosie, clearly not recognising her situation. Rosie smiled to reassure her and spoke softly, even though she knew the old lady wouldn't understand.

'It's OK, it's OK. You just fell asleep. Reverend Lewis is going to take you home in his car now.'

At the mention of Lewis, recognition passed over Agnese's face. Confident that Rosie wasn't about to attack her, she leant forwards to look around the room, taking in her surroundings.

'Reverend Lewis is waiting by the front door to take you home so you can sleep.' Rosie pressed her hands together in prayer and brought them to her left cheek, her head tipped sideways, indicating sleep.

'Ah, *grazie, grazie*,' Agnese said, mirroring the motion and smiling.

With Rosie's help, Agnese managed to get to her feet and Rosie tucked her arm through hers to accompany her to the car. The woman was clearly still half asleep and doddery – the last thing they wanted was her to fall and hurt herself. Slowly and gently, they walked arm in arm from the living room into the hallway, with Fox standing by the front door, ready to open it. Lewis was nowhere to be seen, but Rosie felt that with Fox's help, they could get her down the stairs.

But halfway down the hallway, Agnese looked left and without warning, steered into the spare bedroom that Rosie had slept in last night.

'Er, um, not this way . . .'

Rosie tried to think of some Italian word, any Italian, that would explain to the old woman that she was being taken home, but it was too late. Agnese pulled back the covers and kicked off her little black pumps before climbing in, mirroring the hand signal for sleep that Rosie showed her in the living room. With a tired smile and a little yawn, she lay down and closed her eyes, with Rosie still staring at her.

'Shit,' Rosie whispered before tiptoeing out of the room and up to Fox.

'She's gone to bed.'

'What?' Fox whispered, looking back up the hallway.

'She's gone into the bedroom and climbed into bed,' Rosie said, gesturing for him to follow.

As they tiptoed back into the bedroom, there was a familiar gentle snore rising from Agnese, the covers pulled up to her chin. She was fast asleep. They both tiptoed out.

Back in the hallway, Lewis joined them, emerging from his office.

'Why are you standing here? Where's Agnese?' he whispered.

Both of them pointed behind them at the partially open door and watched as he stepped forwards, to see Agnese snuggled up soundly.

'Why is she in there?' he asked.

'She took herself in there,' Rosie said. 'I tried to stop her, but she obviously didn't understand. She made this gesture and then lay down.'

She mirrored the 'sleep' gesture with her hands and Lewis looked from her to the bedroom to her again. Then he started laughing quietly, his hand raised to try to stifle it. But his laughter was contagious. First, Fox joined him and then within moments, all three of them were giggling in hushed tones, acknowledging the absurdity of the situation. Lewis gestured for them to head back into the living room.

'OK, so it seems we have another house guest for the night,' Lewis said, which made them all laugh again. 'But it does mean we are in a pickle as to where to put you, Rosie. No disrespect, but I don't think it fair to wake Agnese to make her swap places with you. She's been through an awful lot.'

Rosie shook her head. 'I wouldn't dream of it. She stays put. I'll sleep on the floor.'

'No, you won't,' Fox said. 'You have the sofa bed, I'll sleep on the floor.'

'No, that's not fair,' Rosie argued.

'I would offer you my bed with Tabitha,' said Lewis, 'but the boys will be in at the crack of dawn for their stockings and I don't think you'll want waking at 4am. Plus, it would be a bit of a shock for Tabitha to find you in our bed . . .' He tailed off, checking the time on his watch. 'I really need to head off if I'm to have enough time to prepare for midnight Mass.'

'Of course, you go. We'll sort this between ourselves,' Fox said, ushering him out.

Lewis looked hesitant, but checking his watch a second time, he left them alone in the living room. Rosie heard the quiet click of the front door as he left. She looked at Fox awkwardly.

'Honestly, I'm fine on the floor,' she said. 'I'll just grab a pillow from the sofa.'

'Nonsense,' said Fox, grabbing a cushion himself and throwing it onto the floor beside the Christmas tree. 'I'll sleep here. Trust me, I've slept in worse places. It's fine.'

Rosie tried to argue, but he wasn't having any of it. Ten minutes later, she was dressed in her new pyjamas that she'd bought on her shopping spree earlier, removed her make-up and was now lying outstretched in the sofa bed, the covers pulled up to her chin.

She could hear Fox trying to get comfortable on the floor, but he didn't even have a blanket to cover himself. He was using his new coat. Every time he moved, she heard the buttons of his coat smacking hard onto the wooden floor. She even heard the sound of the material shifting from under him, his elbows or knees knocking against the unforgiving wood.

The lamps had been switched off and the only light came in the form of moonlight, but Rosie couldn't sleep. She felt so guilty sleeping in the large sofa bed while he suffered on the floor. She sat up and looked over in his direction.

'Fox,' she whispered, just in case he had fallen asleep.

'Yes?' he whispered back, his body still.

'I've got far too much room in here. The mattress is huge.' She patted the bed to emphasise her point. 'Would you like to share with me? I promise I don't snore.' She realised her heart was pounding hard in her chest as she waited for his response.

'Don't make promises you can't keep,' he joked from the floor. 'I've heard you snore.'

'You haven't!' she said, mortified. 'I don't!'

She heard him laughing and threw a pillow in his direction. She heard it hit him and his reply.

'Oi!'

'You'll be needing that. C'mon, before I change my mind,' she said, patting the bed again.

She heard him rise and pad over towards her. She stayed perfectly still, lying on her back looking up at the ceiling.

The mattress lowered as he climbed in and she could feel the warmth from his skin without him even touching her. He matched her position, on his back, with his arms by his side. It felt incredibly intimate.

'Yep, this is definitely more comfortable than the floor,' he said. 'Thank you.'

'No thanks necessary – it was your bed first.'

He didn't answer. But Rosie could sense he was as alert as she was, with neither of them moving a muscle. The whole apartment felt quiet, still.

'This is the weirdest Christmas I think I've ever had,' Rosie said, hearing the clock in the hallway chime midnight. She counted all twelve chimes.

'I bet. It's up there with one of my strangest Christmases, too,' Fox said. 'I thought I would be spending Christmas alone this year.'

'I'm always alone,' Rosie said without thought, surprising herself.

She heard Fox's head turn on his pillow to look at her.

'Rosie, you're . . . I think that you are . . . I-I want to . . .' he stuttered, clearly struggling with what to say. 'I'm glad I'm getting to spend Christmas with you.'

His voice was barely a whisper, but she heard the ruffle of bedding and the touch of his hand over hers. It felt like an electric current. She continued staring ahead, not trusting herself. His hand enveloped hers before grasping her palm in his and lacing his fingers between hers. It felt nice. His hands were so much bigger than hers, yet they fitted together perfectly.

'I'm glad I'm spending Christmas with you, too,' she replied, finally turning her head to look at him.

His eyes were alive and searching hers, and she knew that if she leant in, he would kiss her. She wanted him to. Every fibre in her body pushed her forwards, yet she didn't move. Couldn't move.

He was wearing a simple grey V-neck T-shirt and she could see small hairs on his chest. Instinctively, she wanted to reach out and stroke those hairs, to lean into that chest. But she didn't. He looked like he was having a hard time resisting, too, his chest rising and falling. She imagined his heart pounding.

'Goodnight, Fox,' she said, her words speaking volumes.

He looked surprised but then resigned and he smiled.

'Goodnight, Rosie. Merry Christmas.'

'Merry Christmas to you, too.'

And that's how they fell asleep, their faces turned towards one another and their hands still clasped. For the first time in a long time, Rosie relaxed into her dreams, feeling safe and protected.

Chapter Forty-five

Rosie blinked open her eyes and took a moment to register her surroundings. It was dark in the room and she felt incredibly comfortable. She snuggled down a little deeper into her warm pillow, which was rhythmically moving up and down with her breaths. *Wait*, Rosie thought. *Pillows don't move.*

She lifted her head to find she was currently wrapped in the arms of Fox, with both his arms around her waist, and her head against his chest. Their legs were touching, and her left arm was wrapped around his torso.

Panicking, she froze. She could make out his closed eyes, still asleep, and his deep breathing, which, on exhale, sounded like a bit like a bear. His face was relaxed and she badly wanted to trace her fingers across his day-old stubble, which made him look both dishevelled and extremely sexy. She decided that if she moved too much, she was in danger of waking him, so she folded herself back into her original position and fell back to sleep almost instantly, a smile on her face.

When Rosie awoke for a second time, it was to the sounds of whispering around her. She opened her eyes to find three gorgeous pairs of sparkly blue eyes staring up close to hers, their three matching blond heads pressed together.

'I think she's awake,' one voice said before being shushed by another.

'Mum says we cannot wake them. She said that if we do, then they might not fall in a-more-ray.'

'What's a-more-ray?' the littlest voice asked, and she could feel them nudging each other as they stood leaning on the duvet with their hands.

'I don't know. Maybe like a stingray? Mrs Aubert says a stingray is a big, flapping fish.'

'Why would Mummy want them to fall into more stingrays? Do they sting?'

'I don't know.'

'Let's go ask Mummy. I don't want Uncle Fox to get stung.'

'Do you remember last year when Mummy got stung by a bee and she said all those no-no words . . .'

Their little voices tailed away as they moved collectively back towards their parents' bedroom and Rosie couldn't help but stifle a giggle, followed by a yawn, just as Fox pulled her a little closer in his sleep. She found herself sinking back into a delicious dream about two red foxes wrapping themselves together in soft bramble . . .

The third time Rosie awoke was with a start.

Her eyes flew open, aware that a large crashing noise had startled her. The crash was followed by furious whispers, which sounded to Rosie like Tabitha and Lewis. She realised she was now facing away from Fox but that they were sleeping in a sideways hug, with his legs tucked into the bend of hers, his large arm wrapped over her shoulders protectively. But his arm didn't feel relaxed like in sleep. It felt frozen in place, as if he were startled.

She tried to edge gently away from him but instinctively knew he was awake. His arm moved and she manoeuvred herself around so that she was facing him. The curtains were still drawn, but the Christmas tree lights had switched on, so they were both bathed in a flashing warm white light. It was evident by Fox's wide, concerned eyes that he was very much awake.

'Morning,' she whispered, already missing the touch of his arm protecting her.

'Morning,' he replied, looking a little sheepish and brushing his fingers through his hair. 'Sorry about the cuddling. I didn't know I was doing it.'

'That's OK,' Rosie said, interrupting. 'It was really nice, actually.'

'Yeah?' he said quietly.

'Yeah,' Rosie said, smiling.

He shuffled closer, not quite touching her but with his face on her pillow.

'Is this OK?'

It was barely audible, but she nodded and he put an arm around her waist, tightening his grip, but in a protective way, urging her to come closer. She did. Their noses were almost touching.

'And this?' He moved in slowly, with Rosie losing focus of his face as his lips touched hers.

He pulled back, searching her face for clues.

She nodded again. He tasted delicious. His lips were so soft and when they touched hers, she felt both fire and ice ripple through her body.

'And this?' He moved towards her again and she closed her eyes, willing him to kiss her, but there was another explosion of noise and they pulled apart, to see the three boys running into the room and heading straight for the Christmas tree and its newly placed presents.

They didn't even stop to glance in Fox's or Rosie's direction. Rosie pulled the covers right up to her chin and sat up, watching as Tabitha almost threw herself into the living room in an effort to grab the boys. The sight was highly amusing and she nudged Fox, who also sat up.

'Morning, sis,' he said, stretching his arms up towards the ceiling. 'Morning, boys. Happy Christmas!'

'Oh, thank goodness you're both awake. I was so worried we would *wake* you.' She emphasised the word *wake* by adding air quotes with her hands.

'Nope, we were rudely awoken by the sound of you clearly attempting to defrost the turkey,' he joked as Tabitha rolled her eyes.

'Ha ha. That was Lewis. He was trying to make a coffee without waking you, but dropped the cafetière, silly fool. A great start to Christmas, no caffeine and glass everywhere.'

She was handing each boy a pillowcase, which appeared to be brimming with presents, watching fondly as they excitedly ripped into the paper, their faces gleefully happy.

'Lewis, they're awake. Grab the camera, will you?'

Rosie watched as the boys, all in matching pyjamas, opened their presents in front of their parents, their faces lit with excitement. Tabitha was wrapped in a red dressing gown and Lewis perched on the arm of her chair, his pyjamas hidden by the clearly new dressing gown that still had the tag attached at the back. Rosie smiled. It was a lovely festive image.

She looked across at Fox to find that he wasn't watching the Christmas scene at all but was looking at her. His face was full of warmth and he slipped a hand back into hers before turning his head back to watch his nephews. As Christmas Day mornings go, Rosie realised this was a good one.

Chapter Forty-six

After another mammoth and impressive meal cooked by Tabitha, they were all reclining in the living room watching the boys play with their new toys. Rosie and Fox were still wearing their paper cracker hats and Rosie was dressed in another new outfit, this time a deep emerald-green tea dress. Thankfully, it had an elasticated waistband, which was definitely needed after the amount of roast potatoes she had ingested.

Fox had also decided on a new outfit, which was a sky-blue long-sleeved shirt with black jeans, and Rosie couldn't help but look at him. How had she not noticed how handsome he was? Perhaps because she had either collided with him, fought with him or become irritated with him. But after the last few days together, she was finding it hard not to fall for him.

She decided to excuse herself and headed to the study, where Lewis had said she was more than welcome to call or email anyone she wanted to wish them a happy Christmas. She knew that both Audrey and Bee would be catering for in-laws' requests and demands like a maniac, so she didn't ring but sent a simple email wishing them both a brilliant Christmas and informing them that a Christmas do-over was 100 per cent happening on her return. She informed them both that she was having a great day, despite her circumstances, and that they needn't worry about her at all. Signing off, she realised how true that statement was.

The door opened and Fox peered in.

'They're handing out the presents for adults now. Tabitha has insisted that you join us.' He gestured for her to get up and follow him.

As she passed by him, he stopped her by the door frame and kissed her gently, pressing his body to hers and then moving away again.

She smiled and looked down nervously, still unused to this level of attention.

'I'll be there in one minute,' she said, turning away from the living room and heading down the long hallway to her room, which she now jointly shared with Agnese, it seemed.

She opened the large built-in wardrobe and removed a bag filled with presents. She adjusted a red bow on the top one, grateful that she had had the foresight to get them professionally wrapped instore at the mall yesterday, and returned to join the others in the living room.

'There she is!' Tabitha declared as Rosie walked in and sat in the empty seat beside Fox.

She placed the bag by her legs in front of the sofa and then waited to watch everyone else share their love through the power of presents.

Tabitha went first, handing out presents to Lewis and Fox, who both childishly ripped them open. Fox had been gifted an expensive designer jumper, which he appeared to love, and also a slate-coloured photo frame with an image of Tabitha and him from when they were children. They were pulling silly faces and wearing matching shell suits, which made Fox howl with laughter. The children came to stare.

Lewis had been gifted a beautiful watch, which he declared he had had his eye on for ages, to which Tabitha rolled her eyes as if stating the obvious. There were little presents, too, and Rosie enjoyed watching them both excitedly open presents as if they were children again.

There were even gifts for Agnese, who looked emotional as she unwrapped a beautiful gold-edged Bible, a bottle of grappa and a box of delicious-looking amaretto biscuits. With tears in her eyes, she blew kisses to them both.

Then it was time for Tabitha. She held out both hands in childish glee, her eyes closed and her smile wide. Fox went first, with a small A5 envelope and a larger present. She opened the envelope first, pulling out a piece of paper and scanning it quickly. Her hand rose to her mouth as she gasped and handed it over to Lewis for him to read.

'Really?' she said to Fox. 'This is huge.'

Fox shrugged. 'Who else am I going to spend money on if not my stupid sister and her awesome but clearly very patient husband?' He smiled as she threw a cushion at him.

Lewis's eyes grew wide. 'Fox, thank you! That's extremely generous. Wow!'

The children badgered them to know what it was, unimpressed by the idea of paper as a present.

'Uncle Fox has been very kind, indeed. He's booked me and Daddy a trip to Rome, including a hotel, hire car and tickets to both the Colosseum and the Vatican.' Tabitha's eyes were misty with tears and she continued, 'The only caveat being that Uncle Fox babysits the boys for the whole weekend. With unlimited ice cream.'

Fox winked at his sister as the boys all jumped up and down in excitement, chanting, 'Ice cream, ice cream!'

The second present was a state-of-the-art coffee machine.

'Because your coffee is terrible and if I have to babysit, then I'll need good-quality caffeine.'

After many hugs, both Lewis and Tabitha sat back down, with Tabitha wiping away her tears while Lewis rummaged under the tree. He pulled out a box wrapped in gold ribbon and handed it to his wife, stating, 'For my love. Merely a token based on the amount of love I have for you.'

Tabitha ripped into the wrapping, tearing off the bow and lifting the lid on a black velvet box. Inside was a ring with a large yellow square diamond surrounded by a cluster of smaller but brilliantly sparkling white diamonds. She fell silent as she stared at the beautiful ring before gazing over at her husband.

'The yellow diamond is for you, shining bright as the centre of our family, and the four stones surrounding it are for each of us. I had it made specially.'

The tears started again for Tabitha; as she slid the ring onto her finger, she couldn't help but cry tears of joy. Rosie found it incredibly emotional and wiped a stray tear from her own cheek.

To lighten the mood, Fox stood up and moved over to the Christmas tree. He pulled out a present tucked behind the trunk and turned back to everyone before declaring, 'For the woman who loses everything.' He handed it to Rosie.

'For me?' she said, surprised but ridiculously excited to have been included.

'For you.'

She opened it excitedly, her fingers tearing the paper off to reveal a small cardboard box. Pulling off the lid, she burst out laughing. Inside, nestled on a plush red velvet cushion, was a silver padlock. It was the type that could be latched onto a suitcase or oversized travel bag.

'Look at the back,' Fox instructed, his face watching hers.

She picked it out of the box and turned it over. There was an engraving in the smooth metal of the lock with the words, 'Lost and Found in Venice.'

'It is meant both physically and metaphorically,' he said.

'It's brilliant!' Rosie said, running her fingers over the engraving and feeling the smooth indents in the metal. 'I love it, thank you.'

She smiled at him, aware that everyone was watching but really wanting to kiss him. Instead, she bent down to her own bag of presents and lifted the one from the top before turning and handing it to him.

'I didn't forget you, either.'

'How on earth did you two manage to get presents?' Tabitha asked, her face confused. 'You travelled here with nothing!'

'We made a little detour to the mall,' Fox said, turning the present over and over before tearing the paper like an excited child.

Rosie watched nervously as he pulled out a new pair of grey running shorts, similar to the ones he was wearing the day they collided at the Santa race.

'These are to replace the ones that ripped,' she said, watching him stare at the shorts with a look of surprise.

'I didn't even know they had ripped until I got home later that day! I can't believe you noticed.' He lay the shorts down on his lap and looked at her with his bright green eyes.

Something passed between them, an invisible current or connection, but it faded as Lewis asked, 'Why were your shorts ripped? And why are you wearing shorts in December?'

Fox looked away from Rosie to his brother-in-law and chuckled. 'That, my friend, is a long story . . .'

Chapter Forty-seven

Once the rest of the presents had been handed out, including toy trucks for the boys, a pretty butterfly hair clasp for Tabitha and a bottle of wine for Lewis, Rosie and Fox decided that a bit of privacy might do them some good, so they decided to go for a stroll around the neighbourhood.

When they mentioned this to Tabitha, she nudged Lewis knowingly and gave Rosie a wink, which resulted in a playful punch in the arm from Fox.

'All I'm saying is that it's nice to see you so . . . relaxed,' Tabitha said to him. 'It's been a while, that's all.'

Fox cleared his throat and headed into the hallway to put on his shoes. Rosie followed and slid on her new ankle boots. Fox seemed distracted, elusive almost. Rosie went to question if he was OK, but as soon as they entered the main stairwell and he'd closed the door to Tabitha's apartment, he placed both hands on her face and pushed her up against the wall before drawing her into a long, deep kiss.

His tongue found hers and his kiss deepened into something that made her entire body want to sink into his. His hands reached inside her coat and found their way around her waist, pulling her even closer.

She responded by letting out a small moan as his hands moved lower down her back. There was a sudden slam of a door in the vicinity and they broke apart, both breathless, both wanting more.

Footsteps approached and Fox gave her a cheeky smile before turning to look at the couple who had just appeared on their landing. Rosie touched her tingling lips gently, feeling the sensation of Fox still on them, aching for more. She felt hot and alive.

'I think we'd better get out for that walk, don't you?' Fox said as the couple passed by to head up the next flight of stairs.

Rosie didn't fancy the walk any more, she just wanted to continue their kisses, but she nodded. He took her hand and they walked side by side down the few flights of stairs until they were outside.

The evening was cold but clear and with their hands still entwined, Fox led the way, passing blocks of flats, small parks and residential buildings. As they walked, they talked, sharing more about one another while intermittently stopping every now and again for another sweet kiss.

Fox sure knew how to kiss, Rosie realised. He could be soft and sweet, leaving her wanting more, or he could show his passion by grabbing her in the shadows of a building and kissing her with an intensity that left them both a little wobbly at the knees.

After an hour's walk, Rosie realised that they had come full circle and were back near Tabitha's apartment once more. They had found the roads quiet and Rosie was charmed by the area. She tried not to think about what would happen over the next few days on their return to Milan.

She had a life back home that was waiting for her, but the longer she stayed here, the more she realised that she wasn't living her life, she was simply existing. She thought she had been protecting herself from further pain since her parents' accident, but in actuality, she was just going through the motions – going to work, returning home, keeping the house as it always had been. Maybe Bee was right – maybe she needed to step outside of her routine and try new things, even if it did terrify her.

She wanted to ask Fox what would happen back in Milan. Was this just a quick fling for him because it was convenient and their normal lives were on pause? Should she ask him?

As he paused to open the communal door to Tabitha's building, she took advantage of the situation and pushed him back against the door with her palms against his chest. It felt strong and muscular, even under the layers of his clothing. His lips on hers felt good, felt right. They seemed to come together like two magnets drawn to one another, their magnetism creating a frisson of heat and passion.

She opened her eyes for a moment and could see the surprised look in his eyes at her pouncing on him. But she could see his response from his dilated pupils and wandering hands. She liked the feeling of control she had over him and pulled away, leaving him wanting more.

'We should get back,' she said softly. 'Tabitha will be wondering where we've got to.'

She could see that he didn't want this moment to stop, but his good manners overtook him and he smiled before leading her into the vestibule and closing the door behind them. They ascended the stairs in silence, Rosie knowing that if she turned to look at him, she'd want to kiss him again. By the time they reached Tabitha's front door, she was itching to kiss him again. He was like the fix she never knew she needed.

With his arms placed either side of her head against the front door, they kissed again, but only moments into the kiss, the door behind her was ripped open suddenly and they almost lost their balance, Fox saving her from falling backwards by grabbing her around the waist. He stared over her head. His look was oddly unsettling. His eyes were no longer misty and sensual; now they were wide open and filled with shock. Before she had a chance to turn around, she heard Tabitha's strained voice approaching and another voice, a voice so smooth and feminine.

'Now, what do we have here? Care to explain?'

Chapter Forty-eight

Fox pulled Rosie up straight and spoke over her shoulder to the female voice behind her, his own voice sounding cross and curt.

'What are *you* doing here?'

'It's Christmas! How could I not come and see *amore mio* on Christmas Day! I'm just sorry I couldn't be here sooner.' The voice was as smooth as cool silk.

'Fox, I didn't know. S-she just turned up . . .'

Rosie recognised Tabitha's voice, but it was strained. She turned around to find herself staring at a beautiful Italian woman, with long, dark, coiffed hair, a tight rollneck knee-length dress and high-heeled knee-high stiletto boots. Despite her narrow frame, her presence seemed to take up most of the width of the hallway, with Tabitha behind her. The woman's make-up was impeccable and Rosie felt the odd sensation that she had met this woman before. Or seen photos of her. Even, she remembered with a flash, stayed in her room.

It was Gabriella.

As if on cue, Fox said, 'Gabriella, you shouldn't have come. We talked on Saturday.' His voice was low, his tone serious.

'I know, I know, but I had to give you your Christmas present!'

Her sing-song voice was sweetness personified and she pulled out a small box from her oversized black handbag.

'What sort of fiancée would I be if I didn't drive all the way over to see my beloved on Christmas Day?'

'Gabriella,' Fox began, his warning tone evident. He didn't move to accept the gift but kept his hands firmly at his side.

'Oh, don't look so guilty. I don't need a present in return.

Just your love is present enough.' Her sing-song voice echoed into the landing, with no attempt to keep quiet.

'Gabriella, seriously. Enough.' Fox's tone was final, but it was too late.

'Fiancée?' Rosie looked from Fox to Gabriella, to Tabitha, who was looking pained.

Fox's face was so strained, she could see a twitch forming by his left eye.

'Yes, fiancée. As in betrothed. As in marriage!' Her smile was superior and smooth, but Rosie could see a flame of anger in her eyes.

'Never my fiancée, Gabriella. Not now, not ever. It's over. Why do you insist on persevering with something that ended months ago?'

Gabriella stepped forwards and pressed a fingertip to his lips, causing him to jump back as if he had been burnt. She was still smiling.

'If it ended months ago, then explain to me what happened two weeks ago at your place.'

'That was a mistake. A drunken one at that.' Fox was answering Gabriella, but he had turned to Rosie as if to persuade her.

'Look,' Tabitha said, passing Gabriella to reach the front door and indicating for them to both come in. 'Let's not do this in the hallway for all of the neighbours to hear. Come inside and we'll chat like grown-ups,' she said, ushering them both inside.

Rosie hesitated for a second, feeling sick and overwhelmed.

Once the front door was closed, they all stood in the narrow hallway awkwardly, with Fox looking back and forth between Gabriella and Rosie. It was a wonder he didn't get whiplash.

'Let's grab a drink and sit down. Thankfully, the kids have gone with Lewis to visit some of his parish so we are alone,' Tabitha said, leading them back into the living room and gesturing for them to sit down.

Rosie noticed that the room was empty of Lewis and Agnese. The Christmas tree was still flashing its warm lights, but watching Fox and Gabriella take a seat, she suddenly found the room incredibly suffocating.

'I just need to go . . . Give me one second . . .' She turned to leave, but not before hearing Gabriella's snide comment.

'That's better, just you and me, my little red fox. Just as it should be.'

Rosie didn't turn back; she didn't want to. She felt nauseous and wanted to lie down. She hurried to the spare bedroom with the intention of locking the door and lying in the dark, but upon opening the door, she jumped as she was met by the concerned face of Agnese sitting on the bed, her legs pressed together and her hands folded neatly on her lap. She looked pained, as if the debacle tonight was affecting her. She had clearly come to escape it by hiding out in the bedroom. Rosie realised that maybe they had more in common than just a shared bedroom.

Agnese gestured for Rosie to close the door and lock it, which she did, and then she patted the space beside her, urging her to take a seat next to her, which she also did, crossing her hands in front of her, mirroring Agnese. The silence was comforting and just having Agnese there brought her a sense of calm. There was no expectation to talk or explain, but having another body in the room made her feel less alone. She liked the feeling of being told what to do, even if it was just simple instructions.

Sitting in silence, she could hear discussions being held in the living room, even through the thick walls that separated them, but she was almost grateful that she couldn't hear the specifics. This wasn't her story. It wasn't her life. She belonged back in the UK, with her large, empty house and travel job. She didn't mix with the Gabriellas of this world, or the Foxes. For the first time in days, she wished she was home. Back living her humdrum life where there were no surprises.

Without realising, she had begun to cry. Her tears fell from her cheeks onto her clasped hands and her nose ran at a steady pace, meaning that she had to use the sleeve of her new coat.

Then, through her tears, she noticed an object being held up in front of her face, a white unfocused object. She blinked a few times to clear the tears and focused on what was a beautiful lace handkerchief, with embroidered red flowers sewn into the fabric. Agnese was holding it out for her to take. Rosie felt it too beautiful to use for her snot and tears, so she shook her head, but Agnese only held it closer to her face, insisting she take it.

She did, but only to be polite. She dabbed at her eyes gently, hoping she wouldn't leave any make-up stains on the pure white fabric, and smiled weakly as a thanks to Agnese. But Agnese was insistent, indicating for her to use it properly. Her eyes were the colour of slate, with tiny flecks of aqua blue up close and Rosie could see a youthfulness to them that she hadn't noticed before. A determination, too. To placate her, Rosie blew her nose with the handkerchief, realising that it actually made her feel better, and managed a watery smile in Agnese's direction.

Without warning, Agnese lifted one arm and began to stroke Rosie's head, her ageing, soft hands combing through Rosie's hair slowly and methodically. It was a gentle, motherly movement and Rosie found herself naturally lowering her chin to her chest and closing her eyes, enjoying the sensation. No one had stroked her head in years, not like this, not since her parents were alive.

Then Agnese began to speak. At first, the words were spoken so quietly that Rosie couldn't make them out. Agnese had a low-pitched tone, each syllable pronounced, each word sounding solemn. She continued her methodical stroking while talking and Rosie could hear the woman's natural speech roll off her tongue in a melodious pattern. She sensed it was a poem or lyrics from a song, but without knowing Italian, she had no idea what was being said.

They stayed this way for a few minutes, with Agnese letting her cry until she was spent. She stopped her stroking and reached for Rosie's hand. Rosie looked over to her to see that Agnese had placed one hand on her own black laced high-neck dress, just over her heart, and she was smiling.

She then proceeded to pull from beneath her collar a long, delicate gold chain with a square locket attached. With aged, trembling hands, she opened the clasp of the locket to reveal a tiny sepia image on either side. She gestured for Rosie to take a look.

Leaning forwards, Rosie noticed the left was a photograph of a beautiful young woman, and even though the quality was grainy and old, she could see the resemblance of the young woman to the woman sitting beside her now. To the right was a photo of a handsome young man, his face kind yet serious. He was wearing a shirt and tie and his hair was combed to one side with precision, indicating propriety. But his eyes were warm and inviting, and Rosie could almost sense an adventurous streak to him.

'Aurelio,' Agnese said softly, pointing at his picture in her locket. Then she patted her chest again, right by her heart. '*Mio* Aurelio.' She was smiling sadly.

She pointed at the wall behind Rosie that they shared with the living room beyond. Rosie looked at the bare wall and back to Agnese with a confused expression, shaking her head and shrugging her shoulders.

'*Tua* Fox,' Agnese said, but Rosie didn't understand. '*Tua* Fox,' she repeated before placing the palm of her right hand on Rosie's heart. '*Tua* Fox.'

But Rosie shook her head. He wasn't her Fox. He wasn't her anything. He was Gabriella's fiancé. She was just an inconvenience that he felt obligated to help. She was nothing more than a lost woman in need of assistance to get home. He was fulfilling his job role and she had latched onto him as if he were her raft in the middle of the ocean. Which, she realised with a jolt, he actually was – her raft.

She was lost. Lost not only geographically, but also in life. And she needed to take charge and find her way.

She looked at the old woman in front of her, a stranger whose grief had enabled Rosie to see clearly. She needed to take charge of her life and to do that, she needed to leave.

'I want to go home,' she said to Agnese, trying to remember any Italian that she could. 'Um, my, er, *mio casa*,' she stuttered, remembering the name for home.

With relief, she could see recognition in Agnese's face and the woman smiled before leaning down to extract her large handbag from beneath the bed. Unzipping it, she pulled out a large, weathered purse that was almost bursting open, its zip half closed and the fabric frayed and worn.

Unzipping it, the contents were evident – wads and wads of notes stuffed inside, their similarity indicating they were of the same denomination. Agnese pulled out a small amount from the fat wad jammed inside and began counting them out slowly onto her lap. Rosie could see that each note was a fifty-euro note.

'Oh, no,' Rosie said, realising what the woman was doing. 'I didn't mean to imply—! I don't need your cash, please.'

But Agnese ignored her and continued counting out the notes as if Rosie wasn't speaking. When she had reached what must have been a pile of at least a dozen notes, she placed the remainder into her purse and zipped it up before placing it delicately back inside her bag. She then scooped up the pile of notes on her lap and gestured for Rosie to take them.

'No, please. Thank you, you're so kind, but I don't need them . . .' Rosie insisted, indicating with her arms that she didn't need anything.

But the old woman didn't move, didn't flinch. She just held out the money, her slate-grey eyes focused and unwavering.

'Agnese, please. I didn't mean to imply—'

But Agnese interrupted her with four words, '*Per te. Tua casa.*' She gestured to the money again, nodding at it, her expression solemn. Her face crinkled as she attempted to speak again, but this time it was clear that the words were unfamiliar on her tongue. 'To get home.'

Chapter Forty-nine

It had taken Rosie approximately two minutes to gather her meagre belongings in her new backpack and gratefully hug Agnese goodbye. With a multitude of whispered appreciations, which the old lady shrugged off, Rosie was ushered silently out of the apartment, with Agnese closing the front door softly behind her.

It had taken Rosie another thirty minutes to catch the next tram back to the train station, where she found herself miraculously in time to immediately hop onto the next train to Milan. Owing to it being Christmas Day, there were hardly any people about, so she found herself travelling for the next few hours in total silence, watching as the dark Italian countryside whizzed by, her heart feeling more wretched as the distance between her and Fox increased.

It had taken Rosie a further hour to wait and board the train from Milan to Venice. This time, the train was a little busier, families clearly travelling home after a festive Christmas Day spent with loved ones. Rosie had never felt more alone. She tried to doze on the journey back to Venice, wanting to shut out the laughter and merriment evident from other travellers.

After a long and tiring journey, it had taken Rosie a further half an hour to catch a water taxi back to the Grandioso Canale Vista Hotel, where, just before the stroke of midnight, she found a surprised Eduardo, the manager of the hotel, standing behind the reception desk in an empty lobby.

'*La signorina* Redbrush! You have returned! Are you safe and well?'

He rushed around from the reception desk to assist her and she found she was incredibly grateful to have reached her destination finally. She smiled weakly.

'Quite well, thank you, Eduardo,' she said, letting him kiss her on both cheeks. 'I don't suppose you happen to have a spare room, do you? I am without accommodation.'

'But of course,' Eduardo said, releasing her and rushing back around the reception desk, where he dutifully began tapping away at his computer.

In the meantime, Rosie pulled out the remaining notes and coins given to her by Agnese. Sadly, travelling on Christmas Day had proved expensive and she found that she was not as flush as she'd hoped to be.

'Um, your smallest and cheapest room, if possible, Eduardo.'

He looked up to see her counting her cash and paused just for a moment before returning his gaze to his computer screen.

'Let me see,' he said, his eyes narrowing in concentration. 'You are in luck. I have one room remaining this evening and it is free for the next five nights. It is probably not to your standards, but it is all we have left . . .' He tailed off, looking regrettably in her direction.

'If it has a bed in it, then it sounds perfect,' she said, gratefully coming forwards to the desk and laying her cash on the counter. 'How much?'

Eduardo looked at the notes and then back at his screen before declaring, 'Fifty euros for one night. But I am afraid you might be a little disappointed.'

'Fifty euros!' Rosie said, delighted, pushing the last of her notes across the counter. She'd worry about paying for the other nights tomorrow. She was too tired to think. 'Fantastic! I'll sleep in a cupboard if you have that available.'

Her spirits lifted slightly at the thought of a comfy bed and some welcome, heart-numbing sleep where she didn't have to think about Fox and his fiancée in each other's arms. She balled up her fists and rubbed them over her eyes in an attempt to clear the image. When she removed them, she found Eduardo staring at her, his face soft and compassionate. He was also holding a key.

'Come, let me take you to your room.'

Before he moved, he picked up the reception phone beside him and spoke swiftly in Italian before ending the call. He walked around the desk and led her to the elevator, with no attempt at small talk, which Rosie appreciated.

Riding the elevator to the top floor, he motioned for her to follow him down a corridor to the very end, where he stopped outside a heavy oak door with an engraved plaque nailed on it stating, Piazza San Marco Suite.

'Er, Eduardo, I think we have the wrong room,' she whispered, not wanting to wake any guests in adjoining rooms.

But he shook his head and unlocked the door before walking in, indicating for her to follow. She did so and found herself in a large circular hallway with adjoining doors, all open. Turning on the spot, she could see a bedroom, separate dining room, bathroom and lounge area. The suite was so large that she wondered if she was dreaming. It made her room last week look like a dingy hostel.

'For you, Miss Redbrush. The Piazza San Marco Suite.'

'But I can't possibly afford this, Eduardo. I don't have any money!' She looked at him but he shrugged, smiling.

'Call it a late Christmas present.'

Before she had a chance to reply, there was a knock at the door and he swiftly answered, letting in two male housekeeping staff members. One was carrying a large cardboard box in both arms and the other was pushing a silver trolley with multiple dishes covered with silver domes, a bottle of wine, a single wine glass and an expensive-looking thick napkin. They headed into the dining room to the left of Rosie and she watched as the food was laid out on the large dining table. The box was placed beside it.

'The box contains the belongings from your previous room,' Eduardo said, pointing, 'along with a few extras added by your party, who have now returned home.' He then pointed to the silver trolley that was being wheeled back out of her suite.

'And that is some dinner for you, compliments of the chef. I am sure you are in need of refreshment after your journey.'

Rosie stood there open-mouthed and before she had a chance to thank him, he gave her a quick nod and ushered the two staff out of the suite, closing the door behind him, leaving Rosie in a state of shock. She looked down at her hands, which were still holding her remaining cash, the notes in one hand and the coins in the other. Mentally counting the money in her head, she realised that despite offering Eduardo a fifty-euro note for a room for the night, he hadn't accepted it. She was still holding it.

Turning full circle, taking in the enormity of the room and the lavish décor, she couldn't help but feel immensely touched. Eduardo had given her this entire suite, along with what smelt like a magnificent dinner, all for free.

Chapter Fifty

After eating the most delicious pasta and managing almost three-quarters of the creamiest tiramisu she had ever tasted, Rosie felt rejuvenated enough to tackle the large box of her belongings.

Pouring herself a second glass of the fruitiest red wine, she stood up and walked over to the cardboard box that was sitting at the far end of the dining table, its plain outer layer revealing nothing of the contents. Rosie wasn't particularly excited by the thought of her belongings; it would probably be just her washbag, make-up (which she had now mostly replaced with Italian equivalents) and some clothes.

Standing in front of it, she pulled off the box lid and peered down to look at the contents. What she saw was not what she expected at all. The box was full to the brim of items wrapped in tissue paper of all colours, some small, some large. She lifted the top item out first and laid it on the table before unravelling the creamy delicate paper slowly and carefully. She gasped at what she found.

It was a traditional Venetian fan. As Rosie gently opened it, the soft fluttering of paper revealed a detailed and colourful map of Venice painted onto its delicate paper. There was a little note within the tissue wrapping with the handwritten words: *A beautiful fan for a beautiful girl. Thank you. Winnie.*

Rosie placed the fan on the table and reached for the next item. This one was smaller and as she unravelled the paper, a postcard of Venice dropped out, along with a metal brooch in the shape of a red lipstick. It was quirky and cool. Rosie turned the postcard over, where Mildred's bold handwriting had scrawled the words: *Rosie – the world is your oyster – explore!*

Next was a lovely Italian pack of cards from Norman, with one card loose in the tissue paper. It was the Queen of Hearts. He had written Rosie's name on the card with an arrow pointing down at the image of the queen. He had signed it simply at the bottom of the card with his name.

As Rosie unpacked each item, she found herself laughing and tearing up, each present so like its giver, all so unique. The next present was from Walter. This was larger and contained a two-pack of Bellini glasses and a jar of peaches in syrup. His note stated simply: *Do not leave Venice without a visit to Harry's Bar. Yours, Walter.*

Next was an Italian bottle of red wine and a beautifully packaged gift of prunes. The card read: *To keep your iron levels up. From Albert.* Rosie properly chuckled at this note, knowing his own struggle with anaemia. Placing it beside the other gifts, Rosie found herself with a lovely collection of presents.

After that was a small A5 rectangular gift. Upon opening it, Rosie laughed loudly as she found herself browsing through a collection of postcards from the Venice Guggenheim Museum, all containing images of naked male statues. Without needing to check the card, she knew it was from Enid. The card enclosed read: *To keep your spirits up, Enid.*

The seventh present was from Dottie. It was a miniature wooden gondola, exquisitely painted. Her note read: *To remember me by. Sorry again! Dottie.*

The eighth gift was a gold-covered, Venetian-style notebook, with the first line on the first page already inscribed. It read: *Rosie's Story* . . . The card was written from Shirley.

The ninth present was another large gift and Rosie found herself holding a beautifully wrapped box of gluten-free pastries. Without needing to see the card, she knew it would be from Olive.

She had reached the last gift now. The box only contained one more tissue-wrapped item and then her belongings folded neatly below, filling up only a third of the large box. She knew who it would be from – there was only one of the group left:

Horace. She unwrapped the gold tissue paper and found herself staring at a palm-sized grey stone. It was smooth but plain. But when Rosie flipped it over, she gasped. An intricate carving of the world had been etched into the smooth surface. Each continent, each country, all delicately inscribed by a clearly talented hand. No wording, no name, just the world as the focal point.

Rosie ran her finger gently over the cool stone, marvelling at the detail, and as she did so, she found her eyes drawn to the ring on her finger. Another gift, another person thinking of her. Both with images of the world at her fingertips. Rosie placed the stone down with the other gifts and took a step back to admire them all.

Despite not being with her loved ones at Christmas, she had still been blessed with presents. Looking at her now complete display, she found herself no longer feeling alone this Christmas. She felt loved.

Chapter Fifty-one

The next morning, Rosie awoke to a feeling of determination for three things. She was going to sort her passport out as soon as she could, she was going to clear her name with Wanderlust Wishes and she was going to forget that she had ever met or fallen for Fox.

However, the small obstacle blocking her from achieving any of these things was the fact that it was Boxing Day. The British Consulate General was still closed for the holidays, as was Wanderlust Wishes, and her vivid dream last night of Fox serenading her from a gondola under her window, a red rose in one hand and a brand-new passport in the other, did not help in her quest to forget him. Nor did lying in bed. So, she pulled back the oh-so-soft covers and decided that her day would be spent admiring Venice. She was stuck there, so she might as well make the most of it.

As she headed to the ridiculously opulent bathroom, she noticed a card had been pushed under the door to her suite. Upon opening it, she found it to be a paid invoice for the room for the next four nights, meaning she had a place to stay while she sorted her passport. The relief was immense. She hadn't realised the tension in her shoulders until she felt them drop from their taut position. She had been given the freedom of time to sort herself out. With a new lightness to her step, she dressed quickly and headed out into the wintery sun.

Venice was glorious at Christmas, Rosie realised a few hours later. She had decided to use some of her money to buy a travel pass for the vaporetto, the public transport system for Venice. It meant that she was able to hop on and off as she pleased. Despite most places being closed, she could still marvel at the architecture and streets as she circumnavigated the various districts.

By the time the sun had risen high into the sky, Rosie found herself pausing beside the Rialto Bridge and taking a seat on the bank of the Grand Canal. With the bridge stretching high above her to her left and the water curving away from her to the right, Rosie sat still for almost an hour. Just watching as the world went by. She had nowhere to be and no one to visit.

The sun caressed her face and the lapping of the water against the bank was so soothing that she closed her eyes instinctively, but an image of Fox smiling at her punctuated her thoughts. It hit her hard in the chest, as if she'd been punched. She missed him. Terribly. She wanted him to sit next to her and tell her facts about Venice. She wanted to hear him humming a tune, which he often did without realising, wanted him to run his fingers through his hair in a way that was so adorable. She wanted Fox.

She wondered where he was right at that minute. Unwanted images of him in Gabriella's arms flashed through her mind like a kaleidoscope of horror – them waking up in bed together, them kissing under the moonlight, her hair cascading down her back, him down on one knee proposing to her, his handsome face excited and in love. Needing to get the images out of her head, she got up and forced herself to walk. Somewhere, anywhere, she didn't care. She just wanted to walk Fox out of her mind and out of her life forever.

Rosie made her way back to the hotel from the Rialto Bridge almost unconsciously. She nodded at the reception staff but didn't stop until she was back inside the silence of her suite. She undressed robotically, ignoring the fresh flowers placed on the dining table and the basket of fruit and pastries sitting on the lounge table. Leaving a trail of clothes behind her, she moved into the bedroom and closed the heavy curtains to block out the last of the late-afternoon sun.

The room was plunged into darkness. She then climbed into bed and closed her eyes shut, willing herself to sleep. Despite her reservations that she would not be able to sleep, her hours of walking and the shock of the last few days had taken their toll and within minutes of laying her head on her pillow, she had fallen into a deep sleep.

When Rosie next awoke, she was shocked to find it was morning. She had effectively slept for over seventeen hours straight. She'd never slept for that long before, even when she had caught flu and was bed-bound for four days.

She instinctively rolled over to check her phone, remembering with a start that she didn't have one. Sighing, she rolled out of bed. She dressed without purpose, wondering how she was going to fill the long, empty day ahead. She ate some fruit from the gift basket, not wanting to spend any more of her precious remaining money on eating out, and made her way down to the foyer.

As the lift doors opened, she glanced ahead, uninterested in the busyness of guests checking out. She decided to slope through them unnoticed, with no desire to look at Eduardo's kind but sympathetic face. She was almost at the revolving doors of the hotel when she heard a voice rising above others. A voice that was instantly recognisable to Rosie anywhere in the world.

She turned to find the source.

'I don't care about client confidentiality. I need to know if she is currently residing in *this* hotel. Her name is Rosie Redbrush and she is all alone . . .' There was a pause while Rosie assumed someone else was speaking. 'No, I will not lower my voice. I need to find my best friend.'

'Bee?' Rosie said, spotting Bee's familiar yellow duffel coat from behind.

Bee turned at the mention of her name and spotted Rosie standing by the doors, almost hidden by a large group of tourists.

'Rosie!' she yelled, causing everyone in the foyer to jump and fall silent.

But Bee didn't even notice as she pushed past people to get to her. Flinging herself at Rosie with the full force of her body, she immediately burst into tears.

'I've been so worried about you!' she cried, through sobs. 'I flew out yesterday to Florence and headed straight to the address you provided, but was told you had left suddenly, with no goodbye, no note . . .' She tailed off as she let go of Rosie to stare at her. 'Are you OK? Why did you run away? The woman, Tabitha, was properly upset. She said she felt it was her fault for letting Gabriella in . . . Rosie, what has happened?' Bee wiped her streaming nose on the back of her yellow sleeve, leaving a slimy trail, but she didn't care.

She looked exhausted, Rosie noted. Her clothes were crumpled and her hair was unwashed. She felt terribly guilty.

'I'll explain everything,' she said, aware that the entire foyer had paused, and was listening in to their conversation. 'But I'm OK. Let's head up to my room and I'll tell you what's happened.'

As she led Bee past the reception desk, she saw Eduardo flash her a concerned look, but she smiled to signal she was fine. He exhaled and gestured via a click of his fingers for the bellboy to collect Bee's luggage that she'd abandoned at the front desk.

Rosie and Bee returned to her suite in silence, with only the sound of a few sobs from Bee interrupting their journey. It was only when the door to the suite had closed and they had slumped onto one of the two sofas in the living room that Rosie retold the story of events since she'd last spoken to Bee.

Bee listened in total silence, which was unusual for her, but when Rosie spoke of Gabriella's return to Tabitha's apartment, Bee's eyes filled with tears, which she brushed away quickly, allowing Rosie to continue. Once her whole sorry tale had been told, Rosie took a deep sigh before looking at her oldest friend in the world for a reply. But she wasn't expecting the response that she gave.

'You love him,' she declared, her eyes bright and serious. 'You love Fox.'

'Don't be ridiculous,' Rosie said quickly, shaking off the insinuation with a determined shake of her head. 'I've only known him a few days.'

'You love him,' Bee repeated, smiling sadly and closing her hand around Rosie's before giving it a squeeze.

'Bee, stop,' Rosie said, pulling her hand back as if she'd been burnt. 'I don't love him. I don't feel anything for him. I just want to go home.'

She thought she'd been strong, but she felt a rogue tear escape her left eye and she mentally berated it. Traitor. Another followed, and another, until she lowered her head into the palms of her hands and sobbed in earnest. Bee jumped forwards and pulled Rosie into her chest, shushing her and gently rubbing her back until the sobbing subsided and Rosie was spent.

'I think,' Bee said, speaking over the top of Rosie's head as she hugged her into her chest, 'that we should get out of here and you should show me the sights of Venice. I didn't come all this way in search of my best friend to spend my time cooped up in a hotel room. However nice it is . . .' she said, tailing off as she properly took in her surroundings. 'Shit, Rosie. How did you land a room as nice as this? It's gorgeous.'

That made Rosie smile weakly, her eyes glassy.

'Yeah, I know. Not too shabby.'

'Nope.' Bee jumped up, her initial panic over and back to her old self. 'We leave in five minutes, so glam up, we're going out.'

She headed in the direction of the bedroom before being interrupted by a knock on the door. Answering it, she found Eduardo holding Bee's luggage.

'Ah, fabulous, thank you!' Bee said, offering him some scrunched-up euros, which he declined.

'Is *Signorina* Rosie here? Is she OK?'

Rosie appeared in the door frame and smiled at him. He was so kind.

'I'm fine, thank you, Eduardo. This is my best friend, Bee, and she is here to rescue me.'

Eduardo looked at Bee and smiled with relief. 'Ah, *Signorina* Bee, a pleasure. Welcome to Venice.' He gave her a curt nod and Bee lit up.

'Well, aren't you a delight! Eduardo,' she said, taking a step closer to him, 'our friend, Rosie, has had the most awful time in the last few days. Most awful. What would you recommend to someone who is stuck in Venice and needs cheering up?'

Eduardo paused before smiling widely. 'Why, free passes, of course!'

Chapter Fifty-two

Eduardo had been true to his word and managed to provide them with free passes to almost all the major tourist sites within Venice. Plus, with his many contacts, not only had they had their tickets upgraded so that they didn't have to queue, but they were also gifted lunch in one of the stunning outdoor cafés in St Mark's Square. Here, they got to sit in the sunshine drinking Aperol spritzes and watching the pigeons and tourists take in the view.

Afterwards, Eduardo had booked a private gondola to take them up and down the Grand Canal, with free champagne and fresh strawberries, before being dropped at Harry's Bar, where they were treated like celebrities and offered the best seat in the house, at Harry's table.

'Walter was right,' Rosie said as she took another sip of the nicest Bellini she had ever tried. The cocktail had a consistency of puréed peaches blended with the sharpness of Prosecco. It was incredibly fresh, sweet yet light, and Rosie sent a silent thanks to Walter for telling her about the place and to Eduardo for knowing the current manager of the bar.

'This place is fantastic.'

'No arguments from me,' Bee said, closing her eyes as she took another sip. 'Worth every cent.'

'If we were paying, which we're not,' Rosie added, chuckling.

'Makes it all the sweeter, then,' Bee said, gesturing to a nearby waiter for two more.

'Do you think Fox ever brought Gabriella here?' Rosie said without thought.

Bee's eyes shot open and she scanned Rosie's face.

'I don't know . . . maybe.'

'Hmm,' Rosie said, thinking of an alternative universe where she would be sat here with Fox, clinking glasses and sharing peachy kisses.

'His sister told me that he left her apartment as soon as they realised you had gone,' Bee said nonchalantly, watching Rosie's face for a response, which she got, as Rosie's eyes widened at the new information.

'Really? With Gabriella?' She rushed her words, almost stumbling over them to get the questions out.

'I dunno,' Bee said, shrugging. 'I guess so.' She was playing it cool, but her face was serious. 'Would it matter?'

'No, not at all,' Rosie replied, taking a deep, long sip of her cocktail. 'He's free to do whatever he wants. They probably wanted to have some privacy so booked into a hotel or something.' The thought made her feel physically sick, so she pushed her cocktail glass away from her on the table.

'Maybe,' Bee said as two more cocktails were placed in front of them. She thanked the waiter.

Rosie groaned and let her head drop onto the table. 'Oh, Bee,' she wailed, her voice muffled against the wood of the table. 'She was stunning. Like Beyoncé stunning. She had the perfect figure, amazing boobs and hair that looked like she'd stepped straight out of a hair commercial. She is everything that I'm not.'

She jumped as Bee slammed her hand onto the table, raising her head and looking at her best friend.

'Enough! You are gorgeous both inside and out. I will not let some gawdy, warbly opera singer with most likely fake hair extensions and a fake personality make you feel shit about yourself. Now, drink up, shut up and let's enjoy today for what it is. I'm child-free, husband-free and getting to spend quality time with my best friend in the best city in the world! *Salute!*' Bee pushed Rosie's glass towards her and encouraged her to clink glasses.

Rosie did so and they both took a long sip. Bee was right: instead of mourning what could have been, she should be celebrating what she had always had. A brilliant, caring and slightly bonkers best friend.

By the time they left Harry's Bar, it was already dark outside, with the large Christmas tree looking magical against the backdrop of St Mark's Square. Rosie and Bee decided that it would be nice to take a long walk back to the hotel, mostly so that Bee could walk the Venetian streets, but also because they were pretty tipsy and the fresh air would do them good.

Passing the designer shops of Calle Larga XXII Marzo, Rosie and Bee linked arms as they admired the clothes, handbags and shoes that taunted them with their sparkly sequins and painful price tags.

They continued through the streets and over the many, many bridges that seemed to appear with every hundred steps or so. Each bridge was unique, some steep and stumpy, some grander and more elegant. But each was beautiful and as they wended their way around the city, they made a game of counting how many they passed.

Veering down a narrow alleyway, which opened up to another dark canal, they came across a bridge that stood out from the others. Built with painted iron railings instead of the usual white brick slabs, the railing itself was swamped in hundreds, if not thousands, of what appeared to be padlocks of every colour and size.

Bee and Rosie stopped to touch the padlocks, Rosie noticing that most of the locks had been decorated with ribbons of multiple colours, along with tags displaying messages or inscriptions on the metal directly. Taking a closer look, they were all declarations of love. Each lock a hint at a love story. Each ribbon a taste of a colourful life. Some were in English, but there appeared to be a multitude of languages. As Bee and Rosie moved from lock to lock in silence, they were touched by the words and the sentiments behind them.

Rosie noticed that some declared young love. Others were in memorandum of a love lost, or indicating unrequited love. Some were inscribed with wedding dates, anniversaries, occasions that meant something to the owner. She felt a lump rise in her throat at being around so much emotion. The moonlight reflected off each lock, their shackles inserted into the mechanism, symbolising the link between the strength and power of the lock and the strength and power of love.

They took their time examining each lock that caught their eye, still both in silence, both feeling honoured to read someone's personal yet public testimony of love to someone unknown. Rosie had no idea how long they spent on that bridge, but when they stepped off it back onto the street, she had made a decision. She didn't mention it to Bee, but she knew that when she woke tomorrow, she needed to venture out alone on her own mission of acceptance.

Chapter Fifty-three

It wasn't hard for Rosie to slope out of bed the next morning and get dressed without waking Bee. She had flaked out the minute they got back to the hotel last night, and a combination of Bellinis and exhaustion meant that she was snoring loudly, with no chance of waking for at least a couple of hours.

Rosie headed to the hotel reception, where, placing a small item on the counter, she asked for directions to the destination that had become ingrained in her mind since last night. The receptionist on duty drew a quick map on a piece of headed paper and then glanced at the item sitting on the counter. Rosie noticed his gaze and quickly removed it, shoving it deep into her coat pocket. With a smile, she thanked him and made her way into the cold outside.

Rosie took her time walking slowly through the quiet streets, taking in the atmosphere of Venice in the early hours. It was almost eight o'clock by the time she reached her destination and she had barely passed more than a handful of people on her whole journey. She liked Venice when it was barely awake, the early rising sun having not yet found its way into the narrow pathways and streets, meaning that the tops of buildings were bathed in an orange hue but the pavements were still enjoying the last moments of the night.

Rosie found her way easily back to the bridge, despite the labyrinthine streets that snaked this way and that. It was like she was being drawn to it by an unknown current. The bridge was empty, which was unsurprising, and the water below the bridge was barely moving. There was a stillness in the air, as if the dawn hadn't quite woken yet.

She made her way to the centre of the bridge and looked down at the dark waters below. Without tourists or boats, the city was silent. The shutters of the buildings surrounding her were closed and as she unzipped her backpack, the sound appeared to stir a small flock of tiny birds to her left. She watched them rise towards the rooftops, no doubt seeking the warm sun.

Carefully extracting the padlock from her bag, she turned it over and over in her outstretched hands. It was shiny and new, its metal untarnished and the inscription clean. She ran a finger over the words that she had now read many times: Lost and Found in Venice. The Christmas present from Fox. Little did she know when he gave it to her that she would find herself giving it back to the city of love only a few days later.

Moving the shackle from the padlock body, she delicately moved the four-number combination lock to 1224 – twelve for the month she met Fox and twenty-four for the year. Choosing an empty spot along the bridge railing, she leant forwards to hook the padlock on, locking the shackle into place with a satisfying click. Letting go, she watched it swing for a moment before coming to a standstill. Just like her encounter with Fox. New, exciting and moving at a rate, before coming to a complete stop at the return of Gabriella.

Running her finger over the engraving one last time, she recited the words quietly out loud:

'Rosie Redbrush. No longer lost but now found.'

She turned to leave, when she stopped suddenly at the solitary image standing at the bottom of the bridge, staring back at her. She closed her eyes tightly, believing she was dreaming, but when she opened her eyes again, he was there. Only this time he had stepped a little closer.

'I've found you,' he said breathlessly. His broad chest was rising and falling quickly as if he'd been running. He took another step towards her. 'Rosie, I—'

'What are you doing here, Fox?' Rosie asked, not believing that he was within touching distance.

She wanted to reach out and feel him but knew that she would find it too painful.

'I've been searching for you ever since you upped and left on Christmas Day. I haven't stopped. I thought you'd head straight to the consulate, but you weren't there, so then I tried the Il Posto Tranquillo Hotel, but again, no sighting of you. So I guessed I'd lost you until the consulate opened again.

'But then my sister received a visit from your friend frantically searching for you and they swapped numbers. Tabitha knew that your friend was planning on heading to Venice, which gave me the idea to head to Venice, too. I hopped on the next train from Milan to Venice yesterday and I've just been wandering the streets looking for you.'

'All night?' Rosie asked, and he nodded, pushing back his hair in a way that made Rosie's legs go weak.

'I'd all but given up hope, when Tabitha received a call from your friend this morning. She'd woken to find you missing from your hotel room and panicked that you'd decided to travel to Milan alone. So she called Tabitha, who called me.

'I then called the hotel, who advised me that a woman of your description was seen leaving the hotel only half an hour earlier. And they knew where you were headed as they'd drawn you a map on a piece of paper. That piece of paper,' he said, pointing at the map that was on the ground under Rosie's bag. 'I ran here as quickly as I could. I just couldn't bear the thought of losing you again . . .' He tailed off, his voice hoarse.

He looked so tired and dishevelled, yet Rosie didn't think he'd ever looked so handsome.

'Where's Gabriella, though? Won't she be cross you've left her to come and look for me?' she said, finding that her heart was racing and her mouth felt dry.

'I couldn't care less where Gabriella is,' Fox said, exasperated. 'We broke up three months ago. I knew it hadn't been working and wanted to finish things even before that, but she refused to accept it. I never had any intention of marrying her. And contrary to what she implied, it was never that serious.'

Rosie looked at him, wondering if what he was saying could possibly be true.

As if on cue, he stepped closer and showed her his phone. There were multiple messages from him to Gabriella, all saying the same thing – he wanted to end their relationship – but she kept arguing against it.

'What about what she said about you both two weeks ago? Did you?'

'We did,' he said, flushing slightly, 'but it was a drunken mistake, nothing more. I promise.'

He was so close to her now that she could feel his warmth.

'Rosie, what I felt for her in the months we were together doesn't compare to what I felt for you after only a few hours together. When you disappeared, I felt like I'd lost my one chance of happiness. My one chance of . . .' He paused. 'Love.'

Rosie tried to breathe, but she was finding it hard. Her heart was in her throat.

'Why did you run away?' This time it was a whisper, his eyes searching her face for answers.

'Because I couldn't bear it.'

'Bear what?'

'The thought of losing you to someone else. So I ran.'

She didn't attempt to stop the tears from forming, didn't try to stop him as he pulled her close to him, so close that she felt his heartbeat, and it was as fast as hers.

'Why?' he asked, kissing her so softly that she almost didn't feel it.

She leant in for more, but he waited for an answer. She shook her head, unable to answer. The tears were flowing down her cheeks.

'Rosie, my Rosie. Promise you won't run away from me again?' he said, raising his hands to her cheeks and kissing away the tears. 'I am deeply, stupidly, race-across-the-country in love with you.'

Rosie's eyes rose to meet his and this time the tears were ones of joy.

Finding her voice, she whispered back, 'I love you, too.'

This time when he kissed her it wasn't light or quick. It was a kiss so deep, so full of love, that the world stopped around them and they became lost in one another. A kiss that both took away the stress and sadness of the last few days and replaced it with a love that settled deep inside their hearts.

Rosie was no longer lost in Venice. With Fox beside her, she had now been found.

Acknowledgements

To my husband, who has always believed in me, even when I wasn't so sure. We make a perfect team. Thanks for chasing Santas with me, for climbing volcanos, for riding the subway while holding my hand, for exploring castles... out of all love stories I've ever written, ours is still my favourite.

To all of my family for their never-ending support, I feel so blessed. To my boys who are my biggest joy; getting to be your mum will forever be my greatest achievement. Every moment with you both is just magic.

To my wonderful mum who has shown me what it takes to be strong, loyal, and love unconditionally. You will always be my favourite shopping partner (but you really don't need another handbag!)

To my dad and Margaret, who have consistently promoted and championed me and my writing. Your joint support is such a tonic when I'm knee-deep in edits! (Dad, you've set a precedent now and I'm fully expecting you to read this next book – cover to cover!)

To my greatest and oldest friends, Debs, Liz, Nikki; always there, always ready to care. Years of love, laughter and joy. I'm not sure who I'd be without you.

To Tara, my beautiful friend. Throughout the last year, you've supported me so much. My life coach for social media, my coffee-provider when I couldn't leave the house, my cheerleader for promoting my book, my talented make-up artist... over a decade of friendship and I count myself lucky to call you my friend.

To my book club gals, you are, and continue to be, totally awesome. Thanks for all the laughs, the wine, and your endless love of books.

To the Clownballs, what a bunch of legends! Victoria, thanks for all the cat noises and daily smiles. You are fiercely loyal, brilliantly funny and just an all-round terrific friend. Sean, thanks for being consistently sarcastic, yet always knowing exactly when I need a hug. Although I'm still waiting on my Starbucks. Stephen, your humour and patience is greatly appreciated, especially when explaining mechanics, science, logic, music, or basic general knowledge to me. And Michelle, thanks for having faith. In God, in me, in life. Your positivity is wonderful to be around and our morning singsong is always a favourite part of my day. From our daily messaging to our competitiveness over wordle, I feel so grateful to work with such a brilliant 'Bunch of Anchors!' Here's to the next quiz night. (And no, for the last time, I am not willing to add in a dastardly, yet dashing gondolier into the story.)

To Rhea. Where do I start? Thank you for giving me the opportunity to continue chasing my dreams. I feel incredibly lucky to have an editor as supportive, as passionate and as creative as you. And thank you for your patience – even when I decide to throw away an entire, completed manuscript and start again, all on a whim and a spark of an idea that I think has potential! A huge thanks to the Orion team too, for transforming a seed of an idea into a completed book, and to Hannah, the illustrator, for the most beautiful book cover; thank you for bringing my story to life. I feel honoured to work with you all.

And finally, to you, the reader. Thank you. It's an honour to know you've invested your time in reading my story. I still find it incredible to think that readers from all around the world might find enjoyment from the fictional characters that I have created. Rosie and Fox have been a joy to write and I hope you fall in love with them, just as I have.